D0107196

BRENDA JACKSON

is a die "heart" romantic who married her childhood sweetheart and still proudly wears the "going steady" ring he gave her when she was fifteen. Because she's always believed in the power of love, Brenda's stories always have happy endings. In her real-life love story, Brenda and her husband of thirty-three years live in Jacksonville, Florida, and have two sons.

A *USA TODAY* bestselling author of over thirty romance titles, Brenda divides her time between, family, writing and working in management at a major insurance company. You may write Brenda at P.O. Box 28267, Jacksonville, Florida 32226; her e-mail address at WriterBJackson@aol.com or visit her Web site at www.brendajackson.net.

ROCHELLE ALERS

is a native New Yorker who lives on Long Island. She admits to being a hopeless romantic, who is in love with life. Rochelle's interests include traveling, music, art and gourmet cooking. She is the first recipient of the Vivian Stephens Career Achievement Award for Excellence in Romance Novel Writing, and the winner of Waldenbooks and Borders Multicultural Bestselling Romance. Her titles are now required reading at several universities. View her biography at www.rochellealers.com, or contact her at roclers@aol.com or P.O. Box 690, Freeport, NY 11520-0690.

Brenda Jackson   Rochelle Alers

When You
LEAST
Expect It

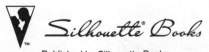
Published by Silhouette Books
America's Publisher of Contemporary Romance

 SILHOUETTE BOOKS

WHEN YOU LEAST EXPECT IT

Copyright © 2005 by Harlequin Books S.A.

ISBN 0-373-28539-6

The publisher acknowledges the copyright holders of the individual works as follows:

A LITTLE DARE
Copyright © 2003 by Brenda Streater Jackson

A YOUNGER MAN
Copyright © 2002 by Rochelle Alers

CONTENTS

A LITTLE DARE

Brenda Jackson

To Pauline Hall,
thanks for your feedback on the book in progress
and for falling in love with Dare.

And most importantly, thanks to my Heavenly Father
who gave me the gift to write.

Prologue

The son Dare Westmoreland didn't know he had, needed him.

Shelly Brockman knew that admission was long overdue as she stood in the living room of the house that had been her childhood home. The last box had been carried in and now the task of unpacking awaited her. Even with everything she faced, she felt good about being back in a place that filled her with many fond memories. Her thoughts were cut short with the slamming of the front door. She turned and met her son's angry expression.

"I'm going to hate it here!" He all but screamed at the top of his lungs. "I want to go back to Los Angeles! No matter what you say, this will never be my home!"

Shelly winced at his words and watched as he threw down the last bag filled with his belongings before racing up the stairs. Instead of calling after him, she closed her eyes, remembering why she had made the move from California to Georgia, and knew that no matter how AJ felt, the move was the best thing for him. For the past year he had been failing in school and hanging out with the wrong crowd. Because of his height, he looked older than a ten-year-old and had begun associating with an older group of boys at school, those known to be troublemakers.

Her parents, who had retired and moved to Florida years ago, had offered her the use of her childhood home rent-free. As a result, she had made three of the hardest decisions of her life. First, deciding to move back to College Park, Georgia, second switching from being a nurse who worked inside the hospital to a home healthcare nurse, and finally letting Dare Westmoreland know he had a son.

More than anything she hoped Dare would understand that she had loved him too much to stand between him and his dream of becoming an FBI agent all those years ago. Her decision, unselfish as it had been, had cost AJ the chance to know his father and Dare the chance to know his son.

Crossing the room she picked up AJ's bag. He was upset about leaving his friends and moving to a place he considered Hicksville, USA. However, his attitude was the least of her worries.

She sighed deeply and rubbed her forehead, knowing she couldn't put off telling Dare much longer since chances were he would hear she'd return to town. Besides, if he took a good hard look at AJ, he would know the truth, and the secret she had harbored for ten years would finally be out.

Deep within her heart she knew that it was time.

One

Two weeks later—early September

Sheriff Dare Westmoreland leaned forward in the chair behind his desk. From the defiant look on the face of the boy standing in front of him he could tell it would be one of those days. "Look, kid, I'm only going to ask you one more time. What is your name?"

The boy crossed his arms over his chest and had the nerve to glare at him and say, "And I've told you that I don't like cops and have no intention of giving you my name or anything else. And if you don't like it, arrest me."

Dare stood to his full height of six-feet-four, feeling every bit of his thirty-six years as he came from behind his desk to stare at the boy. He estimated the kid, who he'd caught throwing rocks at passing cars on the highway, to be around twelve or thirteen. It had been a long time since any kid living in his jurisdiction had outright sassed him. None of them would have dared, so it stood to reason that the kid was probably new in town.

"You will get your wish. Since you won't cooperate and tell me who you are, I'm officially holding you in police custody until someone comes to claim you. And while you're waiting you may as well make yourself useful. You'll start by mopping out the bathroom on the first floor, so follow me."

Dare shook his head, thinking he didn't envy this kid's parents one bit.

Shelly had barely brought her car to a complete stop in front of the sheriff's office before she was out of it. It had taken her a good two hours in Atlanta's heavy traffic to make it home after receiving word that AJ had not shown up at school, only to discover he wasn't at home. When it had started getting late she had gotten worried and called the police. After giving the dispatcher a description of AJ, the woman assured her that he was safe in their custody and that the reason she had not been contacted was because AJ had refused to give anyone his name. Without asking for any further details Shelly had jumped into her car and headed for the police station.

She let out a deep sigh. If AJ hadn't given anyone his name that meant the sheriff was not aware she was AJ's mother and for the moment that was a comforting thought. As she pushed open the door, she knew all her excuses for not yet meeting with Dare and telling him the truth had run out, and fate had decided to force her hand.

She was about to come face to face with Sheriff Dare Westmoreland.

"Sheriff, the parent of John Doe has arrived."

Dare looked up from the papers he was reading and met his secretary's gaze. "Only one parent showed up, Holly?"

"Yes, just the mother. She's not wearing a wedding ring so I can only assume there isn't a father. At least not one that's around."

Dare nodded. "What's the kid doing now?" he asked, pushing the papers he'd been reading aside.

"He's out back watching Deputy McKade clean up his police motorcycle"

Dare nodded. "Send the woman in, Holly. I need to have a long talk with her. Her son needs a lot more discipline than he's evidently getting at home."

Dare moved away from his desk to stand at the window where he could observe the boy as he watched McKade polish his motorcycle. He inhaled deeply. There was something about the boy that he found oddly familiar. Maybe he reminded him of himself and his four brothers when they'd been younger. Although they had been quite a handful for their parents, headstrong and in some ways stubborn, they had known just how far to take it and just how much they could get away with. And they'd been smart enough to know when to keep their mouths closed. This kid had a lot to learn.

"Sheriff Westmoreland, this is Ms. Rochelle Brockman."

Dare swung his head around and his gaze collided with the woman he'd once loved to distraction. Suddenly his breath caught, his mouth went dry and every muscle in his body froze as memories rushed through his spiraling mind.

He could vividly recall the first time they'd met, their first kiss and the first time they had made love. The last time stood out in his mind now. He dragged his gaze from her face to do a total sweep of her body before returning to her face again. A shiver of desire tore through him, and he was glad that his position, standing behind his desk, blocked a view of his body from the waist down. Otherwise both women would have seen the arousal pressing against the zipper of his pants.

His gaze moved to her dark brown hair, and he noted that it was shorter and cut in one of those trendy styles that accented the creamy chocolate coloring of her face as well as the warm brandy shade of her eyes.

The casual outfit she wore, a printed skirt and a matching blouse, made her look stylish, comfortable and ultra-feminine. Then there were the legs he still considered the most gorgeous pair he'd ever seen. Legs he knew could wrap around his waist while their bodies meshed in pleasure.

A deep sigh escaped his closed lips as he concluded that at thirty-three she was even more beautiful than he remembered and still epitomized everything feminine. They'd first met when she was sixteen and a sophomore in high school. He'd been nineteen, a few weeks shy of twenty and a sophomore in college, and had come home for a visit to find her working on a school project with his brother Stone. He had walked into the house at the exact moment she'd been leaning over Stone, explaining some scientific formula and wearing the sexiest pair of shorts he had ever seen on a female. He had thought she had a pair of legs that were simply a complete turn-on. When she had glanced up, noticed him staring and smiled, he'd been a goner. Never before had he been so aware of a woman. An immediate attraction had flared between them, holding him hostage to desires he'd never felt before.

After making sure Stone didn't have designs on her himself, he had made his move. And it was a move he'd never regretted making. They began seriously dating a few months later and had continued to do so for six long years, until he had made the mistake of ending things between them. Now it seemed the day of reckoning had arrived.

"Shelly."

"Dare."

It was as if the years had not passed between them, Dare suddenly thought. That same electrical charge the two of them always generated ignited full force, sending a high voltage searing through the room.

He cleared his throat. "Holly, you can leave me and Ms. Brockman alone now," he thought it best to say.

His secretary looked at Shelly then back at him. "Sure, Sheriff," she murmured, and walked out of the office, pulling the door shut behind her.

Once the door closed, Dare turned his full attention back to Shelly. His gaze went immediately to her lips; lips he used to enjoy tasting time and time again; lips that were hot, sweet and ultra-responsive. One night he had thrust her into an orgasm just from gnawing on her lips and caressing them with the tip of his tongue.

He swallowed to get his bearings when he felt his body begin responding to just being in the same room with her. He then admitted what he'd known for years. Shelly Brockman would always be the beginning and the end of his most blatant desires and a part of him could not believe she was back in College Park after being gone for so long.

Shelly felt the intensity of Dare's gaze and struggled to keep her emotions in check, but he was so disturbingly gorgeous that she found it hard to do so. Wearing his blue uniform, he still had that look that left a woman's mind whirling and her body overheated.

He had changed a lot from the young man she had fallen in love with years ago. He was taller, bigger and more muscular. The few lines he had developed in the corners of his eyes, and the firmness of his jaw made his face more angular, his coffee-colored features stark and disturbingly handsome and still a pleasure to look at.

She noted there were certain things about him that had remained the same. The shape of his mouth was still a total turn-on, and he still had those sexy dimples he used to flash at her so often. Then there were those dark eyes— deep, penetrating—that at one time had had the ability to read her mind by just looking at her. How else had he known when she'd wanted him to make love to her without her having to utter a single word?

Suddenly Shelly felt nervous, panicky when she remembered the reason she had moved back to town. But there was no way she could tell Dare that he was AJ's father—at least not today. She needed time to pull herself together. Seeing him again had derailed her senses, making it impossible for her to think straight. The only thing she wanted was to get AJ and leave.

"I came for my son, Dare," she finally found her voice to say, and even to her own ears it sounded wispy.

Dare let out a deep breath. It seemed she wanted to get right down to business and not dwell on the past. He had no intention of letting her do that, mainly because of what they had once meant to each other. "It's been a long time, Shelly. How have you been?" he asked raspily, failing to keep his own voice casual. He found the scent of her perfume just as sexy and enticing as the rest of her.

"I've been fine, Dare. How about you?"

"Same here."

She nodded. "Now may I see my son?"

Her insistence on keeping things nonpersonal was beginning to annoy the hell out of him. His eyes narrowed and his gaze zeroed in on her mouth; bad timing on his part. She nervously swiped her bottom lip with her tongue, causing his body to react immediately. He remembered that tongue and some of the things he had taught her to do with it. He dragged air into his lungs when he felt his muscles tense. "Aren't you going to ask why he's here?" he asked, his voice sounding tight, just as tight as his entire body felt.

She shrugged. "I assumed that since the school called and said he didn't show up today, one of your officers had picked him up for playing hooky."

"No, that's not it," he said, thinking that was a reasonable assumption to make. "I'm the one who picked him up, but he was doing something a bit more serious than playing hooky."

Shelly's eyes widened in alarm. "What?"

"I caught him throwing rocks at passing motorists on

Old National Highway. Do you know what could have happened had a driver swerved to avoid getting hit?"

Shelly swallowed as she nodded. "Yes." The first thought that came to her mind was that AJ was in need of serious punishment, but she'd tried punishing him in the past and it hadn't seemed to work.

"I'm sorry about this, Dare," she apologized, not knowing what else to say. "We moved to town a few weeks ago and it hasn't been easy for him. He needs time to adjust."

Dare snorted. "From the way he acted in my office earlier today, I think what he needs is an attitude adjustment as well as a lesson in respect and manners. Whose kid is he anyway?"

Shelly straightened her spine. The mother in her took offense at his words. She admitted she had spoiled AJ somewhat, but still, considering the fact that she was a single parent doing the best she could, she didn't need Dare of all people being so critical. "He's my child."

Dare stared at her wondering if she really expected him to believe that. There was no way the kid could be hers, since in his estimation of the kid's age, she was a student in college and his steady girl about the same time the boy was born. "I mean who does he really belong to since I know you didn't have a baby twelve or thirteen years ago, Shelly."

Her gaze turned glacial. "He *is* mine, Dare. I gave birth to him *ten* years ago. He just looks older than he really is because of his height." Shelly watched Dare's gaze sharpen and darken, then his brows pulled together in a deep, furious frown.

"What the hell do you mean *you* gave birth to him?" he asked, a shocked look on his face and a tone of voice that bordered on anger and total disbelief.

She met his glare with one of her own. "I meant just what I said. Now may I see him?" She made a move to leave Dare's office but he caught her arm.

"Are you saying that he was born after you left here?"

"Yes."

Dare released her. His features had suddenly turned to stone, and the gaze that focused on hers was filled with hurt and pain. "It didn't take you long to find someone in California to take my place after we broke up, did it?"

His words were like a sharp, painful slap to Shelly's face. He thought that she had given birth to someone else's child! How could he think that when she had loved him so much? She was suddenly filled with extreme anger. "Why does it matter to you what I did after I left here, Dare, when you decided after six long years that you wanted a career with the FBI more than you wanted me?"

Dare closed his eyes, remembering that night and what he had said to her, words he had later come to regret. He slowly reopened his eyes and looked at her. She appeared just as stricken now as she had then. He doubted he would ever forget the deep look of hurt on her face that night he had told her that he wanted to break up with her to pursue a career with the FBI.

"Shelly, I…"

"No, Dare. I think we've said enough, too much in fact. Just let me get my son and go home."

Dare inhaled deeply. It was too late for whatever he wanted to say to her. Whatever had once been between them was over and done with. Turning, he slowly walked back over to his desk. "There's some paperwork that needs to be completed before you can take him with you. Since he refused to provide us with any information, we couldn't do it earlier."

He read the question that suddenly flashed in her gaze and said, "And no, this will not be a part of any permanent record, although I think it won't be such a bad idea for him to come back every day this week after school for an hour to do additional chores, especially since he mentioned he's not into any after-school activity. The light tasks I'll be assigning to him will work off some of that rebellious energy he has."

He met her gaze. "However, if this happens again, Shelly, he'll be faced with having to perform hours of community service as well as getting slapped with a juvenile delinquent record. Is that understood?"

She nodded, feeling much appreciative. Had he wanted to, Dare could have handled things a lot more severely. What AJ had done was a serious offense. "Yes, I understand, and I want to thank you."

She sighed deeply. It seemed fate would not be forcing her hand today after all. She had a little more time before having to tell Dare the truth.

Dare sat down at his desk with a form in front of him and a pen in his hand. "Now then, what's his name?"

Shelly swallowed deeply. "AJ Brockman."

"I need his real name."

She couldn't open her mouth to get the words out. It seemed fate wouldn't be as gracious as she'd thought after all.

Dare was looking down at the papers in front of him, however, the pause went on so long he glanced up and looked at her. He had known Shelly long enough to know when she was nervous about something. His eyes narrowed as he wondered what her problem was.

"What's his real name, Shelly?" he repeated.

He watched as she looked away briefly. Returning her gaze she stared straight into his eyes and without blinking said, "Alisdare Julian Brockman."

Two

Air suddenly washed from Dare's lungs as if someone had cut off the oxygen supply in the room and he couldn't breathe. Everything started spinning around him and he held on to his desk with a tight grip. However, that didn't work since his hands were shaking worse than a volcano about to explode. In fact his entire body shook with the force of the one question that immediately torpedoed through his brain. Why would she name her son after him? Unless...

He met her gaze and saw the look of guilt in her eyes and knew. Yet he had to have it confirmed. He stood on non-steady legs and crossed the room to stand in front of Shelly. He grasped her elbow and brought her closer to him, so close he could see the dark irises of her eyes.

"When is his birth date?" he growled, quickly finding his equilibrium.

Shelly swallowed so deeply she knew for certain Dare could see her throat tighten, but she refused to let his reaction unsettle her any more than it had. She lifted her chin. "November twenty-fifth."

He flinched, startled. "Two months?" he asked in a pained whisper yet with intense force. "You were two months pregnant when we broke up?"

She snatched her arm from his hold. "Yes."

Anger darkened the depths of his eyes then flared through his entire body at the thought of what she had kept from him. "I have a son?"

Though clearly upset, he had asked the question so quietly that Shelly could only look at him. For a long moment she didn't answer, but then she knew that in spite of everything between them, there was never a time she had not been proud that AJ was Dare's son. That was the reason she had returned to College Park, because she felt it was time he was included in AJ's life. "Yes, you have a son."

"But—but I didn't know about him!"

His words were filled with trembling fury and she knew she had to make him understand. "I found out I was pregnant the day before my graduation party and had planned to tell you that night. But before I got the chance you told me about the phone call you'd received that day, offering you a job with the Bureau and how much you wanted to take it. I loved you too much to stand in your way, Dare. I knew that telling you I was pregnant would have changed everything, and I couldn't do that to you."

Dare's face etched into tight lines as he stared at her. "And you made that decision on your own?"

She nodded. "Yes."

"How dare you! Who in the hell gave you the right to do that, Shelly?"

She felt her own anger rise. "It's not who but what. My love for you gave me the right, Dare," she said and without giving him a chance to say another word, she angrily walked out of his office.

Fury consumed Dare at a degree he had never known before and all he could do was stand there, rooted in place, shell-shocked at what he had just discovered.

He had a son.

He crossed the room and slammed his fist hard on the desk. Ten years! For ten years she had kept it from him. Ten solid years.

Ignoring the pain he felt in his hand, he breathed in deeply when it hit him that he was the father of John Doe. No, she'd called him AJ but she had named him Alisdare Julian. He took a deep, calming breath. For some reason she had at least done that. His son did have his name—at least part of it anyway. Had he known, his son would also be wearing the name Westmoreland, which was rightfully his.

Dare slowly walked over to the window and looked out, suddenly seeing the kid through different eyes—a father's eyes, and his heart and soul yearned for a place in his son's life; a place he rightly deserved. And from the way the kid had behaved earlier it was a place Dare felt he needed to be. It seemed that Alisdare Julian Brockman was a typical Westmoreland male—headstrong and stubborn as hell. As Dare studied him through the windowpane, he could see Westmoreland written all over him and was surprised he hadn't seen it earlier.

He turned when the buzzer sounded on his desk. He took the few steps to answer it. "Yes, Holly?"

"Ms. Brockman is ready to leave, sir. Have you completed the paperwork?"

Dare frowned as he glanced down at the half-completed form on his desk. "No, I haven't."

"What do you want me to tell her, Sheriff?"

Dare sighed. If Shelly for one minute thought she could just walk out of here and take their son, she had another thought coming. There was definitely unfinished business between them. "Tell Ms. Brockman there're a few things I need to take care of. After which, I'll speak with her again in my office. In the meantime, she's not to see her son."

There was a slight pause before Holly replied. "Yes, sir."

After hanging up the phone Dare picked up the form that contained all the standard questions, however, he didn't know any answers about his son. He wondered if he could ever forgive Shelly for doing that to him. No matter what she said, she had no right to have kept him in the dark about his son for ten years.

After the elder Brockmans had retired and moved away, there had been no way to stay in touch except for Ms. Kate, the owner of Kate's Diner who'd been close friends with Shelly's mother. But no matter how many times he had asked Kate about the Brockmans, specifically Shelly, she had kept a stiff lip and a closed mouth.

A number of the older residents in town who had kept an eye on his and Shelly's budding romance during those six years had been pretty damn disappointed with the way he had ended things between them. Even his family, who'd thought the world of Shelly, had decided he'd had a few screws loose for breaking up with her.

He sighed deeply. As sheriff, he of all people should have known she had returned to College Park; he made it his business to keep up with all the happenings around town. She must have come back during the time he had been busy apprehending those two fugitives who'd been hiding out in the area.

With the form in one hand he picked up the phone with the other. His cousin, Jared Westmoreland, was the attorney in the family and Dare felt the need for legal advice.

"The sheriff needs to take care of few things and would like to see you again in his office when he's finished."

Shelly nodded but none too happily. "Is there anyway I can see my son?"

The older woman shook her head. "I'm sorry but you

can't see or talk to him until the sheriff completes the paperwork."

When the woman walked off Shelly shook her head. What had taken place in Dare's office had certainly not been the way she'd envisioned telling him about AJ. She walked over to a chair and sat down, wondering how long would it be before she could get AJ and leave. Dare was calling the shots and there wasn't anything she could do about it but wait. She knew him well enough to know that anger was driving him to strike back at her for what she'd done, what she'd kept from him. A part of her wondered if he would ever forgive her for doing what she'd done, although at the time she'd thought it was for the best.

"Ms. Brockman?"

Shelly shifted her gaze to look into the face of a uniformed man who appeared to be in his late twenties. "Yes?"

"I'm Deputy Rick McKade, and the sheriff wants to see you now."

Shelly stood. She wasn't ready for another encounter with Dare, but evidently he was ready for another one with her.

"All right."

This time when she entered Dare's office he was sitting behind his desk with his head lowered while writing something. She hoped it was the paperwork she needed to get AJ and go home, but a part of her knew the moment Dare lifted his head and looked up at her, that he would not make things easy on her. He was still angry and very much upset.

"Shelly?"

She blinked when she realized Dare had been talking. She also realized Deputy McKade had left and closed the door behind him. "I'm sorry, what did you say?"

He gazed at her for a long moment. "I said you could have a seat."

She shook her head. "I don't want to sit down, Dare. All I want is to get AJ and take him home."

"Not until we talk."

She took a deep breath and felt a tightness in her throat. She also felt tired and emotionally drained. "Can we make arrangements to talk some other time, Dare?"

Shelly regretted making the request as soon as the words had left her mouth. They had pushed him, not over the edge but just about. He stood and covered the distance separating them. The degree of anger on his face actually had her taking a step back. She didn't ever recall seeing him so furious.

"Talk some other time? You have some nerve even to suggest something like that. I just found out that I have a son, a ten-year-old son, and you think you can just waltz back into town with my child and expect me to turn my head and look away and not claim what's mine?"

Shelly released the breath she'd been holding, hearing the sound of hurt and pain in Dare's voice. "No, I never thought any of those things, Dare," she said softly. "In fact, I thought just the opposite, which is why I moved back. I knew once I told you about AJ that you would claim him as yours. And I also knew you would help me save him."

Eyes narrowed and jaw tight, Dare stared at her. She watched as immediate concern—a father's concern—appear in his gaze. "Save him from what?"

"Himself."

She paused, then answered the question she saw flaring in his eyes. "You've met him, and I'm sure you saw how angry he is. I can only imagine what sort of an impression he made on you today, but deep down he's really a good kid, Dare. I began putting in extra hours at the hospital, which resulted in him spending more time with sitters and finding ways to get into trouble, especially at school when he got mixed up with the wrong crowd. That's the reason

I moved back here, to give him a fresh start—with your help."

Anger, blatant and intense, flashed in Dare's eyes. "Are you saying that the only reason you decided to tell me about him and seek my help was because he'd started giving you trouble? What about those years when he was a *good* kid? Did you not think I had a right to know about his existence then?"

Shelly held his gaze. "I thought I was doing the right thing by not telling you about him, Dare."

A muscle worked in his jaw. "Well, you were wrong. You didn't do the right thing. Nothing would have been more important to me than being a father to my son, Shelly."

A twinge of regret, a fleeting moment of sadness for the ten years of fatherhood she had taken away from him touched Shelly. She had to make him understand why she had made the decision she had that night. "That night you stood before me and said that becoming a FBI agent was all you had ever wanted, Dare, all you had ever dreamed about, and that the reason we couldn't be together any longer was because of the nature of the work. You felt it was best that as an agent, you shouldn't have a wife or family." She blinked back tears when she added, "You even said you were glad I hadn't gotten pregnant any of those times we had made love."

She wiped at her eyes. "How do you think I felt hearing you say that, two months pregnant and knowing that our baby and I stood in the way of you having what you desired most?"

When AJ's laughter floated in from the outside, Shelly slowly walked over to the window and looked into the yard below. The boy was watching a uniformed officer give a police dog a bath. This was the first time she had heard AJ laugh in months, and the sheer look of enjoyment on his face at that moment was priceless. She turned back around to face Dare, knowing she had to let him know how she felt.

"When I found out I was pregnant there was no question in my mind that I wouldn't tell you, Dare. In fact, I had been anxiously waiting all that night for the perfect time to do so. And then as soon as we were alone, you dropped the bomb on me."

She inhaled deeply before continuing. "For six long years I assumed that I had a definite place in your heart. I had actually thought that I was the most important thing to you, but in less than five minutes you proved I was wrong. Five minutes was all it took for you to wash six years down the drain when you told me you wanted your freedom."

She stared down at the hardwood floor for a moment before meeting his gaze again. "Although you didn't love me anymore, I still wanted our child. I knew that telling you about my pregnancy would cause you to forfeit your dream and do what you felt was the honorable thing—spend the rest of your life in a marriage you didn't want."

She quickly averted her face so he wouldn't see her tears. She didn't want him to know how much he had hurt her ten years ago. She didn't want him to see that the scars hadn't healed; she doubted they ever would.

"Shelly?"

The tone that called her name was soft, gentle and tender. So tender that she glanced up at him, finding it difficult to meet his dark, piercing gaze, though she met it anyway. She fought the tremble in her voice when she said, "What?"

"That night, I never said I didn't love you," he said, his voice low, a near-whisper. "How could you have possibly thought that?"

She shook her head sadly and turned more fully toward him, not believing he had asked the question. "How could I not think it, Dare?"

Her response made him raise a thick eyebrow. Yes, how

could she not think it? He had broken off with her that night, never thinking she would assume that he had never loved her or that she hadn't meant everything to him. Now he could see how she could have felt that way.

He inhaled deeply and rubbed a hand over his face, wondering how he could explain things to her when he really didn't understand himself. He knew he had to try anyway. "It seems I handled things very poorly that night," he said.

Shelly chuckled softly and shrugged her shoulders. "It depends on what you mean by poorly. I think that you accomplished what you set out to do, Dare. You got rid of a girlfriend who stood between you and your career plans."

"That wasn't it, Shelly."

"Then tell me what was *it*," she said, trying to hold on to the anger she was beginning to feel all over again.

For a few moments he didn't say anything, then he spoke. "I loved you, Shelly, and the magnitude of what I felt for you began to frighten me because I knew what you and everyone else expected of me. But a part of me knew that although I loved you, I wasn't ready to take the big step and settle down with the responsibility of a wife. I also knew there was no way I could ask you to wait for me any longer. We had already dated six years and everyone—my family, your family and this whole damn town—expected us to get married. It was time. We had both finished college and I had served a sufficient amount of time in the marines, and you were about to embark on a career in nursing. There was no way I could ask you to wait around and twiddle your thumbs while I worked as an agent. It wouldn't have been fair. You deserved more. You deserved better. So I thought the best thing to do was to give you your freedom."

Shelly dipped her chin, no longer able to look into his eyes. Moments later she lifted her gaze to meet his. "So, I'm not the only one who made a decision about us that night."

Dare inhaled deeply, realizing she was right. Just as she'd done, he had made a decision about them. A few moments later he said, "I wish I had handled things differently, Shelly. Although I loved you, I wasn't ready to become the husband I knew you wanted."

"Yet you want me to believe you would have been ready to become a father?" she asked softly, trying to make him see reason. "All I knew after that night was that the man I loved no longer wanted me, and that his dream wasn't a future with me but one in law enforcement. And I loved him enough to step aside to let him fulfill that dream. That's the reason I left without telling you about the baby, Dare. That's the only reason."

He nodded. "Had I known you were pregnant, my dreams would not have mattered at that point."

"Yes, I knew that better than anyone."

Dare finally understood the point she'd been trying to make and sighed at how things had turned out for them. Ten years ago he'd thought that becoming a FBI agent was the ultimate. It had taken seven years of moving from place to place, getting burnt-out from undercover operations, waking each morning cloaked in danger and not knowing if his next assignment would be his last, to finally make him realize the career that had once been his dream had turned into a living nightmare. Resigning from the Bureau, he had returned home to open up a security firm about the same time Sheriff Dean Whitlow, who'd been in office since Dare was in his early teens, had decided to retire. It was Sheriff Whitlow who had talked him into running for the position he was about to vacate, saying that with Dare's experience, he was the best man for the job. Now, after three years at it, Dare had forged a special bond with the town he'd always loved and the people he'd known all of his life. And compared to what he had done as an FBI agent, being sheriff was a gravy train.

He glanced out of the window and didn't say anything for the longest time as he watched AJ. Then he spoke. "I take it that he doesn't know anything about me."

Shelly shook her head. "No. Years ago I told him that his father was a guy I had loved and thought I would marry, but that things didn't work out and we broke up. I told him I moved away before I had a chance to tell him I was pregnant."

Dare stared at her. "That's it?"

"Yes, that's it. He was fairly young at the time, but occasionally as he got older, he would ask if I knew how to reach you if I ever wanted to, and I told him yes and that if he ever wanted me to contact you I would. All he had to do was ask, but he never has."

Dare nodded. "I want him to know I'm his father, Shelly."

"I want him to know you're his father, too, Dare, but we need to approach this lightly with him," she whispered softly. "He's going through enough changes right now, and I don't want to get him any more upset than he already is. I have an idea as to how and when we can tell him, and I hope after hearing me out that you'll agree."

Dare went back to his desk. "All right, so what do you suggest?"

Shelly nodded and took a seat across from his desk. She held her breath, suddenly feeling uncomfortable telling him what she thought was the best way to handle AJ. She knew her son's emotional state better than anyone. Right now he was mad at the world in general and her in particular, because she had taken him out of an environment he'd grown comfortable with, although that environment as far as she was concerned, had not been a healthy one for a ten-year-old. His failing grades and the trouble he'd gotten into had proven that.

"What do you suggest, Shelly?" Dare asked again, sitting down and breaking into her thoughts.

Shelly cleared her throat. "I know how anxious you are to have AJ meet you, but I think it would be best, considering everything, if he were to get to know you as a friend before knowing you as his father."

Dare frowned, not liking the way her suggestion sounded. "But I am his father, Shelly, not his friend."

"Yes, and that's the point. More than anything, AJ needs a friend right now, Dare, someone he can trust and connect with. He has a hard time making friends, which is why he began hanging out with the wrong type of kids at the school he attended in California. They readily accepted him for all the wrong reasons. I've talked to a few of his teachers since moving here and he's having the same problems. He's just not outgoing."

Dare nodded. Of the five Westmoreland brothers, he was the least outgoing, if you didn't count Thorn who was known to be a pain in the butt at times. Growing up, Dare had felt that his brothers were all the playmates he had needed, and because of that, he never worried about making friends or being accepted. His brothers were his friends—his best friends—and as far as he'd been concerned they were enough. It was only after he got older and his brothers began seeking other interests that he began getting out more, playing sports, meeting people and making new friends.

So if AJ wasn't as outgoing as most ten-year-old kids, he had definitely inherited that characteristic from him. "So how do you think I should handle it?"

"I suggest that we don't tell him the truth about you just yet, and that you take the initiative to form a bond with him, share his life and get to know him."

Dare raised a dark brow. "And just how am I supposed to do that? Our first meeting didn't exactly get off to a great start, Shelly. Technically, I arrested him, for heaven's sake. My own son! A kid who didn't bat an eye when he informed me he hated cops—which is what I definitely am. Then there's this little attitude problem of his that I feel needs adjusting. So come on, let's be real here. How am I supposed to develop a relationship with *my kid* when he dislikes everything I stand for?"

Shelly shook her head. "He doesn't really hate cops, Dare, he just thinks he does because of what happened as we were driving from California to here."

Dare lifted a brow. "What happened?"

"I got pulled over in some small Texas town and the officer was extremely rude. Needless to say he didn't make a good impression on AJ."

She sighed deeply. "But you can change that, Dare. That's why I think the two of you getting together and developing a relationship as friends first would be the ideal thing. Ms. Kate told me that you work with the youth in the community and about the Little League baseball team that you coach. I want to do whatever it takes to get AJ involved in something like that."

"And he can become involved as my son."

"I think we should go the friendship route first, Dare."

Dare shook his head. "Shelly, you haven't thought this through. I understand what you're saying because I know how it was for me as a kid growing up. At least I had my brothers who were my constant companions. But I think you've forgotten one very important thing here."

Shelly raised her brow. "What?"

"Most of the people in College Park know you, and most of them have long memories. Once they hear that you have a ten-year-old son, they'll start counting months, and once they see him they'll definitely know the truth. They will see just how much of a Westmoreland he is. He favors my brothers and me. The reason I didn't see it before was because I wasn't looking for it. But you better believe the good people of this town will be. Once you're seen with AJ they'll be looking for anything to link me to him, and it will be easy for them to put two and two together. And don't let them find out that he was named after me. That will be the icing on the cake."

Dare gave her time to think about what he'd said before continuing. "What's going to happen if AJ learns that I'm his father from someone other than us? He'll resent us for keeping the truth from him."

Shelly sighed deeply, knowing Dare was right. It would be hard to keep the truth hidden in a close-knit town like College Park.

"But there is another solution that will accomplish the same purpose, Shelly," he said softly.

She met his gaze. "What?"

Dare didn't say anything at first, then he said. "I'm asking that you hear me out before jumping to conclusions and totally dishing the idea."

She stared at him before nodding her head. "All right."

Dare continued. "You said you told AJ that you and his father had planned to marry but that we broke up and you moved away before telling him you were pregnant, right?"

Shelly nodded. "Yes."

"And he knows this is the town you grew up in, right?"

"Yes, although I doubt he's made the connection."

"What if you take him into your confidence and let him know that his father lives here in College Park, then go a step further and tell him who I am, but convince him that you haven't told me yet and get his opinion on what you should do?"

Since Dare and AJ had already butted heads, Shelly had a pretty good idea of what he would want her to do—keep the news about him from Dare. He would be dead set against developing any sort of personal relationship with Dare, and she told Dare so.

"Yes, but what if he's placed in a position where he has to accept me, or has to come in constant contact with me?" Dare asked.

"How?"

"If you and I were to rekindle our relationship, at least pretend to do so."

Shelly frowned, clearly not following Dare. "And just how will that help the situation? Word will still get out that you're his father."

"Yes, but he'll already know the truth and he'll think I'm the one in the dark. He'll either want me to find out the truth or he'll hope that I don't. In the meantime I'll do my damnedest to win him over."

"And what if you can't?"

"I will. AJ needs to feel that he belongs, Shelly, and he does belong. Not only does he belong to you and to me, but he also belongs to my brothers, my parents and the rest of the Westmorelands. Once we start seeing each other again, he'll be exposed to my family, and I believe when that happens and I start developing a bond with him, he'll eventually want to acknowledge me as his father."

Dare shifted in his chair. "Besides," he added smiling. "If he really doesn't want us to get together, he'll be so busy thinking of ways to keep us apart that he won't have time to get into trouble."

Shelly lifted a brow, knowing Dare did have a point. However, she wasn't crazy about his plan, especially not the part she would play. The last thing she needed was to pretend they were falling in love all over again. Already, being around him was beginning to feel too comfortably familiar.

She sighed deeply. In order for Dare's plan to work, they would have to start spending time together. She couldn't help wondering how her emotions would be able to handle that. And she didn't even want to consider what his nearness might do to her hormones, since it had been a long time since she had spent any time with a man. A very long time.

She cleared her throat when she noticed Dare watching her intently and wondered if he knew what his gaze was doing to her. Biting her lower lip and shifting in her seat, she asked, "How do you think he's going to feel when he finds out that we aren't really serious about each other, and it was just a game we played to bring him around?"

"I think he'll accept the fact that although we aren't married, we're friends who like and respect each other. Most boys from broken relationships I come in contact with have parents who dislike each other. I think it's important that a child sees that although they aren't married, his parents are still friends who make his well-being their top priority."

Shelly shook her head. "I don't know, Dare. A lot can go wrong with what you're proposing."

"True, but on the other hand, a lot can go right. This way we're letting AJ call the shots, or at least we're letting him think that he is. This will give him what he'll feel is a certain degree of leverage, power and control over the situation. From working closely with kids, I've discovered that if you try forcing them to do something they will rebel. But if you sit tight and be patient, they'll eventually come around on their own. That's what I'm hoping will happen in this case. Chances are he'll resent me at first, but that's the chance I have to take. Winning him over will be my mission, Shelly, one I plan to accomplish. And trust me, it will be the most important mission of my life."

He studied her features, and when she didn't say anything for the longest time he said, "I have a lot more to lose than you, but I'm willing to risk it. I don't want to spend too much longer with my son not knowing who I am. At least this way he'll know that I'm his father, and it will be up to me to do everything possible to make sure that he wants to accept me in his life."

He inhaled deeply. "So will you at least think about what I've proposed?"

Shelly met his gaze. "Yes, Dare, I'll need time," she said quietly.

"Overnight. That's all the time I can give you, Shelly."

"But, I need more time."

Dare stood. "I can't give you any more time than that. I've lost ten years already and can't afford to lose any more. And just so you'll know, I've made plans to meet with Jared for lunch tomorrow. I'll ask him to act as my attorney so that I'll know my rights as AJ's father."

Shelly shook her head sadly. "There's no need for you to do that, Dare. I don't intend to keep you and AJ apart. As I said, you're the reason I returned."

Dare nodded. "Will you meet me for breakfast at Kate's Diner in the morning so we can decide what we're going to do?"

Shelly felt she needed more time but knew there was no way Dare would give it to her. "All right. I'll meet you in the morning."

Three

Dare reached across his desk and hit the buzzer.

"Yes, Sheriff?"

"McKade, please bring in John Doe."

Shelly frowned when she glanced over at Dare. "John Doe?"

Dare shrugged. "That's the usual name for any unidentified person we get in here, and since he refused to give us his name, we had no choice."

She nodded. "Oh."

Before Dare could say anything else, McKade walked in with AJ. The boy frowned when he saw his mother. "I wondered if you were ever going to come, Mom."

Shelly smiled wryly. "Of course I was going to come. Had you given them your name they would have called me sooner. You have a lot of explaining to do as to why you weren't in school today. It's a good thing Sheriff Westmoreland stopped you before you could cause harm to anyone."

AJ turned and glared at Dare. "Yeah, but I still don't like cops."

Dare crossed his arms on his chest. "And I don't like boys with bad attitudes. To be frank, it doesn't matter whether or not you like cops, but you'd sure better learn to respect them and what they stand for." This might be his son, Dare thought, but he intended to teach him a lesson in respect, starting now.

AJ turned to his mother. "I'm ready to go."

Shelly nodded. "All right."

"Not yet," Dare said, not liking the tone AJ had used with Shelly, or how easily she had given in to him. "What you did today was a serious matter, and as part of your punishment, I expect you to come back every day this week after school to do certain chores I'll have lined up for you."

"And if I don't show up?"

"AJ!"

Dare held up his hand, cutting off anything Shelly was about to say. This was between him and his son. "And if you don't show up, I'll know where to find you and when I do it will only make things a lot worse for you. Trust me."

Dare's gaze shifted to Shelly. This was not the way he wanted to start things off with his son, but he'd been left with little choice. AJ had to respect him as the sheriff as well as accept him as his father. From the look on Shelly's face he knew she understood that as well.

"Sheriff Westmoreland is right," she said firmly, giving Dare her support. "And you *will* show up after school to do whatever he has for you to do. Is that understood?"

"Yeah, yeah, I understand," the boy all but snapped. "Can we go now?"

Dare nodded and handed her the completed form. "I'll walk the two of you out to the car since I was about to leave anyway."

Once Shelly and AJ were in the car and had buckled up their seat belts, Dare glanced into the car and said to the boy, "I'll see you tomorrow when you get out of school."

Ignoring AJ's glare, he then turned and the look he gave

Shelly said that he expected to see her tomorrow as well, at Kate's Diner in the morning. "Good night and drive safely."

He then walked away.

An hour later, Dare walked into a room where four men sat at a table engaged in a card game. The four looked up and his brother Stone spoke. "You're late."

"I had important business to take care of," Dare said grabbing a bottle of beer and leaning against the refrigerator in Stone's kitchen. "I'll wait this round out and just watch."

His brothers nodded as they continued with the game. Moments later, Chase Westmoreland let out a curse. Evidently he was losing as usual, Dare thought smiling. He then thought about how the four men at the table were more than just brothers to him; they were also his very best friends, although Thorn, the one known for his moodiness, could test that friendship and brotherly love to the limit at times. At thirty-five, Thorn was only eleven months younger than him, and built and raced motorcycles for a living. Last year he'd been the only African-American on the circuit.

His brother Stone, known for his wild imagination, had recently celebrated his thirty-third birthday and wrote action-thriller novels under the pen name, Rock Mason. Then there were the fraternal thirty-two-year-old twins, Chase and Storm. Chase was the oldest by seven minutes and owned a soul-food restaurant in downtown Atlanta, and Storm was the fireman in the family. According to their mother, she had gone into delivery unexpectedly while riding in the car with their dad. When a bad storm had come up, he chased time and outran the storm to get her to the hospital. Thus she had named her last two sons Chase and Storm.

"You're quiet, Dare."

Dare looked up from studying his beer bottle and brought his thoughts back to the present. He met Stone's curious stare. "Is that a crime?"

Stone grinned. "No, but if it was a crime I'm sure you'd arrest yourself since you're such a dedicated lawman."

Chase chuckled. "Leave Dare alone. Nothing's wrong with him other than he's keeping Thorn company with this celibacy thing," he said jokingly.

"Shut up, Storm, before I hurt you," Thorn Westmoreland said, without cracking a smile.

Everyone knew Thorn refrained from having sex while preparing for a race, which accounted for his prickly mood most of the time. But since Thorn had been in the same mood for over ten months now they couldn't help but wonder what his problem was. Dare had a clue but decided not to say. He sighed and crossed the room and sat down at the table. "Guess who's back in town."

Storm looked up from studying his hand and grinned. "Okay, I'll play your silly guessing game. Who's back in town, Dare?"

"Shelly."

Everyone at the table got quiet as they looked up at him. Then Stone spoke. "*Our* Shelly?"

Dare looked at his brother and frowned. "No, not *our* Shelly, *my* Shelly."

Stone glared at him. "*Your* Shelly? You could have fooled us, the way you dumped her."

Dare leaned back in his chair. He'd known it was coming. His brothers had actually stopped speaking to him for weeks after he'd broken off with Shelly. "I did not dump her. I merely made the decision that I wasn't ready for marriage and wanted a career with the Bureau instead."

"That sounds pretty much like you dumped her to me," Stone said angrily. "You knew she was the marrying kind. And you led her to believe, like you did the rest of us, that the two of you would eventually marry when she finished college. In my book you played her for a fool, and I've always felt bad about it because I'm the one who introduced the two of you," he added, glaring at his brother.

Dare stood. "I did not play her for a fool. Why is it so hard to believe that I really loved her all those years?" he asked, clearly frustrated. He'd had this same conversation with Shelly earlier.

"Because," Thorn said slowly and in a menacing tone as he threw out a card, "I would think most men don't walk away from the woman they claim to love for no damn reason, especially not some lame excuse about not being ready to settle down. The way I see it, Dare, you wanted to have your cake and eat it too." He took a swig of his beer. "Let's change the subject before I get mad all over again and knock the hell out of you for hurting her the way you did."

Chase narrowed his eyes at Dare. "Yeah, and I hope she's happily married with a bunch of kids. It would serve you right for letting the best thing that ever happen to you get away."

Dare raised his eyes to the ceiling, wondering if there was such a thing as family loyalty when it came to Shelly Brockman. He decided to sit back down when a new card game began. "She isn't happily married with a bunch of kids, Chase, but she does have a son. He's ten."

Stone smiled happily. "Good for her. I bet it ate up your guts to know she got involved with someone else and had his baby after she left here."

Dare leaned back in his chair. "Yeah, I went through some pretty hard stomach pains until I found out the truth."

Storm raised a brow. "The truth about what?"

Dare smirked at each one of his brothers before answering. "Shelly's son is mine."

Early the next morning Dare walked into Kate's Diner.

"Good morning, Sheriff."

"Good morning, Boris. How's that sore arm doing?"

"Fine. I'll be ready to play you in another game of basketball real soon."

"I'm counting on it."

"Good morning, Sheriff."

"Good morning, Ms. Mamie. How's your arthritis?"

"A pain as usual," was the old woman's reply.

"Good morning, Sheriff Westmoreland."

"Good morning, Lizzie," Dare greeted the young waitress as he slid into the stool at the counter. She was old man Barton's granddaughter and was working at the diner parttime while taking classes at the college in town.

He smiled when Lizzie automatically poured his coffee. She knew just how he liked it. Black. "Where's Ms. Kate this morning?" he asked after taking a sip.

"She hasn't come in yet."

He raised a dark brow. For as long as he'd known Ms. Kate—and that had been all of his thirty-six years—he'd never known her to be late to work at the diner. "Is everything all right?"

"Yes, I guess so," Lizzie said, not looking the least bit worried. "She called and said Mr. Granger was stopping by her house this morning to take a look at her hot-water heater. She thinks it's broken and wanted to be there when he arrived."

Dare nodded. It had been rumored around town for years that old man Granger and Ms. Kate were sweet on each other.

"Would you like for me to go ahead and order your usual, Sheriff?"

He rolled his shoulders as if to ease sore muscles as he smiled up at her and said. "No, not yet. I'm waiting on someone." He glanced at his watch. "She should be here any minute."

Lizzie nodded. "All right then. I'll be back when your guest arrives."

Dare was just about to check his watch again when he

heard the diner's door open behind him, followed by Boris's loud exclamation. "Well, my word, if it isn't Shelly Brockman! What on earth are you doing back here in College Park?"

Dare turned around on his stool as other patrons who'd known Shelly when she lived in town hollered out similar greetings. He had forgotten just how popular she'd been with everyone, both young and old. That was one of the reasons the entire town had all but skinned him alive when he'd broken off with her.

A muscle in his jaw twitched when he noticed that a few of the guys she'd gone to school with—Boris Jones, David Wright and Wayland Miller—who'd known years ago that she was off-limits because of him, were checking her out now. And he could understand why. She looked pretty damn good, and she still had that natural ability to turn men on without even trying. Blue was a color she wore well and nothing about that had changed, he thought, as his gaze roamed over the blue sundress she was wearing. With thin straps tied at the shoulders, it was a decent length that stopped right above her knees and showed off long beautiful bare legs and feet encased in a pair of black sandals. When he felt his erection straining against the crotch of his pants, he knew he was in big trouble. He was beginning to feel a powerful and compelling need that he hadn't felt in a long time; at least ten years.

"Is that her, Sheriff? The woman you've been waiting on?"

Lizzie's question interrupted Dare's musings. "Yes, that's her."

"Will the two of you be sitting at the counter or will you be using a table or a booth?"

Now that's a loaded question, Dare thought. He wished—doubly so—that he could take Shelly and use a table or a booth. He could just imagine her spread out on either. He shook his head. Although he'd always been sexually attracted to Shelly, he'd never thought of her with so much lust before, and he couldn't help wondering why. Maybe it was because in the past she'd always been his. Now things were different, she was no longer his and he was lusting hard—and he meant hard!—for something he had lost.

"Sheriff?"

Knowing Lizzie was waiting for his decision, he glanced toward the back of the diner and made a quick decision. "We'll be sitting at a booth in the back." Once he was confident he had his body back under control, he stood and walked over to where Shelly was surrounded by a number of people, mostly men.

Breaking into their conversations he said, "Good morning, Shelly. Are you ready for breakfast?"

It seemed the entire diner got quiet and all eyes turned to him. The majority of those present remembered that he had been the one to break Shelly's heart, which ultimately had resulted in her leaving town, and from the way everyone was looking at him, the last thing they wanted was for her to become involved with him again.

In fact, old Mr. Sylvester turned to him and said, "I'm surprised Shelly is willing to give you the time of day, Sheriff, after what you did to her ten years ago."

"You got that right," eighty-year-old Mamie Potter agreed.

Dare rolled his eyes. That was all he needed, the entire town bringing up the past and ganging up on him. "Shelly and I have business to discuss, if none of you mind."

Allen Davis, who had worked with Dare's grandfather years ago, crossed his arms over his chest. "Considering what you did to her, yes, we do mind. So you better behave yourself where she is concerned, Dare Westmoreland. Don't forget there's an election next year."

Dare had just about had it, and was about to tell Mr. Davis a thing or two when Shelly piped in, laughing, "I can't be-

BRENDA JACKSON   45

lieve all of you still remember what happened ten years ago. I'd almost forgotten about that," she lied. "And to this day I still consider Dare my good friend," she lied again, and tried tactfully to change the subject. "Ms. Mamie, how is Mr. Fred?"

"He still can't hear worth a dime, but other than that he's fine. Thanks for asking. Now to get back to the subject of Dare here, from the way he used to sniff behind you and kept all the other boys away from you, we all thought he was going to be your husband," Mamie mumbled, glaring at Dare.

Shelly shook her head, seeing that the older woman was determined to have her say. She placed a hand on Ms. Mamie's arm in a warm display of affection. "Yes, I know you all did and that was sweet. But things didn't work out that way and we can't worry about spilled milk now can we?"

Ms. Mamie smiled up at Shelly and patted her hand. "I guess not, dear, but watch yourself around him. I know how crazy you were about him before. There's no need for a woman to let the same man break her heart twice."

Dare frowned, not appreciating Mamie Potter talking about him as if he wasn't there. Nor did it help matters that Shelly was looking at him as though she'd just been given good sound advice. He cleared his throat, thinking that it was time he broke up the little gathering. He placed his hand on Shelly's arm and said, "This way, Shelly. We need to discuss our business so I can get to the office. We can talk now or you can join Jared and I for lunch."

From the look on her face he could tell his words had reminded her of why he was meeting Jared for lunch. After telling everyone goodbye and giving out a few more hugs, she turned and followed Dare to a booth, the farthest one in the back.

He stood aside while she slipped into a soft padded seat and then he slid into the one across from her. Nervously she traced the floral designs on the placemat. Dare's nearness was getting to her. She had experienced the same thing in his office last night, and it aggravated the heck out of her that all that anger she'd felt for him had not been able to diffuse her desire for him; especially after ten years.

Desire.

That had to be what it was since she knew she was no longer in love with him. He had effectively put an end to those feelings years ago. Yet, for some reason she was feeling the same turbulent yearnings she'd always felt for him. And last night in her bed, the memories had been at their worse...or their best, depending on how you looked at it.

She had awakened in the middle of the night with her breath coming in deep, ragged gasps, and her sheets damp with perspiration after a hot, steamy dream about him.

Getting up and drinking a glass of ice water, she had made a decision not to beat herself up over her dreams of Dare. She'd decided that the reason for them was understandable. Her body knew Dare as it knew no other man, and it had reminded her of that fact in a not-too-subtle way. It didn't help that for the past ten years she hadn't dated much; raising AJ and working at the hospital kept her busy, and the few occasions she had dated had been a complete waste of her time since she'd never experienced the sparks with any of them that she'd grown accustomed to with Dare.

"Would you like some more coffee, Sheriff?"

Shelly snatched her head up when she heard the sultry, feminine voice and was just in time to see the slow smile that spread across the young woman's lips, as well as the look of wanton hunger in her eyes as she looked at Dare. Either he didn't notice or he was doing a pretty good job of pretending not to.

"Yes, Lizzie, I'd like another cup."

"And what would you like?" Lizzie asked her, and Shelly

couldn't help but notice the cold, unfriendly eyes that were staring at her.

Evidently the same thing you would like, Shelly thought, trying to downplay the envy she suddenly felt, although she knew there was no legitimate reason to feel that way. What was once between her and Dare had ended years ago and she didn't intend to go back there, no matter how much he could still arouse her. Sighing, she was about to give the woman her order when Dare spoke. "She would like a cup of coffee with cream and one sugar."

The waitress lifted her brow as if wondering how Dare knew what Shelly wanted. "Okay, Sheriff." Lizzie placed menus in front of them, saying, "I'll bring your coffee while you take a look at these."

When Lizzie had left, Shelly leaned in closer to the center of the booth and whispered, "I don't appreciate the daggered looks coming from one of your girlfriends." She decided not to tell him that she'd felt like throwing a few daggered looks of her own.

Lifting his head from the menu, Dare frowned. "What are you talking about? I've never dated Lizzie. She's just a kid."

Shelly shrugged as she straightened in her seat and glanced over to where Lizzie was now taking another order. Her short uniform showed off quite nicely the curves of her body and her long legs. Dare was wrong. Lizzie was no kid. Her body attested to that.

"Well, kid or no kid, she definitely has the hots for you, Dare Westmoreland."

He shrugged. "You're imagining things."

"No, trust me. I know."

He rubbed his chin as his mouth tipped up crookedly into a smile. Settling back in his seat, he asked, "And how would you know?"

She met his gaze. "Because I'm a woman." And I know all about having the hots for you, she decided not to add.

Dare nodded. He definitely couldn't deny that she was a woman. He glanced over at Lizzie and caught her at the exact moment she was looking at him with a flirty smile. He remembered the other times she'd given him that smile, and now it all made sense. He quickly averted his eyes. Clearing his throat, he met Shelly's gaze. "I've never noticed before."

Typical man, Shelly thought, but before she could say anything else, Lizzie had returned with their coffee. After taking their order she left, and Shelly smiled and said, "I can't believe you remembered how I like my coffee after all this time."

Dare looked at her. His gaze remained steady when he said, "There are some things a man can't forget about a woman he considered as his, Shelly."

"Oh." Her voice was slightly shaky, and she decided not to touch that one; mainly because what he said was true. He had considered her as his; she had been his in every way a woman could belong to a man.

She took a deep breath before taking a sip of coffee. Emotions she didn't want to feel were churning inside her. Dare had hurt her once and she refused to let him do so again. She would definitely take Ms. Mamie's advice and watch herself around him. She glanced up and noticed Dare watching her. The heat from his gaze made her feel a connection to him, one she didn't want to feel, but she realized they did have a connection.

Their son.

She cleared her throat, deciding they needed to engage in conversation, something she considered a safe topic. "How is your family doing?"

A warm smile appeared on Dare's face. "Mom and Dad and all the rest of the Westmoreland clan are fine."

Shelly took another sip of her coffee. "Is it true what I've heard about Delaney? Did she actually finish medical school and marry a sheikh?" she asked. She wondered

how that had happened when everyone knew how overprotective the Westmoreland brothers had been of their baby sister.

Dare smiled and the heat in his gaze eased somewhat.
"Yeah, it's true. The one and only time we took our eyes
off Laney, she slipped away and hid out in a cabin in the
mountains for a little rest and relaxation. While there she
met this sheikh from the Middle East. Their marriage took
some getting used to, since she up and moved to his country. They have a five-month-old son named Ari."

"Have you seen him yet?"

Dare's smile widened. "Yes, the entire family was there
for his birth and it was some sort of experience." A frown
appeared on his face when he suddenly thought about what
he'd missed out on by not being there when AJ had come
into the world. "Tell me about AJ, Shelly. Tell me how
things were when he was born."

Shelly swallowed thickly. So much for thinking she had
moved to a safe topic of conversation. She sighed, knowing Dare had a right to what he was asking for. "He was
born in the hospital where I worked. My parents were there
with me. I didn't gain much weight while pregnant and that
helped make the delivery easier. He wasn't a big baby, only
a little over six pounds, but he was extremely long which
accounts for his height. As soon as I saw him I immediately
thought he looked like you. And I knew at that moment no
matter how we had separated, that my baby was a part of
you."

Shelly hesitated for a few moments and added. "That's
why I gave him your name, Dare. In my mind he didn't look
like a Marcus, which was the name I had intended to give
him. To me he looked like an Alisdare Julian. A little Dare."

Dare didn't say anything for the longest time, then he
said, "Thank you for doing that."

"You're welcome."

Moments later, Dare cleared his throat and asked, "Does he know he was named after his father?"

"Yes. You don't know how worried I was before arriving at the police station yesterday. I was afraid that you had found out his name, or that he had found out yours. Luckily for me, most people at the station call you Sheriff, and everyone in town still calls you Dare."

Dare nodded. "Except for my family, few people probably remember my real name is Alisdare since it's seldom used. I've always gone by Dare. If AJ had given me his full name I would have figured things out."

After a few brief quiet moments, Dare said, "I told my parents and my brothers about him last night, Shelly."

She nervously bit into her bottom lip. "And what were their reactions?"

Dare leaned back against his seat and met her gaze. "They were as shocked as I was, and of course they're anxious to meet him."

Shelly nodded slowly. She'd figured they would be. The Westmorelands were a big family and a rather close-knit group. "Dare, about your suggestion on how we should handle things."

"Yes?"

She didn't say anything for the longest time, then she said, "I'll go along with your plan as long as you and I understand something."

"What?"

"That it will be strictly for show. There's no way the two of us could ever get back together for any reason. The only thing between us is AJ."

Dare raised a brow and gave her a deliberate look. He wondered why she was so damn sure of that, but decided to let it go for now. He wanted to start building a relationship with his son immediately, and he refused to let Shelly put stumbling blocks in his way. "That's fine with me."

He leaned back in his chair. "So how soon will you tell AJ about me?"

"I plan to tell him tonight."

Dare nodded, satisfied with her answer. That meant they could put their plans into action as early as tomorrow. "I think we're doing the right thing, Shelly."

She felt the intensity of his gaze, and the force of it touched her in a way she didn't want. "I hope so, Dare. I truly hope so," she said quietly.

Four

Dare glanced at the clock again and sighed deeply. Where was AJ? School had let out over an hour ago and he still hadn't arrived. According to what Shelly had told him that morning at breakfast, AJ had ridden his bike to school and been told to report to the sheriff's office as soon as school was out. Dare wondered if AJ had blatantly disobeyed his mother.

Although Shelly had given him her cell-phone number—as a home healthcare nurse she would be making various house calls today—he didn't want to call and get her worried or upset. If he had to, he would go looking for their son himself and when he found him, he intended to—

The sound of the buzzer interrupted his thoughts. "Yes, McKade, what is it?"

"That Brockman kid is here."

Dare nodded and sighed with relief. Then he recalled what McKade had said—*that Brockman kid*. He frowned. The first thing he planned to do when everything settled was to give his son his last name. *That Westmoreland kid* sounded more to his liking. "Okay, I'll be right out."

Leaving his office, Dare walked down the hall toward the front of the building and stopped dead in his tracks when he saw AJ. His frown deepened. The kid looked as though he'd had a day with a tiger. "What happened to you?" he asked him, his gaze roaming over AJ's torn shirt and soiled jeans, not to mention his bruised lip and bloodied nose.

"Nothing happened. I fell off my bike," AJ snapped.

Dare glanced over at McKade. They both recognized a lie when they heard one. Dare crossed his arms over his chest. "You never came across to me as the outright clumsy type."

That got the response Dare was hoping for. The anger flaring in AJ's eyes deepened. "I am not the clumsy type. Anyone can fall off a bike," he said, again snapping out his answer.

"Yes, but in this case that's not what happened and you know it," Dare said, wanting to snap back but didn't. It was apparent that AJ had been in a fight, and Dare decided to cut the crap. "Tell me what really happened."

"I'm not telling you anything."

Wrong answer, Dare thought taking a step forward to stand in front of AJ. "Look, kid, we can stand here all day until you decide to talk, but you *will* tell me what happened."

AJ stuck his hands in the pockets of his jeans and glanced down as if to study the expensive pair of Air Jordans on his feet. When seconds ticked into minutes and he saw that Dare would not move an inch, he finally raised his head, met Dare's gaze, squared his shoulders and said, "Caleb Martin doesn't like me and today after school he decided to take his dislike to another level."

Dare leaned against the counter and raised a brow. "And?"

AJ paused, squared his shoulders again and said, "And I decided to oblige him. He pushed me down and when I got up I made sure he found out the hard way that I'm not someone to mess with."

Dare inwardly smiled. He hated admitting it but what his son had said had been spoken like a true Westmoreland. He didn't want to remember the number of times one of the Westmoreland boys came home with something bloodied or broken. Word had soon gotten around school that those Westmorelands weren't anyone to tangle with. They never went looking for trouble, but they knew how to handle it when it came their way.

"Fighting doesn't accomplish anything."

His son shrugged. "Maybe not, but I bet Caleb Martin won't be calling me bad names and pushing me around again. I had put up with it long enough."

Dare placed his hand on his hips. "If this has been going on for a while, why didn't you say something about it to your mother or to some adult at school?"

AJ's glare deepened even more. "I'm not a baby. I don't need my mother or some teacher fighting my battles for me."

Dare met his son's glare with one of his own. "Maybe not, but in the future I expect you not to take matters into your own hands. If I hear about it, I will haul both you and that Martin kid in here and the two of you will be sorry. Not only will I assign after-school duties but I'll give weekend work duties as well. I won't tolerate that kind of foolishness." Especially when it involved his son, Dare decided not to add. "Now go into that bathroom and get cleaned up then meet me out back."

AJ shifted his book bag to his other shoulder. "What am I supposed to do today?"

"My police car needs washing and I can use the help."

AJ nodded and rushed off toward the bathroom. Dare couldn't hide the smile that lit his face. Although AJ had grumbled last night about having to show up at the police station after school, Dare could tell from his expression that he enjoyed having something to do.

"Sheriff?"

Dare glanced up and met McKade's gaze. "Yes?"

"There's something about that kid that's oddly familiar."

Dare knew what McKade was getting at. His deputy had seen the paperwork he'd completed last night and had probably put two and two together; especially since Rick McKade knew his first and middle names. The two of them were good friends and had been since joining the FBI at the same time years back. When Dare had decided to leave the Bureau, so had McKade. Rick had followed Dare to Atlanta, where he'd met and fallen in love with a schoolteacher who lived in the area.

"The reason he seems oddly familiar, McKade, is because you just saw him yesterday," Dare said, hoping that was the end of it.

He found out it wasn't when McKade chuckled and said, "That's not what I mean and you know it, Dare. There's something else."

"What?"

McKade paused a moment before answering. "He looks a lot like you and your brothers, but *especially* like you." He again paused a few moments then asked, "Is there anything you want to tell me?"

Dare's lips curved into a smile. He didn't have to tell McKade anything since it was obvious he had figured things out for himself. "No, there's nothing I want to tell you."

McKade chuckled again. "Then maybe I better tell you, or rather I should remind you that the people in this town don't know how to keep a secret if that's what you plan to do. It won't be long before everyone figures things out, and when they do, someone will tell the kid."

Dare's smile widened when he thought of that happening. "Yes, and that's what his mother and I are counting on." Knowing what he'd said had probably confused the

hell out of McKade, Dare turned and walked through
the door that led out back.

The kid was a hard worker and a darn good one at that,
Dare decided as he watched AJ dry off the police cruiser.
He had only intended the job to last an hour, but he could
tell that AJ was actually enjoying having something to do.
He made a mental note to ask Shelly if AJ did any chores
at home, and if not, maybe it wouldn't be a bad idea for
her to assign him a few. That would be another way to keep
him out of trouble.

"Is this it for the day?"

AJ's statement jerked Dare from his thoughts. AJ had
placed the cloth he'd used to dry off the car back in the
bucket. "Yes, that's it, but make sure you come back tomorrow—and I expect you to be on time."

A scowl appeared on AJ's face but he didn't say anything
as he picked up his book bag and placed it on his shoulder.
"I don't like coming here after school."

Dare shook his head and inwardly smiled, wondering
who the kid was trying to convince. "Well, you should
have thought of that before you got into trouble."

Their gazes locked for a brief moment and Dare detected
a storm of defiance brewing within his son. "How much
longer do I have to come here?" AJ asked in an agitated
voice.

"Until I think you've learned your lesson."

AJ's glare deepened. "Well, I don't like it."

Dare raised his gaze upward to the sky then looked back
to AJ. "You've said that already kid, but in this case what
you like doesn't really matter. When you break the law you
have to be punished. That's something I suggest you remember. I also suggest that you get home before your mother
starts worrying about you," he said, following AJ inside the
building.

"She's going to do that anyway."

Dare smiled. "Yeah, I wouldn't put it past her, since mothers are that way. I'm sure my four brothers and I worried my mother a lot when we were growing up."

AJ raised a brow. "You have four brothers?"

Dare's smile widened. "Yes, I have four brothers and one sister. I'm the oldest of the group.

AJ nodded. "It's just me and my mom."

Dare nodded as well. He then stood in front of the door with A. J. "To answer your question of how long you'll have to come here after school, I think a full week of this should make you think twice about throwing rocks at passing cars the next time." Dare rubbed his chin thoughtfully then added, "Unless I hear about you getting involved in a fight again. Like I said, that's something I won't tolerate."

AJ glared at him. "Then I'll make sure you don't hear about it."

Not giving Dare a chance to respond, AJ raced out of the door, got his bike and took off.

"Ouch, that hurts!"

"Well, this should teach you a lesson," Shelly said angrily, leaning over AJ as she applied antiseptic to his bruised lip. "And if I hear of you fighting again, I will put you on a punishment like you wouldn't believe."

"He started it!"

Shelly straightened and met her son's dark scowl. "Then next time walk away," she said firmly.

"People are going to think I'm a coward if I do that. I told you I was going to hate it here. Nobody likes me. At least I had friends in L.A."

"I don't consider those guys you hung around with back in L.A. your friends. A true friend wouldn't talk you into doing bad things, AJ, and as far as anyone thinking you're a coward, then let them. I know for a fact that you're one of the bravest persons I know. Look how long you've had to be the man of the house for me."

AJ shrugged and glanced up at his mother. "But it's different with you, Mom. I don't want any of the guys at school thinking I'm a pushover."

"Trust me, you're not a pushover. You're too much like your father." She then turned to walk toward the kitchen.

Shelly knew she had thrown out the hook and it wouldn't take long for AJ to take the bait. She heard him draw in a long breath behind her and knew he was right on her heels.

"Why did you mention him?"

She looked back over her shoulder at AJ when she reached the kitchen. "Why did I mention who?"

"My father."

She leaned against the kitchen cabinet and raised a curious brow. "I'm not supposed to mention him?"

"You haven't in a long time."

Shelly nodded. "Only because you haven't asked about him in a long time. Tonight when you said something about being a pushover, I immediately thought of him because you're so much like him and he's one of the bravest men I know."

AJ smiled. He was glad to know his father was brave. "What does he do, fly planes or something?"

Shelly smiled knowing of her son's fixation with airplanes and spaceships. "No." She inhaled deeply. "I think it's time we had a talk about your father. I've been doing a lot of thinking since moving back and I need you to help me make a decision about something."

AJ lifted a brow. "A decision about what?"

"About whether to tell your father about you."

Surprised widened AJ's eyes. "You know where he is?"

Shelly shook her head. "AJ, I've always known where he is. I've always told you that. And I've always told you if you ever wanted me to contact him to just say the word."

Uncertainty narrowed his eyes, then he glanced down as if to study his sneakers. "Yeah, but I wasn't sure if you really meant it or not," he said quietly.

Shelly smiled weakly and reached out and gently gripped his chin to bring his gaze back to hers. "Is that why you stopped asking me about him? You thought I was lying to you about him?"

He shrugged. "I just figured you were saying what you wanted me to believe. Nick Banner's mom did that to him. She told him that his dad had died in a car accident when he was a baby, then one day he heard his grandpa tell somebody that his dad was alive and had another family someplace and that he didn't want Nick."

Shelly's breath caught in her throat. She felt an urgent need to take her son into her arms and assure him that unlike Nick's father, his father did want him. But she knew he was now at an age where mothers' hugs were no longer *cool*. Her heart felt heavy knowing that AJ had denied himself knowledge of his father in an attempt to save her from what he thought was embarrassment.

"Come on, let's sit at the table. I think it's time for us to have a long talk."

AJ hung his head thoughtfully then glanced back at her. His eyes were wary. "About him?"

"Yes about him. There are things I think you need to know, so come on."

He followed her over to the table and they sat down. Her gaze was steady as she met his. "Now then, just to set the record straight, everything I've ever told you about your father was true. He was someone I dated through high school and college while I lived here in College Park. Everyone in town thought we would marry, and I guess that had been my thought, too, but your father had a dream."

"A dream?"

"Yes, a dream of one day becoming an FBI agent. You have your dream to grow up and become an astronaut one day, don't you?"

"Yes."

"Well, your father had a similar dream, but his was one

day to become an FBI agent, and I knew if I had told him that I was pregnant with you, he would have turned his back on his dream for us. I didn't want him to do that. I loved him too much. So, without telling him I was pregnant with you, I left town. So he never knew about you, AJ."

Shelly sighed. Everything she'd just told AJ was basically true. However, this next part would be a lie; a lie Dare was convinced AJ needed to believe. "Your father still doesn't know about you, and this is where I need your help."

AJ looked confused. "My help about what?"

"About what I should do." When his confusion didn't clear she said, "Since we moved back, I found out your father is still living here in College Park."

She could tell AJ was momentarily taken aback by what she'd said. He stared at her with wide, expressive eyes. "He's here? In this town?" he asked in a somewhat shaky yet excited voice.

"Yes. It seems that he moved back a few years ago after he stopped working for the FBI in Washington, D.C." Shelly leaned back in her chair. "I want to be fair to the both of you. You're getting older and so is he. I think it's time that I finally tell him about you, just like I'm telling you about him."

AJ nodded and looked her and she saw uncertainty in his eyes. "But what if he doesn't want me?"

Shelly smiled and then chuckled. "Trust me, when he finds out about you he will definitely want you. In fact I'm a little concerned about what his reaction will be when he realizes that I've kept your existence from him. He is a man who strongly believes in family and he won't be a happy camper."

"Had he known about me, he would have married you?"

Shelly's smiled widened, knowing that was true. "Yes, in a heartbeat, which is the reason I didn't tell him. And although it's too late for either of us to think of ever having a life together again, because we've lived separate lives for so long, there's no doubt in my mind that once I tell him about you he'll want to become a part of your life. But I need to know how you feel about that."

AJ shrugged. "I'm okay with it, but how do you feel about it. Mom?"

"I'm okay with it, too."

AJ nodded. He then lowered his head as his finger made designs across the tablecloth. Moments later he lifted his eyes and met her gaze. "So when can I get to meet him?"

Shelly took a deep breath and hoped that her next words sounded normal. "You've already met your father, AJ. You met him yesterday."

She inhaled deeply then broke it down further by saying, "Sheriff Dare Westmoreland is your father."

Five

"Sheriff Westmoreland!" AJ shouted as he jumped out of his seat. He stood in front of his mother and lifted his chin angrily, defiantly. "It can't be him. No way."

Shelly smiled slightly. "Trust me, it *is* him. I of all people should know."

"But—but, I don't want *him* to be my father," he huffed loudly.

Shelly looked directly at AJ, at how badly he was taking the news, which really wasn't unexpected, considering the way he and Dare had clashed. "I'm sorry you feel that way because he is and there's nothing you can do about it. Alisdare Julian Westmoreland *is* your father."

When she saw the look that crossed his face, she added. "And I didn't make up that part, either. You really were named after him, AJ. He merely shortens the Alisdare to Dare."

She felt AJ's need to deny what she'd just told him, but there was no way she could let him do that. "The question is, now that you know he's your father, what are we going to do about it?"

She watched his forehead scrunch into a frown, then he said, "We don't have to do anything about it since he doesn't have to know. We can continue with things the way they are."

She lifted a brow. "Don't you think he has every right to know about you?"

"Not if I don't want him to know."

Shelly shook her head. "Dare will be very hurt if he ever learns the truth." She studied her son. "Can you give me a good reason why he shouldn't be told?"

"Yes, because he doesn't like me and I don't like him."

Shelly met his gaze. "With your disrespectful attitude, you probably didn't make a good impression on him yesterday, AJ. However, Dare loves kids. And as far as you not liking him, you really don't know him, and I think you should get to know him. He's really a nice guy, otherwise I would not have fallen in love with him all those years ago." A small voice whispered that that part was true. Dare had always been a caring and loving person. "How did things go between the two of you today?"

AJ shrugged. "We still don't like each other, and I don't want to get to know him. So please don't tell him, Mom. You can't."

She paused for a moment knowing what she would say, knowing she would not press him anymore. "All right, AJ, since you feel so strongly about it, I won't tell him. But I'm hoping that one day *you* will be the one to tell him. I'm hoping that one day you'll see the importance of him knowing the truth."

She stood and walked over to AJ and placed her hand on his shoulder. "There's something else you need to think about."

"What?"

"Dare is a very smart man. Chances are he'll figure things out without either one of us telling him anything."

He frowned and his eyes grew round. "How?"

Shelly smiled. "You favor him and his four brothers. Although he hasn't noticed it yet, there's a good chance that he will. And then there's the question of your age. He knows I left town ten years ago, the same year you were born."

AJ nodded. "Did he ask you anything when you saw him yesterday?"

"No. I think he assumes your father is someone I met after leaving here, but as I said, there's a chance he might start putting two and two together."

AJ's features drew in a deeper frown at the thought of that happening. "But we can't let him figure it out."

She shook her head. Shelly hated lying to AJ although she knew it was for a good reason. She had to remember that. "Whoa. Don't include me in this, AJ. It's strictly your decision not to let Dare know about you, it isn't mine. I'm already in hot water for not having told him that you exist at all. But I'll keep my word and not tell him anything if that's the way you want it."

"Yes, that's the way I want it," AJ said, not hiding the relief on his face.

His lips were quivering, and Shelly knew he was fighting hard to keep his tears at bay. Right now he was feeling torn. A part of him wanted to be elated that his father did exist, but another part refused to accept the man who he'd discovered his father was, all because of that Westmoreland pride and stubbornness.

Shelly shook her head when she felt tears in the back of her own eyes. Dare's mission to win his son's love would not be easy.

Later that night, after AJ had gone to bed Shelly received a phone call from Dare.

"Did you tell him?"

She leaned against her kitchen sink. "Yes, I told him."

There was a pause. "And how did he take it?"

Shelly released a deep sigh. "Just as we expected. He

doesn't want you to know that he's your son." When Dare didn't respond, she said, "Don't take it personally, Dare. I think he's more confused than anything right now. Tonight I discovered why he had stopped asking me about you."

"Why?"

"Because he didn't really believe you existed, at least not the way I'd told him. It seems that a friend of his had shared with him the fact that his mother had told him his father had died in a car accident when he was a baby, and then he'd discovered that his father was alive and well and living somewhere with another family. So AJ assumed what I had told him about you wasn't true and that I really didn't know how to contact you if he ever asked me to. And since he never wanted to place me in a position that showed me up as a liar, he just never bothered."

Again she released a sigh as she fought back the tears that threaten to fall. "And to think that he probably did want to know you all this time but refrained from asking to save me embarrassment in being caught in a lie."

A sob caught in her throat as she blinked back a tear. "Oh, Dare I feel so bad for him, and what he's going through is all my fault. I thought I was making all the right decisions for all the right reasons and now it seems I caused more harm than good."

Dare lay in bed, his entire body tense. He could no longer hold back the anger he felt for Shelly, even knowing he had made a couple of mistakes himself in handling things ten years ago. Had he not chosen a career over her then, things would have worked out a whole lot differently. So, in reality, he was just as much to blame as Shelly, but together they had a chance to make things work to save their son.

"Things are going to work out in the end, Shell, you'll see. You've done your part tonight, now let me handle things from here. It might take months, but in the end I believe that AJ will accept me as his father. In my heart I believe that one day he'll want me to know the truth."

Shelly nodded, hearing the confidence in Dare's voice and hoping he was right. "So now we move to the second phase of your plan?"

"Now we move to the second phase of *our* plan."

The next morning, after AJ had left for school, a gentle knock on the door alerted Shelly that she had a visitor. Today was her day off and she had spent the last half hour or so on the computer paying her bills online, and was just about to walk into the kitchen for a cup of coffee.

Crossing the living room she glanced out of the peephole. Her breath caught. Dare was standing on her porch, and his tall, muscular frame was silhouetted by the mid-morning sunlight that was shining brightly behind him. He looked gorgeous; his uniform, which showcased his solid chest, firm stomach and strong flanks, made him look even more so.

She shivered as everything about her that was woman jolted upward from the soles of her feet, to settle in an area between her legs. She inhaled and commanded her body not to go there. Whatever had been between her and Dare had ended ten years ago, and now was not the time for her body to go horny on her. She'd done without sex for this long, and she could continue to go without it for a while longer. But damn if Dare Westmoreland didn't rattle and stir up those urges she'd kept dormant for ten years. She couldn't for the life of her forget how it had felt to run her hands over his chest, indulging in the crisp feel of his chair and the masculine texture of his skin.

She closed her eyes and took a deep breath at the memory of his firm stomach rubbing against her own and the feel of his calloused palm touching her intimately on the sensitive areas of her body. She remembered him awakening within her a passion that had almost startled her.

His second knock made her regain her mental balance, and warning signals against opening the door suddenly went off in her head as she opened her eyes. A silent voice reminded her that although she might want to, there was no way to put as much distance between herself and Dare as she'd like. No matter how much being around him got to her, their main concern was their son.

Inhaling deeply, she slowly opened the door and met his gaze. Once again she felt every sexual instinct she possessed spring to life. "Dare, what are you doing here?" she asked, pausing afterwards to take a deep, steadying breath.

He smiled, that enticingly sexy smile that always made her want to go to the nearest bed and get it on with him. There was no way she couldn't see him and not think of crawling into bed next to him amidst rumpled sheets while he reached out and took her into his arms and…

"I tried calling you at the agency where you worked and they told me you were off today," he said as he leaned in her doorway, breaking into her wayward thoughts and sending her already sex-crazed mind into turmoil. Why did he still look so good after ten years? And why on earth was her body responding to the sheer essence of him this way? But then she and Dare always had had an abundant amount of overzealous hormones and it seemed that ten years hadn't done a thing to change that.

"Why were you trying to reach me?" she somehow found her voice to ask him. "Is something wrong?"

He shook his head, immediately putting her fears to rest. "No, but I thought it would be a good idea if we talked."

Shelly's eyebrows raised. "Talk? But we talked yesterday morning at Kate's Diner and again last night. What do we have to talk about now?" she asked, trying not to sound as frustrated as she felt.

"I thought you'd like to know how my meeting went with Jared yesterday."

"Oh." She had completely forgotten about his plans to meet with his attorney cousin for lunch. She'd always liked his cousin Jared Westmoreland, who, over the years, had become something of a hotshot attorney. "I would." She took a step back as she fought to remain composed. "Come in."

He stepped inside and closed the door behind him and then glanced around. "It's been years since I've been inside this house. It brings back memories," Dare said meeting her gaze once again.

She nodded, remembering how he used to stand in that same spot countless times as he waited for her to come down the stairs for their dates. And even then, when she breezed down the stairs her mind was filled with thoughts of their evening, especially how it would finish. "Yes, it does."

A long, seemingly endless moment of silence stretched between them before she finally cleared her throat. "I was about to have a cup of coffee and a Danish if you'd like to join me," she offered.

"That's a pretty tempting offer, one that I think I'll take you up on."

Shelly nodded. If he thought *that* was tempting he really didn't know what tempting was about. *Tempting* was Dare Westmoreland standing in the middle of her living room looking absolutely gorgeous. And it didn't help matters one iota when she glanced his way and saw a definite bulge behind his fly. Apparently he was just as hot and bothered as she was.

She quickly turned around. "Follow me," she said over her shoulder, wondering how she was going to handle being alone in the house with him.

Following Shelly was the last thing Dare thought he needed to do. He tried not to focus on the sway of the backside encased in denim shorts in front of him. He was suddenly besieged with memories of just how that backside had felt in his hands when he'd lifted it to thrust inside her. Those thoughts made his arousal harden even more. He suppressed a groan deep in his throat.

He tried to think of other things and glanced around. He liked the way she had decorated the place, totally differently from the way her parents used to have it. Her mother's taste had been soft and quaint. Shelly's taste made a bold statement. She liked colors—bright cheery colors—evident in the vivid print of the sofa, loveseat and wingback chair. Then there were her walls, painted in a variety of colorful shades, so different from his plain off-white ones. He was amazed how she was able to tie everything together without anything clashing. She had managed to create a cozy and homey atmosphere for herself and AJ.

As they entered the kitchen, Dare quickly sat down at the table before she could note the fix his body was in, if she hadn't done so already. But he soon discovered that sitting at the table watching her move around the kitchen only intensified his problem. He was getting even more turned on by the fluid movements of her body as she reached into a cabinet to get their coffee cups. The shorts were snug, a perfect fit, and his entire body began throbbing in deep male appreciation.

"You still like your coffee black and your Danish with a lot of butter, Dare?"

"Yes," he managed to respond. He began to realize that he had made a mistake in dropping by. Over the past couple of days when they'd been together there had been other people around. Now it was just the two of them, alone in this house, in this room. He had to fight hard to dismiss the thought of taking her right there on the table.

He inhaled deeply. If Shelly knew what thoughts were running through his mind she would probably hightail it up the stairs, which wouldn't do her any good since he would only race up those same stairs after her and end up making love to her in one of the bedrooms.

That was something they had done once before when her parents had been out of town and he had dropped by unexpectedly. A slow, lazy smile touched the side of his mouth as he remembered the intensity of their lovemaking that day. That was the one time they hadn't used protection. Perhaps that was the time she had gotten pregnant with AJ?

"What are you smiling about?"

Her question invaded his thoughts and he shifted in the chair to alleviate some of the tension pressing at the zipper of his pants. He met her gaze and decided to be completely honest with her, something he had always done. "I was thinking about that time that we made love upstairs in your bedroom without protection, and wondered if that was the time you got pregnant."

"It was."

He regarded her for a second. "How do you know?"

She stared at the floor for a moment before meeting his gaze again. "Because after that was the first time I'd ever been late."

He nodded. The reason they had made love so recklessly and intensely that day was because he had received orders a few hours earlier to leave immediately for an area near Kuwait. It was a temporary assignment and he would only be gone for two months. But at the time, two months could have been two years for all she cared. Because of the danger of his assignment, the news had immediately sent her in a spin and she had raced up the stairs to her bedroom so he wouldn't see her cry. He had gone after her, only to end up placing her on the bed and making frantic, uncontrolled love to her.

"What did Jared have to say yesterday?" Shelly asked him rather than think about that particular day when they had unknowingly created their son. Straightening, she walked over to the table and placed the coffee and rolls in front of him, then sat down at the table.

He took a sip of coffee and responded, "Jared thinks that whatever we decide is the best way to handle letting AJ know I'm his father is fine as long as we're in agreement. But he strongly thinks I should do whatever needs to be done to compensate you from the time he was born. And I agree. As his father I had certain responsibilities to him."

"But you didn't know about him, Dare."

"But I know about him now, Shelly, and that makes a world of difference."

Shelly nodded. She knew that to argue with Dare would be a complete waste of her time. "All right, I have a college fund set up and if you'd like to contribute, I have no problem with that. That is definitely one way you can help."

Dare leaned back in his chair and met her gaze. "Are you sure there's no other way I can help?"

For a moment she wondered if he was asking for AJ or for her. Could he detect the deep longing within her, the sexual cravings, and knew he could help her there? She sighed, knowing she was letting her mind become cluttered. AJ was the only thing between them, and she had to remember that.

"Yes, I'm sure," she said softly. "My job pays well and I've always budgeted to live within my means. The cost of living isn't as high here as it is in L.A., and my parents aren't charging me any rent, so AJ and I are fine, Dare, but thanks for asking."

At that moment the telephone rang; she hoped he didn't see the relief on her face. "Excuse me," she said, standing quickly. "That's probably the agency calling to let me know my hours and clients for next week."

As Shelly listened to the agency's secretary tell her what her schedule would be for the following week, she tried to get her thoughts back together. Dare had stirred up emotions and needs that she'd thought were dead and buried until she'd seen him two days ago. His presence had blood racing through her body at an alarming speed.

"All right, thanks for calling," she said before hanging up the phone. She quickly turned and bumped into a massive solid chest. "Oh."

Dare reached out and quickly stopped Shelly from falling. "Sorry, I didn't mean to scare you," he said, his words soft and gentle.

She took a step back when he released her. Each time he touched her she was reminded of the sensual feelings he could easily invoke. "I thought you were still sitting down."

"I thought it was time for me to leave. I don't want to take you from your work any longer."

She rubbed her hands across her arms, knowing it was best if he left. "Is that all Jared said?"

He nodded. That was all she needed to know. There was no need to tell her that Jared had suggested the possibility of him having legal visitation rights and petitioning for joint custody of AJ. Both suggestions he had squashed, since he and Shelly had devised what they considered a workable plan.

His gaze moved to her hands and he watched her fingers sliding back and forth across her arms. He remembered her doing that very thing on a certain part of his anatomy several times. The memory of the warmth of her fingers touching him so intimately slammed another arousal through his body that strengthened the one already there.

At that moment, he lost whatever control he had. Being around her stirred up memories and emotions he could no longer fight, nor did he want to. The only thing he wanted, he needed, was to kiss her, taste her and reacquaint the insides of his mouth, his tongue, with hers.

Shelly was having issues of her own and took a steadying breath, trying to get the heated desire racing through her body under control. She swallowed deeply when she saw that Dare's gaze was dead-centered on her mouth, and fought off the panic that seized her when he took a step forward.

"I wonder..." he said huskily, his gaze not leaving her lips.

She blinked, refocused on him. "You wonder about

what?" she asked softly, feeling the last shreds of her composure slipping.

"I wonder if your mouth still knows me."

His words cut through any control she had left. Those were the words he had always whispered whenever they were together after being apart for any length of time, just moments before he took her into his arms and kissed her senseless.

He leaned in closer, then lowered his mouth to hers. Immediately, his tongue went after hers in an attempt to lure her into the same rush of desire consuming him. But she was already there, a step ahead of him, so he tried forcing his body to calm down and settle into the taste he'd always been accustomed to. He had expected heat, but he hadn't expected the hot, fiery explosion that went off in his midsection. It made a groan erupt from deep in his throat.

His hands linked around her waist to hold her closer, thigh-to-thigh, breasts to chest. Sensation after sensation speared through him, making it hard to resist eating her alive, or at least trying to, and wanting to touch her everywhere, especially between her legs. Now that he had rediscovered this—the taste of her mouth—he wanted also to relive the feel of his fingers sliding over her heated flesh to find the hot core of her, swollen and wet.

That thought drove a primitive need through him and the erection pressing against her got longer and harder. The thought of using it to penetrate the very core of her made his mind reel and drugged his brain even more with her sensuality.

A shiver raced over Shelly and a semblance of control returned as she realized just how easily she had succumbed to his touch. She knew she had to put a halt to what they were doing. She had returned to College Park not for herself but for AJ.

She broke off their kiss and untangled herself from his arms. When he leaned toward her, to kiss her again, she pushed him back. "No, Dare," she said firmly. "We shouldn't have done that. This isn't about you or me or our inability to control overzealous hormones. It's about our son and doing what is best for him."

And why can't we simultaneously discover what is best for us, he wanted to ask but refrained from doing so. He understood her need to put AJ first and foremost, but what she would soon realize was that there was unfinished business between them as well. "I agree that AJ is our main concern, Shelly, but there's something you need to realize and accept."

"What?"

"Things aren't over between us, and we shouldn't deceive ourselves into thinking there won't be a next time, so be prepared for it."

He saw the frown that appeared in her eyes and the defiance that tilted her lips reminded him of AJ yesterday and the day before. "No, Dare, there won't be a next time because I won't let there be. You're AJ's father, but what was between us is over and has been for years. To me you're just another man."

He lifted a brow. He wondered if she had kissed many men the way she'd kissed him, and for some reason he doubted it. She had kissed him as though she hadn't kissed anyone in years. He had felt the hunger that had raged through her. He had felt it, explored it and, for the moment, satisfied it. "You're sure about that?"

"Yes, I'm positive, so I suggest you place all your concentration on winning your son over and forget about your son's mother."

As he turned to cross the room to leave, he knew that he would never be able to forget about his son's mother, not in a million years. Before walking out the door he looked back at her. "Oh, yeah, I almost forgot something."

She lifted a brow. "What?"

"The brothers four. They're dying to see you. I told them

of our plans for AJ and they agreed to be patient about seeing him, but they refuse to be patient about seeing you, Shelly. They want to know if you'll meet them for lunch one day this week at Chase's restaurant in downtown Atlanta?"

She smiled. She wanted to see them as well. Dare's brothers had always been special to her. "Tell them I'd love to have lunch with them tomorrow since I'll be working in that area."

Dare nodded, then turned and walked out the door.

AJ saw the two boys standing next to his bike the moment he walked out the school door. Since his bike was locked, he wasn't worried about the pair taking it, but after his fight with Caleb Martin yesterday the last thing he wanted was trouble. Especially after the talks the sheriff and his mother had given him.

The sheriff.

He shook his head, not wanting to think about the fact that the sheriff was his father. But he had thought about it most of the day, and still, as he'd told his mother last night, he didn't want the sheriff to know he was his son.

"What are you two looking at?" he asked in a tough voice, ignoring the fact that one of the boys was a lot bigger than he was.

"Your bike," the smaller of the two said, turning to him. "We think it's cool. Where did you get it?"

AJ relaxed. He thought his bike was cool, too. "Not from any place around here. My mom bought it for me in California."

"Is that where you're from?" the largest boy asked.

"Yeah, L.A. That's where I was born, and I hope we move back there." He sized up the two and decided they were harmless. He had seen them before around school, but neither had made an attempt to be friendly to him until now. "My name is AJ Brockman. What's yours?"

"My name is Morris Sears," the smaller of the two said, "and this is my friend Cornelius Thomas."

AJ nodded. "Do you live around here?"

"Yeah, just a few blocks, not far from Kate's Diner."

"I live just a few blocks from Kate's Diner, too, on Sycamore Street," AJ said, glad to know there were other kids living not far away.

"We saw what happened with you and Caleb Martin yesterday," Morris said, his eyes widening. "Boy! Did you teach him a lesson! No one has ever done that before and we're glad, since he's been messing with people for a long time for no reason. He's nothing but a bully."

AJ nodded, agreeing with them.

"Would you like to ride home with us today?" Cornelius asked, getting on his own bike. "We know a short cut that goes through the Millers' land. We saw a couple of deer on their property yesterday."

AJ's eyes lit up. He'd never seen a deer before, at least not a real live one. He then remembered where he had to go after school. "I'm sorry but today I can't. I have to report directly to the sheriff's office now."

"For fighting yesterday?" Morris asked.

AJ shook his head. "No, for cutting school two days ago. I was throwing rocks at cars and the sheriff caught me and took me in."

Cornelius eyes widened. "You got to ride in the back of Sheriff Westmoreland's car?" he asked excitedly.

AJ raised a brow. "Yes."

"Boy, that's cool. Sheriff Westmoreland is a hero."

AJ gave a snort of laughter. "A hero? And what makes him a hero? He's nothing but a sheriff who probably does nothing but sit in his office all day."

Morris and Cornelius shook their head simultaneously.

"Not Sheriff Westmoreland," Morris said as if he knew that for a fact. "He was in all the newspapers last week for catching those two bad guys the FBI has been looking for.

My dad says Sheriff Westmoreland got shot at bringing them in and that a bullet barely missed his head."

"Yeah, and my dad said," Cornelius piped in, "that those bad guys didn't know who they were messing with, since everyone knows the sheriff doesn't play. Why, he used to even be an FBI agent. My dad went to school with him and graduated the same year Thorn Westmoreland did."

AJ looked curiously at Cornelius. "What does Thorn Westmoreland have to do with anything?"

Cornelius lifted a shocked brow. "Don't you know who Thorn Westmoreland is?"

Of course AJ knew who Thorn Westmoreland was. What kid didn't? "Sure. He's the motorcycle racer who builds the baddest bikes on earth."

Cornelius and Morris nodded. "He's also the sheriff's brother," Morris said grinning, happy to be sharing such news with their new friend. "And have you ever heard of Rock Mason?"

"The man who writes those adventure-thriller books?" AJ asked, his mind still reeling from what he'd just been told—Thorn Westmoreland was the sheriff's brother!

"Yes, but Rock Mason's real name is Stone Westmoreland and he's the sheriff's brother, too. Then there are two more of them, Chase and Storm Westmoreland. Mr. Chase owns a big restaurant downtown and Mr. Storm is a fireman."

AJ nodded. He wondered how Morris and Cornelius knew so much about a family that he was supposed to be a part of, yet he didn't know a thing about.

"And I forgot to mention that their sister married a prince from one of those faraway countries," Morris added, interrupting AJ's thoughts.

"How do you two know so much about the Westmorelands?" AJ asked, wrinkling his forehead.

"Because the sheriff coaches our Little League team and his brothers often help out."

"The sheriff coaches a baseball team?" AJ asked, thinking now he'd heard just about everything. The only time the people in L.A. saw the sheriff was when something bad happened and he was needed to make a statement on TV.

"Yes, and we're on the team and bring home the trophies every year. If you're good he might let you join."

AJ shrugged, not wanting to be around the sheriff any more than he had to. "No thanks, I don't want to join," he said. "Well, I've got to go, since I can't be late."

"How long do you have to go there?" Morris asked standing aside to let AJ get to his bike.

"The rest of the week, so I'll be free to ride home with you guys starting Monday if you still want me to," AJ said, getting on his bike.

"Yes," Cornelius answered. "We'll still want you to. What about this weekend? Will your parents let you go look at the deer with us this weekend? Usually Mr. Miller gives his permission for us to come on his property as long as we don't get into any trouble."

AJ was doubtful. "I'll let you know tomorrow if I can go. My mom is kind of protective. She doesn't like me going too far from home."

Morris and Cornelius nodded in understanding. "Our moms are that way, too," Morris said. "But everyone around here knows the Millers. Your mom can ask the sheriff about them if she wants. They're nice people."

"Do you want to ride to school with us tomorrow?" Cornelius asked anxiously. "We meet at Kate's Diner every morning at seven-thirty, and she gives us a carton of chocolate milk free as long as we're good in school."

"Free chocolate milk? Hey, I'd like that. I'll see you guys in the morning." AJ put his bike into gear and headed for the sheriff's office, determined not to be late for a second time.

Six

Her mouth still knew him.

A multitude of emotions tightened Dare's chest as he sat at his desk and thought about the kiss he and Shelly had shared. Very slowly and very deliberately, he took his finger and rubbed it across his lips, lips that a few hours ago had tasted sweetness of the most gut-wrenching kind. It was the kind of sweetness that made you crave something so delightful and pleasurable that it could become habit forming.

But what got to him more than anything was the fact that even after ten years, her mouth still knew him. That much was evident in the way her lips had molded to his, the familiarity of the way she had parted her mouth and the ease in which his tongue had slid inside, staking a claim he hadn't known he had a right to make until he had felt her response.

He leaned back in the chair. When it came to responding to him, that was something Shelly could never hold back from doing. He'd always gotten the greatest pleasure and enjoyment from hearing the sound of her purring in bed. He used to know just what areas on her body to touch, to caress and to taste. Often, all it took was a look, him simply meeting her gaze with deep desire and longing in his eyes, and she would release an indrawn sigh that let him know she knew just what he wanted and what he considered necessary. Those had been the times he hadn't been able to keep his hands off her, and now it seemed, ten years later, he still couldn't. And it didn't help matters any that she had kissed him as though there hadn't been another man inside her mouth in the ten years they'd been apart. Her mouth had ached for his, demanded everything his tongue could deliver, and he'd given it all, holding nothing back. He could have kept on kissing her for days.

Dare ran his hand over his face trying to see if doing so would help him retain his senses. Kissing Shelly had affected him greatly. His body had been aching and throbbing since then, and the painful thing was that he didn't see any relief in sight.

Over the past ten years he had dated a number of women. His sister Delaney had even painted him and his brothers as womanizers. But he felt that was as far from the truth as it could be. After he and Shelly had broken up, he'd been very selective about what women he wanted in his bed. For years he had looked for Shelly's replacement, only to discover such a woman didn't exist. He hadn't met a woman who would hold a light to her, and he'd accepted that and moved on. The women he'd slept with had been there for the thrill, the adventure, but all he'd gotten was the agony of defeat upon realizing that none could make him feel in bed the way he'd always felt with Shelly. Oh, he had experienced pleasure, but not the kind that made you pound your chest with your fists and holler out for more. Not the kind that compelled you to go ahead and remain inside her body since another orgasm was there on the horizon. And not the kind you could still shudder from days later, just thinking about it.

He could only get those feelings with Shelly.

Closing his eyes, Dare remembered how she had broken off their kiss and the words she'd said before he'd left her house. *"You're AJ's father, but what was between us is over and has been for years. To me you're just another man."*

He sighed deeply and reopened his eyes. If Shelly believed that then she was wrong. Granted, AJ was their main concern, but what she didn't know and what he wouldn't tell her just yet was that his mission also included her. He hadn't realized until she had walked into his office two days ago that his life had been without direction for ten years. Seeing her, finding out about AJ and knowing that he and Shelly were still attracted to each other made him want something he thought he would never have again.

Peace and happiness.

The buzzer interrupted his thoughts. Leaning forwarding he pushed the button for the speakerphone. "Yeah, Holly, what is it?"

"That Brockman kid is here, Sheriff. Do you want me to send him in?"

Dare again sighed deeply. "Yes, send him in."

Dare felt AJ watching him. The kid had been doing so off and on since he'd finished the chores he'd been assigned and had come into his office to sit at a table in the corner and finish his homework.

Dare had sat behind his desk, reading over various reports. The only sound in the room was AJ turning the pages of his science book and Dare shuffling the pages of the report. More than once Dare had glanced up and caught the kid looking at him, as if he were a puzzle he was trying to figure out. As soon as he'd been caught staring, the kid had quickly lowered his eyes.

Dare wondered what was going through AJ's mind now that he knew he was his father? The only reason Dare could come up with as to why he'd been studying him so intently was that he was trying to find similarities in their features. They were there. Even Holly had noticed them, although she hadn't said anything, merely moving her gaze between Dare and AJ several times before comprehension appeared on her face.

Dare glanced up and caught AJ staring again and decided to address the issue. "Is something wrong?" he asked.

AJ glanced up from his science book and glared at him. "What makes you think something is wrong?"

Dare shrugged. "Because I've caught you staring several times today like I've suddenly grown two heads or something."

He saw the corners of AJ lips being forced not to smile. "I hate being here. Why couldn't I just go home after I finished everything I had to do instead of hanging around here?"

"Because your punishment was to come here for an hour after school and I intend to get my hour. Besides, if I let you leave earlier, you might think I'm turning soft."

"That will be the day," AJ mumbled.

Dare chuckled and went back to reading his reports.

"Is Thorn Westmoreland really your brother?"

Dare lifted his head and gazed back across the room at AJ. My brother and your uncle, he wanted to say. Instead he responded by asking, "Who told you that?"

AJ shrugged. "Morris and Cornelius."

Dare nodded. He knew Morris and Cornelius. The two youngsters usually hung together and were the same age and went to the same school as AJ. "So you know Morris and Cornelius?"

AJ turned the page on his book before answering, pretending the response was being forced from him. "Yeah, I know them. We met today after school."

Dare nodded again. Morris and Cornelius were good kids. He knew their parents well and was glad the pair were developing a friendship with AJ, since he considered them a good influence. Both got good grades in school, sung in the youth choir at church and were active in a number of sports he and his brothers coached.

"Well, is he?"

Dare heard the anxiousness in AJ's voice, although the kid was trying to downplay it. "Yes, Thorn's my brother."

"And Rock Mason is, too?"

"Yes. I told you the other day I had four brothers and all of them live in this area."

AJ nodded. "And they help you coach your baseball team?"

Dare leaned back in his chair. "Yes, pretty much, although Thorn contributes to the youth of the community by teaching a special class at the high school on motorcycle safety and Stone is involved with the Teach People to Read program for both the young and old."

AJ nodded again. "What about the other two?"

Dare wondered at what point AJ would discover they were holding a conversation and revert back to his I-don't-like-cops syndrome? Well, until he did, Dare planned to milk the situation for all it was worth. "Chase owns a restaurant and coaches a youth basketball team during basketball season. His team won the state championship two years in a row."

Dare smiled when he thought of his younger brother Storm. "My youngest brother Storm hasn't found his niche yet." Other than with women, Dare decided not to add. "So he helps me coach my baseball team and he also helps Chase with his basketball team."

"And your sister married a prince?"

Dare's smile widened when he thought of the baby sister he and his brothers simply adored. "Yes, although at the time we weren't ready to give her up."

AJ's eyes grew wider. "Why? Girls don't marry princes every day."

Dare chuckled. "Yes, that may be true, but the Westmorelands have this unspoken code when it comes to family. We stick together and claim what's ours. Since Delaney was the only girl, we claimed her when she was born and weren't ready to give her up to anyone, including a prince."

AJ turned a few pages again, pretending further disinterest. A few moments later he asked, "What about your parents?"

Dare met AJ's stare. "What about them?"

"Do they live around here?"

"Yes, they live within walking distance. Their only complaint is that none of us, other than Delaney, have gotten married. They're anxious for grandkids and since they don't see Delaney's baby that often, they would like one of us to settle down and have a family."

Dare knew that what he'd just shared with AJ would get the kid to thinking. He was about to say something else when the buzzer on his desk sounded.

"Yes, McKade, what is it?"

"Ms. Brockman is here to see you."

Dare was surprised. He hadn't expected Shelly to drop by, since AJ had ridden his bike over from school. A quick glance across the room and he could tell by AJ's features that he was surprised by his mother's unexpected visit as well. "Send her in, McKade."

Dare stood as Shelly breezed into his office, dressed in a skirt and a printed blouse. "I hate to drop in like this, but I received an emergency call from one of my patients living in Stone Mountain and need to go out on a call. Ms. Kate has agreed to take care of AJ, and I have to drop him off at her place on my way out. I thought coming to pick him up would be okay since his hour is over."

Dare glanced at the clock on the wall which indicated

AJ's hour had been over ten minutes ago. At some point the kid had stopped watching the clock and so had he.

"Since you're in a rush, I can save you the time by dropping him off at Ms. Kate's myself. I was getting ready to leave anyway."

Dare then remembered that since tonight was Wednesday night, his parents' usual routine was to have dinner with their five sons at Chase's restaurant before going to prayer meeting at church. He knew his family would love meeting AJ, and since they'd been told of his and Shelly's strategy about AJ knowing Dare was his father, there was no risk of someone giving anything away.

"And I have another idea," he said, meeting Shelly's gaze, trying not to notice how beautiful her eyes were, how beautiful she was, period. Just being in the same room with her had his mouth watering. She stood in the middle of his office silhouetted by the light coming in through his window and he thought he hadn't seen anything that looked this good in a long time.

"What?" she asked, interrupting his thoughts.

"AJ is probably hungry and I was on my way to Chase's restaurant where my family is dining tonight. He's welcome to join us, and I can drop him off at Ms. Kate's later."

Shelly nodded. Evidently Dare felt he'd made some headway with AJ for him to suggest such a thing. She glanced across the room at AJ who had his eyes glued to his book, pretending not have heard Dare's comment, although she knew that he had.

"AJ, Dare has invited you to dine with his family before dropping you off at Ms. Kate's. All right?"

It seemed AJ stared at her for an endless moment, as if weighing her words. He then shifted his gaze to Dare, and Shelly felt the sudden clash of two very strong personalities, two strong-willed individuals, two people who were outright stubborn. But then she saw something else, something that met her breath catch and her heart do a flip—

two individuals who, for whatever reason, were silently agreeing to a give a little, at least for this one particular time.

AJ then shifted his gaze back to her. He shrugged. "Whatever."

Shelly let out a deep sigh. "Okay, then, I'll see you later." She walked across the room to place a kiss on AJ's forehead; ignoring the frown he gave her. "Behave yourself tonight," she admonished.

She turned and smiled at Dare before walking out of his office.

"The only reason I decided to come with you is because I want to meet Thorn Westmoreland. I think he is so cool." AJ said, and then turned his attention back to the scenery outside the vehicle's window.

Instead of using the police cruiser, Dare had decided to drive his truck instead, the Chevy Avalanche he'd purchased a month ago. He glanced over at AJ when he brought the vehicle to a stop at a traffic light. He couldn't help but chuckle. "I figured as much, but you won't be the first kid who tried getting on my good side just to meet Thorn."

AJ scowled. "I'm not trying to get on your good side," he mumbled.

Dare chuckled again. "Oh, sorry. My mistake."

For the next couple of miles the inside of the vehicle was quiet as Dare navigated through evening traffic with complete ease.

"So, how was your day at school?" Dare decided to ask when the vehicle finally came to a complete standstill as he attempted to get on the interstate.

AJ glanced over at him. "It had its moments."

Dare smiled. "What kind of moments?"

AJ glared. "Why are you asking me all these questions?"

Dare met his gaze. "Because I'm interested."

AJ's glare deepened. "Are you interested in me or in my mother? I saw the way you were looking at her."

Dare decided the kid was too observant, although he was falling in nicely with their plans. "And what way was I looking at her?"

"One of those man-like-woman looks."

Dare chuckled, never having heard it phrased quite that way before. "What do you know about a man-like-woman look?"

"I wasn't born yesterday."

"Not for one minute did I think you had been." After a few moments he glanced back at AJ. "Did you know your mom used to be my girlfriend some years back?"

"So?"

"So, I thought you should know."

"Why?"

"Because she was very special to me then."

When Dare exited off the interstate, AJ spoke. "That was back then. My mother doesn't need a boyfriend, if that's what you're thinking."

Dare gave his son a smile when he brought the vehicle to a stop at a traffic light. "What I think, AJ, is that you should let your mom make her own decisions about those kinds of things."

AJ glared at him. "I don't like you."

Dare shrugged and gave his son a smile. "Then I guess that means nothing has changed." But he knew something *had* changed. As far as he was concerned, AJ consenting to go to dinner with him to meet his family was a major breakthrough. And although the kid claimed that Thorn was the only reason he was going, Dare had no problem using his brother to his advantage if that's what it took. Besides, AJ would soon discover that of all the Westmorelands, Thorn was the one who was biggest on family ties and devotion, and if you accepted one Westmoreland, you basically accepted them all, since they were just that thick.

At that moment Dare's cell phone rang and he answered it. After a few remarks and nods of his head, he said,

"You're welcome to join us for dinner if you'd like. I know for a fact that everyone would love to see you." He nodded again and said, "All right. I'll see you later.

Moments later he glanced over at AJ when they came to a stop in front of Chase's restaurant. "That was your mother. The emergency wasn't as bad as she'd thought, and she is on her way back home. I'm to take you there after dinner instead of to Ms. Kate's house."

AJ narrowed his eyes at Dare. "Why did you do that?"

"Do what?" Dare asked, lifting a brow.

"Invite her to dinner?"

"Because I figured that like you, she has to eat sometime, and I know that my family would have love seeing her again." He hesitated for a few moments, then added, "And I would have liked seeing her again myself. Like I said, your mom used to mean a lot to me a long time ago."

Their gazes locked for a brief moment, then AJ glared at him and said angrily, "Get over it."

Dare smiled slightly. "I don't know if I can." Before AJ had time to make a comeback, Dare unsnapped his seat belt. "Come on, it's time to go inside."

Shelly pulled onto the interstate, hoping and praying that AJ was on his best behavior. No matter what, she had to believe that all the lessons in obedience, honor and respect that he'd been taught at an early age were somewhere buried beneath all that hostility he exhibited at times. But right now she had to cope with the fact that he was still a child, a child who was getting older each day and enduring growing pains of the worst kind. But one thing was for certain, Dare was capable of dealing with it, and for that she was grateful.

When she thought of Dare, she had no choice but to think of her traitorous body and the way it had responded to him earlier that day at her house. As she'd told AJ, Dare was smart. He was also very receptive, and she knew he had picked up on the fact that she had wanted him. All it had taken was one mindblowing kiss and she'd been ready to get naked if he'd asked.

When she came to a traffic light she momentarily closed her eyes, asking for strength where Dare was concerned. If she allowed him to become a part of her life, she could be asking for potential heartbreak all over again, although she had to admit the new Dare seemed more settled, less likely to go chasing after some other dream. But whatever the two of them had once shared was in the past, and she refused to bring it to the present. She had enough to deal with in handling AJ without trying to take on his father, too.

She had to continue to make it clear to Dare that it was his son he needed to work on and win over and not her. Their first and foremost concern was AJ, and no matter how hot and bothered she got around Dare, she would not give in again. She had to watch her steps and not put any ideas into Dare's head. More than anything, she had to stop looking at him and thinking about sex.

Her body was doing a good job reminding her that ten years was a long time to go without. She'd been too busy for the abstinence to cross her mind, but today Dare had awakened desires she'd thought were long buried. Now she felt that her body was under attack—against her. It was demanding things she had no intention of delivering.

Her breath caught and she felt her nipples tingle as she again thought about the kiss they had shared. Once more she prayed for the strength and fortitude to deal with Alisdare Julian Westmoreland.

Seven

"Dad, Mom, I'd like you to meet, AJ. He's Shelly's boy." Dare knew his father wouldn't give anything away, but he wasn't so convinced about his mother as he saw the play of emotions that crossed her features. She was looking into the face of a grandson she hadn't known she'd had; a grandson she was very eager to claim.

Luckily for Dare, his father understood the strategy that he and Shelly were using with AJ and spoke up before his wife had a chance to react to the emotions she was trying to hold inside. "You're a fine-looking young man, but I would expect no less coming from Shelly." He reached out and touched AJ's shoulder and smiled. "I'm glad you're joining us for dinner. How's your mother?"

"She's fine," AJ said quietly, bowing his head and studying his shoes.

Dare wondered what kind of docile act the kid was performing, but then another part of him wondered if when taken out of his comfort zone, AJ had a tendency to feel uneasy around people he didn't know. Dare recalled a conversation he'd had with Shelly about AJ not being all that out-going.

When Dare saw Thorn enter the restaurant he beckoned him over saying, "Thorn, I'd like you to meet someone. From what I gather, he's a big fan of yours."

AJ's mouth literally fell open and the size of his eyes increased. He tilted his head back to gaze up at the man towering over him. "Wow! You're Thorn Westmoreland!"

Thorn gave a slow grin. "Yes, I'm Thorn Westmoreland. Now who might you be?"

To Dare's surprise, AJ grinned right back. It was the first look of happiness he'd seen on his son's face, and a part of him regretted he hadn't been the one to put it there.

"I'm AJ Brockman."

Thorn tapped his chin with his finger a couple of times as if thinking about something. "Brockman. Brockman. I used to know a Shelly Brockman some years ago. In fact she used to be Dare's girlfriend. Are you related to that Brockman?"

"Yes, I'm her son."

Thorn chuckled. "Well, I'll be," he said, pretending he didn't already know that fact. "And how's your mother?"

"She's fine."

At that moment Dare looked up and saw his other brothers enter. More introductions were made, and, just like Thorn, they pretended they were surprised to see AJ, and no one gave anything away about knowing he was Dare's son.

When they all sat down to eat, with AJ sitting between Thorn and Dare, it was obvious to anyone who cared to notice that the boy was definitely a Westmoreland.

Shelly put aside the novel she'd been reading when she heard the doorbell ring. A glance out the peephole confirmed it was AJ, but he wasn't alone. Dare had walked him to the door, and with good reason. AJ was half asleep and barely standing on his feet.

She quickly opened the door to AJ's mumblings. "I told you I could walk to the door myself without your help," he was saying none too happily.

"Yeah, and I would have watched you fall on your face, too," was Dare's response.

Shelly stepped aside and let them both enter. "How was dinner?" she asked, closing the door behind them.

AJ didn't answer, instead he continued walking and headed for the stairs. She gave a quick glance to Dare, who was watching AJ as he tried maneuvering the stairs. "That kid is so sleepy he can't think straight," he said. "You might want to help him before he falls and breaks his neck. I would do it, but I think he's had enough of me for one evening."

Shelly nodded, then quickly provided AJ a shoulder to lean on while he climbed the stairs.

Dare moved to stand at the foot of the stairs and watched Shelly and AJ until they were no longer in sight. He sighed deeply, thinking how his adrenaline had pumped up when Shelly had opened the door. She'd been wearing the same outfit she'd worn to his office that evening, and his gaze had been glued to her backside all the while she'd moved up the stairs, totally appreciating the sway of her hips and the way the skirt intermittently slid up her thighs with each upward step she took.

He thought that he would do just about anything to be able to follow right behind her and tumble her straight into bed, but he knew that wasn't possible, especially with AJ in the house. Not to mention the fact that she was still acting rather cautiously around him.

He knew it would probably take her a while to get AJ ready for bed, and since he didn't intend leaving until they had talked, he decided to sit on the sofa and wait for her. He picked up the book she'd been reading, Stone's most recent bestseller, and smiled, thinking it was a coincidence that he was reading the same book.

Making sure he kept the spot where she'd stopped reading marked, he flipped a couple of chapters ahead and picked up where he'd left off last night before sleep had overtaken him.

Shelly paused on the middle stair when she noticed Dare sitting on her sofa reading the book she had begun reading earlier that day. She couldn't help noticing that her living room appeared quiet and seductive, and the light from a floor lamp next to where he sat illuminated his features and created an alluring scene that was too enticing to ignore.

She silently studied him for a long time, wondering just how many peaceful moments he was used to getting as sheriff. He looked comfortable, relaxed and just plain sexy as sin. His features were calm, yet she could tell by the way his eyes were glued to the page that he was deeply absorbed in the action-thriller novel his brother had written.

He shifted in his seat while turning the page and crossed one leg over the other. She knew they were strong legs, sturdy legs, legs that had held her body in place while his had pumped relentlessly into her, legs that had nudged hers apart again when he wanted a second round and a third.

Swallowing at the memory, she felt her heart rate increase, and decided the best way to handle Dare was to send him home—real quicklike. She didn't think she could handle another episode like the one they had shared earlier that day.

He must have heard the sound of her heavy breathing, or maybe she had let out a deep moan without realizing she'd uttered a single word. Something definitely gave her away, and she felt heat pool between her legs when he lifted his gaze from the book and looked at her. It wasn't just an ordinary look either. It was a hot look, a definite scorcher and a blatant, I-want-to-take-you-to-bed look.

She blinked, thinking she had misread the look, but then she knew she hadn't. He wouldn't say the words out loud, but he definitely wanted her to know what he was thinking. She breathed in deeply. Dare was trouble and she was determined to send him packing.

He stood when she took the last few steps down the stairs. "He's out like a light," she said quietly when he came to stand in front of her. "I could barely get him in the shower and in bed without him falling asleep again. Thanks for taking him to dinner and for making sure he got back home."

Shelly paused, knowing she had just said a mouthful, but she wasn't through yet. "I know you've had a busy day today and need your rest as much as I do, so I'll see you out now. In fact you didn't have to wait around for me to finish upstairs."

"Yes, I did."

She stared at him. "Why?"

"I thought you'd want to know how tonight went."

Shelly inwardly groaned. Of course she wanted to know how tonight went, but she'd been so intent on getting Dare out the door she had forgotten to ask. "Yes, of course. Did he behave himself? How did he take to your family?"

Dare glanced up at the top of the stairs then returned his gaze to her. "Is there somewhere we can talk privately?"

The first place Shelly thought about was the kitchen, and then she remembered what had happened between them earlier that day. She decided the best place to talk would be outside on the porch. That way he would definitely be out of the house. "We can talk outside on the porch," she said, moving in that direction.

Without waiting for his response, she took the few steps to the door and stepped outside.

The night air was crisp and clear. The first thing Shelly noticed was the full moon in the sky, and the next was the zillions of stars that sparkled like diamonds surrounding it.

She went to stand next to a porch post, since it was the best spot for the glow of light from the moon. The last thing she needed was to stand in some dark area of the porch with Dare.

She heard him behind her when he joined her, however, instead of standing with her in the light, he went and sat in the porch swing that was located in a darkened corner. She sucked in a breath. If he thought for one minute that she would join him in that swing, he had another thought coming. As far as she was concerned, they could converse just fine right where they were.

"So how did AJ behave tonight?" she asked, deciding to plunge right in, since there was no reason to prolong the moment.

She heard the swing's slow rocking when he replied, "To my surprise, very well. In fact, his manners were impeccable, but then it was obvious that he was trying to impress Thorn." Dare chuckled. "He pretty much tried ignoring me, but my brothers picked up on what he was doing and wrecked those plans. Whenever he tried excluding me from the conversation, they counteracted and included me. Pretty soon he gave up, after finding out the hard way an important lesson about the Westmorelands."

"Which is?"

"We stick together, no matter what."

Shelly nodded. She'd known that from previous years.

"But I must admit there was this one time when they were ready to disclaim me as their brother," Dare said, chuckling.

Shelly rested her back against the post and crossed her legs. "And what time was that?"

"The night I ended things with you. They thought I was crazy to give you up for any reason. And that included a career."

She nervously rubbed her hands up and down her arms, not wanting to talk about what used to be between them.

"Well, all that's in the past, Dare. Is there anything else about tonight I should know?" she asked, trying to keep their conversation moving along.

"Yes, there is something else."

She sought out his features, but could barely make them out in the darkened corner of the porch. "What?"

"I gave AJ reason to believe that I'm interested in you again."

Shelly nodded. "And how did he handle that?"

Dare smiled. "He had something to say about it, if that's what you're asking. Just how far he'll go to make sure nothing develops between us I can't rightly say."

Shelly nodded again. Neither could she. Personally, she thought AJ's dislike of Dare was a phase he was going through, but a very important phase in his life, and she didn't want to do anything to make things worse with him. "In that case, more than likely he'll have a talk with me about it."

Dare leaned back against the swing. "And what do you plan to say when he does?"

Shelly sighed. "Basically, everything we agreed I should say. I'm to let him know he's the one who has a beef with you, not me, and therefore I don't have a problem with re-establishing our relationship."

Dare heard her words. Although they were fabricated for AJ's benefit, they sounded pretty damn good to him, and he wished they were true, because he certainly didn't have a problem reestablishing anything with her.

He looked over at Shelly and saw how she leaned against the post while silhouetted by the glow from the moon. His gaze zeroed on the fact that she stood with her legs crossed. Tight. She had once told him that she had a tendency to stand with her legs crossed really tight whenever she felt a deep throbbing ache between them. Evidently she had forgotten sharing that piece of information with him some years ago.

"Well, if that about covers everything, then we'd best call it a night."

Her words interrupted his thought, and he figured they could do better than just call it a night. Calling it a "night of seduction" sounded more to his liking. Some inner part of him wanted to know if she wanted him as much as he wanted her, and there was only one way to find out.

"Come sit with me for a while, Shelly," he said, his voice husky.

Shelly swallowed and met his gaze. "I don't think that's a good idea, Dare."

"I do. It's a beautiful night and I think we should enjoy it before saying good-night."

Enjoy it or enjoy each other? Shelly was tempted to ask, but decided she wouldn't go there with Dare. Once he got her in that swing that would be the end of it. Or the beginning of it, depending on the way you looked at it. Her body was responding to him in the most unsettled and provocative way tonight. All he had to do was to touch her one time and…

"Let me give you what you need, Shelly."

He saw her chin lift defiantly, and he saw the way she frowned at him. "And what makes you think that you know what I need?"

"Your legs."

She raised a confused brow. "What about my legs?"

"They're crossed, and pretty damn tight."

Shelly's heart missed a beat and the throbbing between her legs increased. He had remembered. A long, seemingly endless moment of silence stretched out between them. She could see his features. They were as tight as her legs were crossed. And the gaze that held hers was like a magnet, drawing her in, second by tantalizing second.

She shook her head, trying to deny her body what it wanted, what it evidently needed, but it had a mind of its own and wasn't adhering to any protest she was making.

The man sitting on the swing watching her, waiting for her, had a history of being able to pleasure her in every possible way. He knew it and she knew it as well.

Breathing deeply, she found herself slowly crossing the porch toward him, out of the light and into the darkness, out from temptation and into a straight path that led to seduction. She came to a stop between his spread knees and when their legs touched, she sucked in a deep breath at the same time she heard him suck in one, too. And when she felt his hand reach under her skirt skimming her inner thigh, her knees almost turned to mush.

His voice was husky and ultra sexy when he spoke. "This morning I had to know if your mouth still knew me. Now I want to find out if this," he said, gliding his warm hand upward, boldly touching the crotch of her panties, "knows me as well."

Her eyes fluttered closed and she automatically reached out and placed both hands on his shoulders for support. A part of her wanted to scream Yes! Her body knew him as the last man…the only man…to stake a claim in this territory, but she was incapable of speech. All she could do was stand there and wait to see what would happen next and hope she could handle it.

She didn't have to wait long; the tips of Dare's fingers slowly began messaging the essence of her as he relentlessly stroked his hand over the center of her panties.

"You're hot, Shelly," he said, his voice huskier than before. "Sit down in my lap facing me."

Dare had to move his body forward then sideways for her to accommodate his request. The arrangement brought her face just inches from his. His hand was still between her legs.

He leaned forward and captured her mouth, giving her a kiss that made the one they'd shared that morning seemed complacent. Her senses became frenzied and aroused, and the feel of his hand stroking her only added to her turmoil.

And when she felt his fingers inch past the edge of her bikini panties, she released a deep moan.

"Yeah, baby, that's the sound I want to hear," he said after releasing her lips. "Open your legs a little wider and tell me how you like this."

Before she could completely comply with his request, he slid three fingers inside her, and when he found that too tight a fit, backed out and went with two. "You're pretty snug in there, baby," he whispered as his fingers began moving in and out of her in a rhythm meant to drive her insane. "How do you like this?"

"I love it," she whispered, clenching his shoulders with her hands. "Oh, Dare, it's been so long."

He leaned closer and traced the tips of her lips with his tongue before moving to nibble at her ear. She was about to go up in smoke, and he couldn't help but wonder how long it had been for her, since this was making her come apart so quickly and easily. He asked, "How long has it been, Shelly?"

She met his gaze and drew in a trembling breath. "Not since you, Dare."

His fingers went still; his jaw tightened and his gaze locked with hers. "You mean that you haven't done this since we…"

She didn't let him finished as she closed her mouth over his, snatching his words and his next breath in the process. But the thought that no other man had touched her since him sent his mind escalating, his entire body trembling. No wonder her legs had been crossed so tightly and he intended to make it good for her.

His fingers began moving inside her again and her muscles automatically clenched around them. She was tight and wet and the scent of her arousal was driving him insane. He broke off the kiss, desperately needing to taste her.

"Unbutton your top, Shelly."

She released her hands from his shoulders and slowly unbuttoned her blouse, then unsnapped the front opening of her bra. As soon as her breasts poured forth, looming before him, he began sucking, nibbling and licking his way to heaven. He moved his fingers within her using the same rhythm his tongue was using on her breasts.

He felt the moment her body shook and placed his mouth over hers to absorb her moans of pleasure when spasms tore into her. Her fingernails dug into his shoulders as he continued using his fingers to pleasure her. And when it started all over again, and more spasms rammed through her, signaling a second orgasm, she pulled her mouth from his, closed her eyes and leaned forward to his chest, crying out into the cotton of his shirt.

"That's it baby, let go and enjoy."

And as another turbulent wave of pleasure ripped through her and she fought to catch her breath, Shelly let go and enjoyed every single moment of what Dare was doing to her.

And she doubted that after tonight her life would ever be the same.

Eight

"Mom? Mom? Are you okay?"

Shelly heard the sound of AJ's voice as he tried gently to shake her awake.

"Mom, wake up. Please say something."

She quickly opened her eyes when her mind registered the panic in his tone. She blinked, feeling dazed and disoriented, and tried to focus on him, but at the moment she felt completely wrung out. "AJ? What are you doing out of bed?"

Confusion appeared in his face. "Mom, I'm supposed to be out of bed. It's morning and I have to go to school today. You forgot to wake me up. And why did you sleep on the sofa all night in the same clothes you had on yesterday?"

Somehow, Shelly found the strength to sit up. She yawned, feeling bone-tired. "It's morning already?" The last thing she remembered was having her fourth orgasm in Dare's arms and slumping against him without any strength left even to hold up her head. He must have brought her into the house and placed her on the sofa, thinking she would eventually come around and go up the stairs. Instead, exhausted, depleted and totally satisfied, she had slept through the night.

"Mom, are you all right?

She met AJ's concerned gaze. He had no idea just how all right she was. Dare had given her just what her body had needed. She had forgotten just what an ace he was with his fingers on a certain part of her. "Yes, AJ, I'm fine." She glanced at the coffee table and noticed the book both she and Dare had been reading and considered it the perfect alibi. "I must have fallen asleep reading. What time is it? You aren't late are you?" She leaned back against the sofa's cushions. After a night like last light, she could curl up and sleep for the entire day.

"No, I'm not late, but you might be if you have to go to work today."

Shelly shook her head. "I only have a couple of patients I need to see, and I hadn't planned on going anywhere until around ten." She decided not to mention that she was also having lunch with Dare's brothers today. She yawned again. "What would you like for breakfast?"

He shrugged. "I'll just have a bowl of cereal. I met these two guys at school yesterday and we're meeting up to ride our bikes together."

Shelly nodded. She hoped AJ hadn't associated himself with the wrong group again. "Who are these boys?"

"Morris Sears and Cornelius Thomas. And we're going to meet at Kate's Diner every morning for chocolate milk." As an afterthought he added. "And it's free if we let her know we've been good in school."

Shelly made a mental note to ask Dare about Morris and Cornelius when she saw him again. Being Sheriff he probably knew if the two were troublemakers.

"They're real cool guys and they like my bike," AJ went on to say. "Yesterday they told me all about the sheriff and his brothers." His eyes grew wide. "Why didn't you tell me that Thorn Westmoreland is my uncle?"

"Because he's not."

At AJ's confused frown, Shelly decided to explain. "Until you accept Dare as your father you can't claim any of the Westmorelands as your uncles."

AJ glared. "That doesn't seem fair."

"And why doesn't it? You're the one who doesn't want Dare knowing he's your father, so how can you tell anyone that Thorn and the others are your uncles without explaining the connection? Until you decide differently, to the Westmorelands you're just another kid."

She stood. "Now, I'm going upstairs to shower while you eat breakfast."

AJ nodded as he slowly walked out of the room and headed for the kitchen. Shelly knew she had given him something to think about.

"Is it true?" Morris asked excitedly the moment AJ got off his bike at Ms. Kate's Diner.

AJ raised a brow. "Is what true?"

It was Cornelius who answered, his wide, blue eyes expressive. "That you had dinner with the sheriff and his family last night?"

AJ shrugged, wondering how they knew that. "Yeah, so what about it?"

"We think it's cool, that's what about it. The sheriff is the bomb. He makes sure everyone in this town is safe at night. My mom and dad say so," Cornelius responded without wasting any time.

AJ and the two boys opened the door and walked into the diner. "How did you know I had dinner with the sheriff?" he asked as they walked up to the counter where cartons of chocolate milk had been placed for them.

"Mr. and Mrs. Turner saw all of you and called my grandmother who then called my mom and dad. Everyone was wondering who you were and I told my mom that you were a kid who got in trouble and had to report to the sheriff's office after school every day. They thought you were a family member or something, but I told them you weren't."

AJ nodded. "My mom had to go to work unexpectedly last night and the sheriff offered to take me to dinner with him since I hadn't eaten."

"Wow! That was real nice of him, wasn't it?"

AJ hadn't really thought about it being an act of kindness and said, "Yeah, I guess so."

"Do you think he'll mind if we go with you to his office after school?" Morris asked excitedly.

AJ scrunched his face, thinking. "I guess not, but he might put you to work."

Morris shrugged. "That's all right if he does. I just want him to tell us about the time he was an FBI agent and did that undercover stuff to catch the bad guys."

AJ nodded. He didn't want to admit it, but he wouldn't mind hearing about that himself. He smiled when the nice lady behind the counter handed them each a donut to go along with their milk.

Shelly's hands tightened on the steering wheel after she brought her car to a stop next to the police cruiser marked Sheriff. She'd had no idea Dare would be joining his brothers for lunch. How would she manage a straight face around him and not let anyone know they had spent close to an hour in a darkened area of her porch last night doing something deliriously naughty?

She opened the car door and took a deep breath, thinking that the things Dare had done to her had turned her inside out and whetted her appetite. To put it more bluntly, sixteen hours later she was still aroused. After having gone without sex for so long she now felt downright hungry. In fact *starving* was a better word to use. Would Dare look at her and detect her sexually-excited state? If anyone could, it would be Dare, a man who'd once known her better than she'd known herself.

And to think she'd even admitted to him that she hadn't slept with another soul since their breakup ten years ago. Now that he knew, she had to keep her head on straight and keep Dare's focus on AJ and not her.

With a deep sigh she opened the door and went inside.

She paused and watched all five men stand the moment she entered the restaurant. They must have seen her drive up and were ready to greet her. Tears burned the back of her eyes. It had been too long. When she'd been Dare's girl-friend, the brothers had claimed her as an honorary sister, and since she'd been an only child, she'd held that attachment very dear. One of the hardest things about leaving College Park had been knowing that in addition to leaving Dare she'd also left behind a family she had grown very close to.

As she looked at them now, she began to smile. They stood in a line as if awaiting royalty and she walked up to them, one by one. "Thorn," she said to the one closest to Dare in age. She gladly accepted the kiss he boldly placed on her lips and the hug he fondly gave her.

"Ten years is a long time to be gone, Shelly," he said with a serious expression on his face. "Don't try it again."

She couldn't help but smile upon seeing that he was bossy as ever. "I won't, Thorn."

She then moved to Stone, the first Westmoreland she had come to know; the one who had introduced her to Dare. Without saying a word she reached for him, hugging him tightly. After they released each other, he placed a kiss on her lips as well.

"I'm so proud of your accomplishments, Stone," she said smiling through her tears. "And I buy every book you write."

He chuckled. "Thanks, Shell." His face then grew serious. "And I ditto what Thorn said. Don't leave again." His gaze momentarily left hers and shifted to where Dare was standing. He glared at his brother before returning his gaze to hers and added, "No matter what the reason."

She nodded. "All right."

Then came the twins, who were a year younger than she. She remembered them getting into all sorts of mischief, and from the gleams in their eyes, it was evident they were still up to no good. After they both placed chaste pecks on her lips, Storm said, smiling. "We told Dare that he blew his chance with you, which means you're now available for us."

Shelly grinned. "Oh, am I?"

"Yeah, if you want to be," Chase said, teasingly, giving her another hug.

When Chase released her she drew a deep breath. Next came Dare.

"Dare," she acknowledged softly, nervously.

She figured since she'd already been in his company a few times, not to mention what they had done together last night, that he would not make a big production of seeing her. She soon discovered just how wrong that assumption was when he gently pulled her into his arms and captured her lips, nearly taking her breath in the process. There was nothing chaste about the kiss he gave her and she knew it had intentionally lasted long enough to cause his brothers to speculate and to give anyone who saw them kiss something to talk about.

When he released her mouth, it was Stone who decided to make light of what Dare had done by saying, "What was that about, Dare? Were you trying to prove to Shelly that you could still kiss?"

Dare answered as his gaze held hers. He smiled at Stone's comment and said, "Yeah, something like that."

Shelly never had problems getting through a meal before. But then she'd never had the likes of Dare Westmoreland on a mission to seduce her. And it didn't matter that she was sitting at a table in a restaurant next to him, surrounded by his brothers, or that the place was filled to lunch-crowd capacity.

She took several deep breaths to calm her racing heart, but it did nothing to soothe the ache throbbing through her. It all started when she caught herself staring at his hand as he lifted a water goblet to his lips. Seeing his fingers had reminded her how she had whimpered her way into ecstasy as those same fingers had stroked away ten years of sexual frustration.

She had caught his eyes dark with desire, over the water glass, and had realized he had read her thoughts. And, as smooth as silk, when he placed the glass down he took that same hand and without calling attention to what he was doing, placed it under the table on her thigh.

At first she'd almost jerked at the cool feel of his hand, then she'd relaxed when his hand just rested on her thigh without moving. But then, moments later, she had almost gasped when his hand moved to settle firmly between her legs. And amidst all conversations going on around them, as the brothers tried to bring her up to date on what had been going on in their lives over the past ten years, no one seemed to have noticed that one of Dare's hands was missing from the table while he gently stroked her slowly back and forth through the material of her shorts. He'd tried getting her zipper down, a zipper that, thanks to the way she was sitting, wouldn't budge.

Thinking that she had to do something, anything to stop this madness, she leaned forward and placed her elbows on the table and cupped her face in her hands as she tried to ignore the multitude of sensations flowing through her. She glanced around wondering if any of the brothers had any idea what Dare was up to, but from the way they were talking and eating, it seemed they had more on their minds than Dare not keeping his hands to himself.

"We want you to know that we'll do everything we can to help you with AJ, Shelly."

Shelly nodded at Stone's offer and then felt her cheeks grow warmer when another one of Dare's fingers wiggled its way inside her shorts. "I appreciate that, Stone."

"He's my responsibility," Dare spoke up and glanced at his brothers, keeping a straight face, not giving away just what sidebar activities he was engaged in.

"Yeah, but he belongs to us, too," Thorn said. "He's a Westmoreland, and I think that you did a wonderful job with him, Shelly, considering the fact that you've been a single parent for the past ten years. He's going through growing pains now, but once he sees that he has a family who cares deeply for him, he'll be just fine."

She nodded. She had to believe that as well. "Thanks, Thorn."

"Well, although I truly enjoyed all your company, it's time for me to get back to the station," Dare said, finally removing his hand from between her legs. When he stood she glanced up at him knowing that regardless of whether it was a dark, cozy corner on her porch at night or in a restaurant filled with people in broad day light, Dare Westmoreland did just what he pleased, and it seemed that nothing pleased him more than touching her.

"So, what did you do next, Sheriff?"

Dare shook his head. When AJ had shown up after school, he had brought Morris and Cornelius with him and explained that the two had wanted to tag along. Dare had made it clear that if they had come to keep AJ company then they might as well help him with the work, and he had just the project for the three of them.

He had taken them to the basement where the police youth athletic league's equipment was stored, with instructions that they bring order to the place. That past year a number of balls, gloves and bats had been donated by one of the local sports stores.

Deciding to stay and help as well to supervise, he had not been prepared for the multitude of questions that Morris and Cornelius were asking him. AJ didn't ask him anything, but Dare knew he was listening to everything that was being said.

"That's why it pays to be observant," Dare said, unloading another box. "It's always a clue when one guy goes inside and the other stays out in the car with the motor running. They had no idea I was with law enforcement. I pretended to finish filling my tank up with gas, and out of the corner of my eye I could see the man inside acting strangely and I knew without a doubt that a robbery was about to take place."

"Wow! Then what did you do?" Morris asked, with big, bright eyes.

"Although I worked for the Bureau, we had an unspoken agreement with the local authorities to make them aware of certain things and that's what I did. Pretending to be checking out a map, I used my cell phone to alert the local police of what was happening. The only reason I became involved was because I saw that one of the robbers intended to take a hostage, a woman who'd been inside paying for gas. At that point I knew I had to make a move."

"Weren't you afraid you might get hurt?" AJ asked.

Dare wondered if AJ was aware that he was now as engrossed in the story as Morris and Cornelius were. "No, AJ, at the time the only thing I could think about was that an innocent victim was at risk. Her safety became my main concern at that point, and whatever I did, I had to make sure that she wasn't hurt or injured."

"So what did you do?"

"In the pretense of paying for my gas, I entered the store at the same time the guy was forcing the woman out. I decided to use a few martial arts moves I had learned in the marines, and—"

"You used to be in the marines?" AJ asked.

Dare smiled. The look of total surprise and awe on his son's face was priceless. "Yes, I served in the marines for four years, right after college."

AJ smiled. "Wow!"

"My daddy says the marines only picks the most bravest and the best men," Morris said, also impressed.

Dare smiled. "I think all the branches of the military selects good men, but I do admit that marines are a very special breed." He glanced at his watch. "It's a little over an hour, guys. Do I need to call any of your parents to let them know that you're on your way home?"

All three boys shook their heads, indicating that Dare didn't have to. "All right."

"Sheriff, do you think you can teach us some simple martial arts moves?" Cornelius asked.

"Yeah, Sheriff, with bad people kidnapping kids we need to know how to protect ourselves, don't we?" Morris chimed in.

Dare grinned when he saw AJ vigorously nodding his head, agreeing with Morris. "Yes, I guess that's something all of you should know, some real simple moves. Just as long as you don't use it on your classmates for fun or to try to show off."

"We wouldn't do that," Morris said eagerly.

Dare nodded. "All right then. I'll try to map out some time this Saturday morning. How about checking with your parents, and if they say it's all right, then the three of you can meet me here."

He glanced at his watch again. Shelly didn't know it yet, but he intended to see her again tonight, no matter what excuse he had to make to do so. He smiled, pleased with the progress he felt he'd made with AJ today. "Okay, guys, let's get things moving so we can call it a day. The three of you did an outstanding job and I appreciate it."

"Mom, did you know that the sheriff used to be in the marines?"

Shelly glanced up from her book and met AJ's excited gaze. He was stretched out on the floor by the sofa doing his homework. "Yes, I knew that. We dated during that time."

"Wow!"

She lifted a brow. "What's so fantastic about him being a marine?"

AJ rolled his eyes to the ceiling. "Mom, everyone knows that marines are tough. They adapt, improvise and overcome!"

Shelly smiled at her son's Clint Eastwood imitation from one of his favorite movies. "Oh." She went back to reading her book.

"And Mom, he told us about the time he caught two men trying to rob a convenience store and taking a hostage with them. It was real cool how he captured the bad guys."

"Yeah, I'm sure it was."

"And he offered to teach us martial arts moves on Saturday morning at the police station so we'll know how to protect ourselves," he added excitedly in a forward rush.

Shelly lifted her head from her book again. "Who?"

"The sheriff."

She nodded. "Oh, your father?"

Their gazes locked and Shelly waited for AJ's comeback, expecting a denial that he did not consider Dare his father. After a few minutes he shrugged his shoulders and said softly, "Yes." He then quickly looked away and went back to doing his homework.

Shelly inhaled deeply. AJ admitting Dare was his father

was a start. It seemed the ice surrounding his heart was slowly beginning to melt, and he was beginning to see Dare in a whole new light.

Nine

Dare walked into Coleman's Florist knowing that within ten minutes of the time he walked out, everyone in College Park would know he had sent flowers to Shelly. Luanne Coleman was one of the town's biggest gossips, but then he couldn't worry about that, especially since for once her penchant to gab would work in his favor. Before nightfall he wanted everyone to know that he was in hot pursuit of Shelly Brockman.

Due to the escape of a convict in another county, he had spent the last day and a half helping the sheriff of Stone Mountain track down the man. Now, thirty-six hours after the man had been recaptured, Dare was bone tired and regretted he had missed the opportunity to see Shelly two nights ago as he'd planned. The best he could do was go home and get some sleep to be ready for the martial arts training he had promised the boys in the morning.

He also regretted that he had not been there when AJ had arrived after school yesterday. It had officially been the last time he was to report to him. According to McKade, AJ had come alone and had been on time. He had also done the assignment Dare had left for him to do without having much to say. However, McKade had said AJ questioned him a couple of times as to why he wasn't there.

Dare walked around the shop, wondering just what kind of flowers Shelly would like, then decided on roses. According to Storm, roses, especially red ones, said everything. And everyone knew that Storm was an ace when it came to wooing women.

"Have you decided on what you want, Sheriff?"

He turned toward Mrs. Coleman. A woman in her early sixties, she attended the same church as his parents and he'd known her all of his life. "Yes, I'd like a dozen roses."

"All right. What color?"

"Red."

She smiled and nodded as if his selection was a good one, so evidently Storm was right. "Any particular type vase you have in mind?"

He shrugged. "I haven't thought about that."

"Well, you might want to. The flowers say one thing and the vase says another. You want to make sure you select something worthy of holding your flowers."

Dare frowned. He hadn't thought ordering flowers would be so much trouble. "Do you have a selection I can take a look at?"

"Certainly. There's an entire group over on that back wall. If you see something that catches your fancy, bring it to me."

Dare nodded again. Knowing she was watching him with those keen eyes of hers, he crossed the room to stand in front of a shelf containing different vases. As far as he was concerned one vase was just as good as any, but he decided to try and look at them from a woman's point of view.

A woman like Shelly would like something that looked special, soft yet colorful. His gaze immediately went to a white ceramic vase that had flowers of different colors painted at the top. For some reason he immediately liked it and could see the dozen roses arranged really prettily in it. Without dallying any further, he picked up his choice and walked back over to the counter.

"This is the one I want."

Luanne Coleman nodded. "This is beautiful, and I'm sure she'll love it. Now, to whom will this be delivered?"

Dare inwardly smiled, knowing she was just itching to bits to know that piece of information. "Shelly Brockman."

Her brows lifted. "Shelly? Yes, I heard she was back in town, and it doesn't surprise me any that you would be hot on her heels, Dare Westmoreland. I hope you know that I was really upset with you when you broke things off with her all those years ago."

You and everybody else in this town, Dare thought, leaning against the counter.

"And she was such nice girl," Luanne continued. "And everyone knew she was so much in love with you. Poor thing had to leave town after that and her parents left not long after she did."

As Luanne accepted his charge card she glanced at him and said, "I understand she has a son."

Dare pretended not to find her subject of conversation much to his interest. He began fidgeting with several key rings she had on display. "Yes, she does."

"Someone said he's about eight or nine."

Dare knew nobody had said any such thing. The woman was fishing, and he knew it. He might as well set himself up to get caught. "He's ten."

"Ten?"

"Yes." Like you didn't already know.

"That would mean he was born soon after she left here, wouldn't it?"

Dare smiled. He liked how this woman's mind worked. "Yes, it would seem that way."

"Any ideas about his father?"

"No."

"No?"

Dare wanted to chuckle. "None."

She frowned at him. "Aren't you curious?"

"No. What Shelly did with her life after she left here is none of my business."

Dare couldn't help but notice that Luanne's frown deepened. She handed his charge card back to him and said, "I have Shelly's address, Sheriff, since she's staying at her parents' old place."

Dare nodded, not surprised that she knew that. "When will the flowers be delivered?"

"Within a few hours. Will that be soon enough?"

"Yes."

"Sheriff, can I offer you a few words of advice?"

He wondered what she would do if he said no. She would probably give him the advice anyway. He could tell she was just that upset with him right now. "Why sure, Ms. Luanne. What words of advice would you like to offer me?"

She met his gaze without blinking. "Get your head out of the sand and stop overlooking the obvious."

"Meaning?"

She frowned. "That's for you to figure out."

Shelly looked at Mr. Coleman in surprise. She then looked at the beautiful arrangement of flowers he held in his hand. "Are you sure these are for me?"

The older man beamed. "Yes, I'm positive. Luanne said for me to get them to you right away," he said handing them to her.

"Thanks, and if you just wait a few minutes I'd like to give you a tip."

Mr. Coleman waved his hand as he went down the steps. "No need. I've already been tipped real nice for delivering them," he said with a grin that said he had a secret that he wouldn't be sharing with her.

"All right. Thanks, Mr. Coleman." She watched as he climbed into his van and drove off. Closing the door she went into the living room and placed the flowers on the first table she came to. Someone had sent her a dozen of the most beautiful red roses that she had ever seen. And the vase they were in was simply gorgeous; she could tell the vase alone had cost a pretty penny.

She quickly pulled off the card and read it aloud. "You're in my thoughts. Dare."

Her heart skipped a beat as she lightly ran her fingers over the card. Even the card and envelope weren't the standard kind that you received with a floral arrangement. They had a rich, glossy finish that caused Dare's bold signature to stand out even more.

For a moment, Shelly could only stare at the roses, the vase they were in and the card and envelope. It was obvious that a lot of time and attention had gone into their selection, and a part of her quivered inside that Dare would do something that special for her.

You're in my thoughts.

She suddenly felt tears sting her eyes. She didn't know what was wrong with her. It seemed that lately her emotions were wired and would go off at the least little thing. Ever since that day of Dare's visit and what he'd done to her on the porch, not to mention that little episode he'd orchestrated at the restaurant, she'd been battling the worst kind of drama inside her body. He had done more than open Pandora's box. He had opened a cookie jar that had been kept closed for ten years, and now she wanted Dare in the worst possible way.

"Who sent the flowers, Mom?"

Shelly lifted her head and met her son's gaze. "Your father."

He shrugged. "The sheriff?"

"One and the same." She glanced back over at the flowers. "Aren't they beautiful?"

AJ came to stand next to her. It was obvious they couldn't see the arrangement through the same eyes when he said, "Looks like a bunch of flowers to me."

She couldn't help but laugh. "Well, I think they're special, and it was thoughtful for him to send them to let me know I was in his thoughts."

AJ shrugged again. "He's looking for a girlfriend, but I told him you weren't interested in a boyfriend."

Shelly arched a brow. "AJ, you had no right to say that."

His chin jutted out. "Why not? You've never had a boyfriend before, so why would you care about one now? It's just been me and you, Mom. Isn't that enough?"

Shelly shook her head. Her son had years to learn about human sexuality and how it worked. She was just finding out herself what ten years of abstinence could do to a person. "AJ, don't you think I can get lonely sometimes?" she asked him softly.

He didn't say anything for a little while. Then he said, "But you never got lonely before."

"Yes, and I worked a lot before. That's how you got into all that trouble. I was putting in extra hours at the hospital when the cost of living got high. I needed additional money so the two of us could afford to live in the better part of town. I didn't have time to get lonely. Now with my new job, I can basically make my own hours so I can spend more time with you. But you're away in school a lot during the days, and pretty soon you'll have friends you'll want to spend time with, won't you?"

AJ thought of Morris and Cornelius and the fun they'd had on the playground that day at school. "Yes."

"Well, don't you think I need friends, too?"

"Yes, but what's wrong with having girlfriends?"

"There's nothing wrong with it, but most of the girls I went to school with have moved away, and although I'm sure I'll meet others, right now I feel comfortable associating with people I already know, like Dare and his brothers."

"But it's the sheriff who wants you as his girlfriend. He likes you."

She smiled. Dare must have laid it on rather thick. "You think so?"

"Yes. He said you used to be his special girl. His brothers and parents said so, too. And I've got a feeling he wants you to be his special girl again. But if you let him, he'll find out about me."

"And you still see that as a bad thing, AJ?"

He remained silent for a long time, then he hunched his shoulders. "I'm still not sure he would want me."

Shelly felt a knot forming in her stomach. She wondered if he was using his supposed dislike of Dare as an excuse to shield himself from getting hurt. "And why wouldn't he want you?"

"I told you that he didn't like me."

And you also said you didn't like him, she wanted to remind him, but decided to keep quiet about that. "Well, I know Dare, and I know that he likes you. He wouldn't have invited you to dinner with him and his family if he didn't. He would have taken you straight to Ms. Kate's house knowing she would have fed you."

She watched AJ's shoulders relax. "You think so?"

If you only knew, she thought. "Yes, I think so. I believe you remind Dare of himself when he was your age. I heard he was a handful for his parents. All the brothers were."

AJ nodded. "Yes, he said that once. He has a nice family."

She smiled. "Yes, he has."

AJ stuck his hands inside his pockets. "So, he's back now?"

"Who?"

"The sheriff. He left town to help another sheriff catch a guy who escaped from jail. Deputy McKade said so."

"Oh." Shelly had wondered why she hadn't heard from him since the luncheon on Thursday. Not that she had been looking for him, mind you. "Well, in that case, yes, I would say that he's back, since he ordered these flowers."

"Then our lessons for tomorrow morning are still on."

"Your lessons?"

"Yeah, remember, I told you he had said he would teach me, Morris and Cornelius how to protect ourselves at the police station in the morning."

"Oh, I'd almost forgotten about that." She wanted to meet her son's new playmates and ask Dare about them. "Will they need a ride or will their parents bring them?"

"Their parents will be bringing them. They have to go to the barbershop in the morning."

Shelly nodded, looking at the long hair on her son's head. She'd allowed him to wear it in twists, as long as they were neat-looking. Maybe in time she would suggest that he pay a visit to the barbershop as well.

"And after our class they have to go to church for choir practice."

AJ's words recaptured Shelly's attention. Morris and Cornelius were active in church? The two were sounding better and better every minute. "All right then. Go get cleaned up for dinner."

He nodded. "Do you think the sheriff will call tonight or come by?" AJ asked as he trotted up the stairs.

I wish. "I'm not sure. If he just got back into town he's probably, tired so I doubt it."

"Oh."

Although she was sure he hadn't wanted her to, she had heard the disappointment in his voice anyway. He sounded just how she felt.

Dare couldn't sleep. He felt restless. Agitated. Horny.

He threw back the covers and got out of bed, yanked a T-shirt over his head and pulled on his jeans. His body was a nagging ache, it was throbbing relentlessly and his arousal strained painfully against his jeans. He knew what his problems was, and he knew just how he could fix it.

He sighed deeply, thinking he definitely had a problem, and wondered if at two in the morning, Shelly was willing to help him solve it.

Shelly couldn't sleep and heard the sound of a pebble the moment it hit her window. At first she'd thought she was hearing things, but when a second pebble hit the window she knew she wasn't. She also knew who was sending her the signals to come to the backyard.

That had always been Dare's secret sign to let her know he was back in town. She would then sneak past her parents' bedroom and slip down the stairs and through the back door to race outside to his arms.

She immediately got out of bed, tugged on her robe and slipped her feet into her slippers. Not even thinking about why he would be outside her window this time of night, she quickly tiptoed down the stairs. Without turning on a light, she entered the kitchen and opened the back door, and, although it was too dark for her to see, she knew he was there. Her nostrils immediately picked up his scent.

"Dare?" she whispered, squinting her eyes to see him.

"I'm here."

And he was, suddenly looming over her, gazing down at her with a look in his eyes that couldn't be disguised. It was desperate, hot, intense, and it made her own eyes sizzle at the same time the area between her legs began to throb. "I heard the pebbles," she said, swallowing deeply.

He nodded as he continued to hold her gaze. "I was hoping you would remember what it meant."

Oh, she remembered all right. Her body remembered, too. "Why are you here?" she asked softly, feeling her insides heat up and an incredible sensation flow between her legs. Desire was surging through every part of her body and she was barely able to stand it. "What do you want, Dare?"

He reached out and placed both hands at her waist, intentionally pulling her closer so she could feel his large, hard erection straining against his jeans. "I think that's a big indication of what I want, Shelly," he murmured huskily, leaning down as his mouth drew closer to hers.

Ten

Shelly felt a moment of panic. One part of her mind tried telling her that she didn't want this, but another part, the one ruled by her body, quickly convinced her that she did. Her mind was swamped with the belief that it didn't matter that it hadn't been a full week since she laid eyes on Dare again after ten years. Nor did it matter that there were issues yet unresolved between them. The only thing that mattered was that this was the man she had once loved to distraction, the man she had given her virginity to at seventeen; the man who had taught her all the pleasures a man and woman could share, and the man who had given her a son. And, she inwardly told herself, this has nothing to do with love but with gratifying our needs.

Realizing that and accepting it, her body trembled as she lifted her face to meet his, and at that moment everything, including the ten years that had separated them, evaporated and was replaced by hunger, intense, sexual hunger that was waiting to explode within her. He felt it, too, and his body reacted, drawing her closer and making a groan escape from her lips.

He covered her mouth with his, zapping her senses in a way that only he could do. Fueled by the greed they both felt, his kiss wasn't gentle. It displayed all the insatiability he was feeling.

And then some.

Dare didn't think he could get enough. He wanted to get inside her, reacquaint her body with his and give her the satisfaction she had denied herself for ten years. He wanted to give her *him*. He felt his blood boil as he pulled his mouth from hers with a labored breath. She was shaking almost violently. So was he.

"Come with me. I've got a place set up for us."

Nodding, she let him lead her off the back porch and through a thicket of trees to a spot hidden by low overhanging branches, a place they had once considered theirs. It was dark, but she was able to make out the blanket that had been spread on the ground. As always, he had thought ahead. He had planned her seduction well this night.

"Where did you park your car?" she asked wondering how he had managed things.

"At the station. I walked from there, using the back way. And nobody saw me."

She nodded. Evidently he had read her mind. From the information she had gotten from Ms. Kate earlier today, the town was buzzing about AJ, wondering if Dare was actually too dim-witted to figure out her son was his.

She met his gaze, which was illuminated by the moonlight. "Thanks for the flowers. They're beautiful. You didn't have to send them."

"I wanted to send them, Shelly."

He drew in a deep breath, and she saw that his gaze was glued to her mouth just as hers was glued to his. She couldn't help but think of the way he tasted, the hunger and intense desire that was still blatant in his loins, making his erection even bigger. Their need for each other had never been this sharp, all-consuming.

"I want you, Shelly," he whispered gently, pulling her down to the blanket with him.

She went willingly, without any resistance, letting him know that she wanted the intimacy of this night as much as he did. She wanted to lose herself in him in the same way he wanted to lose himself in her. Totally. Completely.

She didn't say a word as he gently pushed her robe from her shoulders, and then pulled her nightgown over her head. Nor did she utter a sound when his fingers caressed her breasts then tweaked her nipples before moving lower, past her rib cage and her stomach until he reached the area between her legs.

When he touched her there, dipped into her warmth, her breathing quickened and strained and she almost cried out.

"You're so wet," his voice rumbled against her lips. "All I could think about over the last couple of days is devouring you, wanting the taste of you on my tongue."

Heat built within her body as he pushed her even more over the edge, making her whimper in pleasure. And when pleasure erupted inside her with the force of a tidal wave, he was there to intensify it.

He kissed the scream of his name from her lips, again taking control of her mouth. The kiss was sensual, the taste erotic and it fueled her fire even more. She had ten years to make up for, and somehow, she knew, he was well aware of that.

When her body ceased its trembling, he pulled back, ending their kiss, and stood to remove his clothes. She looked up at him as he tossed his T-shirt aside. He appeared cool and in control as he undressed in front of her, but she knew he was not. His gaze was on her, and she again she connected with it. It felt like a hot caress.

She watched as he eased down his jeans, and she gasped. Her mouth became moist, her body got hungrier. He wasn't wearing any underwear and his erection sprang forth—full of life, eager to please and ready to go. The tip seemed to point straight at her, and the only thing she could think about was the gigantic orgasm she knew Dare would give her.

Anticipation surged within her when he kicked his jeans aside and stood before her completely naked. And her senses began overflowing with the scent of an aroused man.

An aroused man who was ready to mate with an aroused woman.

She then noticed the condom packet he held in his hand. It seemed he had planned her seduction down to the last detail. She watched as he readied himself to keep her safe. Inhaling deeply when the task was done, he lifted his head and met her gaze.

"This is where you tell me to stop, Shelly, and I will."

She knew him, trusted him and realized that what he'd said was true. No matter how much he wanted her, he would never force himself on her. But then, he need not worry about her turning him down. Her body was on fire for him, the area between her legs throbbed. He had given her relief earlier, but that hadn't been enough. She wanted the same thing he wanted.

Deep penetration.

They had discovered a long time ago that they were two intensely sexual human beings. Anytime he had wanted her, all he had to do was touch her and he would have her hot, wet and pulsing within minutes. And anytime they mated, neither had control other than to make sure she was protected from pregnancy, except for that one time when they hadn't even had control for that.

When he dropped down to rejoin her on the blanket, she drew in a deep breath and automatically wrapped her arms around him as he poised his body over hers. He leaned down and placed a kiss on her lips.

"Thank you for my son."

A groan gently left her throat when she felt the head of him pressed against her entrance. Hot and swollen. He nudged her legs apart a little wider with his knees as his gaze continued to hold hers. "Ten years of missing you and not sharing this, Shelly."

And then he entered her, slowly, methodically, trembling as his body continued to push into hers as he lifted her hips. He let out a deep guttural moan. In no time at all he was planted within her to the hilt. The muscles of her body were clenching him. Milking him. Reclaiming him.

She held his gaze and when he smiled, so did she.

And then he began an easy rhythm. Slowly, painstakingly, he increased the pace. And with each deep thrust, he reminded her of just how things used to be between them, and how things still were now.

Hungry. Intense. Overpowering.

His gaze became keen, concentrated and potently dark each time he thrust forward, drove deeper into her, and she felt her body dissolve, dissipate then fuse into his. She felt the muscles of his shoulders bunch beneath her hands, heard the masculine sound of his growl and knew he was fighting reaching sexual fulfillment, waiting for her, refusing to leave her behind. But he couldn't hold back any longer, and, with one last, hard, deep thrust his body began shaking as he reached the pinnacle of satisfaction.

His orgasm triggered hers, and when her mouth formed a chilling scream, he quickly covered it with his, denying her the chance to wake the entire neighborhood. But he couldn't stop her body from quivering uncontrollably. Nor could he stop her legs from wrapping around him, locking their bodies together, determined that they continue to share this. She closed her eyes as a feeling of unspeakable joy and gratification claimed her in the most provocative way, restitution, compensation for ten years of not having access to any of this.

And when the last of the shudders subsided and they both continued to shiver in the aftermath, he sank down, lowered his head to the curve of her neck, released a deep satisfied sigh, and wondered what words he could say to let her know just how overwhelmed he felt.

He forced himself to lift up, to meet her gaze, and she opened her eyes and looked at him. And at that moment, in that instant, he knew words weren't needed. There was no way she couldn't know how he felt.

And as he leaned down and kissed her, he knew that the rest of the night belonged to them.

"Mom? Mom? Are you all right?"

Shelly opened her eyes as she felt AJ nudge her awake. Once again he had found her sleeping on the sofa. After several more bouts of intense lovemaking, they had redressed, then Dare had gathered her into his arms and carried her inside the house. Not wanting to risk taking her upstairs to her own bed and running into AJ, just in case he had awakened during the night to use the bathroom or something, she had asked Dare to place her on the sofa.

Now she turned over to meet AJ's gaze and felt the soreness between her legs as she did so. She had used muscles last night that she hadn't used in over ten years. "Yes, sweetheart, I'm fine."

He lifted a brow. "You slept on the sofa again."

She glanced at the book that was still where it had been the last time she had used it for an alibi. "I guess I fell asleep reading again." She glanced at the clock on the wall. It was Saturday which meant it wasn't a school day so why was he up so early? "Isn't this your day to sleep late?"

He smiled sheepishly, and that smile reminded her so much of Dare that her breath almost caught. "Yeah, but the sheriff is giving us martial arts lessons today, remember?"

Yes, she remembered, then she wondered if after last night Dare would be in any physical shape to give the boys anything today. But then he was a man, and men recovered from intense sessions of lovemaking a lot quicker than most women. Besides, she doubted if he'd gone without sex for ten years as she had. She forced the thought from her mind, not wanting to think about Dare making love to other women.

She shifted her attention back to AJ. "You're excited about taking lessons from Dare aren't you?"

He shrugged. "Yes, I guess. I've always wanted to learn some type of martial arts, but you never would let me take any classes. Morris said his father told him that the sheriff is an ace when it comes to that sort of stuff, and I'm hoping he'll be willing to give us more than one lesson."

Shelly wondered if AJ would ever stop referring to Dare as "the sheriff." But then, to call him Dare was even less respectful. "All right, do you want pancakes this morning?"

"Yes! With lots and lots of butter!"

She smiled as she stood, wincing in the process. Her sore muscles definitely reminded her of last night. "Not with lots and lots of butter, AJ, but I'll make sure you get enough."

Shelly saw Dare the moment she pulled her car into the parking lot at the sheriff's office. He walked over to the car and met them. She wasn't surprised to discover that he'd been waiting for them.

"Are we late?" AJ asked quickly, meeting Dare's gaze.

Dare smiled at him. "No, Cornelius isn't here yet, but I understand he's on his way. Morris's mother just dropped him off a few minutes ago. He's waiting inside."

He then looked at Shelly, and his smile widened. "And how are you doing this morning, Shelly?"

She returned his smile, thinking about all the things the two of them had done last night while most of College Park slept. "I'm fine, Dare, what about you?"

"This is the best I've felt in years." He wanted to say ten years to be exact, but didn't want AJ to catch on to anything.

Shelly glanced at her watch. "How long will the lessons last today?"

"At least an hour or so. Why? Is there something you need to do?"

Shelly placed an arm around AJ's shoulders. "Well, I was hoping I'd have enough time to get my nails done in addition to getting my hair taken care of."

"Then do it. I'm going over to Thorn's shop when I leave here to check out the new bike that he's building. AJ is welcome to go with me if he likes and I can bring him home later."

He shifted his glance from Shelly to AJ. "Would you like to go to Thorn's shop to see how he puts a motorcycle together?"

The expression in AJ's eyes told Dare that he would. "Yes, I'd love to go!" He turned to Shelly. "Can I, Mom?"

Shelly met Dare's gaze. "Are you sure, Dare? I wouldn't want to put you out with having to—"

"No, I'd like his company."

AJ's eyes widened in surprise. "You would?"

Dare grinned. "Sure, I would. You did a great job with all the chores that I assigned to you this week, and I doubt that you'll be playing hooky from school anytime soon, right?"

AJ lowered his head to study his sneakers. "Right."

"Then that does it. My brothers will be there and I know for a fact they'd like to see you again."

AJ smiled. "They would?"

"Yes, they would. They said they enjoyed having you at dinner the other night. Usually on Saturday we all pitch in to give Thorn a hand to make sure any bike he's building is ready to be delivered on time. The one he's working on now is for Sylvester Stallone."

"Wow!"

Dare laughed at the astonishment he heard in AJ's voice and the look of awe on his face. What he'd said about his brothers wanting to see AJ again was true. They were biting at the bit for a chance to spend more time with their nephew.

"Well, I guess that's settled," Shelly said, smiling at Dare and the son he had given her. "I'd better get going if I want to make my hair appointment on time." She turned to leave.

"Shelly?"

She turned back around. "Yes?"

"I almost forgot to mention that Mom called this morning. She heard from Laney last night. She, Jamal and the baby are coming for a visit in a couple of weeks and will stay for about two months. Then they will be moving to stay at their place in Bowling Green, Kentucky, while Laney completes her residency at the hospital there."

Shelly smiled. When she'd last seen Dare's baby sister, Delaney was just about to turn sixteen and the brothers were having a time keeping the young men away. Now she had graduated from medical school and had landed herself a prince from the Middle East. She was a princess and the mother to a son who would one day grow up to be a king. "That's wonderful! I can't wait to see her again."

Dare grinned. "And she can't wait to see you, either. Mom told her that you had moved back and she was excited about it."

Without having to worry about AJ, Shelly decided to throw in a pedicure after getting her hair and nails done. Upon returning home, she collapsed on the bed and took a nap. The lack of sleep the night before still had her tired. After waking up, she was about to go outside on the porch and sit in the swing when she heard a knock at the door. She glanced through the peephole and saw it was Dare and AJ. Both of them had their hands and, faces smeared with what looked like motor oil. She frowned. If they thought they were coming inside her house looking like that, they had another thought coming.

"Go around back," she instructed, opening the door just a little ways. "I'll bring you washcloths and a scrub brush to clean up. You can also use the hose." She then quickly closed the door.

She met them in the backyard where they were using the hose to wash oil from their hair. It was then that she noticed several oil spots on AJ's outfit as well. "What on earth happened?"

"Storm happened," Dare grumbled, taking the shampoo and towel she handed him. His frown indicated he wasn't all that happy about it either. "You know how he likes to play around? Well, for some reason he decided to fill a water gun with motor oil, and AJ and I became his victims."

She shifted her gaze from Dare to AJ. Whereas Dare was not a happy camper because of Storm's childish antics, it seemed AJ was just the opposite. "Storm is so much fun!" He said, laughing, "He told me all about how he had to save this little old lady from a burning house once."

Shelly smiled. "Well, I'm glad you enjoyed yourself, but those clothes can stay out here. In fact, we may as well trash them."

AJ nodded. "Storm said to tell you that he's going to buy me another outfit and he'll call to find out when he can take me shopping."

Shelly crossed her arms over her chest and lifted a brow. "Oh, he did, did he?"

"Yes."

She shifted her gaze back to Dare. "What are we going to do about that brother of yours?"

Dare shrugged, smiling. "What can I do? I guess we could try marrying him off, except so far there's not a woman around who suits his fancy except for Tara, but she's Thorn's challenge."

A bemused look covered Shelly face. "What?"

"Tara Matthews. She's Laney's friend—a doctor who works at the same hospital in Kentucky where Delaney plans to complete her residency. I'll explain about her being Thorn's challenge at another time."

Shelly nodded, planning to hold him to that. She glanced down at her watch. "I was about to cook burgers and fries, if anyone is interested."

Dare looked pleased. "Only if you let me grill the burgers."

"And I'll help," AJ chimed in, volunteering his services.

Shelly shook her head. "All right, and I'll cook the fries and make some potato salad and baked beans to go along with it. How does that sound?"

"That sounds great, Mom."

Shelly nodded, liking the excitement she heard in her son's voice. "Dare?"

He chuckled. "I agree with AJ. That sounds great."

Dare remained through dinner. He got a call that he had to take care of, but returned later with Chase and Storm close on his heels. They brought a checkers game, intent on showing AJ how to play. It was almost eleven before AJ finally admitted he was too tired to play another game. Chase and Storm left after AJ went to bed, leaving Dare to follow later after they mentioned they were headed over to Thorn's place to wake him up to play a game of poker.

An hour or so later, Shelly walked Dare to the door. He had spent some time telling her how Tara Matthews was a feisty woman that only Thorn could tame and that was why the brothers referred to her as Thorn's challenge. "So you think this Tara Matthews has captured the eye of Thorn Westmoreland?"

Dare chuckled. "Yes, although he doesn't know it yet, and I feel sorry for Tara when he does."

Shelly nodded. Moments later she said, "I hope you know your leaving late is giving the neighbors a lot to say."

He smiled. "Yeah, I heard from McKade that a lot of

people around town are questioning my intelligence. They think I haven't figured out that AJ's my son."

Shelly nodded. "Yes, that's what I'm hearing, too, from Ms. Kate."

"How do you think AJ is handling things?"

"I don't think anyone has said anything to him directly, but I know a couple of people have asked him about his father in a roundabout way."

Dare lifted a brow. "When?"

"A couple of days ago at Kate's Diner. He goes there every morning on his way to school."

Dare nodded. "Damn, Shelly, I'm ready to end this farce and let this whole damn town know AJ's mine."

"I know, Dare, but remember we decided to let him be the one to determine when that would be. Personally, I think it'll be sooner than you think, because he's slowly coming around."

Dare raised a questioning brow. "You think so?"

"Yes. The two of you are interacting together a lot better. That's obvious. I can tell, and I know your brothers picked up on it tonight as well."

"Yes, but for some reason he still holds himself back from me," Dare said in a frustrated tone. "I sense it, Shelly, and it bothers the heck out of me. I don't know why he's doing it."

Shelly smiled slightly. "I think I do."

Dare met her gaze. "Then tell me—why?"

She sighed. "I think AJ is beginning to wonder if he's good enough to be your son."

Dare frowned. "Why would he wonder about a thing like that?"

"Because basically he's beginning to see you through a new set of eyes, the same eyes Morris and Cornelius see you with, and AJ's concerned about the way the two of you met. He knows it wasn't a good start and that you were disappointed with him. Now he's afraid that he won't be able to wipe the slate clean with you."

Dare rubbed a hand down his face. "There'll never be a time that I wouldn't want my son, Shelly."

She wrapped her arms around his waist upon hearing the frustration in his voice. She heard the love there as well. "I know that and you know that, but he has to know that, too. Now that you've broken the ice with him, it's time for you to get to know him and for him to get to know you. Then he'll see that no matter what, you'll always be there for him."

Dare let out a deep sigh. "And I thought winning him over would be easy."

She smiled. "In a way, it has been. To be honest with you, I really didn't expect him to come around this soon. Like you, he has somewhat of a stubborn streak about certain things. Him coming around the way he has just goes to show that you evidently have a way with people."

Dare smiled and brought her closer to him. "And do I have a way with you, Shelly?" The only reason he wasn't making love to her again tonight was that he was well aware of the fact that her body was sore. He couldn't help noticing how stiff her movements were when she'd dropped AJ off that morning and again this evening at dinner.

"After last night how can you even ask that, Dare? You know I was putty in your hands," she said, recapturing his attention.

"Then that makes us even, because I was definitely putty in yours as well." He leaned down and kissed her, thinking of just how right she felt in his arms.

Just like always.

Eleven

Shelly stretched out in her bed with a sensuous sigh. Almost two weeks had passed since she and Dare had spent the night together on a blanket in her backyard. Since then, nightly meetings in the backyard on a blanket had become almost a ritual. He had become almost a fixture in her home, dropping by for dinner, and inviting her and AJ to a movie or some other function in town.

AJ was beginning to let his guard down around Dare, but as yet he had not acknowledged him as his father. Shelly knew Dare's patience was wearing thin; he was eager to claim his son, but as she had explained to Dare weeks ago, AJ had to believe in his heart that his father wanted him for a son before he could give Dare his complete love and trust.

She then thought about her own feelings for Dare. She had to fight hard to keep from falling in love with Dare all over again. She had to remember they were playacting for AJ's sake. To anyone observing them, it seemed that he was wooing her. He was giving the townspeople something to talk about with the different flower arrangements that he sent her each week.

A couple of people had taken her aside and warned her not to be setting herself up for heartbreak all over again, since everyone knew Dare Westmoreland was a staunch bachelor. But there were others who truly felt he was worthy of another chance, and they tried convincing her that if anyone could change Dare's bachelor status, she could.

What she couldn't tell them was that she was not interested in changing Dare's bachelor status. Although she had detected some changes in him, she could not forget that at one time he had been a man driven to reach out for dreams that had not included her. And she could never let herself become vulnerable to that type of pain again. For six years she had believed she was the most important thing in Dare's life, and to find out that she hadn't been had nearly destroyed her. She had enough common sense to know that what she and Dare were sharing in the backyard at night was not based on emotional but on physical needs, and as long as she was able to continue to know the difference, she would be all right.

She pulled herself up in bed when she heard the knock on her bedroom door. "Come in, AJ."

It was early still, an hour before daybreak, but she knew he was excited. Today was the day that Dare's sister Delaney and her family were arriving from the Middle East. The Westmoreland brothers were ecstatic and had talked about their one and only sister so much over the past two weeks that AJ had gotten caught up in their excitement; after all, the woman was his aunt, although he assumed Delaney didn't know it.

He opened the door and stood just within the shadows of the light coming in from the hallway. Again, Shelly couldn't help but notice just how much he looked like Dare. No wonder the town was buzzing. "What is it, AJ?"

He shrugged. "I wanted to talk to you about something, Mom."

She nodded and scooted over in bed, but he went and sat in the chair. Evidently, he thought he was past the age to get into his mother's bed. Shelly's heart caught. Her son was becoming a young man and with his budding maturity came a lot of issues that Dare would be there to help her with. Not only Dare but the entire Westmoreland family.

He remained silent for a few minutes, then he spoke. "I've decided to tell the sheriff I'm his son."

Shelly's heart did a flip, and she swallowed slowly. "When did you decide that?"

"Yesterday."

"And what made you change your mind?"

"I've been watching him, Mom. I was in Kate's Diner one morning last week when he came in, but he didn't see me at first. When he walked in, all the people there acted like they were glad to see him, and he knew all their names and asked them how they were doing. Then it hit me that he really wasn't a bad cop or a mean cop at all. No one would like him if he was, and everybody likes him, Mom."

Shelly blinked away the tears from her eyes. AJ was right. Everyone liked Dare and thought well of him. AJ had had to discover that on his own, and it seemed that he had. "Yes, everyone likes Dare. He's a good sheriff and he's fair, AJ."

"Most of the kids at school thinks he's the bomb and feel that I'm lucky because you're his girlfriend."

Shelly made a surprised face. "The kids at your school think I'm his girlfriend?"

AJ nodded. "Well, aren't you?"

Shelly smiled slightly. She didn't want to give him hope that things would work out between her and Dare, and that once he admitted to being Dare's son they would miraculously become a loving family. "No, AJ, although we're close, Dare and I are nothing more than good friends. We always have been and always will be."

"But he wants you for his girlfriend, I can tell. Everyone can tell and they're all talking about it, as well as the fact they think I'm his son, although they don't want me to hear that part, but I do. The sheriff spends a lot of time with us and takes us places with him. The kids at school say their parents think it's time for him to settle down and marry, and I can tell that he really likes you, Mom. He always treats you special and I like that."

Shelly inhaled deeply. She liked it, too, but she knew a lot more about why Dare was spending time with her than AJ did. It was all part of his plan to gain his son's love and trust. She refused to put too much stock into anything else, not even the many times they had slept together. She knew it had to do with their raging hormones and nothing more. "So, when are you going to tell him?" she asked quietly.

AJ shrugged. "I still don't know that yet. But I wanted to let you know that I would be telling him."

She nodded. "Don't take too long. Like I said, Dare won't be a happy camper knowing we kept it from him, but I believe he'll be so happy about you that he'll quickly come around."

AJ's eyes lit up. "You think so?"

"Yes, sweetheart, I do."

He nodded. "Then I might tell him today. He asked if I'd like to go with him to meet his sister and her family at the airport. I might tell him then."

Shelly nodded again, knowing that if he did, it would certainly make Dare's day.

AJ thought Dare's truck was really cool. He had ridden in it a couple of times before, and just like the other times, he thought it was a nice vehicle for a sheriff to have when you wanted to stop being sheriff for a little while. But as he looked at Dare out of the corner of his eyes, he knew that the sheriff was always the sheriff. There was probably never a time he when he wasn't on the job, and that included times like now when he wasn't wearing his uniform.

"So are you looking forward to that day out of school next Friday for teachers' planning day?" Dare asked the moment he'd made sure AJ had snapped his seat belt in place. Once that was done, he started the engine.

"Yes, although Mom will probably find a lot of work for me to do that day." He didn't say anything else for a little while, then he asked quickly, "Do you like kids?"

Dare glanced over at him and smiled. "Yes, I like kids."

"Do you ever plan to have any?"

Dare lifted his brow. "Yeah, one day. Why do you ask?"

AJ shrugged. "No reason."

Dare checked the rearview mirror as he began backing out of Shelly's driveway. He was headed for the airport like the rest of his family to welcome his sister home. He couldn't help wondering if AJ had started quizzing him for some reason and inwardly smiled, ready for any questions that his son felt he needed to ask.

Princess Delaney Westmoreland Yasir clutched her son to her breast and inhaled sharply. She leaned against her husband's side for support. Her mother had said Shelly's son favored Dare, but what she was seeing was uncanny. There was no way anyone could take a look at the boy standing next to Dare and not immediately know they were father and son. They had the same coffee coloring, the same dark intense eyes and the same shape mouth and nose. AJ Brockman was a little Dare; a small replica of his father, there was no doubt of that.

"And who do we have here?" she asked after regaining her composure and giving her parents and brothers hugs.

"This is AJ," Dare said, meeting his sister's astonished gaze. "Shelly Brockman's son. I think Mom mentioned to you that she had returned to town."

Delaney nodded. "Yes, that's what I heard." She smiled down at AJ and immediately fell in love. He was a Westmoreland, and she was happy to claim him. "And how are you, AJ?" she asked her nephew, offering him her hand.

"I'm fine, thank you," he said somewhat shyly.

"And how is your mother?"

"She's doing fine. She said she couldn't wait to see you later today."

Delaney smiled. "And I can't wait to see her. She was like a big sister to me."

With love shining in her eyes, Delaney then glanced at the imposing figure at her side and smiled. "AJ, this is my husband, Jamal Ari Yasir."

AJ switched his gaze from Delaney to the tall man standing next to her. He wasn't sure what he should do. Was he supposed to bow or something? He let out a deep sigh of relief when the man stooped down to his level and met his gaze. "And how are you, AJ?" he asked in a deep voice, smiling.

AJ couldn't help but return the man's smile, suddenly feeling at ease. "I'm fine, sir."

When the man straightened back up, AJ switched his gaze to the baby Delaney held in her arms. "May I see him?"

Delaney beamed. "Sure. His name is Ari Terek Yasir." She leaned down and uncovered her son for AJ to see. The baby glanced at AJ and smiled. AJ smiled back, and so did everyone else standing around them at the airport. Delaney looked over at her mother, in whose eyes tears of happiness shone at seeing her two grandsons together getting acquainted.

Suddenly Prince Jamal Ari Yasir cleared his throat. Everyone had become misty-eyed and silent, and he decided to put the spark and excitement back into the welcome gathering. This was the family he had come to love, thanks to his wife who he truly cherished. His dark eyes shone with amusement as he addressed the one brother who he hadn't completely won over yet. "So, Thorn, are you still being a thorn in everyone's side these days?" he asked smiling.

Twelve

Shelly smiled as she looked at the young woman sitting in the chair across from her on the patio at Dare's parents' home. The last time she had seen Delaney Westmoreland she'd been a teenager, a few months shy of her sixteenth birthday, a rebellious, feisty opponent who'd been trying to stand up to her five overprotective and oftentimes overbearing brothers.

Now she was a self-assured, confident young woman, a medical doctor, mother to a beautiful baby boy and wife to a gorgeous sheikh from a country in the Middle East called Tahran. And from the looks the prince was constantly giving his wife, there was no doubt in her mind that Delaney was also a woman well loved and desired.

And, Shelly thought further, Delaney was breathtakingly stunning. Even all those years back there had never been any doubt in Shelly's mind that Delaney would grow up to become a beauty. She was sure there hadn't been any doubt in the brothers' minds of that as well, which was probably the reason they had tried keeping such a tight rein on her.

But clearly they had not been a match for Prince Jamal Ari
Yasir.

Delaney and Shelly were alone on the patio. Mrs. Westmoreland was inside, singing Ari to sleep, and AJ had gone
with his father and grandfather to the store to buy more
charcoal. The brothers and Jamal had taken a quick run to
Thorn's shop for Jamal to take a look at Thorn's latest
beauty of a bike.

"I'm glad you returned, Shelly, to bring AJ home to Dare
and to us. I don't think you know how happy you've made
my parents. They thought Ari was their only grandchild and
were fretting over the fact they wouldn't be able to see him
as often as they wanted to. I felt awful about that, but knew
my place was with Jamal, which meant living in his country the majority of the time. One good thing is that as long
as his father is king, we have the luxury of traveling as
much as we want. But things will change once Jamal be-
comes king."

When Shelly nodded, she continued, "We hope that
won't happen for a while. His father is in excellent health
and has no plans to turn things over to Jamal just yet."

After a long moment of silence, Shelly said, "I want to
apologize for leaving the way I did ten years ago, Delaney,
and for not staying in touch."

Delaney's eyes shone in understanding. "Trust me, we all
understood your need to put distance between you and
Dare. Everyone got on his case after you left, and for a while
there was friction between him and my brothers."

Shelly nodded. Dare had told her as much.

"Mom explained the situation to me about AJ," Delaney added, breaking into Shelly's thoughts. "She told me
how you and Dare have decided to let him be the one to
tell Dare the truth. What's the latest on that? Is he softening any toward Dare? As someone just arriving on the
scene, I'd say they seem to be getting along just fine."

Shelly nodded, remembering AJ's intense dislike of Dare

in the beginning. "I think he's discovered Dare isn't the mean cop that he thought he was, and yes, he is definitely softening. He even told me this morning that he plans to tell Dare that he's his father."

A huge smile touched Delaney's features. "When?"

"Now, that I don't know. From what I gather he'll tell Dare when they get a private moment and when he feels the time is right. He's battling his fear that Dare may not want him because of the way he behaved in the beginning."

Delaney shook her head. "There's no way Dare would not want his son."

"Yes, I know, but AJ has to realize that for himself."

Delaney nodded, knowing Shelly was right.

AJ stood next to Dare in the supermarket line. He watched as the sheriff pulled money from his wallet to pay for his purchases. When they walked outside to wait for Mr. Westmoreland, who was still inside buying a few additional items he'd discovered he needed, AJ decided to use that time to ask Dare a couple more questions.

"Can I ask you something?"

Dare looked at him. "Sure. Ask me anything you want to know, AJ."

"Earlier today you said you liked kids. If you ever marry, do you think you'd want more than one child?"

Dare wondered about the reason for that question. Was AJ contented being an only child? Would he feel threatened if Dare told him that he relished the thought of having other children—if Shelly would be their mother? He sighed, deciding to be completely honest with his son.

"Yes, I'd want more than one child. I'd like as many as my wife would agree to give me."

AJ's face remained expressionless, and Dare didn't have a clue if the answer he'd given would help him or hang him. "Any more questions?"

For a long moment, AJ didn't say anything. Then he met Dare's gaze and asked, "Is Dare your real name?"

Dare shook his head. "No, my real name is Alisdare Julian Westmoreland." He continued to hold his son's gaze. "Why do you ask?"

AJ placed his hands into his pockets. "Because my name is Alisdare Julian, too. That's what the AJ stands for."

Dare wasn't sure exactly what he was supposed to say, but knew he should act surprised, so he did. He raised his dark brows as if somewhat astonished. "Your mother named you after me?"

AJ nodded. "Yes."

Dare stared at AJ for a moment before asking. "Why did she do that?"

He watched as his son drew a deep breath. "Because—"

"Sorry I took so long. I bet your mom thinks the three of us have been kidnapped."

Both Dare and AJ turned to see Mr. Westmoreland walking toward them. But Dare was determine his son would finish what he'd been about to say. He returned his gaze to AJ. "Because—?"

AJ looked at the older man walking toward them, and then at Dare and, after losing his nerve, quickly said, "Because she liked your name."

"Because she liked your name."

Later that night Dare shook his head, remembering the reason AJ had given him for Shelly's choice of his name. He knew without a shadow of a doubt that AJ had come within a second of finally telling him he was his son before his father had unintentionally interrupted them, destroying that chance. But Dare was determined he would get it again.

Once they'd returned to his parents' home, there had been no private time, and on more than one occasion he'd been tempted to suggest that the two of them go back to the store and pick up some item his mother just had to have, but since his brothers and Jamal hadn't yet returned, his mother put him to work helping his father grill the ribs and steaks.

Now it was past eleven and Shelly was gathering her things to take a tired and sleepy AJ home. He had gotten worn out playing table tennis with his uncles for the past couple of hours.

Dare studied Shelly, as he'd been doing most of the night. She was wearing a pair of jeans that molded to her curvaceous hips and a blue pullover top that, to him, emphasized her lush breasts. Breasts he'd been kissing and tasting quite a lot over the past few weeks. Her body had always been a complete turn-on to him, and nothing had changed. He'd been fighting an arousal all night. The last thing he needed was for his brothers to detect what a bad way he was in, although from the smirks they had sent him most of the evening, he was well aware that they knew.

"AJ and I are going to have to say good-night to everyone," Shelly said smiling. "Thanks again for inviting us." She met Dare's gaze and blinked at his unspoken message. He was letting her know that he would be seeing her later tonight.

He slowly crossed the room to her. "I'll walk the two of you out."

She nodded before turning to give Delaney and Jamal, the elder Westmorelands and finally the brothers hugs.

Dare frowned at Storm when he deliberately kissed Shelly on the lips, trying to get a rise out of him and knowing it had worked. As far as Dare was concerned Shelly was his, and he didn't appreciate anyone mauling her. He had put up with it the first time they'd seen her at Chase's restaurant, but now he figured that it was time Storm learned to keep his hands and his lips to himself.

When Shelly and AJ walked ahead of him going out the

door, he hung back and growled to Storm. "If you ever do that again, I'll break your arm."

He ignored Storm's burst of laughter and followed Shelly and AJ outside.

It was a beautiful night. The air felt crisp, pleasantly cool as Shelly closed the back door behind her and raced across the backyard to the place where she knew Dare was waiting for her. She hadn't bothered to put on a robe, since he would be taking it off her anyway, and she hadn't bothered to put on a gown, preferring to slip into an oversized T-shirt instead.

It had taken her some time to get AJ settled and into bed after arriving home from the Westmorelands. They had talked; he had told her that he'd come close to telling Dare the truth tonight, but that he'd been interrupted. She knew the longer he put it off, the harder it was going to be for him.

"Shelly?"

She sucked in a deep breath when Dare emerged from the shadows, dazzling her senses beneath the glow of a full moon. She immediately walked into his arms. Dark, penetrating eyes met hers and then, in a deep, ragged breath, he tipped her head back as his lips captured hers.

The whimpered sounds erupting from deep within her throat propelled him forward, making the urge for them to mate that more intense, urgent, imperative. He gently lifted her T-shirt and touched her, discovering she was completely bare underneath. With unerring speed he lifted her off her feet, wrapped her legs around his waist and walked a few steps to a nearby tree.

She saw it was another seduction, planned down to every detail. Evidently he'd kept himself busy while waiting for her, she thought, noticing he had securely tied a huge pillow around the tree trunk. It served as a cushion for her backside when he pressed her against it. And then he was breathing hard and heavy while unzipping his pants and reaching inside to free himself. "I knew I couldn't wait, so I've already taken care of protection," he whispered as he thrust forward, entering her.

At her quick intake of breath, he covered her mouth with his, sipping the nectar of surprise from her lips, playing around in her mouth with his tongue as if relishing the taste of her. How long ago had they last kissed? Hadn't it been just last night? You couldn't tell by the way he was eating away at her mouth and the way she eagerly responded, wanting, needing and desiring him with a vengeance.

She opened he legs wider, wrapped them around his waist tighter when he went deeper, sending shock waves of pleasure racing through her. She felt close, so very close to the edge, and she knew she wanted him to be with her when she fell.

She broke off their kiss. "Now, Dare!"

Dare began moving. Throwing his head back he inhaled a deep whiff of her scent—hot, enticing, sensually hers—and totally lost it. His jaw clenched as he thrust deeper, moved faster, when she arched her back. Desperately, he mated with her with quick, precise strokes, giving her all he had and taking all she had to give.

He was past the point of no return and she was right there with him. And when he felt her body tighten and the spasm rip through her, bringing with it an orgasm so powerful that he felt the earth shake beneath his feet, he held her gaze and thrust into her one final time as he joined her in a climax that just wouldn't stop. The sensations started at the top of his head and moved downward at lightning speed, building intense pressure in that part of his body nestled deep inside her, and making him clench his teeth to keep from screaming out her name and stomping his feet.

The sensations kept coming and coming and he leaned forward to kiss her again, capturing the essence of what they were sharing. As his body continued to tremble while buried deep inside of her, he knew that even after ten long years, he was still seductively, passionately and irrevocably hers. She was the only woman he would ever want. The only woman he would ever need. The only woman who could make him understand and appreciate the difference between having mindblowing sex and making earth-shattering, soul-stirring, deep-down-in-your-gut love.

She was the only woman.

And he also knew that she was the only woman he would ever love and that he still loved her.

Moments later, Dare pulled his body from Shelly's and, gathering her gently into his arms, walked over to place her on the blanket. He stretched out on his side facing her as he waited for the air to return back to his lungs and the blood to stop rushing fast and furious through his veins.

"I was beginning to think you weren't coming," he finally said some time later, the tone of his voice still quivering from the afterglow of what they'd just shared.

He couldn't help touching her again, so he slid his hand across her stomach, gently stroking her. He remembered the question AJ had asked him about wanting other children, and he remembered thinking that he'd want more children only if Shelly were their mother. He wouldn't hesitate putting another child of his inside her, in the womb he knew he had touched tonight. Not only had he touched it, he had branded it his.

Shelly slowly opened her eyes as her world settled, and the explosion she'd felt moments ago subsided. She gazed up at him and wondered how was it possible that each time they did this it was better than the time before. She always felt cherished in his arms.

Treasured.

Loved.

She silently shook that last thought away, refusing to let

her mind go there; refusing to live on false hope. And she refused to give in to the want, need and desire to give him her heart again, no matter how strong the pull was to do so. She broke eye contact with him and looked away.

"Shelly?"

She returned her gaze to him, to respond to what he'd said. "It took a little longer than expected to get AJ settled tonight. He wanted us to have a long talk."

Dare asked, "Is he all right?"

"Yes. But I think he's somewhat disappointed that he didn't get the chance to tell you the truth today. He had planned to do so."

Dare sighed deeply. His gut instincts had been right. "Do you think I should talk to him tomorrow?"

Shelly shook her head. "No, I think the best thing to do is to wait until he gets up his courage again. But I suggest you make things a bit easier on him by making sure the two of you have absolute privacy without any interruptions. However, you're also going to have to make sure he doesn't think things are being orchestrated for that purpose. He still has to feel as though he's in control for a while longer, Dare, especially with this. Right now, telling you that he's your son is very important to him."

Dare nodded. It was important to him as well. He slumped down on his back beside her and looked up at the stars. "I think I have an idea."

"What?"

"The brothers and I, along with Jamal, had planned on going to the cabin in the North Carolina mountains to go fishing. AJ knows about it since he heard us planning the trip, so he won't think anything about it. What if I invite him to come along?"

Shelly raised a brow. "Why would you want to take AJ with you guys? I'd think the six of you had planned it as a sort of guys' weekend, right?"

"Right. But I remember AJ mentioning to Thorn that

he'd never gone fishing before, and I know that Thorn came close to inviting him. The only reason he didn't was because he knew we would he playing poker in addition to fishing and Storm's mouth can get rather filthy when he starts losing."

Shelly nodded. "But how will this help your situation with AJ? The two of you still won't have any privacy."

"Yes, we will if the others don't come. After AJ and I arrive, the others can come up with an excuse as to why they couldn't make it."

Shelly raised a doubtful brow. "All five of them?"

"Yes. It has to be a believable reason for all of them though, otherwise AJ will suspect something."

Shelly had to agree. "And while you and AJ are there alone for those three days, you think he'll open up to you?"

Dare sighed deeply. "I'm hoping that he will. At least I'm giving him the opportunity to do so." He met Shelly's stare. "What do you think?"

Shelly shrugged. "I don't know, Dare. It might be just the thing, but I don't want you to get your hopes up and be disappointed. I know for a fact that AJ wants you to know the truth, but I also know that for him the timing has to be perfect."

Dare nodded as he pulled her into his arms. "Then I'm going to do everything in my power to make sure that it is."

Thirteen

Dare hung up the phone and met AJ's expectant gaze.

"That was Chase. One of his waitresses called in sick. He'll have to pitch in for the weekend and won't be able to make it."

He saw the disappointment cloud AJ's eyes. So far since arriving at the cabin they had received no-show calls from everyone except Thorn, and he expected Thorn to call any minute.

"Does that mean we have to cancel this weekend?" AJ asked in such a disappointed voice that a part of Dare felt like a heel.

"Not unless you want to. There's still a possibility that Thorn might show."

Although he'd said the words, Dare knew they weren't true. His brothers and Jamal had understood his need to be alone with AJ this weekend and had agreed to bow out of the picture and plan something else to do.

When AJ didn't say anything, Dare said. "You know what I think we should do?"

AJ lifted a brow. "What?"

"Enjoy the three days anyway. I've been looking forward to a few days of rest and relaxation, and I'm sure you're glad to have an extra day off school, as well, right?"

AJ nodded. "Right."

"Then I say that we make the most of it. I can teach you how to fish in the morning and, tomorrow night we can camp outside. Have you ever gone camping?"

"No."

Dare sadly shook his head at the thought. When they were kids his father had occasionally taken him and his brothers camping for the weekend just to get them out of their mother's hair for a while. "We can still do all the things that we'd planned to do anyway. How's that?"

AJ was clearly surprised. "You'll want to stay here with just me?"

A lump formed in Dare's throat at the hope he heard in his son's voice. He swallowed deeply. If only you knew how much I want to stay here with just you, he thought. "Yes," he answered. "I guess I should be asking you if you're sure that you want to stay here with just me."

AJ smiled. "Yes, I want to stay."

Dare returned that smile. "Good. Then come on. Let's get the rest of the things out of the truck."

The next morning Dare got up bright and early and stood on the porch enjoying a cup of coffee. AJ was still asleep, which was fine, since the two of them had stayed up late the night before. Thorn had finally called to say he couldn't make it due to a deadline he had to meet for a bike he had to deliver. So it was final that it would only be the two of them.

After loading up the supplies in the kitchen after Thorn's call, they'd gathered wood for a fire. Nights in the mountains meant wood for the fireplace and they had gathered enough to last all three days. Then, while he left AJ with the task of stacking the wood, Dare had gone into the kitchen to prepare chili and sandwiches for their dinner.

They hadn't said much over their meal, but AJ'd really started talking while they washed dishes. He'd told him about the friends he had left behind in California, and how he had written to them. They hadn't written back. He'd also talked about his grandparents, the Brockmans, and how he had planned to spend Christmas with them.

Now, Dare glanced around, deciding he really liked this place. It had once been jointly owned by one of their cousins and a friend of his, but Jamal had talked the two men into selling it to him and had then presented it to Delaney as one of her wedding gifts. It was at this cabin that Delaney and Jamal had met. While she was out of the country, Delaney had graciously given her brothers unlimited use of it, and all five had enjoyed getting away and spending time together here every once in a while.

Dare turned when he heard a noise behind him and smiled. "Good morning, AJ."

AJ wiped sleep from his eyes. "Good morning. You're up early."

Dare laughed. "This is the best time to catch fish."

AJ's eyes widened. "Then I'll be ready to go in a second." He rushed back into the house.

Dare chuckled and hoped his son remembered not only to get dressed but to wash his face and brush his teeth. He inhaled deeply, definitely taking a liking to this father business.

Dare smiled as he looked at the sink filled with fish. AJ had been an ace with the fishing pole and had caught just as many fish as he had. He began rolling up his sleeves to start cleaning them. They would enjoy some for dinner today and tomorrow and what was left they would take home with them and split between his mother and Shelly.

Maybe he could talk Shelly into having a fish fry and inviting the family over.

His gaze softened as he thought how easy it was to want to include Shelly in his daily activities. He suppressed a groan thinking of all their nighttime activities and smiled as it occurred to him they had yet to make love in a bed. He had to think of a way to get her over to his place for the entire night. Sneaking off to make love in her backyard under the stars had started off being romantic, but now he wanted more than romance, he wanted permanence...forever. He wanted them to talk and plan their future, and he wanted her to know just how greatly she had enriched his life since she had returned.

He shifted his thoughts to AJ. So far they'd been together over twenty-four hours and he hadn't brought up the topic of their relationship. They had spent a quiet, leisurely day at the lake talking mostly about school and the Williams sisters. It seemed his son had a crush on the two tennis players in a big way, especially Serena Williams. Dare was glad he'd let Chase talk him into taking tennis lessons with him last summer; at least he knew a little something about the game and had been able to contribute to AJ's conversation.

Dare sighed, anxious to get things out in the open with AJ, but as Shelly had said, AJ would have to be the one to bring it up. He glanced over his shoulder when he heard his son enter the kitchen. He had been outside putting away their fishing gear.

"You did a good job today with that fishing rod, AJ," Dare said smiling over his shoulder. "I can't wait to tell Stone. The rod and reel you used belongs to him. He swears only a Westmoreland can have that kind of luck with it," he added absently.

"Then that explains things."

Dare turned around. "That explains what?"

"That explains why I did so good today—I *am* a Westmoreland."

Dare's breath caught and he swallowed deeply. He leaned back against the sink and stared at AJ long and hard, waiting for him to stop studying his sneakers and look at him. Moments later, AJ finally lifted his head and met his gaze.

"And how are you a Westmoreland, AJ?" Dare asked quietly, already knowing the answer but desperately wanting to hear his son say it anyway.

AJ cleared his throat. "I—I really don't know how to tell you this, but I have to tell you. And I have to first say that my mom wanted to tell you sooner, but I asked her not to, so it's not her fault so please don't be mad at her about it. You have to promise that you won't be mad at my mom."

Dare nodded. At that moment he would promise almost anything. "All right. I won't be mad at your mom. Now tell me what you meant about being a Westmoreland."

AJ put his hands into his pockets. "You may want to sit down for this."

Dare watched AJ's face and noticed how nervous he'd become. He didn't want to make him any more nervous than he already was, so he sat at the kitchen table. "Now tell me," he coaxed gently.

AJ hesitated, then met Dare's gaze, and said, "Although my last name is Brockman, I'm really a Westmoreland…because I'm your son."

Dare's breath got lodged in his throat. He blinked. Of course, the news AJ was delivering to him didn't surprise him, but the uncertainty and the caution he saw in his son's gaze did. Shelly had been right. AJ wasn't sure if he would accept him as his son, and Dare knew he had to tread lightly here.

"You're my son?" he asked quietly, as if for clarification.

"Yes. That's why I'm ten and that's why we have the same name." He looked down at his sneakers again as he added, "And that's why I look like you a little, although you haven't seemed to notice but I'll understand if you don't want me."

Dare stood. He slowly crossed the room to AJ and placed what he hoped was a comforting hand, a reassuring hand, a loving hand on his shoulder. AJ looked up and met his gaze, and Dare knew he had to do everything within his power to make his son believe that he wanted him and that he loved him.

Choosing his words carefully and speaking straight from his heart and his soul, he said, "Whether you know it or not, you have just said words that have made me the happiest man in the entire world. The very thought that Shelly gave me a son fills me with such joy that it's overwhelming."

AJ searched his father's gaze. "Does that mean you want me?"

Dare chuckled, beside himself in happiness. "That means that not only do I want you, but I intend to keep you, and now that you're in my life I don't ever intend to let you out of it."

A huge smile crept over AJ's features. "Really?"

"Yes, really."

"And will my name get changed to Westmoreland?"

Dare smiled. "Do you want your name changed to Westmoreland?"

AJ nodded his head excitedly. "Yes, I'd like that."

"And I'd like that, too. We'll discuss it with your mother and see what her feelings are on the matter, all right?"

"All right."

They stared at each other as the reality of what had taken place revolved around them. Then AJ asked quietly, "And may I call you Dad?"

Dare's chest tightened, his throat thickened and he became filled with emotions to overpowering capacity. He knew he would remember this moment for as long as he lived. What AJ was asking, and so soon, was more than he could ever have hoped for. He had prayed for this. A smile dusted across his face as parental pride and all the love he felt for the child standing in front of him poured forth.

"Yes, you can call me Dad," he said, as he reached out and pulled his son to him, needing the contact of father to son, parent to offspring, Westmoreland to Westmoreland. They shared a hug of acceptance, affirmation and acknowledgement as Dare fought back the tears in his eyes. "I'd be honored for you to call me that," he said in a strained voice.

Moments later, Dare sighed, thinking his mission should have been completed, but it wasn't. Now that he had his son, he realized more than ever just how much he wanted, loved and needed his son's mother. His mission wouldn't be accomplished until he had her permanently in his life as well.

Later that night Dare placed calls to his parents and siblings and told them the good news. They took turns talking with AJ, each welcoming him to the family. After dinner Dare and AJ had talked while they cleaned up the kitchen. Already plans were made for them to return to the cabin in a few months, and Dare suggested that they invite Shelly to come with them.

"She won't come," AJ said, drying the dish his father had handed him.

Dare raised a brow. "Why wouldn't she?"

"Because she's not going to be your girlfriend," he said softly. "Although now I wish that she would."

Dare turned and folded his arms across his chest and looked at his son. "And what makes you think your mother won't be my girlfriend, AJ?" he asked, although the title of wife was more in line with what he was aiming for.

"She told me," he said wryly. "That same night we had a cookout at Grandma and Grandpa Westmoreland's house. After we got home we talked for a long time, and I told her that I had come close to telling you that night that I was your son. I asked if the three of us would be a family after I told you and she said no."

Dare remembered that night well. Shelly had been late coming to the backyard and had mentioned she and AJ had had a long talk. He sighed deeply as he tilted his head to the side to think about what AJ had said, then asked, "Did she happen to say why?"

AJ shook his head. "Yes. She said that although the two of you had been in love when you made me, that now you weren't in love anymore and were just friends. She also said that chances were that one day you would marry someone nice and I'd have a second mother who would treat me like her son."

Dare frowned. He and Shelly not being in love was a crock. How could she fix her lips to say such a thing, let along think it? And what gave her the right to try and marry him off to some other woman? Didn't she know how he felt about her? That he loved her?

Then it suddenly hit him, right in the gut that, no, Shelly had no idea how he felt, because at no time had he told her. For the past month they had spent most of their time alone together, at night in her backyard under the stars making love. Did she think all they'd been doing was having sex? But then why would she think otherwise? He sucked in a breath, thinking that he sure had missed the mark.

"Is that true, Dad? Will you marry someone else and give me a second mother?"

Dare shook his head. "No, son. Your mother is the only mother you'll have, and she's the only woman I ever plan to marry."

Mimicking his father, AJ placed his arms across his chest and leaned against the sink. "Well, I don't think she knows that."

Dare smiled. "Then I guess I'm just the person to convince her." He leaned closer to his son and with a conspiratorial tone, he said. "Listen up. I have a plan."

Fourteen

The first thing Shelly noticed as she entered the subdivision where Dare's home was located was that all the houses were stately and huge and sat on beautiful acreages. This was a newly developed section of town that had several shopping outlets and grocery stores. She could vividly remember it being a thickly wooded area when she had left town ten years ago.

She glanced at her watch. Dare had called and said that he and AJ had decided to return a day early and asked that she come over to his place and pick up AJ because Dare needed to stay at home and wait for the arrival of some important package. All of it sounded rather secretive, and the only thing she could come up with was that it pertained to some police business.

After reading the number posted on the front of the mailbox, she knew the regal-looking house that sat on a hill with a long, circular driveway belonged to Dare. She and Delaney had spent the day shopping yesterday and one of the things Delaney had mentioned was that Dare had banked most of his salary while working as a federal agent, and when he moved back home he had built a beautiful home.

Moments later, after parking her car Shelly strolled up the walkway and rang the doorbell. It didn't take long for Dare to answer.

"Hi, Shelly."

"Hi, Dare." Her heart began beating rapidly, thinking she would never tire of seeing him dressed casually in a pair of jeans and a chambray shirt. As she met his gaze, she thought that she had definitely missed him during the two days he and AJ had gone to North Carolina.

"Come on in," he invited, stepping aside.

"Thanks." She glanced around Dare's home when he closed the door behind her. Nice, she thought. The layout was open and she couldn't help noticing how chic and expensive everything looked. "Your home is beautiful, Dare."

"Thanks, and I'm glad you like it."

Shelly saw that he was leaning against the closed door staring at her. She cleared her throat. "You mentioned AJ finally got around to admitting that you're his father."

Dare shook his head. "Yes."

Shelly nodded. "I'm happy about that, Dare. I know how much you wanted that to happen."

"Yes, I did."

A long silence followed, and, with nothing else to say, Shelly cleared her throat again, suddenly feeling nervous in Dare's presence, mainly because he was still leaning against the door staring at her with those dark penetrating eyes of his. Breaking eye contact, she glanced at her watch and decided to end the silence. "Speaking of AJ, where is he?"

Dare didn't say anything for a moment, then he spoke. "He isn't here."

Shelly raised a brow. "Oh? Where is he?"

"Over at my parents'. They dropped by and asked if he could visit with them for a while. I didn't think you would mind, so I told them he could."

Shelly nodded. "Of course I don't mind." After a few minutes she cleared her throat for the third time and said, "Well, I'm sure you have things to do so I'll—"

"No, I don't have anything to do, since the important package I was waiting for arrived already."

"Oh."

"In fact, I was hoping that you and I could take in a movie and have dinner later."

Her dark gaze sank into his. "Dinner? A movie?"

"Yes, and you don't have to worry about AJ. He'll be in good hands."

With a slight shrug, she said, "I know that, Dare. Your parents are the greatest."

Dare smiled. "Well, right now they think their oldest grandson is the greatest. Now that the secret is out, you should have seen my mom. She can't wait to go around bragging to everyone about him since it's safe to do so."

Shelly's stomach tightened. Now that the secret was out, things would be changing...especially her relationship with Dare. He wouldn't have to pretend interest in her any longer. Even now, she knew that probably the only reason he was inviting her to the movies and to dinner was out of kindness.

"Well, what about the movies and dinner?" Dare asked, reclaiming her attention.

She met his gaze. This would probably be the last time they would be together, at least out in public. There was no doubt in her mind that until they got their sexual needs under control they would still find the time to see each other at night in private.

"Yes, Dare. I'll go out to the movies and to dinner with you."

"Thanks for going out with me tonight, Shelly."

"Thanks for inviting me, Dare. I really enjoyed myself." And she had. They had seen a comedy featuring Eddie

Murphy at the Magic Johnson Movie Theater near the Greenbriar Mall. Afterward, they had gone to a restaurant that had served the best-tasting seafood she'd ever eaten. Now they were walking around the huge shopping mall that brought back memories of when they had dated all those years ago and had spent a lot of their time there on the weekends.

Dare claimed the reason he was in no hurry to end their evening was because he wanted to give his parents and siblings a chance to bond with AJ, and he thought the stroll through Greenbriar Mall would kill some time.

"How do you like the type of work you're doing now, working outside the hospital versus working inside?"

This was the first time he had ever asked her anything about her job since she'd moved back. "It took some getting used to, but I'm enjoying it. I get to meet a lot of nice people and because of the hours I work, I'm home with AJ more."

Dare nodded. "I never did tell you why I stopped being an agent for the Bureau, did I?"

Shelly shook her head. "No, you didn't."

Dare nodded again. He then told her all the things he had liked about working for the FBI and those things he had begun to dislike. Finally he told her the reason he had returned home.

"And do you like what you're doing now, Dare?" she couldn't help but ask him, since she of all people knew what a career with the FBI had meant to him.

"Yes, I like what I'm doing now. I feel I'm making more of a difference here than I was making with the Bureau. It's like I'm giving back to a community that gave so much to my brothers and me while we were growing up. It's a good feeling to live in a place where you have history."

Shelly had to agree. She enjoyed being back home and couldn't bear the thought of ever leaving again. Although she had lived in L.A. for ten years, deep down she had never considered it as her home.

She sighed and glanced down at her watch. "It's getting late. Don't you think it's time for us to pickup AJ? I don't want him to wear out his welcome with your folks."

Dare laughed, and the sound sent sensations up Shelly's body, making her shiver slightly. He thought she had shivered for a totally different reason and placed his arm around her shoulders, pulling her closer to him for warmth. "He'll never be able to wear out his welcome with my family, Shelly. Come on, let's go collect our son."

Three weeks later, Shelly sat outside alone on her porch swing as it slowly rocked back and forth. It was the third week in October and the night air was cool. She had put on a sweater, but the stars and the full moon were so beautiful she couldn't resist sitting and appreciating them both. Besides, she needed to think.

Ever since that night Dare had taken her to a movie and to dinner, he had come by every evening to spend time with AJ. But AJ wasn't the only person he made sure he spent time with. Over the past few weeks he had often asked her out, either to a movie, dinner or both. Then there was the time he had asked her to go with him to the wedding of one of his deputies.

She sighed deeply. Each time she had tried putting distance between them, he would succeed in erasing the distance. Then there were the flowers he continued to send each week. When she had asked him why he was still sending them, he had merely smiled and said because he enjoyed doing so. And she had to admit that she enjoyed receiving them. But still, she didn't want to put too much stock in Dare's actions and continued to see what he was doing as merely an act of kindness on his part. It was evident that he wanted them to get along and establish some sort of friendly relationship for AJ's sake.

The other thing that confused her was the fact that he no longer sought her out at night. Their late-night rendezvous in her backyard had abruptly come to an end the night Dare had taken her on their first date. He had offered her no explanation as to why he no longer came by late at night, and she had too much pride to ask him.

He came by each afternoon around dinnertime and she would invite him to stay, so she still saw him constantly. And at night, after AJ went to bed, he would sit outside on the porch swing with her and talk about how her day had gone, and she would ask him about his. Their talks had become a nightly routine, and she had to admit that she rather enjoyed them.

She shifted her thoughts to AJ. He was simply basking in the love that his father and the entire Westmoreland family were giving him. Dare had been right when he'd said all AJ had needed was to feel that he belonged. Each time she saw her son in one of his happy moods, she knew that he was glad as well as proud to be a part of the Westmoreland clan, and that she had made the right decision to return to College Park.

She stood, deciding to go inside and get ready for bed. Dare had left immediately after dinner saying he had to go to the station and finish up a report he was working on. As usual, before he left he had kissed her deeply, but otherwise he had kept his hands to himself. However, whenever he pulled her into his arms, she knew he wanted her. His erection was always a sure indicator of that fact. But she knew he was fighting his desire for her, which made things confusing, because she didn't understand why.

As she got ready for bed she continued to wonder what was going on with Dare. Why had he ended all sexual ties between them? Had he assumed she thought things were more serious between them than they really were because of their nightly meetings in her backyard?

As she closed her eyes she knew that if reality could not find her in his arms making love, that she would be there with him in the dreams she knew she would have that night.

* * *

Shelly smiled at Ms. Mamie. The older woman had broken her ankle two weeks ago and Shelly had been assigned as her home healthcare nurse. "I thought we had talked about you staying off your foot for a while, Ms. Mamie."

Ms. Mamie smiled. "I tried, but it isn't easy when I have so much to do."

Shelly shook her head. "Well, your ankle will heal a lot quicker if you follow my instructions," she said, rewrapping the woman's leg. She made it a point to check on Ms. Mamie at least twice a week, and she enjoyed her visits. Even with only one good leg, the older woman still managed to get around in her kitchen and always had fresh cookies baked when Shelly arrived.

"So, how are things going with you and the sheriff?"

Shelly looked up. "Excuse me?"

"You and the sheriff. How are the two of you doing? Everyone is talking about it."

Shelly frowned, not understanding. "They are talking about Dare and AJ or about me and Dare?"

"They are talking about you and Dare. Dare and AJ is old news. Everyone knew that boy was Dare's son even if Dare was a little slow in coming around and realizing that fact." Shelly's mind immediately took in what Ms. Mamie had said. She'd had no idea that she and Dare were now the focus of the townspeoples' attention. "Why are people talking about me and Dare?"

"Because everyone knows how hard he's trying to woo you."

Shelly stilled in her task and looked at Ms. Mamie. She couldn't help but grin at something so ridiculous. "Why would people think Dare is trying to woo me?"

"Because he is, dear."

The grin was immediately wiped from Shelly's face. Woo her? Dare? She shook her head. "I think you're mistaken."

"No, I'm not," Ms. Mamie answered matter-of-factly.

"In fact, me and the ladies in my sewing club are taking bets."

Shelly raised a brow. "Bets?"

"Yes, bets as to whether or not you're going to give him a second chance. All of us know how much he hurt you before."

Shelly's head started spinning. "But I still don't understand why you all would think he was wooing me."

Ms. Mamie smiled. "Because it's obvious, Shelly. Luanne tells us each time he sends you flowers, which I understand is once, sometimes twice a week. Then, according to Clara, who lives across the street from you, he comes to dinner every evening and he takes you out on a date occasionally." The woman's smile widened. "Clara also mentioned that he's protecting your reputation by leaving your house at a reasonable time every night so he won't give the neighbors something to talk about."

Shelly shook her head. "But none of that means anything."

Ms. Mamie gently patted her hand. "That's where you're wrong, Shelly. It means everything, especially for a man like Dare. The ladies and I have watched him over the years ignore one woman after another, women who threw themselves at him. He never got serious about any of them. When you came back things were different. Anyone with eyes can see that he is smitten with you. That boy has always loved you, and I'll be the first to say he made a mistake ten years ago, but I feel good knowing he's trying real hard to win you back." She then grinned conspiratorially. "It even makes me feel good knowing that you're making it hard for him."

Making it hard for him? She hadn't even picked up on the fact that he was trying to win her back. Shelly opened her mouth to say something, then closed it, deciding that she needed to think about what Ms. Mamie had said. Was it true? Was Dare actually wooing her?

That question was still on her mind half an hour later when she pulled out of Ms. Mamie's driveway. She sighed deeply. The only person who could answer that question was Dare, and she decided it was time that he did.

Thunder rumbled in the distance as Dare placed a lid on the pot of chili he'd just made. He had tried keeping himself busy that afternoon since thoughts of Shelly weighed so heavily on his mind.

He knew one of the main reasons for this was that AJ would be spending the weekend with Morris and Cornelius, which meant Shelly would be home all alone, and Shelly all alone was too much of a temptation to think about. He sighed deeply, wondering just how much longer he could hold out in his plan to prove to her that what was between them was more than sex and that he cared deeply for her. For the past three weeks he had been the ardent suitor as he tried easing his way back into her heart. The only thing about it was that he wasn't sure whether his plan was working and exactly where he stood with her.

He paused in what he was doing when he heard his doorbell ring and wondered which of his brothers had decided to pay him a visit. It would be just like them to show up in time for dinner. Leaving the kitchen, he made his way through the living room to open the front door. His chest tightened with emotion when he looked through his peephole and saw that it wasn't one of his brothers standing outside on his porch, but Shelly.

He quickly opened the door and recognized her nervousness. A man in his profession was trained to detect when someone was fidgety or uneasy about something. "Shelly," he greeted her, wondering what had brought her to his place.

"Dare," she said returning the greeting in what he considered a slightly skittish voice. "May I come in and talk to you about something?"

He nodded and said, "Sure thing," before stepping aside to let her enter.

His gaze skimmed over her as she passed him, and he thought there was no way a woman could look better than this, dressed in a something as simple as a pullover V-neck sweater and a long flowing skirt; especially if that skirt appeared to have been tailor-made just for her body. It flowed easily and fluidly down all her womanly curves.

He locked the door and turned to find her standing in the middle of his foyer as though she belonged in his house, every day and every night. "We can go into the living room if you like," he said, trying not to let it show just how much he had missed being alone with her.

"All right."

He led her toward the living room and asked, "Are you hungry? I just finished making a pot of chili."

"No, thanks, I'm not hungry."

"What about thirsty? Would you like something to drink?"

She smiled at him. "No, I don't want anything to drink. I'm fine."

He nodded. Yes, she was definitely fine. He didn't know another woman with a body quite like hers, and the memories of being inside that body made his hands feel damp. The room suddenly felt warmer than it should be.

He inhaled as he watched her take a seat on the sofa. He, in turn, took the chair across from her. Once she had gotten settled, he asked, "What is it you want to talk to me about, Shelly? Is something wrong with AJ?"

She shook her head. "Oh, no, everything with AJ is fine. I dropped him off at the Sears's house. I think he's excited about spending the weekend."

Dare nodded. He thought AJ was excited about spending the weekend as well. "If it's not about AJ then what do you want to talk about?"

His gaze held hers, and she hesitated only a moment before responding. "I paid a visit to Ms. Mamie today to check on her ankle. I'll be her home healthcare nurse for a while."

Dare nodded again, thinking there had to be more to her visit than to tell him that. "And?"

She hesitated again. "And she mentioned something that I found unbelievable, but I was concerned since it seems that a lot of the older women in this town think it's true."

He searched her features and detected more nervousness than before. "What do they think is true?"

Dare became concerned when seconds passed and Shelly didn't answer. Instead, she moved her gaze away from his to focus on some object on his coffee table. He frowned slightly. There had never been a time that Shelly had felt the need to be shy in his presence, so why was she now?

Standing, he crossed the room to sit next to her on the sofa. "All right, Shelly, what's this about? What do Ms. Mamie and her senior citizens' club think is true?"

Shelly swallowed deeply and took note of how close Dare was sitting next to her. Every time she took a breath she inhaled his hot male scent, a scent she had grown used to and one she would never tire of.

She breathed in and decided to come clean. Making light of the situation would probably make it easier, she thought, especially if he decided to laugh at something so absurd. She smiled slightly. "For some reason they think you're trying to woo me."

His gaze didn't flicker, but remained steadily on her face when he asked. "Woo you?"

She nodded. "Yes, you know—pursue me, court me."

Sitting so close to her, Dare could feel her tension. He also felt her uncertainty. "In other words," he said softly, "they think I'm trying to win you over, find favor in your eyes, in your heart and in your mind and break down your resistance."

Shelly nodded, although she didn't think Dare needed to

break down her resistance since he had successfully done that a month or so ago. "Yes, that's it. That's what they believe. Isn't that silly?"

Dare shifted his position and draped his arms across the back of the sofa. He met Shelly's gaze, suddenly feeling hungry and greedy with an appetite that only she could appease. He studied her face for a little while longer, then calmly replied. "No, I don't think there's anything silly about it, Shelly. In fact, their assumptions are right on target."

She blinked once, twice, as the meaning of his words sank in. He watched as her eyebrows raised about as high as they could go, and then she said, "But why?"

Keeping his gaze fixed on hers, he asked, "Why what?"

"Why would you waste your time doing something like that?"

Dare drew in a deep breath. "Mainly because I don't consider it a waste of my time, Shelly. Other than winning my son's love and respect, winning your heart back is the most important thing I've ever had to do."

Shelly swallowed, and for the first time in weeks she felt a bubble of hope grow inside her. Her heart began beating rapidly against her ribs. Was Dare saying what she thought he was saying? There was only one way to find out. "Tell me why, Dare."

He leaned farther back against the sofa and smiled. His smile was so sexy, so enticing, and so downright seductive that it almost took her breath away. "Because I wanted to prove to you that I knew the difference between having sex and making love. And I had the feeling that you were beginning to think I didn't know the difference, and that all those times we spent in your backyard on that blanket were about sex and had nothing to do with emotions. But emotions were what it was all about, Shelly, each and every time I took you into my arms those nights. I have never just had sex with you in my life. There has never been a time that I didn't make love to you. For us there will always be a difference."

Tears misted Shelly's eyes. He was so absolutely right. For them there would always be a difference. She had tried convincing herself that there wasn't a difference and that each time they made love it was about satisfying hormones and nothing more. But she'd only been fooling herself. She loved Dare. She had always loved him and would always love him.

"AJ made me realize what you might have been thinking when we spent time at the cabin together," Dare said, interrupting Shelly's thoughts.

"He told me what you had said about the possibility of me getting married one day, and I knew then what you must have been thinking to assume that you and AJ and I would never be a family."

Shelly nodded. "But we will be a family?" she asked quietly, wanting to reach out and touch Dare, just to make sure this entire episode was real and that she wasn't dreaming any of it.

"Yes, we will be a family, Shelly. I made a mistake ten years ago by letting you go, but I won't make the same mistake twice. I love you and I intend to spend the remainder of my days proving just how much." Sitting forward, his smile was tender and filled with warmth and love when he added, "That is, if you trust me enough to give me another chance."

Shelly reached out and cupped his jaw with her hands. She met the gaze of the man she had always loved and who would forever have her heart. "Are you sure that is what you want, Dare?"

"Yes, I haven't been more sure of anything in my life, Shelly, so make me the happiest man in the world. I love you. I always have and always will, and more than anything, I want you for my wife. Will you marry me?"

"Oh, Dare, I love you, too, and yes, I will marry you."

She automatically went into his arms when he leaned forward and kissed her. His kiss started off gentle, but soon it began stoking a gnawing hunger that was seeping through both of their bodies and became hard and demanding. And then suddenly Dare broke the kiss as he stood and Shelly found herself lifted off the sofa and cradled close to his body.

While she slowly ran her lips along his jaw, the corners of his mouth and his neck, he took the stairs two at a time, his breath ragged, as he carried her to his bedroom. Once there, he placed her in the middle of his bed and began removing his shirt. Her mouth began watering as he exposed a hard-muscled chest. All the other times since she'd been back they had made love in the dark, and although she had felt his chest she hadn't actually seen it. At least not like this. It was daylight and she was seeing it all, the thatch of hair that covered his chest then tapered down into a thin line as it trailed lower to his...

She swallowed and realized that his hand had moved to the snap on his jeans. He slowly began taking them off. She swallowed again. Seeing him like this, in the light, a more mature and older Dare, made her see just how much his body had changed, just how much more physical, masculine and totally male he was.

And just how much she appreciated being the woman he wanted.

She watched as he reached into the nightstand next to the bed to retrieve a condom packet, and how he took the time to prepare himself to keep her safe. With that task done, he lifted his gaze and met hers. "I'd like other children, Shelly."

She smiled and said, "So would I, and I know for a fact that AJ doesn't like being an only child, so he would welcome a sister or brother as well."

Dare nodded, remembering the question AJ had asked about whether he wanted other children. He was glad to hear AJ would welcome the idea. Dare walked the few steps back over to the bed and, leaning down, he began removing every stitch of clothing from Shelly's body, almost unable to handle the rush of desire when he saw her exposed skin.

"You're beautiful, Shelly," he whispered breathless, smiling down at her when he had finished undressing her and she lay before him completely naked.

She returned his smile, glowing with his compliment. As he joined her in bed and took her into his arms, she knew that this was where she had always been meant to be.

Shelly felt the heat of desire warm her throat the moment Dare joined his mouth to hers, and all the love she had for him seeped through every part of her body as his kiss issued a promise she knew he would fulfill.

They hadn't made love in over a month so she wasn't surprised or shocked by the powerful emotions surging through her that only intensified with Dare's kiss. He wasn't just kissing her, he was using his tongue to stroke a need, deliver a promise and strip away any doubt that it was meant for them to be together.

Dare dragged his mouth from hers, his breath hard, shaky and harsh. "I need you now, baby," he said, reaching down and checking her readiness and finding her hot and wet. He settled his body over hers as fire licked through his veins, love flowed from his heart and a need to be joined with her drove everything within him.

He inhaled sharply as the tip of his erection pressed her wet and swollen flesh and it seemed that every part of his being was focused there, and when she opened her legs wider for him, arched her back, pushed her hips up and sank her nails deep in his shoulder blades, he couldn't help but groan and surge forward. The sensation of him filling her to the hilt only made him that much more hungrier, greedy. And she was there with him all the way.

He thrust into her again and again, each stroke more

hard and determined than the one before; the need to mate life staining, elemental, a necessity. And when he felt her thighs begin to quiver with the impact of her release, he followed her, right over the edge into oblivion. This woman who had given him a little Dare, who gave him more love than he rightly deserved would have his heart forever.

A shiver of awareness course down the length of Shelly's spine when Dare placed several kisses there. She opened her eyes and met his warm gaze.

"Do you know this is the first time we've made love in a bed since you've been back," he said huskily, as an amused smile touched his lips.

She tipped her head to the side and smiled. "Is that good or bad?"

His long fingers reached out and begin skimming a path from her waist toward the center of her legs. "It's better." He leaned down and placed a kiss on her lips. "Stay with me tonight."

The heat shimmering in his eyes made her body feverish. With AJ spending the weekend away there was no problem with her staying with him. "Umm, what do I get if I stay?" She closed her eyes and sighed when his fingers touched her, caressed her, intent on a mission to drive her insane.

"Do you have to ask?" he rasped, his voice low and teasing against her lips.

"No, I don't," she replied in breathless anticipation.

She trembled as Dare began inflaming her body the same way he had inflamed her heart. They had endured a lot, but through it all their love had survived and for the first time since returning to College Park, she felt she had finally come home.

Epilogue

Shelly couldn't help but notice the frown on the Dare's face. It was a frown directed at Storm, who had just kissed her on the lips.

"I thought I warned you about doing that, Storm," Dare said in a very irritated tone of voice.

"But I can get away with it today because she's the bride and any well-wisher can kiss a bride on her wedding day."

Dare raised a brow. "Are you also willing to kiss the groom?"

Now it was Storm who frowned. "Kiss you? Hell, no!"

Dare smiled. "Then I suggest you keep your lips off the bride," he said, bringing Shelly closer to his side. "And there's enough single women here for you to kiss so go try your lips on someone else."

Storm chuckled. "The only other woman I'd want to kiss is Tara and I'm not crazy enough to try it. You're all talk, but Thorn really *would* kill me."

Shelly chuckled at Storm's comment as her gaze went to the woman the brothers had labeled Thorn's challenge, Tara Matthews. She was standing across the room talking to Delaney. Shelly thought that Tara was strikingly beautiful in an awe-inspiring, simply breathtaking way, and she couldn't help noticing that most of the men at the reception, both young and old, were finding it hard to keep their eyes off her. Every man except for Thorn. He was merely standing alone on the other side of the room looking bored.

"How can the two of you think that Thorn is interested in Tara when he hasn't said anything to her at all, other than giving her a courtesy nod? And he's not paying her any attention."

Dare chuckled. "Oh, don't let that nonchalant look fool you. He's paying her plenty of attention, right down to her painted toenails. He's just doing a good job of pretending not to."

"Yeah," Storm chimed in, grinning. "And he's been brooding ever since Delaney mentioned at breakfast this morning that Tara is moving to Atlanta to finish up her residency at a hospital here. The fact that she'll be in such close proximity has Thorn sweating. The heat is on and he doesn't like it at all."

A short while later Dare and Shelly had a talk with their son. "It's almost time for us to leave for our cruise, AJ. We want you on your best behavior with Grandma and Grandpa Westmoreland."

"All right." AJ looked at his father with bright eyes. "Dad, Uncle Chase and Uncle Storm said all of us are going fishing when you get back."

Dare smiled. He had news for his brothers. If they thought for one minute that he would prefer spending a weekend with them rather than somewhere in bed with his wife, they had another thought coming. "Oh, they did, did they?"

"Yes."

He nodded as he glanced over at his brothers who were talking to Tara—all of them except for Thorn. He also noted the Westmoreland cousins—brothers Jared, Durango, Spencer, Ian and Reggie—were standing in the group as well. The only one missing was Quade, and because of his covert activities for the government, there was no telling where that particular Westmoreland was or what he was doing at any given moment. "We'll talk about it when I get back," Dare said absently to AJ, wondering at the same time just where Thorn had gone off to. Although he didn't see him, he would bet any amount of money that he was somewhere close by with his eyes on Tara.

Dare shrugged. He was glad Tara was Thorn's challenge and not his. He then returned his full attention to his son. "When school is out for the holidays, your mom and I are thinking about taking you to Disney World."

"Wow!"

Dare chuckled. "I take it you'd like that?"

"Yes, I'd love it. I've been to Disneyland before but not Disney World and I've been wanting to go there."

"Good." Dare pulled Shelly into his arms after checking his watch. It was time for them to leave for the airport. They would be flying to Miami to board the cruise ship to St. Thomas. "And keep an eye on your uncles, AJ, while I'm gone. They have a tendency to get a little rowdy when I'm not here to keep them in line."

AJ laughed. "Sure, Dad."

Dare clutched AJ's shoulder and pulled him closer. "Thanks. I knew that I could count on you."

He breathed in deeply as he gathered his family close. With Shelly on one side and AJ on the other, he felt intensely happy on this day, his wedding day, and hoped that each of his brothers and cousins would one day find this same happiness. It was well worth all the time and effort he had put into it.

When he met Shelly's gaze one side of his mouth tilted into a hopelessly I-love-you-so much smile, and the one she returned said likewise. And Dare knew in his heart that he was a very happy man.

His mission had been accomplished. He had won the hearts of his son and of the woman that he loved.

* * * * *

A YOUNGER MAN

Rochelle Alers

For Brenda J. Woodbury—
"He sets the time for sorrow and the time for joy...."

He sets the time for sorrow and the time for joy,
the time for mourning and the time for dancing,
the time for making love and the time for not making love,
the time for kissing, and the time for not kissing.
                                    —*Ecclesiastes* 3: 4-5

One

"Do you need help?"

Veronica Johnson-Hamlin stared at the large man sitting astride a motorcycle. He removed a black shiny helmet, tucking it under one arm. "No, thanks. I've already called road service." Raising her right hand, she showed him her cellular telephone.

"How long have you been waiting?"

"Not too long."

"How long is not too long?"

She glanced at her watch. "About twenty minutes."

Kumi shook his head. "That's a long time to be stranded here."

His protective instincts had surfaced without warning. She was a lone female, stuck along a stretch of road that was not heavily trafficked, in an expensive vehicle.

Swinging a denim-covered leg over the bike, he pushed it off the road, propping it against a tree. Looping the strap of his helmet over one of the handlebars, he made his way around to the back of the Lexus SUV, peering into the cargo area before returning to the driver's side again.

"Do you have a jack and a spare?"

Vertical lines appeared between Veronica's large clear brown eyes. "I told you that I've called for road service."

Kumi moved closer, staring directly at her for the first time. He hadn't realized he was holding his breath until he felt tightness in his chest. The woman staring back at him had the most delicately feminine features he'd ever seen. A slender face claimed a pair of high cheekbones that afforded her an exotic appearance. Her slanting eyes, a light brown with flecks of amber-gold, were clear—clear enough for him to see his own reflection in their mysterious depths, and they were the perfect foil for her flawless umber-brown skin. Her nose was short, the bridge straight, the nostrils flaring slightly as she pressed her full, generously curved lips together. He wasn't able to discern the color or texture of the hair concealed under a navy blue cotton bandana. His gaze slipped lower to a white man-tailored shirt she'd tucked into a pair of jeans.

"Do you have any perishable items in the back?" he asked, gesturing with his thumb.

Veronica's eyelids fluttered. There was no doubt some of her frozen purchases had begun defrosting when she'd turned off the engine. She forced a smile. "They should keep until the service station sends someone."

Kumi rested his hand on the door. "Look, miss, I'm just trying to help you. You're stuck here in a very expensive truck. I'd hate to read about someone coming along and jacking you for your ride. And you'd be lucky if they only took your vehicle."

She registered his warning as she studied his face—feature by feature. His black hair was cropped close to his scalp, and she suspected the stubble covering his perfectly shaped head was new growth from what recently had been a shaved dark brown pate. He had a strong face with prominent cheek-bones, a bold nose and a lush full mouth. She couldn't see his eyes behind his mirrored sunglasses, but she still felt their intense heat. He was tall, no doubt several inches above six feet, and built like a professional athlete. She estimated that he was somewhere in his midthirties. Her gaze lowered to his powerful arms. There was a small tattoo on the left bicep, but she couldn't quite make out the design.

"What's it going to be, miss? Do you want to wait here by yourself, or do you want me to fix your flat?"

Veronica took another glance at her watch. It was at least half an hour since she'd dialed the number to her automobile club. Reaching over, she removed the key.

"I have a spare and a jack in the cargo area."

Kumi took the key from her outstretched fingers. By the time he'd rounded the truck and opened the rear door, she'd stepped out and stood alongside the Harley.

He glanced over at her, silently admiring the way her jeans clung to her curvy waist and hips. She wasn't tall, but then she couldn't be called short, either. There was a mature lushness about her body that epitomized her femininity. His sensitive nose caught a whiff of the perfume on her body and clothing and a muscle quivered in his jaw. The fragrance was perfect for her, reminding him of an overripe lush peach bursting with thick, sweet juice.

Moving several bags, he found the jack and spare tire. He bounced the tire on the asphalt, making certain it was inflated. Working quickly, Kumi removed the flat, replacing it with the spare. His biceps bulged under his suntanned skin as he tightened lug nuts. It had taken him less than fifteen minutes to change the tire and store the flat behind the front seats.

"I suggest you get this one repaired as soon as possible, because it's not safe to ride around without a spare."

Veronica nodded at the same time she reached into the front pocket of her jeans. She withdrew two twenties. "Thank you for your help."

He stared at the money as if it were a venomous reptile. "I don't want *that*."

"It's the least I can do," she countered.

Turning on his heel, Kumi walked over to his bike and swung a leg over it. "I didn't help you because I expected to be paid."

A flush swept over her face. "If you won't take any money, then how can I repay you?"

Behind his sunglasses, his gaze moved leisurely over her body. He smiled for the first time and displayed large, straight and startling white teeth. "How about a home-cooked meal?"

Veronica's jaw dropped at the same time her eyes narrowed. "What?"

His smile widened. "I've been out of the country for ten years, and what I've missed most is a home-cooked Southern meal."

She arched dark eyebrows. "What if I can't cook?"

It was his turn to lift his eyebrows. "You sure bought a lot of food for someone who can't cook."

She smiled, her eyes crinkling attractively. Veronica didn't know why, but there was some thing quite charming about the young man sitting on the Harley. He had gone out of his way to help her. If he hadn't come along, she still would be waiting for road service.

He angled his head. "Well?"

"Well what?" The two words were layered with a thread of annoyance.

"Are you going to fix that meal?"

What Veronica wanted to do was jump in her truck, drive away and leave him sitting on his bike watching her taillights.

"What do you want?"

His gaze shifted to her Georgia license plate. "Surprise me, Miss Georgia Peach."

"What if I met you at a restaurant?"

Kumi wagged a finger. "No fair. I want home-cooked."

Her temper flared without warning. "If you think I'm going to invite you—a stranger to my home—then you're crazy."

Folding massive arms over a broad chest, he glared at her behind the lenses of his sunglasses. "What do you think I'm going to do to you? Rape you? If I was going to assault you I would've done that already."

Heat stole into her cheeks. "Don't put words in my mouth! I didn't say anything about rape."

"Speaking of mouths—I still want a home-cooked meal."

Folding her hands on her hips, Veronica glared back at him. "Do you ride around looking for hapless women to rescue in exchange for food?"

Throwing back his head, Kumi laughed loudly, the sound coming deep from within his wide chest. "I kind of like that idea."

"Look, Mr...."

"Walker," he supplied. "The name is Kumi Walker."

"Mr. Walker."

"Yes, miss?" He lifted his thick black curving eyebrows in a questioning expression.

"It's Ms. Johnson." She'd given him her maiden name. "Okay," she said, deciding to concede.

What harm would there be in cooking a meal for him? And he was right about attacking her. If he'd wanted to attack her and take her vehicle, he could've done it easily.

Kumi flashed a victorious grin. "How about Sunday around four?"

"Sunday at four," she repeated, holding out her hand. "I need my key."

He removed the car key from the back pocket of his jeans and dangled it in front of her. "Where do you live?" She grabbed for the key, but he pulled it away from her grasp. "Your address, Ms. Johnson."

Swallowing back the curses threatening to spill from her lips, Veronica counted slowly to three. "Do you know Trace Road?" He nodded. "I live at the top of the hill." She held out her hand, palm upward. "Now give me my damn key."

Kumi dropped the key in her hand, then picked up his helmet and placed it on his head. He waited, watching the gentle sway of her hips as she walked over to the SUV and got into the driver's seat. He was still waiting when she slammed the door to the Lexus, started up the engine and sped away. As she disappeared from view he glanced at his watch. He would have to exceed the speed limit if he were to make it back to his cottage to shower and change his clothes in time.

Twenty minutes later he stood under the spray of a cool shower, recalling his interaction with Ms. Johnson. He didn't know what had drawn him to her, but he intended to find out.

It wasn't until later that night when he lay in bed that he thought perhaps there could be a Mr. Johnson. Even though she hadn't worn a ring, he knew instinctively she would've mentioned a husband—if he did indeed exist.

Closing his eyes, Kumi tried recalling her incredible face and body, and much to his chagrin he couldn't.

Veronica left the warmth of her bed, walking across the smooth, hardwood parquet floor on bare feet to a set of double French doors. Daybreak had begun to breathe a blush over the night sky, depositing feathery streaks of pinks, blues, violet and mauve. Rays from the rising sun cut a widening swath across the navy blue canvas, as ribbons of light crisscrossed the Great Smoky Mountains and painted the verdant valley with delicate hues from a painter's palette. With a trained eye, Veronica witnessed the breathtaking splendor.

Opening the doors, she stepped out onto the second-story veranda and leaned against the waist-high wooden railing. She closed her eyes, shivering slightly against the early morning chill sweeping over her exposed flesh. Her revealing nightgown was better suited for sultry Atlanta, not the cooler temperatures of the western North Carolina mountain region. Despite the softly blowing wind molding the delicate silken garment to her curvy body, she felt the invisible healing fingers massaging the tension in her temples, dissolving the lump under her heart and easing the tight muscles in her neck and shoulders.

Breathing in the crisp mountain air, she watched the sun inch higher—high above the haze rising from the deep gorges. The sight was more calming and healing than any prescribed tranquilizer.

Why had it taken her so long to return to this mountain retreat? Why hadn't she returned after burying her husband Dr. Bramwell Hamlin? Why had she lingered in Atlanta, Georgia, a year after defending her legal claim to his estate?

She knew the answers even before she'd formed the questions in her mind. She hadn't wanted to leave Atlanta— leave a way of life that had become as necessary to her as breathing. It was where she'd been born, raised and had set up a successfully thriving art gallery; it was also where she'd married and had been widowed.

It hadn't mattered that Bram had been old enough to be her father. In fact, he'd been several years older than her own father, but she'd come to love him—not as a father figure but as a husband. She'd married Bram at thirty-four, was widowed at forty and now at forty-two had to determine whether she truly wanted to leave the glamour of Atlanta and relocate to her vacation retreat in the North Carolina mountains.

Pushing away from the railing, she stepped back into the bedroom and closed the doors. It was Sunday and she had to decide what she was going to prepare for dinner. It was the first time in two years that she would cook for a man. Cooking dinner for Kumi Walker would be a unique and singular experience. After she fed the arrogant young man his requested home-cooked meal, she would show him the door. And that was certain to be an easy task, because since becoming a wealthy widow, she had become quite adept at rejecting men.

Easing the narrow straps of the nightgown off her shoulders, she let it float to the floor. She stepped out of it, bending down and picking up the black silk garment. Straightening gracefully, she headed for the bathroom.

The sun had shifted behind the house, leaving the kitchen cooler. Overhead track lighting cast a warm gold glow on stark white cabinets and black-hued appliances. Veronica had adjusted the air conditioner to counter the buildup of heat from the oven. She'd spent nearly four hours preparing oven-fried chicken, smothered cabbage with pieces of smoked turkey, candied sweet potatoes, savory white rice, cornbread and a flavorful chicken giblet gravy. Dessert was homemade strawberry shortcake.

Glancing up at the clock on the built-in microwave oven, she noted the time. Kumi was expected to arrive within forty-five minutes. All she had to do was set the table in the dining area off the kitchen, take another shower and select something appropriate to wear.

Kumi hung his jacket on a hook behind his seat and placed a bouquet of flowers on the passenger seat alongside a bottle of champagne. Slipping behind the wheel of his brother-in-law's car, he turned the key in the ignition and headed in the direction of Trace Road.

Warm air flowing through the open vents feathered over his freshly shaven face. He wanted to enjoy the smell of his home state. He hadn't realized how much he'd missed Asheville and North Carolina until he'd sat on the bike and rode through towns and cities he'd remembered from his childhood. Memories—good and bad—had assailed him.

He'd left the States at twenty-two, returning a decade later as a stranger.

He'd been back for eight days, yet had not seen or spoken to his two older brothers or his parents. His sister Deborah had disclosed that the elder Walkers were vacationing abroad, and were expected to return to the States for the Memorial Day weekend. And that meant he had ten days before he would come face-to-face with his father—Dr. Lawrence Walker—a man who was as tyrannical as he was unforgiving. A man who'd hung up on him whenever he called home. A man who had symbolically buried his last-born because Kumi would not follow his edict. After a while, Kumi had stopped calling.

Concentrating on his driving, he turned off the local road and onto a narrowed one identified by a sign as Trace. He reached the top of the hill, slowing and searching for Ms. Johnson's house. He saw one house, and then another.

He swallowed an expletive. He hadn't asked her the house number. His frustration escalated as he steered with one hand, driving slowly, while peering to his right at structures set several hundred feet back from the winding road. There were a total of six along the half-mile stretch of Trace Road. He drove another quarter of a mile into a wooded area before reversing direction. As soon as the houses came into view again, he saw her Lexus.

Kumi turned into the driveway behind her SUV, shifted into Park and turned off the engine. He retrieved his jacket, the flowers and the champagne.

He felt her presence seconds before he saw her, and when he turned to stare at the woman who'd promised to cook for him, he almost dropped the flowers and the wine.

She stood in the open doorway dressed in off-white. His gaze was fused to the outline of her body in a sheer organdy blouse she'd paired with tailored linen slacks. A delicate lacy camisole dotted with tiny pearls showed through the fabric of the airy shirt. Her feet were pushed into a pair of low-heeled mules in a matching pale linenlike fabric covering.

Kumi forced himself to place one foot in front of the other as he approached her, mouth gaping. Her hair—it was thick, chemically straightened, and worn in a blunt-cut pageboy that curved under her delicate jawline. It wasn't the style that held his rapt attention, but the color. It was completely gray! A shimmering silver that blended perfectly with her flawless golden-brown face.

Two

Veronica knew she'd shocked the arrogant young man when he wouldn't meet her amused gaze. He'd come on to her thinking she was only a few years older than he was. But it was her gray hair that had left this swaggering mahogany Adonis gaping, slack-jawed.

"Good afternoon, Kumi."

The sound of her voice shattered his entrancement. He smiled. "Good afternoon, Ms. Johnson."

Veronica returned his smile, capturing his gaze with her brilliant amber one. His eyes were large, alert, deep-set and a mysterious glossy black.

"You may call me Veronica." She stepped back, permitting him entrance to her home.

He walked into the living room, staring up at the towering cathedral ceiling and winding wrought-iron staircase leading to a loft. Streams of sunlight from floor-to-ceiling windows highlighted the highly waxed bleached pine floors with a parquetry border of alternating pine and rosewood inlay.

Shifting slightly, he turned and stared down at Veronica Johnson staring up at him. The fragrance of Oriental spice clinging to her flesh, hair and clothes swept around him, making him a prisoner of her startling beauty and femininity.

Veronica's eyes crinkled in a smile. "I think you'd better give me the flowers before you shred them."

He looked at the bouquet he'd clutched savagely in his right hand. The petals from some of the roses and lilies had fallen off the stems within the cellophane covering.

"I'm—I'm sorry. But...these are for you." He handed her the flowers and the bottle of champagne, chiding himself for stuttering like a starstruck adolescent. What he did not want to admit was that seeing Veronica Johnson again had left him more shaken than he wanted to be.

"Thank you. The flowers are beautiful." Her gaze shifted from the bouquet to Kumi. "Is something wrong?" Her voice was soft, comforting.

"No...I mean yes." He decided to be honest with her and himself. "You surprised me."

She arched a questioning eyebrow. "How?"

"Your hair. The color shocked me. I didn't expect the gray."

Her expression was impassive. "In other words, you didn't expect me to be *that* old."

His mouth tightened slightly before he said, "I was talking about your hair color, not your age."

"I'm gray because I'm old enough to claim gray hair." She knew she didn't owe him an explanation, but decided to teach him a lesson. The next time he met a woman, he would be less apt to flirt with her. "I began graying prematurely at twenty-eight," she continued, "and by the time I was thirty-eight I was completely gray."

"There's no need for you to address me as if I were a child," he retorted sharply.

"I did not call you a child, Kumi. But if you feel that way, then I can't help it."

Closing his eyes briefly, Kumi struggled to control his temper. It had begun all wrong. He hadn't come to Veronica Johnson's house to debate age differences. He'd come because there was something about her that drew him to her. She was older than he was, but that didn't bother him as much as it appeared to disturb her.

"The flowers need water, the champagne should be chilled and I'd like to eat. The only thing I've eaten all day is a slice of toast and a cup of coffee. Meanwhile, you seem out of sorts because you're a few years older than me."

It was Veronica's turn for her delicate jaw to drop. Kumi was beyond arrogant. "I'm not out of sorts."

Kumi flashed a sensual smile, disarming her immediately. She returned his smile.

"Can we discuss age after we've eaten?" he asked.

"No," she said quickly. "There's no need to discuss it at all, except to say that I'll turn forty-three on September 29." To her surprise he showed no reaction.

"And I'll celebrate my thirty-third birthday next January, which means there's only a ten-year difference in our ages," he countered in a lower, huskier tone.

Which makes you too young to be my mother, he added silently.

Veronica wanted to yell at him, *Only ten years.* Ten years was a decade; a lot of things, people and events changed within a decade. Her life was a perfect example.

She displayed a bright polite smile—one Atlanta residents recognized whenever she and Bramwell Hamlin—African-American plastic surgeon to the rich and famous—had entertained in their opulent home.

"Everything is ready. If you follow me I'll show you where you can wash up before we dine."

Kumi noticed that she'd said "dine" instead of "eat." He liked that. Following her, he admired her hips as she walked across the yawning space of a living and dining room, to a screened-in room off the corner of the expansive kitchen. A delicate pewter chandelier lit up a large table with seating for six. Two place settings were set with fine china, silver, crystal stemware and damask napkins. Water goblets filled with sparkling water were positioned next to wineglasses.

Attractive lines fanned out around his dark eyes. "You set a beautiful table."

She nodded, acknowledging his compliment. "Thank you. The bathroom is over there." She pointed to a door several feet from the dining space.

Kumi walked over, opened the door and stepped into a small half bath. Potted plants lined a ledge under a tall, narrow window, a profusion of green matching the tiny green vines decorating the pale pink wallpaper. The room was delightful and feminine with its dusky rose furnishings and leaf-green accessories. He washed and dried his hands, then left the bathroom.

Returning to the table, he braced his hands on the back of a chair, staring openly at Veronica's back as she bent from the waist and peered into a kitchen cabinet.

"Is there anything I can help you with?"

"No. Everything's done. Please sit down."

He complied, watching as she retrieved a vase and crystal ice bucket from a cabinet under a countertop. She half filled the bucket with ice from the ice maker in the refrigerator door, then inserted the bottle of champagne. Her movements were fluid as she unwrapped the flowers and arranged them in the vase, filling it with water.

Rising quickly to his feet, Kumi closed the space between them, grasping the vase and the bucket. He placed them on the table. Ignoring her warning look, he carried several platters and covered dishes from the countertop to the table. After Veronica had placed a gravy boat on the table, he came around and pulled out a chair for his hostess. She sat, and he lingered over her head, inhaling the scent emanating from her body. Curbing the urge to press a kiss on her luminous silvery hair, he took his seat.

Staring at her hands, he noted their fragility. And like the rest of her they were beautifully formed. She uncovered several dishes, halting when she glanced up and caught him staring at her.

Veronica knew she intrigued Kumi. There was something in his gaze that communicated that her being older than him was not an issue. She shrugged a shoulder, thinking perhaps he just liked older women. Dropping her gaze, she returned her attention to uncovering the platter of chicken.

"You are incredible," Kumi crooned when he saw the cabbage, fluffy white rice, sweet potatoes and the thick slices of buttery cornbread.

"Voilà, a home-cooked meal." Veronica handed him several serving pieces. "Please help yourself."

Reaching across the table, he picked up her plate. "What do you want?"

A smile trembled over her lips. She was clearly surprised that he'd offered to serve her. "A little bit of everything, thank you."

"White or dark meat?"

"I eat both."

Kumi speared a leg, and then spooned a portion of rice, cabbage and sweet potato onto her plate. He rose slightly and placed it in front of her before serving himself.

Placing a napkin over her lap, Veronica gestured to the bottle of chilled white wine already on the table. "Would you like wine or the champagne?"

"Is there another alternative?"

She gave him a direct stare. "*Homemade* lemonade."

His dark gaze roamed leisurely over her features, lingering on the tempting curve of her lower lip before returning to fuse with the amber orbs with flecks of darker lights. He marveled at her brilliant eyes, her sexy mouth and her flawless skin.

He forced his gaze not to linger below her throat where the outline of full breasts pushed against the silk under the gossamer material of her blouse. Within seconds his body betrayed him; a rush of desire hardened the flesh pulsing between his thighs. Clenching his fists tightly, he clamped his teeth together. He couldn't speak or move as he waited in erotic agony for the swelling to ease.

"Wine, champagne or lemonade?" Veronica asked again.

Kumi shifted uncomfortably on his chair, praying she wouldn't ask him to get up. The pressure of his engorged flesh throbbing against the fabric of his briefs was akin to a pleasurable pain he did not want to go away.

"Wine," he gasped, eliciting a questionable look from her.

Noting his pained expression, she asked, "Are you all right?"

"Yes," he replied a little too quickly. Reaching for the bottle of wine and a nearby corkscrew, he uncorked the bottle with a minimum of effort.

Leaning against the cane-back chair, Veronica gave him a critical squint. "How did you do that so quickly?"

"I've had a lot of experience."

"How?"

"Working in restaurants."

And he had. After leaving the Marine Corps, instead of returning to Asheville, he'd traveled to Paris and fell in love with the City of Lights on sight. A monthlong vacation became two months, then three, and after a while he discovered he didn't want to leave. His decision to live in France had changed him and his life forever.

Veronica studied the impassive expression of the man sitting opposite her. His face was a work of art. High cheekbones, a chiseled jaw, a dark brown complexion with rich red undertones and large deep-set black eyes made for an arresting visage.

"Do you still work in restaurants?" Her tone was soft, but layered with sarcasm.

Kumi filled her wineglass and then his own, a slight smile tugging at the corners of his mouth. He'd picked up on her disdain. It was the same question his mother had asked the last time he'd spoken to her.

Jerome, darling, are you still working in restaurants?

And his response had been, *Yes, Mother, I'm still working in restaurants.*

What he hadn't disclosed to anyone was that he hoped to open his own restaurant within the next eighteen months. He'd worked hard, saved his money and now looked forward to running his own business.

He knew Jeanette Walker wanted him to return to the States, go to college and apply to medical school. This had been his parents' dream after their two older sons had not exhibited the aptitude for a career in medicine. Their focus then shifted to their last-born, hoping and praying that Jerome Kumi Walker would follow the Walker tradition of becoming a doctor like his father, grandfather and great-grandfather had been.

Capturing the questioning amber gaze and holding it with his own, he nodded. "Yes, I still work in restaurants. Right now I'm helping out my sister and brother-in-law."

Veronica picked up a fork. "Do they own a restaurant?"

He shook his head. "No. They're setting up a bed-and-breakfast."

This disclosure intrigued her. "Where?"

"It's about five or six miles outside of Asheville. Two years ago Debbie and Orrin bought a run-down seventeen-room Victorian and began restoring it to its original state."

"Are they doing all the work themselves?"

He nodded. "Yes. Debbie's an interior decorator and my brother-in-law is a general contractor. The project has become a labor of love for them, and they expect to be fully operational by mid-July."

Veronica's gaze narrowed slightly. "And are you going to work in their kitchen?"

It was the second time within a minute he'd picked up the censure in her voice. He stared at her through half-lowered lips, gorging on her blatant feminine beauty. Her white attire made her appear innocent, almost virginal. But he knew Veronica Johnson was not a virgin. She couldn't be. Not with her face and body. She was lush, ripe, like a piece of fruit bursting with thick, sweet juices.

He wanted to taste her, lick her until satiated. He'd lived in Europe for the past decade, traveling to every country, while taking side trips to Asia and Africa. But never had he ever seen or encountered a woman whose femininity cried out to his masculinity the way Veronica Johnson's did. The wild, uninhibited part of him wanted her!

"Yes, *Veronica*. I'm going to work in their kitchen." He'd planned to remain in North Carolina long enough to hire and train the chefs for the elegant bed-and-breakfast.

Her name on his lips became a caress, one that sent a shiver of warning up Veronica's spine. Kumi was flirting with her. He was very subtle, but she sensed that he was coming on to her.

And she had to admit it. She was flattered. Older *and* younger men still found her attractive. Lowering her head slightly, she said a silent grace, and then began eating.

Kumi also blessed his food, then reaching for his wine-

glass he held it aloft. "I'd like to make a toast." He waited
for Veronica to raise her glass, touching his to hers, a clear
chime echoing in the awaiting silence. "It's a quote from Ecclesiastes." She nodded. "Everything that happens in this
world happens at the time God chooses. He has set the right
time for everything. He has given us a desire to know the
future, but never gives us the satisfaction of fully understanding what He does. All of us should eat and drink and enjoy
what we have worked for. It's God's gift."

Staring wordlessly across the table, Veronica's expression
mirrored her shock. *Who was Kumi Walker?* she asked herself. Who was the young man who rode a Harley and quoted
Bible verses?

"Amen," she whispered softly after recovering her voice.
She sipped her wine, savoring its dry fruity taste. Her dinner guest was much more complex than she'd originally
thought. Veronica smiled. This Sunday dinner was certain
to be a very interesting encounter.

Kumi cut a small portion of chicken breast, biting into the
moist succulent meat. Chewing slowly, he savored the distinctive taste of buttermilk with a hint of chili, cumin and
oregano. He took another bite. The chicken had been
dredged in finely ground cornmeal instead of flour.

Closing his eyes, he shook his head. "Unbelievable," he
said after opening them.

Veronica shrugged a shoulder, smiling. "It's different."

"No, it's wonderful," he argued laughingly. "You fried it
in the oven?"

"Yes."

She watched the play of emotions on his face. There was
no doubt he was pleased and surprised with her recipe for
spicy oven-fried chicken. It was only one of many recipes
she'd inherited from her paternal grandmother.

Kumi took a sip of wine, his eyebrows lifting slightly. Even the wine was excellent. "Would you mind sharing the recipe?" He probably could duplicate the recipe on his own, but only after several exhaustive taste tests.

"Not at all," she replied after swallowing a mouthful of sweet potato.

"I'm certain it would be a favorite if Debbie added it as one of the selections on her menu."

"You said they're opening a bed-and-breakfast. Do they intend to serve dinner also?"

He nodded. "They're calling it a B and B, but I see it more like a country inn. Of course they'll offer the customary breakfasts during the week, brunch on the weekends and dinner every night."

A smile softened her mouth. "It sounds very exciting."

His smile matched hers in liveliness. "It is."

The liquid gold in Veronica's eyes flickered with interest. Suddenly she wanted to know more about the man sharing her table. "You said you've been out of the country for ten years. Where were you living?"

For a long moment, he looked back at her. "France."

She sat up straighter. "Where in France?"

"Paris."

Her lids lowered at the same time a soft gasp escaped her. "What a wonderful city."

He leaned forward. "You've been there?"

It was her turn to nod. "I spent two summers there studying art."

Kumi stared, complete surprise on his handsome face. "You're an artist?" he asked in French.

"No. I always wanted to be an artist, but what I lacked in talent I made up in enthusiasm. I studied drawing for two years, but abandoned it to become an art history teacher," she replied in English.

She'd taught art history at a college level for five years before she left academia to open her gallery in Atlanta. She'd
specialized in showing the work of up-and-coming African-
American artists. Two weeks ago she'd sold the gallery to a
consortium of artists who'd pooled their meager earnings to
display their work.

"Do you paint?" he asked, again speaking French.

"The closest I get to painting is sketching. I must have
dozens of pads filled with incomplete sketches."

"Which medium?"

"Charcoal, pastels and colored pencils."

Excitement shimmered in his dark gaze. "Do you have
anything to show? Because Debbie hasn't decided what type
of art she wants to display in some of the rooms."

"Parlez plus lentement, s'il vous plaît," she said, speaking French for the first time. It had been years since she'd
spoken the language and Kumi was speaking it too quickly
for her to understand every word.

He chuckled softly. "I'll try to speak more slowly."

"Your French is flawless. You speak it like a native."

Inclining his head, he said, "Thank you. I've come to believe that it is the most beautiful language in the world."

Veronica had to agree with him. "I'd studied the language in high school and college, but it wasn't until I lived
in Paris that first summer that I truly came to understand
the intricacies of the spoken language. I once overheard two
men screaming at each other on a street corner, not realizing they were insulting each other's mothers with references
to them being donkeys and camel dung. But to me it was just
a passionate heated exchange until my mentor translated the
profanity for me."

Kumi laughed, the deep warm sound bubbling up from
his broad chest. "It's the only language in which curses
sound like words of love."

"You're right," she agreed. "After all, it is called the language of love."

Sobering, he thought of the city he now called home. He lived in the City of Lights, spoke the language of love, yet had never been in love. But, on the other hand, he hadn't lived a monkish existence, either. There were women in his past, but none he liked or loved enough to make a permanent part of his life. Most of the women he'd been involved with claimed he was too aloof and moody. What they hadn't understood was his driving ambition. He'd spent the past six years working and saving his money because he was committed to establishing his own unique dining establishment in a city that boasted hundreds of restaurants, bistros and cafés.

"Who did you study with?" he asked, lapsing fluidly into English.

"Garland Bayless."

"The Garland Bayless who passed away four years ago?"

Attractive lines appeared at the corners of her eyes with her broad smile. "The same."

"The man has become a legend in France."

"I doubt whether he would've become a legend if he'd remained in the States. As a college freshman, I went to his first showing at a gallery in New York, absolutely stunned by his genius. Several noted critics panned his work as amateurish. Their attack was so scathing that Garland packed up and left the country two days after the show closed. He moved to Paris and began selling his work at a fraction of what it was worth at that time.

"I wrote to him once I completed my sophomore year, asking if I could study with him for a summer. Much to my surprise, he wrote back, encouraging me to come to Paris and stay with him at his flat. My father threw a fit."

Kumi swallowed a forkful of cabbage. "Did your father know Bayless was gay?"

"No. And I didn't tell him until after I returned home," she said.

Anyway her father needn't have worried. It wouldn't have mattered what Garland Bayless's sexual preference had been, she thought. At that time Veronica had been so traumatized by a near date-rape episode that she wouldn't permit any man to touch *any* part of her body. She'd been too embarrassed to report the incident and for years she'd lived with the disturbing fear of being raped. It wasn't until later, after she'd married Bramwell, that she knew her reason for marrying a man thirty years her senior was because he was safe. Her husband had been impotent. She wasn't a virgin, but she hadn't had sex with a man in more than twenty years.

"Garland taught me the language, how to choose an inexpensive quality wine and the differences in cheese. I wore my hair in cornrows before they became fashionable in the United States, dressed in funky clothes and shoes, and soaked up everything he taught me."

Kumi didn't know why, but suddenly he envied the time Garland Bayless had spent with Veronica Johnson.

"How many summers did you spend with him?"

"My junior and senior years. I went back to visit him once after I got married."

Here it comes, Kumi groaned inwardly. Now it was time for her to talk about her husband. At first it hadn't bothered him if there was a Mr. Johnson, but after interacting with Veronica, he now resented the man.

He sat across the table from a woman, enjoying an exquisitely prepared meal by another man's wife, a woman who'd turned him on just because she existed. And despite the ten-year age difference, they shared many things in common: both had lived in Paris, spoke French and were devotees of an expatriate African-American artist who had become an icon in his adopted homeland.

"Garland no longer lived in the loft, but had purchased a pied-à-terre in the heart of the city," Veronica continued. "His work hung in museums, were part of private collections, and he managed to find happiness with a sensitive and devoted lover. He threw a lavish party in my honor, telling everyone that I was the only woman that he'd ever considered making love to."

"What did your husband say when he heard this?" Kumi asked with a staid calmness. He didn't think he would appreciate *any* man—gay or straight—openly admitting that he'd wanted to sleep with *his* wife.

Veronica registered a change in Kumi. His tone was coolly disapproving. "Bram couldn't say anything because he'd hadn't gone with me."

Momentarily speechless in his surprise, Kumi finally said, "You traveled to Europe without your husband?"

She bristled noticeably. He had no right to be critical or disapproving. After all, he knew nothing about her or her relationship with her late husband. "There were several occasions when we did not travel together."

Vertical lines appeared between Kumi's eyes. "Were or are?"

A tense silence enveloped the room and Veronica and Kumi stared at each other. The silence loomed between them like a heavy fog.

He waited, half in anticipation and half in dread. He wanted—no needed—to know if this encounter with Veronica Johnson would be his last. If she was actually married, then he would retreat honorably. It had never been his style to pursue a married woman.

"I am a widow," Veronica said in a voice so soft, he had to strain his ears to hear her. "My husband died two years ago."

Slumping back on his chair, Kumi's eyelids fluttered

wildly. She *wasn't* married. That meant he could court her. That is, if she didn't rebuff his advances.

"I'm sorry," he said, quickly regaining his composure.

"Are you really sorry?"

Sitting up straighter, he met her direct stare. A frown furrowed his smooth forehead as his long fingers toyed with the stem of his wineglass.

"Do you really want to know the truth?"

Her expression did not change. "Yes."

His gaze bore into hers. "The truth is that I'm not sorry, because I didn't know your husband. What I am sorry about is that you had to go through the loss."

Veronica stared at a spot over his broad shoulder. She liked Kumi Walker. In fact, she liked him a lot, especially his straightforward manner. Unlike a lot of men she'd met over the years, he was not afraid to speak his mind.

She shifted her gaze to his perfectly symmetrical features. "Thank you for your honesty."

Lowering his gaze, he smiled. "I know no other way to be."

"Then you're truly exceptional."

Long lashes that touched the ridge of his high cheekbones swept up, and his black eyes impaled her, not permitting her to move or breathe. He shook his head slowly.

"I'm not worthy of the compliment."

"I beg to differ with you," she argued softly. "Honesty is something I value and admire in a human being." What she didn't say was *especially in a man.*

He noticed she'd said "human being" and not "a man." Picking up the bottle of wine, he said, "Would you like more wine?"

Running the tip of her tongue over her lower lip, Veronica smiled. "Yes, please."

Kumi wanted to put the bottle down and pull Veronica across the table and kiss her lush mouth. Didn't she know what she was doing to him? What he did instead was fill her glass, then his own. He concentrated on eating the food on his plate, and then took a second helping of everything. She could've easily become a chef. Her cooking skills were exceptional. Everything he'd observed and she'd shown him thus far was exceptional.

"I hope you left room for dessert," she said as Kumi touched the corners of his mouth with his napkin.

Groaning audibly, he shook his head. "Why didn't you mention dessert before I had seconds?"

"I know you haven't been gone so long that you've forgotten that a Southern Sunday dinner is not complete until there's pecan pie, lemon pound cake, strawberry shortcake, the ubiquitous sweet potato pie or jelly-roll cake."

Reaching across the table, Kumi caught her hand, holding it firmly within his larger, stronger grip. "Which one did you make?"

She felt a jolt of energy snake up her arm, and wanted to extract her fingers from his, but the sensations were much too pleasurable. What was it about this younger man that touched her the way no other man had ever been able to do? What was happening to her at forty-two that hadn't been there at twenty-two or thirty-two?

Her last gynecological visit revealed that there hadn't been a drastic drop in her estrogen level, so she wasn't what doctors had referred to as perimenopausal. What the doctor hadn't known was that she hadn't experienced any sexual desire since a college student attempted to rape her after she'd rebuffed his advances. In other words, there never had been a sexual pinnacle for her.

A teasing smile played at the corners of her mouth, bringing Kumi's gaze to linger on the spot. "It's a wonderful complement for champagne."

"It has to be the strawberry shortcake."

"Did you peek in the refrigerator?"

"When did I get the opportunity to peek in your refrigerator?" She gave him a skeptical look, her eyes narrowing slightly. "Don't tell me you don't like to lose?"

Veronica wrinkled her delicate nose. "I hate losing."

"Then I'll let you win the next time."

Her expression stilled, becoming serious. "What next time?"

Releasing her hand, Kumi crossed his arms over his chest. "I want to return the favor and cook for you."

She shook her head, the silvery strands sweeping around her delicate jaw. "That's not necessary."

"I want to."

"Kumi…"

"When was the last time you ate authentic French cuisine?" he said, interrupting her. "I could prepare chicken with Calvados, chicken paillard or a succulent saffron chicken with capers. If you don't want poultry, then I'll make something with lamb, beef or fish." He would agree to cook anything just to see her again.

"Stop!" There was a hint of laughter in the command.

He affected a hopeful look. "Will you let me cook for you?"

"Yes. But…" Her words trailed off.

"But what?"

"Only if you let me assist you. I'd like to learn to perfect a few dishes."

She'd totally ignored her own vow to share only one meal with the man. That was before she'd found him so charming. Besides, he was someone with whom she could practice her French.

"Agreed." His smile was dazzling. "Next Sunday?" She nodded. "What time should I come over? Unless you wouldn't mind coming to my place."

A wave of apprehension swept through her. She'd once

gone to a man's home alone and had been sexually assaulted. "You can cook here."

"At what time?"

"Anytime. I'm always up early."

Pushing back her chair, she stood and reached for Kumi's plate and silverware, but was thwarted when his fingers curved around her wrist. "I'll clear the table."

"That's not necessary," she said.

"You cooked, so I'll clean up." He gave her a warning look. "Sit and relax."

Veronica pretended not to understand his look. "But you're a guest in my home."

He refused to relent. "That may be true, but I was raised to show my appreciation for anyone who has gone out of their way to offer kindness. And that translates into my clearing the table."

A wave of heat flooded her cheeks. "And I repaid your kindness for changing my tire with dinner."

Kumi recognized willfulness in Veronica's personality— a trait that was so apparent in his own. "You offered to repay me by offering me money. Therefore, dinner wasn't your first choice."

Her eyes darkening, she struggled to control her temper. "Then you should've taken the money, *Mr. Walker.*"

He let go of her wrist, gathering the silverware and placing it on his plate. Kumi felt the heat from Veronica's angry gaze as he stacked the plates and carried them to the sink. She was still glaring at him, hands folded on her hips, as he returned to the table to retrieve the serving dishes. What would've taken her three or four trips, he'd accomplished in only two.

Standing in front of the refrigerator, he smiled sweetly. "May I open it and get dessert?"

Taking a half-dozen steps, she moved over to stand near

Kumi. She tilted her chin, staring up at him staring down at her. His body's heat intensified the scent of his aftershave. It was as potent and intoxicating as the man who wore it. Her heart fluttered wildly in her breast as her dormant senses leapt to life.

What was it about this boy-man that quickened her pulse and made her heart pound an erratic rhythm?

Clearing her throat, she pretended not to be affected by his presence. "You may open the champagne."

Kumi went completely still as he held his breath. She stood close enough for him to feel the feminine heat and smell of her body. A warming shiver of desire skipped along his nerve endings as he counted the beats of the pulse in her throat. Time stood still as they shared an intense physical awareness of each other.

"Do you have a towel?" His request broke the spell.

Veronica moved to her right, making certain no part of her body touched his, and opened a drawer under the countertop. She withdrew a black-and-white striped terry-cloth towel, and handed it to him.

He mumbled a thank-you, walking back to the table while she opened the refrigerator to remove a dish with a whipped-cream-covered cake topped with fresh strawberries. By the time she reached the table, he'd opened the bottle of champagne without spilling a drop. The only sound in the silence had been the soft popping sound of the cork as it was removed from the bottle.

Three

Veronica squared her shoulders and turned to face Kumi.

"Would you mind sitting on the patio now that the sun is on the other side of the house?"

Turning his head slightly, he smiled at her, and he wasn't disappointed when she returned his smile. The tense encounter was behind them.

"I'd like that very much."

"Please come with me."

He followed her out of the kitchen, through a narrow hallway and into a screened-in, glass-enclosed room spanning the length of the rear of the house. He was completely stunned by the panorama unfolding before his gaze. Hanging, flowering and potted plants, a large portable waterfall, rattan furniture covered with colorful kente-cloth cushions and a rug made of woven straw fibers were reminiscent of a rain forest. The soothing sound of the gurgling water blended with the relaxing strains of music flowing from a stereo system discreetly hidden under a table.

Nodding his approval, Kumi said, "I feel as if I'm in a jungle."

"That's the effect I wanted to create."

He turned slowly, his gaze sweeping over the meticulously chosen furnishings. "How long does it take for you to water all the plants?"

She placed the cake on a small round glass-topped rattan table with two pull-up matching chairs. "I don't know yet. They were delivered yesterday."

"You just moved here?"

Meeting his questioning gaze, she shook her head. "No. We purchased this house three years ago, ordered the furniture, but I hadn't added the touches that would make it feel like home. I've been away for two years."

He clutched the towel-covered champagne bottle tighter to his chest. "Do you plan to live here permanently?"

"I'm not certain," she replied honestly. "What I plan to do is stay the summer and relax."

What she did not tell him was that she needed to put some distance between herself, the Atlanta gossipmongers and her late husband's adult children. They'd challenged their father's will, accusing her of manipulation. Dr. Hamlin hadn't disinherited his two sons and daughter, but had divided his estate with: one-fourth to be divided between his three children, one-fourth to Veronica and the final half to establish a scholarship foundation bearing his name for exceptional African-American undergraduate students who planned for careers in medicine.

There had been no mention of Martha Hamlin, the first Mrs. Hamlin. After the divorce, Bramwell had given Martha a generous settlement, which should've permitted her to continue the comfortable lifestyle she'd established as the wife of the most prominent black plastic surgeon in the country. Bramwell had established his reputation and vast wealth whenever a superstar athlete or entertainer of color sought out his specialized cosmetic or corrective surgical procedures.

However, within six months of her separation and eventual divorce, Martha found solace in her prized vodka cocktails, losing herself in a drunken haze that usually lasted for days. And whenever she was under the influence, she wrote countless checks in staggering amounts to her overindulgent children.

Less than a year after Veronica married Bramwell, Martha came to her gallery, sobbing uncontrollably that she was going to lose her million-dollar home because she hadn't paid property taxes for two years. Veronica wrote the woman a check from her own personal account. Both had sworn an oath that no one would ever know of their private business transaction.

Martha had kept her word, but of course her children hadn't known that their father's second wife had kept their mother from becoming homeless. None of that mattered when they verbally attacked her after the reading of Bram's will.

Yes—she had made the right decision to close her home and leave Atlanta for North Carolina. She'd had enough of the Hamlins, their lies, harassment and assaults on her character.

Kumi stared at the thickly forested area in the distance. "This is the perfect setting for relaxation."

"That it is," she concurred. "We can sit over there." She motioned to the table with the cake. "Make yourself comfortable while I get the flutes, plates and forks."

He removed his jacket and placed it over the back of one chair. He was still standing in the same spot when she returned. A vaguely sensuous current passed between them as she moved closer. He took the flutes from her loose grip, then the dessert plates and forks. She gasped when his right arm curved around her waist, pulling her against his middle.

With a minimum of effort, he led her to the center of the room. Her startled gaze reminded him of a deer frozen by an automobile's headlights. "Dance with me," he whispered close to her ear. "This song is a favorite of mine."

Veronica forced herself to relax as she sank into his comforting protective embrace. The runaway beating of her heart slowed. She recognized the instrumental version of "I Can't Make You Love Me."

She felt a flicker of something so frightening that she wanted to pull away. It had been twenty years since a man had held her to his body. Twenty years ago it had been an act of violence, unlike the gentle touch of the hands caressing her back through the delicate fabric of her blouse. She was frightened and curious at the same time when she felt Kumi's hardness pressing against her thighs. She realized the strange feeling was desire. It had taken her two decades to feel desire again. And she wanted to cry because it was with a man ten years her junior.

Why now? Why not with some of the other men she'd met before or after her marriage?

Pressing her face against his solid shoulder, Veronica breathed in the masculine scent. The motion caused Kumi's arm to tighten around her waist, pulling her even closer. Dropping his hand, she wound her arms around his neck, certain he felt her trembling.

This time it wasn't from fear, but from a need—a desperate need to experience the passion she hadn't felt in a very long time. The musical piece ended, and they still swayed to their own private song. She finally found the strength to lower her arms and push firmly against his chest.

Lowering his head, Kumi breathed a kiss under her ear. "Thank you for the dance."

She smiled shyly. "You're welcome." She should've been the one thanking him. Raising her chin, she looked up at him as he stared down at her under lowered lids. She wanted to see his eyes. "Kumi?" His name was a breathless whisper.

"*Oui?*"

"The champagne is getting warm and the cream on the cake is melting."

He blinked as if coming out of a trance. Cradling her hand in his, he led her over to the table, pulled out a chair and seated her. He sat down, silently cursing himself for not kissing her. He'd been provided with the perfect opportunity to taste the confection of her generously curved mouth.

The next time, he mused. And there would be a next time. That she'd promised.

Veronica lay in bed Monday morning, staring up at the sheer mosquito netting flowing sensuously around the massive four-poster, loathing getting up. The feeling of being wrapped in a silken cocoon of bottomless peace persisted. She closed her eyes and smiled. The person who'd helped her achieve that feeling was Kumi Walker.

They'd lingered over dessert, drinking champagne and talking for hours about Paris, she experiencing an overwhelming nostalgia for Le Marais, Champs-Élysées, St. Germain-des-Prés, and the Chaillot, Latin, Luxembourg and Jardin des Plantes Quarters. And it was the first time in a very long time that she truly missed Paris—a city wherein each section claimed its own charm and artistic enclave.

She'd recalled restaurants, cafés, art galleries and museums she'd visited while Kumi offered her an update on each. What had surprised her was that he exhibited an exhaustive knowledge of art and architecture. Later he admitted he'd spent hundreds of hours in many of the museums his first year in Paris.

The sun had set and the late-spring night sky was painted with thousands of stars when Kumi finally prepared to leave, and at that moment Veronica hadn't wanted him to go. She'd wanted him to stay and talk—about anything. After he left she realized she was lonely—lonely for male companionship. Lonely because she missed her husband and their nightly chats. There had never been a time when she and Bram weren't able to bare their souls to each other. She'd been able to discuss anything with him—all except for the sexual assault that made it impossible for her to share her body with a man.

She'd met the elegant older man when he'd come into the tiny gallery she'd opened only six months before, looking for a gift for a colleague's birthday. She'd suggested a watercolor of a seascape. Dr. Bramwell Hamlin was more than satisfied with his purchase and quite taken with the woman who'd recommended the painting.

He returned to the gallery the following month, this time to ask her assistance in helping him select artwork for his new home. She'd selected several landscapes and a magnificent still life, and a year later shock waves swept through Atlanta, Georgia's black privileged class when Dr. Hamlin married Veronica Johnson, a woman thirty years his junior.

Veronica opened her eyes, rolling over on her side and peering at the face of the clock on a bedside table. It was ten-thirty. She hadn't slept that late in years. Throwing off the sheet, she sat up, parted the netting and swung her legs over the side of the bed. Her feet hadn't touched the floor when the telephone rang. She picked up the receiver before the second ring.

"Hello."

"Why did I have to hear it from our mother that you now live in the sticks?"

Veronica cradled the cordless instrument under her chin,

smiling. "You wouldn't have to hear it secondhand if you stopped stalking your husband."

Candace Johnson-Yarborough's husky laugh came through the earpiece. "Bite your tongue, big sis. You know I wouldn't permit Ivan to go away on a three-day business trip without making him check in every hour, so what makes you think I'd be apart from him for three months?"

It was Veronica's turn to laugh. Candace had married, what she and thousands of other Georgia black women had referred to, as the "world's sexiest brother." And she had to agree with her sister—Ivan Yarborough was not only good-looking but also a brilliant businessman. Ivan headed a consulting firm whose focus was setting up consortiums of small businesses in predominately African-American communities. He was always a much-sought-after speaker at corporate seminars, colleges and high schools. Candace, a former schoolteacher, had resigned her position to homeschool their two sons while they all traveled together as a family.

"Bite your tongue, little sis. I'll have you know that I don't live in the sticks."

"Yeah, right. Your closest neighbor is at least a mile away."

Veronica wasn't going to argue with Candace, who had always said she preferred living in the middle of a thriving metropolis. Her younger sister craved bright lights, honking automobile horns and blaring music. Besides, she wanted to tell Candace that Trace Road was only half a mile long.

"When are you coming to visit me and see for yourself that it's quite civilized here? There's even a shopping mall less than three miles away."

"I can't now. I have to prepare the kids for final exams. I'm calling for two reasons. One to say hello and let you know we're back, and the other is to let you know the family reunion has been confirmed for the second weekend in August. Aunt Bette is hosting it this time."

She wanted to tell her sister that she was going to conveniently come down with a strange illness for that particular weekend. Their mother's sister was the most annoying and exasperating woman in the entire state of Georgia.

Instead, Veronica agreed to mark the calendar and then asked about her preteen nephews, telling Candace to give them her love.

Kumi showed the middle-aged cook to the door.

"Thank you so much for applying, Mr. Sherman. You'll be informed of our decision before the end of the month."

Waiting until the man walked out of the office his sister and brother-in-law had set up as their office, Kumi shook his head. He'd spent the past two days interviewing applicants, all who were more suited to cooking for a roadside café, than a full-service kitchen offering gourmet meals.

Deborah Walker-Maxwell entered the office seconds later, a pained expression distorting her attractive features. She sat down on a love seat and closed her eyes. "How many does that make?" she asked.

Kumi stared at his sister. The strain of trying to get the B and B ready for opening was beginning to wear on her. The puffiness under her large dark eyes was the most obvious sign. Deborah, the only daughter of Lawrence and Jeanette Walker, was also the most ambitious.

A very successful interior decorator, Deborah had resigned her position at one of the country's leading design firms to go into business for herself. At thirty-eight, she'd taken her life savings, purchased the abandoned dilapidated property and with her contractor-husband, Orrin Maxwell, had begun renovating the former showplace to its original elegance.

Orrin had replaced the floors, walls, hung wallpaper and installed light fixtures, while his wife visited estate sales, an-

tique shops and the many North Carolina furniture mak-
ers for furnishings. Each room now had its own name and
personality.

"He was the eighth one." Kumi's tone mirrored his disappointment. He shook his head. "You advertised for chefs,
yet you're getting cooks. There's a big difference in a short-
order cook and a graduate from a culinary school." So far
he'd filled one position—pastry chef.

Tears filled Deborah's eyes. "What am I going to do?
We're opening in eight weeks."

Rising to his feet, Kumi moved to sit beside her. Dropping
an arm over her shoulder, he cradled her head to his chest.
"I'm going to contact several culinary schools and ask for
their recommendations. A recent graduate would be provided the perfect opportunity to showcase their talent and
training. If you're not fully staffed by the time you open, then
I'll act as executive chef."

Deborah smiled up at her brother through her tears. Large
dark eyes so much like Kumi's crinkled in a smile. "How can
I thank you? I know you're losing millions of francs—"

"Euros," he corrected, interrupting her.

"Okay." She laughed. "Euros. You're still losing tons of
money not working because you're here helping me out. I'm
going to make it up to you, Kumi. I swear I will."

He placed a forefinger over her lips. "No swearing, Debbie." Lowering his head, he removed his finger and brushed
a light kiss on her cheek. "If I was worried about losing
money I never would've agreed to help you and Orrin."

He'd taken a four-month leave from his position as exec-
utive chef at a five-star Parisian hotel to help his sister. He
loved Debbie enough to put his own plans on hold for her.
She'd always been there for him when they were children.
She was the only one who'd protected him from Dr.
Lawrence Walker, who punished her for her insubordina-

tion, but it hadn't seemed to matter to her. She simply spent the time in her room either building dollhouses or reading.

Kumi stared down at Debbie. She'd been a pretty girl, but she was a beautiful woman. She looked just like their mother: petite and delicate with cinnamon-colored skin, large dark eyes and a quick smile. In marrying Orrin Maxwell, she'd rebelled against her parents' wishes. Orrin hadn't been the college graduate their parents hoped she would marry. When Debbie decided to devote herself to her career rather than start a family, she once again shocked her parents.

"When are you going to settle down?" Deborah asked Kumi.

"I have settled down. I have a career and I own a home."

"Not that settling down. When are you going to get married?"

He glanced over her head, his gaze fixed on a massive armoire concealing a television and stereo components. "I don't know, Debbie. Perhaps I'm not cut out for marriage."

"Are you seeing someone?"

He shook his head. "No."

"Don't you ever get lonely? Don't you miss home?"

"I work too many hours to get lonely." Four days of the week he worked at the hotel. On his days off he often catered private parties. "And don't forget that France is my home now."

Her fingertips grazed his smooth-shaven jaw. "Have you ever considered moving back to the States?"

He exhaled audibly. "The first two years I spent in Paris I thought about it a lot. I used to wander the streets all night, while spending my days in museums staring at the same painting for hours. When the money I'd earned in the marines began to run out, I got a job in a restaurant. I waited tables and eventually found myself helping out in the kitchen. I discovered I had a knack for cooking, so I enrolled in a culinary school. The rest is history."

A slight frown furrowed Deborah's smooth forehead. "Why didn't you tell me this in your letters? You always wrote that life in Paris was perfect, and that you were wonderful."

"It was and still is wonderful, Debbie." What he wouldn't say was that anything was wonderful as long as he didn't have to interact with his father. At that time exile was preferable to exclusion.

Removing his arm, he pushed to his feet and extended his hand. She placed her hand in his and he pulled Deborah up in one strong motion. "I'm going out. I'll see you later."

She stared at his broad back under an expertly tailored jacket. "Are you coming back for dinner?"

Smiling at her over his shoulder, he said, "I don't know."

And he didn't know. Right now he felt as jumpy and finicky as a cat. It was a restlessness he hadn't felt in a long time, and he knew it had something to do with Veronica Johnson. They weren't scheduled to see each other again until Sunday, but he did not want to wait another three days.

He was scheduled to interview two more candidates the following day, and he shuddered at the thought. His only confirmed hire was a pastry chef, and he still needed someone to oversee the sautéed items, and one who would be responsible for pasta and accompanying sauces. The B and B was designed to have a full-service kitchen for dinner, which meant it would need at least four assistant chefs.

He walked back to his cottage, his arms swinging loosely at his sides. He was bored out of his skull. If he hadn't been in the States, either he would be working at the hotel's restaurant, catering a private party or relaxing in the courtyard of his modest home in the Luxembourg Quarter. In his spare time he usually prowled the corridors of a museum. And it was on an even rarer occasion that he entertained women in his home.

He covered the distance between the B and B and his cottage in less than fifteen minutes. Unlocking the door, he walked into the parlor, past a tiny kitchen and into his bedroom and changed out of the shirt, tie, jacket and slacks and into a pair of jeans, T-shirt and boots. Returning to the parlor, he picked up the keys to his bike from a table near the front door. Closing the door behind him, he headed for the Harley parked under a carport. Within minutes he was astride the large motorcycle, the wind whipping the shirt on his back as trees, cars and telephone poles became a blur.

His body pulsed with pleasure—a delightful excitement similar to what he'd felt when he'd cradled Veronica Johnson to his chest. He wanted to see her once more before their scheduled Sunday encounter.

Downshifting, he maneuvered up the steep hill to Trace Road. Once at the top he slowed until he came to Veronica's house. The Lexus was parked in the driveway.

She was home!

Four

He came to a complete stop behind her truck, shutting off the engine. The front door stood open, and as he neared the screen door he saw the outline of Veronica's body as she came closer.

His steady gaze bore into her in silent expectation. *Come to me, Veronica. Open the door,* his inner voiced implored. What he didn't want was for her to send him away.

Kumi had registered the expression of surprise freezing Veronica's features before it was replaced by indecision. Had he made a mistake in stopping by without calling her? Had he felt so comfortable with her that he'd assumed that she would open her door and her arms, welcoming him into her home and her life?

Veronica saw him, and a shiver of awareness raced through her body. She'd been thinking about Kumi, and suddenly there he was at her door as if she'd conjured him up.

She felt the heat of his gaze on her face as he watched her intently through the finely woven mesh. She felt the tingling in the pit of stomach, because as she watched Kumi staring at her she saw something so maddeningly arrogant in the man standing at her front door that it rendered her motionless and speechless for several long seconds.

Struggling to maintain her composure, her eyelids fluttered. She'd wanted to see him again, but on her terms. She'd spent most of the morning working in her garden and had just come in to shower and change her clothes when she heard the roar of his Harley.

Here she was standing less than a foot away from him, only a screen door separating them, dressed in a pair of shorts, a revealing tank top and a pair of tattered running shoes.

"Good afternoon, Kumi." Her voice was low, husky, sounding strange even to her ears.

He inclined his head, a half smile tilting the corners of his mobile mouth. "Afternoon, Veronica. I just came by to see if you wanted to go for a ride in the country."

Her gaze narrowed. "On your bike?"

Placing his left hand over his heart, he bowed from the waist, the motion incredibly graceful for a man his height and size. "Yes. I apologize for showing up unannounced, but it would be a shame to waste this beautiful day indoors. Besides, I didn't have your telephone number, so I couldn't call you."

She wanted to tell him that she'd just spent more than two hours working outdoors in her flower garden, but did not want to hurt his feelings. Despite his arrogance, there was something in Kumi Walker's gaze that hinted of vulnerability. It was as if he was waiting for her to reject him. And she wondered if someone he cared for had rejected him, wounding him deeply.

"I'd like to go, but I'm afraid of motorcycles," she admitted honestly.

He lifted a thick black eyebrow. "Have you ever ridden before?"

"No."

"Then how do you know you're afraid?"

"It's too open. I need something around me to make me feel safe, protected."

He stood a step closer—close enough for her to feel his moist breath whisper over her forehead through the barrier of mesh separating them. "I'll protect you, Veronica. I promise I won't let anything happen to you." Her golden gaze widened, and for a long moment she stared at him, giving him the advantage he sought. "Go change your clothes," he ordered softly. "I'll be here waiting for you." The sight of her wearing the revealing attire tested his self-control. Seeing so much of her flesh made him feel as randy as an adolescent boy.

She blinked once. "I don't have a helmet."

"You can use mine."

"What will you use?"

"Nothing."

Veronica shook her head, a silver ponytail swaying gently with the motion. "No. I'm not going if you're not going to wear a helmet. I don't want to be responsible for you cracking your skull if we have an accident."

"I've never had an accident."

"There's always the first time, Mr. Walker."

He glared at her. "Are you using my not wearing a helmet as an excuse not to go?"

"If I didn't want to go, then I'd just come out and say so. Go get another helmet, Kumi Walker, or get lost."

His eyes darkened dangerously as he returned her hostile glare. He knew it was useless to argue with her. If she were afraid for herself, then it probably would go without saying that she'd be afraid for him to ride without protective headgear.

"Okay. But I'll be back."

Veronica watched him as he returned to the motorcycle,

swinging his right leg over the bike in one, smooth motion. Straddling the bike, he placed the shiny black helmet over his head. Raising his chin in a gesture of challenge and defiance, he started up the engine. It took only seconds for him to go from zero to forty as he took off down Trace Road, the roar of the powerful engine fading quickly as man and bike disappeared from view.

Veronica had showered, changed into a pair of jeans, white camp shirt and a pair of low-heeled leather boots by the time Kumi returned with a smaller helmet painted in vivid shades of reds and pinks. He placed the helmet on her head, adjusted the strap and helped her straddle the seat behind him. She curved her arms loosely around his waist.

"Hold me tighter," he said over his shoulder.

She tightened her grip, her breasts pressing against the wide expanse of his back. She wasn't given the opportunity to inhale once he shifted into gear and maneuvered out of the driveway.

Closing her eyes, Veronica pressed her cheek to Kumi's shoulder, certain he could feel the pounding of her heart through the shirt on his back. Her fright and fear eased as he turned off onto a two-lane highway. Five minutes into the ride she felt what he experienced each time he rode his bike—absolute and total freedom.

She was flying, soaring unfettered as the world whizzed by. Suddenly there was only Veronica, Kumi and the steady humming of the powerful machine under their bodies. A rising heat penetrated the layer of cotton covering his upper body; her sensitive nostrils inhaled the natural scent of his skin and that of the sensual cologne that complemented his blatant masculinity. She savored the feel of lean hard muscle under her cheek. There wasn't an ounce of excess flesh on his hard body.

A contented smile curved Kumi's mouth as he peered through the protective shield of his helmet. The soft crush of Veronica's breasts against his back had aroused him. Shifting into higher gear, he increased his speed. Riding with Veronica was like making love. It had begun slowly, tentatively at first, but as the speed accelerated so did his passion.

Veronica Johnson had become the Harley; he'd straddled her, riding faster, harder and deeper. They seemed to leap off the asphalt, the machine eating up the road in voracious gulps. The vibration of the engine had become her body, pulsing faster and faster until he found himself sucked into a vortex of ecstasy from which he never wanted to escape.

Is that how it would be? Would making love to her be slow, methodical, parochial, then wild, frenzied and completely uninhibited?

They'd gone about fifteen miles when he slowed and left the highway, heading up a steep hill to a wooded clearing. It was where he'd learned to ride a motorcycle for the first time; he'd begun racing dirt bikes at twelve, then graduated to motorized bikes before he finally learned to handle the larger, more powerful Harley-Davidson.

He reached the top of the hill and came to a complete stop. Removing his helmet, he stared down at the countryside dotted with trees, houses and narrow, winding streams, breathing deeply. Reaching behind him, he caressed Veronica's arm as she slid off.

Supporting the bike on its stand, he unbuckled her helmet and pulled it gently from her head. Her gleaming hair was pressed against her moist scalp. Anchoring the helmets on the handlebars, he cradled her face between his hands, his fingers curving around the column of her slender neck. He saw a shimmer of excitement in her sun-lit eyes.

Smiling, he asked, "How did you like it?"

"Fantastic." She shrugged a shoulder. "That is once I got over the fright of going so fast."

He tightened his grip along her delicate jawline. "Didn't I tell you that I wouldn't let anything happen to you?"

Her fingers closed around his thick wrists as she sought to pull his hands away from her face. A rising panic wouldn't permit her to breathe. The image of the student seizing her throat, while pressing her against a wall as he fumbled with the zipper to his slacks, came rushing back with vivid clarity, and she panicked.

"No, Kumi. Don't—don't touch me."

He stared at her, baffled as vertical lines appeared between his eyes. "What?"

Closing her eyes against his intense stare, she shook her head. "Please, don't hurt me," she pleaded in a shivery whisper.

Kumi felt as if someone had just doused him with cold water as his hands fell, at the same time his fingers curling into tight fists.

Why would Veronica plead with him not to hurt her? He'd only touched her once before, and that was to dance with her.

He moved closer, this time making certain not to touch her. Leaning down, he whispered close to her ear, "I would never hurt you, Ronnie."

Her breasts trembled above her rib cage, her chest rising and falling heavily under her blouse. She'd made a fool of herself; her greatest fear had surfaced the instant Kumi touched her throat—a chilling, paralyzing fear she'd lived with for more than twenty years, a fear she'd successfully repressed until now.

She wrapped her arms around her body in a protective gesture. Closing her eyes, she shook her head. "It's not you, Kumi."

"Who is it, Veronica?"

She opened her eyes, seeing concern and tenderness in his midnight gaze. Everything that was Kumi Walker communicated itself to her: strong, protective and trusting. But could she trust him? Would she be able to tell him what she hadn't been able to disclose to anyone in two decades? That it had been her fault that she was almost raped?

Tell him, the inner voice whispered, but she ignored it.

"I can't tell you."

He came closer without moving. "Do you think you'll ever be able to tell me?"

Shaking her head, she whispered even though there was no one else around to hear them, "I don't know."

A sad smile touched Kumi's strong mouth. "It's okay, Ronnie."

What he wanted to tell her was that it wasn't okay, not when he wanted to touch her, make love to her. The realization that he wanted to make love to Veronica Johnson had shaken him to the core earlier that morning. It had been years since he'd awakened, hard and throbbing from an erotic dream. The dream had been so vivid that he'd sat up gasping, his body moist and her name on his lips.

And he had yet to discover what had drawn him to Veronica other than her startling natural beauty. She was older than he was, yet he didn't view her as a mother figure. In fact, she was nothing like the other women he'd been attracted to in the past. There was a strength about her that did not lessen her femininity.

He'd found her composed, confident—until now.

"Are you ready to go back?"

Veronica forced a smile she did not feel. She wasn't ready to get back on the bike—not until she was back in control. "Not yet. I'd like to stay and enjoy the scenery."

Kumi nodded, extending his right hand. He watched Veronica staring at his outstretched fingers for a long moment, then trustingly placed her smaller hand in his. He closed his fingers around hers, tightening slightly before he floated down to the grass, gently pulling her down to sit beside him. They sat, shoulders only inches apart, staring out at the picturesque panorama of the Great Smoky Mountains rising in the background. A massive oak tree provided a canopy of natural protection from the fiery rays of the sun.

Pulling his knees to his chest, Kumi wrapped his arms around his denim-covered legs as he replayed the eerie scene they'd just experienced over and over in his head. He could still hear the fear in her voice when she'd pleaded with him not to hurt her. Had he held her that tightly? Had he not known his own strength?

He stood six-two, weighed two hundred and ten pounds and had been trained to bring a man to his knees with a single blow. But each time he'd touched Veronica it had only been in gentleness and protection.

His expression hardened as he considered another possibility. Had she ever been hit by a man, been a victim of domestic violence? And had that man been a boyfriend, or even her late husband?

Why, he wondered, had she waited two years after her husband's death to take up residence in North Carolina? Whom or what in Georgia prompted her to spend the summer in another state? What or whom was she running from?

He'd asked her to tell him of her fear and she had refused. That meant he had to wait—wait for her to feel comfortable or trusted him enough to perhaps open up to him. He wanted and needed her to trust him, because he knew he couldn't continue to see her and not touch her. Not when all of his sleeping and waking moments were filled with the images of her shimmering silver hair, delicately defined feminine face and her temptingly lush body.

He would give himself three months. It was now late

May, and he had secured reservations to return to Paris mid-September. If his relationship with Veronica Johnson remained the same, he would return to Paris—with memories of her and what might have been.

Veronica turned her head slightly, staring at Kumi's profile. His expression was impassive; he was so still he could've been carved out of stone.

A refreshing mountain breeze filtered through the leaves of the tree, cooling her moist face. Her gaze swung back to the valley. The view was magnificent. She wished she'd had a sketch pad. Even though some of her art instructors had labeled her drawings as immature and amateurish, that hadn't stopped her from attempting to capture images on a blank sheet of paper. Pulling her knees to her chest, she executed a pose similar to Kumi's, willing her mind blank.

They sat side by side in silence for more than twenty minutes until Veronica raised her hand, trailing her fingertips over his forearm. Kumi jumped as if she'd burned him and placed his hand over hers, tightening his grip when she attempted to pull away from him.

"I'm ready to go back now."

She was ready and he wasn't. He'd enjoyed sitting with her, her closeness, while marveling in the panorama of the landscape. At no time had he felt the need to initiate conversation. Veronica offered him what he'd sought most of his life—a quiet, healing, calming peace that made him want to stay with her forever.

Releasing her hand, he stared at her, his eyes dark and unfathomable. "Are you certain you're ready?" *Are you ready for me?* his inner voice asked.

Veronica's gaze lingered on the curve of his beautifully shaped mouth. "Yes."

Kumi went completely still. There was something about

his expression that made it impossible for her to look away. Something undeniably magnetic was building between them and binding them together. She felt drugged by his clean and manly scent as he lowered his head.

He came closer and closer; she was unable to move because she did not want to. Shivering despite the heat, she inhaled his moist breath the instant his lips brushed against hers, the touch as soft as a butterfly's gossamer wings.

He kissed her without touching any other part of her body. The warmth of his mouth, the slight pressure of his lips pressing against hers ignited spirals of ecstasy throughout her body. The fingers of her left hand grasped long blades of thick grass, pulling them from their roots. Kumi's kiss sang through her veins, heating her blood.

As quickly as it had begun it was over. Kumi pulled back, leaving her mouth burning with a lingering, smoldering fire. Her eyes were dark, pupils dilated with a rising passion as she stared at the man sitting inches from her.

Kumi smiled once he noted her soft, moist, parted lips. She hadn't kissed him back, but more importantly she hadn't pulled away or panicked, either. He'd risked everything, kissing her when less than half an hour before she'd pleaded with him not to touch her.

"You asked me not to touch you, and I didn't. But you never said I couldn't kiss you."

Veronica studied the lean dark-skinned face, entranced by what she saw. What was it about Kumi Walker that made her feel like a breathless girl of sixteen? She thought him charming *and* arrogant—an arrogance that was compelling and exciting.

"You're right, Kumi." Her voice was soft, seductive. "I never said you couldn't kiss me."

He stared at her and then burst out laughing. Curving an arm around her waist, he stood, pulling her up with him.

He did not drop his arm as he led her back to the bike. Three minutes later the wind tore at their clothes, caressed their moist flesh and sang a nameless song in their ears as man, woman and machine became one.

Five

Images of Kumi and the kiss they'd shared lingered with Veronica over the next two days. She'd given him her telephone number while he had insisted she keep the brightly colored helmet for their next outing. She hung the helmet on a hook in the mudroom at the rear of the house, and each time she saw it she was reminded of his broad back, trim waist and the wildly intoxicating fragrance of sandalwood mingling with his body's natural scent.

She'd established a habit of rising early and slipping outside for a morning walk. By the time she'd walked the length of Trace Road, the sun had risen above the peaks of the mountains, the rays penetrating the haze hovering over the deep gorges and valleys. After showering and a light breakfast of fruit, raisin toast and a cup of decaffeinated coffee, she slipped behind the wheel of her SUV, touring the mountain region and stopping in Cherokee and other small towns in the High Country.

She spent hours in the Museum of the Cherokee Indian,

studying artifacts in the art gallery and the outdoor living exhibit depicting Cherokee life in several eras, returning home with a handmade basket, mask and a wood carving from the Qualla Arts and Crafts Mutual, the cooperative set up across the street from the museum.

The last day she lingered at the Oconaluftee Indian Village, observing demonstrations of traditional skills such as weaving, pottery making, canoe construction and hunting techniques.

The tiny town of Dillsboro was added to her itinerary once she boarded a steam locomotive for a ride on the Great Smoky Mountains Railway, berating herself for not bringing a camera once she realized the open-side cars were ideal for taking pictures of the mountain scenery. She returned home late Saturday afternoon, and unlocked the door to the sound of the ringing telephone. By the time she picked up the receiver, the caller had hung up before the answering machine switched on. Too exhausted to think about who may have been calling, she headed for the staircase leading to her bedroom, showered and lay across her bed completely nude, falling asleep as soon as her head touched the pillow.

Veronica woke up Sunday morning, completely rejuvenated. She'd left the French doors open and crisp mountain air filled the room with the scent of pine and rain. Stretching her bare arms above her head, she stared up at the mosquito netting covering the bed. Bram had hated sleeping with the netting, claiming it had reminded him of a burial shroud.

However, she loved the drapery. It provided the protective cloaking she sought whenever she lay in bed. It made her feel as if she'd retreated to a shadowy fairy-tale world, a make-believe world in which she could sleep and shut out her fear.

Parting the sheer fabric, she swung her legs over the side of the antique bed and headed for the adjoining bathroom. Despite the rain, she would take her walk, then return home to shower and shampoo her hair.

If she'd been in Atlanta she would've worked out at a downtown sports club where she'd been a member for years. However, she found the Trace Road walk a lot more peaceful and invigorating. The solitude provided her with time to think and reflect on what she wanted to do with her life. She hadn't decided whether she would teach again, only because earning a salary wasn't a factor because Bram had left her with enough money to last her well into old age, providing she did not squander it.

She owned the house her late husband had bequeathed her in Buckhead, Atlanta's wealthiest neighborhood, and the three-bedroom, two-and-a-half bath mountain retreat in North Carolina. She'd invested the proceeds from the sale of the gallery in a risk-free mutual fund based upon the recommendation of her family's longtime investment banker.

Even without the money Bram had left her, Veronica Johnson was a wealthy woman. She was old Atlanta, fourth-generation and had grown up in the right neighborhood, earned the right degrees, she had held a prestigious position as an assistant college professor and had married into the right family.

Two priceless Garland Bayless paintings, one she'd purchased and the other a gift from the talented artist, along with a velvet pouch filled with precious baubles she'd inherited from her paternal grandmother lay in an Atlanta bank vault. She'd removed the jewelry and paintings from the Buckhead residence a week before she'd closed the house.

Despite her prestigious pedigree, a few of her more conservative relatives thought her less than proper because she'd expressed a desire to become an artist, had lived with a gay man then married another man, older than her own father. There had been a few occasions when her mother, Irma Johnson, had thrown up her hands saying Veronica was going to be the death of her. Irma had recently celebrated her seventieth birthday and was healthier and more attractive than she'd ever been.

Veronica brushed her teeth, splashed water on her face and slipped into her workout attire. Heavy fog and a falling mist greeted her as she stepped out the back door. She doubted whether the sun would put in an appearance during the daylight hours but that was okay. She hadn't planned any outdoor activities today because Kumi had promised to cook for her.

"I'm coming," Veronica called out seconds after the doorbell echoed through the house, while simultaneously, the clock on the fireplace mantel chimed twelve noon.

Approaching the door, she spied Kumi cradling two plastic crates to his chest, smiling.

After her walk she'd showered, shampooed her hair, blown it out and then curled it in tiny spiral curls that fell in seductive disarray around her face. In deference to the cloudy day, she'd elected to wear a simple linen sheath in a sunny yellow color. On her feet she wore a pair of black ballet-type slippers.

Pushing open and holding the door, she smiled at Kumi. He wore the type of loose-fitting tunic worn by the chefs she'd viewed on the Food Network channel. He'd exchanged his jeans for a pair of sharply creased khakis.

"Please come in."

He hesitated, leaning down to press a kiss to her velvety cheek. "*Bonjour.* I like your hair," he said in French.

Veronica wrinkled her pert nose. "*Merci.*" She peered into the crates, trying to discern what they contained. "What on earth did you bring?" she asked in English.

His eyes crinkled attractively. Not seeing him for two days made him more attractive than she'd remembered. He looked different, and as she stared at him she realized his hair was growing out. It was a glossy black, curling softly over his scalp.

"Lunch and dinner are in one crate, and some of my pots are in the other." He continued to speak French, but slow enough for Veronica to understand.

"Some?"

He stared at her over his shoulder. "The rest are in the trunk of the car."

Veronica stared at his retreating back as he walked in the direction of the kitchen. He returned within minutes, going back to the late-model sedan parked behind her vehicle. He retrieved another plastic crate, shutting the trunk with a solid thunk.

He walked back into the house. "That does it."

She closed the screen door and locked it, then joined Kumi in the kitchen where he'd begun emptying the crates. She stood, stunned, as he set a variety of pots and pans on the countertop. Soon every inch of counter space was taken up with cooking utensils and foodstuffs: a large aluminum bowl was filled with live lobsters, crab, clams and mussels; there was a platter of assorted cheeses; bottles of cooking and drinking wine; champagne; the ingredients for a salad; a container of bright green asparagus; and last but certainly not least a large uncooked duck. Her shock was complete when he turned out a mound of dough sealed in plastic wrap into a large ceramic bowl.

Folding her hands on her hips, she shook her head. "Do you really expect the two of us to eat all of *that*?"

"*Oui, madame.*"

Kumi withdrew two aprons from the last crate, tying one around his waist. He motioned to Veronica. "Come here, and turn around."

She walked over and presented him with her back, suffering his closeness as he looped a strap around her neck, then wrapped the apron around her waist, tying it securely.

Kumi wanted to take her in his arms and kiss her until she pleaded with him to stop. His need to taste the sweetness of her lush mouth again was overwhelming. Resisting the urge to press his mouth to the nape of her neck, he turned and walked into the half bath to wash his hands.

Veronica spent the next two hours exchanging French phrases with Kumi while he washed the clams and mussels, ground dried lavender blossoms, savory thyme, peppercorns and salt together to season the duck before he rolled out dough for two loaves of French bread.

It was only after she saw him wield a knife with rapid precision as he sliced lardoons into tiny pieces before frying them in a skillet for a salad that she realized Kumi Walker couldn't be a waiter or a busboy in a restaurant, he must be a trained chef. Moving the skillet rhythmically up and down, and then back and forth over a flame, he flipped the diced bacon, turning it with a quick flip of his wrist.

He threw Veronica a knowing glance, winking and offering her a wicked grin. "Please check to see if the bread dough has doubled in size."

She rolled her eyes at him. "'I've been out of the country for ten years, and what I've missed most is a home-cooked Southern meal,'" she mumbled, repeating what he'd said to her after he'd fixed her flat.

Blowing her a kiss, he said, "Don't be such a sore loser."

"Why didn't you tell me you were a chef?"

He shrugged a broad shoulder. "You didn't ask."

He was right. She hadn't asked. She'd just assumed he was a waiter. She'd misjudged him, believing he was a cocky young man who was so aware of his virility that he flaunted it like a badge of honor. And riding the Harley had only served to reinforce the macho image.

She was guilty of what so many in Atlanta had done to her—misjudged her when she married Dr. Bramwell Hamlin. But she'd loved Bram—loved him enough to marry him. It had nothing to do with his social standing or his wealth.

After checking on the fragrant-smelling dough under a towel, she returned to the stove. "It's ready."

Curving an arm around Veronica's waist, Kumi pulled her closer, handing her the skillet. "Try flipping it."

She took the pan, attempting to shake and turn the lardoons at the same time and failed.

Standing behind her, Kumi grasped her right wrist. "Loosen your grip on the handle," he said close to her ear. "That's it. Now move the skillet back and forward over the flame while tossing the contents so that they move toward you."

A brilliant smile lit up her golden eyes. "I did it!"

"Yes, you did," he crooned, kissing the side of her neck. She went completely still for several seconds before the tense moment vanished. "When they're golden brown, strain them and then let them drain on some paper towels. We'll warm them up slightly before topping off the salad."

Veronica and Kumi moved comfortably around the large functional kitchen, baking bread and tearing leaves for a salad. He mixed herbs and spices for a dressing, while she unwrapped a square of creamy goat cheese from a layer of cheesecloth. She watched as he dropped two small lobsters, two crabs, half a dozen clams and the same number of mussels into a large pot of boiling water.

It was two-thirty when they sat down at the table in the dining area off the kitchen to enjoy a lunch of freshly baked French bread, a country salad with goat cheese and diced crispy lardoons in a vinaigrette dressing, and the lobster, mussels, crabs and clams in a sauce flavored with wine, butter, garlic and parsley.

Veronica had turned off the overhead recessed lights and the chandelier, lit several votives, turned on a radio on a countertop and enjoyed the exquisitely prepared meal and the man responsible for its creation. The soft sounds of a muted trumpet punctuated the comfortable silence.

She'd suggested Bram buy the North Carolina property so they could come and spend time there and relax from their Atlanta social obligations, but doubted whether she and her late husband had come to the house more than four times since they'd purchased it. What she was sharing with Kumi was what she'd wanted to experience with Bram.

It had taken less than week for Veronica to realize that she was attracted to Kumi. What she would not permit herself to do was fantasize about sleeping with him, even though she wanted to see him—everyday.

Her eyes widened as she stared at her dining partner staring back at her. The flickering light from the votives threw flattering shadows over his dark brown face, accentuating the curve of his strong jaw and chin. Her gaze moved to his mouth, remembering how hers had burned in the aftermath of his brief possession.

Resting an elbow on the table, she cradled her chin in the heel of her left hand. "What made you decide to become a chef?"

His lids came down as he flashed a sensual smile. "I sort of fell into it?"

"How?"

Kumi's expression changed, becoming almost somber. "It's a long story. Are you certain you want to hear it?"

"Of course." She wanted to tell Kumi that she wanted to

know everything about him, hoping she would be able to identify what it was about him that drew her to him.

"I enlisted in the marines and—"

"At what age did you enlist?" she asked, interrupting him.

"Eighteen. This really ticked my parents off because I was scheduled to enter Morehouse that September. My father and I did not get along well, so I saw the marines as an escape."

"Didn't you see leaving North Carolina for Georgia as an escape?"

He shook his head. "No. I still would've been under my father's thumb. And there was no doubt that he would've constantly reminded me that it was his money that kept a roof over my head, clothes on my back and food in my belly. What I did was shift that responsibility from Lawrence Walker to the United States Marine Corps.

"I served four years, then instead of coming back here I went to Europe. I'd planned to spend about three months touring and visiting most European capitals, but something happened to me my first day in Paris."

Leaning forward, Veronica gave him an expectant look. "What happened?" Her voice was a velvety whisper.

His expression brightened as he flashed a warm smile. "I fell in love."

She recoiled as if he'd slapped her. Her breath quickened, her cheeks becoming warm. He had a woman—perhaps a wife. While she wasn't quite lusting after him, what Veronica was beginning to feel for Kumi Walker was quickly approaching that.

"Did you marry her?" she asked, recovering her composure.

"Every Parisian is married to the City of Lights."

She was almost embarrassed at how happy his statement made her. He was talking about Paris, not a woman.

"Once I recovered I realized I needed a job, and because the money I'd saved wasn't going to last more than another month I secured a position working in a restaurant's kitchen. I washed dishes and bused tables before moving up to waiter. One of the chefs befriended me, suggesting I should try cooking. He eventually became my mentor. I attended classes during the day and worked at the restaurant at night." What he didn't tell Veronica was that he'd created several dishes that had won numerous awards.

"How about you, Veronica?" Kumi asked, "What did you feel when you visited Paris for the first time?"

"It took me a week to stop walking around with my mouth gaping. I found it hard to believe everything looked so old yet so incredibly beautiful. The photographs in my art textbooks did not prepare me for the magnificence of Notre Dame or the Jardin des Tuileries. It was if I'd stepped back in time, while at the same time I had every modern convenience at my fingertips."

Kumi took a sip of a dry white wine. "What made you decide to study art?"

The animation left her face. "For as long I could remember I wanted to be an artist. As a child I always had a pad and pencil, drawing everything I saw. My parents were pleased with my artistic talent, but freaked when I told them I wanted to become an artist. They believed a career in law, medicine or education was a more respectable profession, but in the end they supported me.

"My work was good enough for me to be accepted into Parsons School of Art and Design in New York. I'd earned an A in studio drawing and a B in landscape and still-life drawing my freshman year. I knew I'd never be a Picasso, Henry Tanner or Romare Bearden, but I was quite secure with my talent. Everything changed when…"

Her words dropped off; she couldn't continue. It was

halfway through her sophomore year that everything changed—she and her life had changed with a single act attributed to poor judgment.

Kumi saw fear—wild and naked—fill Veronica's eyes. "What happened, Ronnie?" She closed her eyes, shaking her head. Glistening silver curls bounced around her cheeks and over her forehead with the motion.

"I can't," she gasped.

Wiping his mouth with a linen napkin, he pushed back his chair and rounded the table. She gasped a second time. She was sitting, and then without warning she was swept up in Kumi's arms as he cradled her effortlessly to his chest.

"It's all right," he crooned over and over in her ear, walking out of the kitchen and making his way to the patio. "I am not going to hurt you."

Panic rendered Veronica motionless and speechless. She wanted to believe Kumi, but the fear she'd repressed for two decades would not permit her to trust him completely.

Kumi carried Veronica into the comforting space. The overcast day and steadily falling rain cast dusky shadows over all of the furnishings. He sat on a rattan sofa covered in dark-green-and-orange kente-cloth cushions, still cradling her to his chest. The pressure of her hips against his groin failed to arouse him. He wanted to comfort Veronica, not seduce her. He held her, his chest rising and falling in unison with hers. Closing his eyes, he smiled. She'd begun to relax.

Veronica lay in Kumi's arms, absorbing his warmth and strength. She counted the strong steady beats of his heart under her cheek. Inhaling deeply, she breathed in the scent of his aftershave. The sandalwood was the perfect complement for his body's natural scent. Kumi Walker was perfect from his beautiful masculine face, to his perfectly proportioned physique.

Her left arm moved up and curved around his neck the way she'd done to her father when she was a young child. It was a gesture that indicated trust.

Her eyelids fluttered wildly before closing. Could she trust Kumi—trust him enough to tell him of her fear? Tell him that she'd almost been raped and that it had been her own fault?

Swallowing, she drew in a deep breath and said, "I stopped drawing because something happened to me."

Kumi held his breath before he let it out in an audible sigh. Cradling her chin in his hand, he stared down into her wounded gaze. "What happened, Ronnie?"

"I was... Someone tried to rape me."

He blinked once, completely freezing his features. The shock of what she'd disclosed caused the words to wedge in his throat. What was she talking about? His sharp mind recalled her saying that she'd switched her major from drawing to art history. And she hadn't been married when she spent the two summers in Paris living with Garland Bayless. Did someone attempt to rape her before she left for Paris, or had it happened years later?

Lowering his head, he pressed his lips to hers, caressing her mouth more than kissing it. "Tell me about it, sweetheart," he crooned softly.

Six

Veronica opened her mouth and the words came pouring out, words she had never uttered to another human being.

"My college roommate introduced me to this guy, and he eventually became my first serious boyfriend. I was eighteen and he was twenty-two. He was born and raised in New York, so he took me everywhere, showing me places that I never would've visited on my own.

"We talked about what we wanted for our futures—places and things we wanted to see and do together. One weekend he canceled a date, claiming he didn't feel well. Being young, impulsive and very much in love I decided to cook dinner. I wanted to surprise him.

"I was the surprised one, because when he opened the door there was another woman in his apartment with him. He'd tried to explain that she was just a friend, but I didn't want to hear it. He'd thrown on a robe, but his *friend* came out of the bedroom butt naked. Within seconds he wore the robe *and* the dinner.

"I left, tears streaming down my face. I'd trusted him. I'd slept with him because I truly loved him. Not wanting to go back to my apartment and explain everything to my roommate, I decided to go to a bar frequented by students who attended New York University.

"Three drinks later I found myself in a stranger's dorm room with his hands around my throat and my skirt up around my waist." She ignored Kumi's gasp of horror. "I thought he was going to strangle me until he had to release my throat to tear off my panties while he fumbled to pull his pants down. That gave me the advantage I needed. I kneed him in the groan, punched him in an eye and then made my escape. I took a taxi back to my apartment, snuck in quietly so I wouldn't wake my roommate and spent the night in the bathroom.

"The next day my neck was swollen and so bruised that I couldn't talk above a whisper. A colorful scarf concealed the bruises and I told everyone I had laryngitis. Jeff called, but I wouldn't talk to him. He waited for me after class, but I ignored him. After a while he took the hint and left me alone.

"After the attack I discovered I couldn't draw. Something in my head just shut down. That's when I decided to go to Paris—to get away, and to study with Garland. I was desperate to see if I could recapture my muse."

Tilting her chin, she stared up at the man holding her so protectively in his strong embrace. "I'd just turned twenty and I was old enough to know better. It was all my fault. I should've never gone anywhere with a stranger, especially if my reasoning was impaired by alcohol."

"Don't beat up on yourself."

"Who do I blame? Certainly not the student who tried to rape me."

"It wasn't your fault, Veronica. No man has a right to

force a woman to have sex with him if she doesn't want it. I don't care how intoxicated she is."

Her chin quivered as she fought back tears. "He ruined me, Kumi. He ruined me for any man."

Kumi stared at her, baffled. What was she talking about? She hadn't been raped. "How did he ruin you? You're perfect. You're so incredibly beautiful that you take my breath away whenever I look at you."

Her mind refused to register the significance of his words. She wasn't talking about her looks. It was the inside that mattered. What she didn't feel.

"I don't feel anything when a man touches me. Something inside of me died that night."

Kumi struggled with his inner thoughts. "But…" His words trailed off. A pregnant silence ensued, engulfing them. "You married."

She forced a smile when she saw blatant confusion cross his features. "Yes. I did marry. It was a marriage in name only. And before you ask, yes, I did love my husband. If I hadn't I wouldn't have married him."

Kumi's expression darkened with an unreadable emotion. How ironic. It had taken him years to find a woman he wanted in *and* out of bed, and he doubted whether she would ever offer him the intimacy he sought from her.

He knew he had to make a decision—quickly. Would he continue to see Veronica Johnson after today, or would he walk away from her, leaving her to confront her fears—alone?

His eyes moved slowly over her face as lovingly as a caress, seeing what she could not see. She was beautiful and sexy. Sexier than any woman he'd ever met.

Something greater than Jerome Kumi Walker had forced him to ride along that deserted road almost two weeks ago, something that made him stop and help Veronica Johnson. And that something had put the words in his mouth when he'd asked her to cook for him when he knew he could cook for himself. And he also believed and treasured the verse from Ecclesiastes: a time for making love and a time for *not* making love.

He was falling in love with Veronica, and if he did love her then he would have to accept whatever she was able to offer him. At thirty-two he wasn't ready to become a monk, but there were ways a man could relieve himself without benefit of a woman.

Burying his face in her luminous curls, he breathed a kiss on her scalp. "You may believe he ruined you for all of the other men in your life, but actually you were saving yourself for me."

The heavy lashes that shadowed her eyes flew up. "What are you saying?"

"I'm saying that I like you, Veronica Johnson. I want to see you and not just for Sunday dinner."

"No, Kumi. That's not a good idea."

"That's your opinion. I happen to think it's a wonderful idea."

"I don't know what you want from me, but whatever it is I can't give it to you."

His hand moved over her breast, measuring its shape and firmness. "Do I want your body? Yes. I'd be a liar if I said I didn't. But I'd never ask or take from you what you're not willing to give me."

Veronica's body pulsed with new life with his touch, her breast swelling under the fabric of her bra. The sensation was so exquisitely pleasurable she gasped.

"But I'm older than you, Kumi," she whispered.

He smiled, shaking his head. "I thought we settled that last week."

"It's not going to work."

"Why not?"

"I know nothing about you."

"I'm not married, if that's bothering you. I'm neither an absent or deadbeat dad because I don't have any children."

"That's not what's bothering me."

"Then what is it?" When she didn't answer him, he decided to press his assault. "You're the first woman I've met that I can talk to without censoring my thoughts or my words."

Veronica fought the dynamic vitality he exuded and failed miserably. Kumi exhibited a calm and self-confidence men twice his age hadn't acquired. And she'd felt comfortable enough with him that she'd revealed a secret she'd hidden away from everyone—including her sister *and* her parents.

"Why is that, Kumi?"

Tilting his head, he regarded her for a long moment, his near-black eyes peering into her soul. "I believe it's because I'm falling in love with you."

She shook her head. "You don't know me."

"I know what I see and what I like," he said, showing no signs of relenting in his pursuit of her. "Your first lover may have screwed up when you caught him with another woman, but he also screwed up a second time when he didn't get you to forgive him for his indiscretion. You're not going to worry about me screwing up, Veronica Johnson, because there's not going to be another woman."

And there's nothing you can do or say to make me stay away from you, he added silently.

Placing her fingertips over his mouth, Veronica leaned in closer and her mouth replaced her fingers. She kissed him, tentatively at first, then became bolder as she parted her lips, capturing his breath and drinking in his nearness.

Shifting her on his lap, Kumi cradled her face between his large hands. He returned her kiss, resisting the urge to push his tongue into her mouth. What they shared was too new, too frightening to rush.

He wanted to press her down to the cushions, remove her dress and undergarments. The urge to feast on her lush beauty, to run his tongue over her body until she begged him to take her was so strong it frightened him. If ever he claimed her body, he knew he was capable of taking her with all of the gentleness and love she deserved. But he would wait—for another time and when she was ready for him.

Pulling back, he brushed a kiss over her forehead and eyelids, before returning to her moist parted lips.

The kiss ended with both of them breathing heavily. Resting her head on his solid shoulder, Veronica closed her eyes, smiling. She'd believed she was unable to give herself completely to any man. Kumi had proven her wrong. She knew she wasn't ready to take off her clothes and lie with him, because she couldn't forget the ordeal that had happened twenty-two years earlier.

Her unexpected response to the man holding her to his heart was as shocking as the depth of his feelings for her. He was falling in love with her and what he didn't know was that she also was falling in love with him.

The fingers of Kumi's right hand toyed with the buttons of her dress, and one by one he undid the buttons until he bared an expanse of flesh to her waist. She froze as he caressed the silken flesh over her ribs, her breathing quickening.

He eased her onto her back, his hand working its magic, and leaned over her. For a moment he studied her intently, searching for a sign of the fear. A slight smile tilted the corners of his strong mouth.

"Are you all right?"

Veronica's chest rose and fell under the sensual assault on her bare flesh. She nodded rather than speak. His fingers burned her breasts through the sheer fabric of her bra. Her flesh was on fire; she was on fire. It was all she could do not to squirm and writhe under his touch.

Lowering his body, Kumi supported his greater weight on his elbows as he buried his face against the side of her neck, inhaling the distinctive scent that was Veronica's.

"I won't do anything you don't want me to do," he crooned in her ear, when all he wanted was to touch, kiss and taste her.

Veronica felt as if she were standing outside of herself looking on as a spectator. This wasn't happening to her. She'd permitted a man, a stranger she'd known less than two weeks, to touch and kiss her, and she'd kissed him in return.

This stranger had come into her home and into her life to make her feel something she'd thought long dead—desire. She met his gaze. His eyes alone betrayed his ardor. In the raven gaze there was an open invitation she recognized immediately. He was waiting—waiting for her to grant him permission to make love to her.

He pressed closer, her soft curves molding to the contours of his hard body. Her hands slipped up his arms, curling around his strong neck. Closing her eyes, she smiled. "What am I going to do with you?" she whispered.

Kumi laughed deep in his chest. "You can start by permitting me to call on you, Miss Johnson."

Her soft laugher joined his. "You sound so proper, Mr. Walker."

"That's because I was brought up proper," he said truthfully.

It hadn't escaped her notice that Kumi was an absolute gentleman. He always made certain to seat her, and when she stood up, he also rose to his feet. His mother had done a fine job raising him. And if she did agree to go out with him publicly, she knew Kumi would never embarrass her.

Wrapping his arms around her midriff, he held her close—close enough for her to feel the outline of his extraordinary arousal. Her blood warmed and raced through her veins.

Suddenly her body was alive, throbbing with a need that resulted in a gush of wetness between her thighs. She lay panting, her chest heaving as she surrendered to the raw sensations pulsing throughout her lower body.

Kumi watched the play of emotions cross Veronica's face as she breathed through parted lips. He wanted to take her, easing his hardened flesh into her celibate body. But he knew that would not become a reality—not yet. He wanted her to get used to him, the weight of his body. He wanted to be able to touch her and not have her pull away. They had time— at least three full months to get to know each other—in and out of bed.

He reversed their positions, settling her over his chest. "I'm going to keep you prisoner until you grant my wish, princess."

"You are most arrogant, Sir Knight."

"Aye, mistress," he countered, "that I am."

"If I grant your wish, then what can I expect?"

"Grant the wish, princess, and you'll find out."

She punched him softly on the shoulder. "That's not fair, Kumi."

"Yes, it is, because I'm willing to give you all of myself while asking nothing in return." She sobered, a slight frown furrowing her smooth forehead. He brushed a kiss over her lips. "By the time the summer's over you'll know exactly what I mean."

Veronica hummed along with the sultry voice of Lena Horne singing "Stormy Weather." Veronica had left North Carolina at eight, hoping to make it to Atlanta within four hours, because she'd promised her parents she would arrive in time to share lunch with them.

She hadn't planned to return to Atlanta until her family reunion weekend, but the board of the Bramwell Hamlin

Scholarship Foundation had requested she present a check to an impoverished Atlanta high school senior at an awards dinner. The young woman had been accepted into an historically black college's premed program. The check would underwrite the cost of four years of tuition, books and room and board.

The fact that half of Bram's estate had been set aside for the foundation further angered his children. Clinton, the eldest son felt that Veronica had deliberately talked his father into endowing the scholarship fund to cut him out of his rightful inheritance. In a heated discussion with the enraged man, she had quietly reminded Clinton that his father did not owe him one copper penny, and if he'd received anything from the estate then he should've considered it a gift. It was only after the surrogate court had upheld the contents of Bramwell Hamlin's last will and testament that Veronica had become aware of more Hamlin addictions: Clinton's gambling and Norman's drinking. Cordelia seemed to be the only one of Bram's children that was free of the addictive personality of her mother and brothers.

The haunting image of Kumi penetrated her musings. *By the time the summer's over you'll know exactly what I mean.* She would be the last to openly admit it, but she was looking forward to the summer. She wanted to share with Kumi what she should've experienced in her twenties and thirties.

After her Sunday afternoon confessional, she had consented to seeing him. Over the next three days, they'd taken in a movie, and then ate the most delicious chiliburgers in the state at a small roadside café that boasted sawdust floors and loud music blaring from a colorful jukebox. They'd sat in a booth in the back, laughing uncontrollably when she attempted to drink beer from a longneck bottle for the first time in her life, spilling some of the rich brew down her chin. Kumi had moved from sitting opposite her to next to her and surreptitiously used the tip of his tongue to lick the beer from her chin. She'd sat motionless, glorying in the erotic gesture.

She'd ridden home on the back of the Harley, her face pressed against his back, her body tingling from a heightened sexual awareness that had never been there before—not even with her first lover.

She didn't know how, but Jerome Kumi Walker had overwhelmed her with his sexy, compelling personality, leaving her off balance and gasping whenever he touched or kissed her. She'd been able to keep every man at a distance—all except for the motorcycle-riding master chef.

A sensual smile softened her mouth as she thought of how much she'd come to like Kumi. He was even-tempered and generous, and more importantly he was a good listener and very easy to talk to. His above-average intelligence was more than apparent by his fluent French and his vast knowledge of art and architecture. He'd reluctantly admitted he'd been valedictorian of his high school graduating class.

How ironic, she thought, as the skyline of downtown Atlanta came into view. She was scheduled to present a scholarship to a deserving high school graduating senior, a student who planned for a career in medicine, while Kumi, who had been given the opportunity to become a doctor, had deliberately rejected it.

Veronica sat at the lace-covered table on the patio of the home where she'd grown up, enjoying her second glass of iced tea. She had to admit that Irma Johnson brewed the best pitcher of iced, or sweet, as Southerners referred to it, tea in the state.

Smiling, Irma's gold eyes sparkled like citrines. "I must admit you look wonderful, darling." She called everyone darling, and no one took offense because of the way the word rolled off her tongue like watered silk.

She returned her mother's smile. "Thank you, Mother."

Harold Johnson, two years his wife's senior, reached over and patted his daughter's hand. "I have to agree with your mother. You do look wonderful."

Leaning over, she kissed her father's smooth cheek. "Thank you, Daddy."

A tall, spare man, Harold still claimed a head filled with softly curling white hair that contrasted beautifully with a complexion that always reminded Veronica of a sweet potato. Her genes had compromised when she'd inherited her mother's eyes, and body, and her father's hair, coloring and height. Petite, seventy-year-old Irma Wardlaw-Johnson's thick black hair was streaked with only a few silver strands. A former schoolteacher, Irma had met Harold at a fundraiser for the NAACP and had fallen madly in love on sight. Irma's parents had thought widely traveled Harold too urbane for their twenty-two-year old daughter, but reconsidered once they discovered Harold was heir to an insurance company that sold policies to Georgia's Negro populace. Harold and Irma had recently celebrated their forty-eighth wedding anniversary.

"How long do you intend to live in that godforsaken place, darling?"

Veronica rolled her eyes at her mother. "You make it sound as if I live hundreds of miles from civilization."

"You live at the top of a mountain where, if you screamed, your so-called neighbor would never hear you. For heaven's sake, Veronica, you could be dead for a month before someone discovered your body."

"Don't be so melodramatic, Irma." There was obvious censure in Harold's tone.

"Thank you, Daddy," Veronica crooned, winking at Harold.

Veronica did not intend to argue *again* with her mother

about where she'd chosen to live. But then, for as long as she could remember, Irma had always been critical of her lifestyle. It was her mother who had dissented loudly about her becoming an artist and spending the summers in Paris. It was Irma who protested vocally when Veronica had announced her intent to marry Bramwell—a man older than her own father.

She was forty-two, independent and capable of running her life and making her own decisions, despite Irma's objections. She'd been labeled a rebel and a renegade, while her younger sister, Candace, had been the good daughter.

Staring at a pair of eyes that were an exact match for her own, Veronica wondered how Irma would react if she saw her daughter riding on the back of the Harley—or if Veronica invited Kumi to accompany her to their annual family reunion celebration? A mysterious smile lifted her corners of her mouth. Perhaps she would invite him and find out.

Candace Yarborough's expression spoke volumes as she opened the door to Veronica's ring. "You look absolutely fabulous. Why, you're practically glowing." Throwing her arms around her older sister's neck, she kissed her cheek.

Veronica pressed her cheek to Candace's, feeling blissfully happy and wonderfully alive. The awards dinner had been a rousing success. The first recipient of the Bramwell Hamlin Scholarship Foundation award hadn't able to deliver her prepared speech because she hadn't been able to stop sobbing out her joy. The emotional moment had most in attendance crying, as well—Veronica included.

Candace pulled her into the entryway. "Come in and make yourself comfortable."

Following her sister into an expansive living room, Veronica said, "Where are the boys?" She'd been in Atlanta for two days, but had yet to reconnect with her brother-in-law and her nephews.

"They went with Ivan to see his mother. She's not doing too well after her hip-replacement surgery, because she refuses to listen to her orthopedist. I keep reminding Ivan that his sons are as hardheaded as his mother." Glancing at her watch, Candace, said, "They should return sometime around eleven."

Sitting down on an off-white silk club chair, Veronica silently admired the furnishings in the Yarborough living room. Candace had employed the services of a professional interior decorator to make her home a magazine layout designer showplace.

"How did Bobby and Will do on their final exams?"

Candace ran a manicured hand through her short coiffed hair. "They aced them. I initially had my doubts about them being homeschooled, but after seeing their grades this year I'm glad I decided to go through with it."

Veronica studied Candace's round face. She claimed a pair of large, dark eyes, bright smile and a flawless golden complexion; she saw the serenity that had become so apparent in her sister's life. Candace had taken one look at Ivan Yarborough, declared herself in love and embarked on a relentless crusade to become his wife and the mother of his children. She'd loved teaching school, but loved being a wife and mother more. She homeschooled her children and the family traveled together whenever Ivan spent more than three weeks away from home. Candace was determined not to raise her sons alone because of an absentee father.

"Do you want anything?"

Veronica waved her hand. "No, thank you." She'd eaten at the awards dinner.

"Are you sure?"

"Yes, I'm sure."

"When are you going back to North Carolina?"

"Tomorrow."

"What time tomorrow?"

Veronica paused for several seconds. "Probably around noon. Why?"

"Come shopping with me. I need to replenish my lingerie."

"Where do you want to go?"

"To your favorite boutique in Buckhead. I love their selections."

"You or Ivan?"

A rush of color suffused Candace's golden skin. "Well, I do get to model them before he undresses me."

"Be careful, little sis, before you make me an aunt for a third time."

"Bite your tongue, Veronica. At thirty-eight I'm through making babies. It's your turn."

"Bite your tongue back. At forty-two I'm much too old to think about having a baby."

Candace lifted her eyebrows, shaking her head. "Not! Remember Helene had her first one last year, and she was older than you."

"Didn't Andy James say that his son was born with a gray beard?"

"Andy was drunk as skunk for a week after celebrating his son's birth, so he could've said anything. You need to find a man, get married, settle down and have at least one baby."

"What if I have a baby without getting married?" Veronica teased. She'd given up all hope of ever having a child. At first it had bothered her when her sister and girls she'd grown up with had married and became mothers. But after a while she conceded herself that she was still a woman even if she never bore a child.

Candace groaned. "Don't let Mother hear you say that. It would kill her if her daughter was to become an unwed mother."

"I wouldn't be an unwed mother—I'd be a single mother."

"Is there a difference?"

"Big difference, Candace. What if I'd had a child with Bram? I wouldn't be an unwed mother, but a widow and a single mother."

Candace gave her a skeptical look before changing the subject.

The two sisters talked for hours, stopping only when Ivan called Candace to inform her he and their sons had planned to spend the night in Athens and would return the following morning. Veronica left minutes after midnight, promising to meet Candace at the mall in downtown Atlanta at ten that morning.

Seven

The afternoon sun had shifted, sending pinpoints of gold through the leaves of trees flanking Trace Road. The cargo area of Veronica's truck was crowded with shopping bags from several of the boutiques she and Candace had visited. Much to her surprise she'd purchased quite a few sheer and lace-trimmed undergarments. On a dare from her sister, she had bought a lacy black thong panty and matching bra. She would wear the bra, but doubted whether she'd ever wear the thong. The cooler mountain air flowing through the vents of the Lexus was refreshing, unlike the humidity smothering Atlanta like a weighted blanket.

She pulled into the driveway to her home, smiling. Shutting off the engine, she left the SUV, retrieving the shopping bags from the rear; a minute later she unlocked the front door. She'd been away for three days, and it felt good to be back.

Walking up the staircase to her bedroom, she dropped her purchases on a chair in her sitting room, checked the messages on the telephone on the bedside table, listening while undressing.

She raised an eyebrow when Kumi's voice came through the speaker, greeting her in French and telling her that he'd enjoyed spending time with her. The next message was also from him. In this one he confessed to missing her, hoping she would return his call. He left a number. The third and final message stunned her with his intensity. "I miss you, Veronica. Please call me when you get this message." Then there was a pause before he spoke again. "I love you."

Sinking to the bed, clad only in her bra and panties, she stared at the French doors. Each time she saw Kumi, her feelings for him intensified. She was totally entranced whenever he was near and she ached for the protectiveness of his strong embrace. Her eyelids fluttered wildly as she reached for the telephone.

Kumi paced the floor in the small cottage like a caged cat. His initial reunion with his father hadn't gone well. While his mother clung to him weeping inconsolably, his father had stood off to the side glaring. He'd acknowledged Dr. Lawrence Walker's presence with a nod, and then walked out.

He had expected the reunion to be strained, but thought his father would have at least said something—even if he were to just yell at him, proving that his relationship with his father would never change, not even after a fourteen-year separation. Kumi had ridden back to his cabin saddened, tears not for himself but for his mother, because she'd always ended each of her letters to him with a prayer of reconciliation for him and his father. It was apparent that all of her prayers were in vain.

He stopped pacing long enough for his thoughts to stray to Veronica. He hadn't seen her in three days, although he'd left several messages on her answering machine for her to call him. When she hadn't his frustration level had gone off the chart. After the third message he thought perhaps she had taken ill or injured herself and he had ridden over to her house. When he didn't see her truck he knew she had gone away.

He refused to believe that she'd returned to Atlanta. She'd said she planned to spend the summer in North Carolina. He could handle any disappointment—his father's alienation and his mother's tears as long as he had Veronica in his life.

When, he mused, had he become so dependent on her? What was there about her that sent his emotions into overdrive? Why had he fallen in love with her and not some other woman in his past?

The phone on a table in the parlor chimed softly. Turing slowly, he stared at it as if it were a foreign object as it rang again. It rang a third time and he was galvanized into action. Taking three long strides, he picked up the receiver.

"Hello."

"*Bonjour,* Kumi."

His smile matched the warm glow flowing through his body. "How are you, darling?"

"A little tired, but glad to be home. If you're not busy tomorrow evening I'd like to take you out to dinner. My treat."

"I can't."

"You can't what?"

"I can't permit you to pay."

"Why not? Every time we go out you pay for everything."

"I'm an old-fashioned Southern guy—"

"You're more French than Southern and you know it," Veronica said, interrupting him.

"I'm French on the outside and Southern inside."

She laughed softly. "What if we compromise?"

"What are you proposing?"

"We split the check."

"I'm only agreeing because I want to see you," Kumi admitted softly. "What time is dinner?"

"Be here at around five-thirty."

"I'll see you then."

Kumi ended the call, exhaling a long sigh of contentment. It would be less than twenty-four hours before he saw Veronica again.

A threat of rain persisted throughout the next day with dark clouds and an intermittent roll of thunder. Veronica had made dinner reservations at Gabrielle's. The restaurant, with its beautiful Victorian dining room, offered Southern dishes that were transformed into classic entrées without losing their roots. The highlight of dining at Gabrielle's was a splendid view of Asheville from the restaurant's wraparound porch.

She'd spent the day putting up several loads of laundry, dusting and weeding and pruning her flower garden. Now she looked forward to relaxing and spending time with Kumi. She smiled when she thought of the man who'd put the glow back in her cheeks and her eyes. He'd become her friend and confidant—someone she'd confided her most closely guarded secret. There was so much about him she liked—so much she could love if only he'd been older. She still had to convince herself the ten-year difference in their ages wasn't an issue.

When, she thought, had she become so insular and narrow-minded? Had she become like the very people she'd left Atlanta to avoid? Could she open her mind and her heart to accept whatever life was offering her? A knowing smile softened her delicate features.

Yes, her heart sang.

"Yes, I can," she whispered softly.

The doorbell rang and she left her bedroom, made her way down the winding staircase and crossed the living room to the front door. A bright smile tilted her eyes at the corners when she opened to the door to find Kumi staring at her as if she were a stranger. Her penetrating gaze lingered on his impassive expression.

Unlatching the screen door, she pushed it open. "Come in."

Kumi stepped into the living room, his gaze fixed on Veronica's face. She looked beautiful, but fragile and untouchable.

Moving closer, he curved an arm around her waist, pulling her up close. His free hand cradled her chin, raising her face to his. "I missed you like crazy," he whispered seconds before he claimed her mouth with an explosive kiss that sucked the breath from her lungs.

He kissed her with the passion of a predator tearing into its prey, holding her in a strong grip that brooked no resistance. The uneasiness and frustration that had welled up in Kumi overflowed as he staked his claim. He'd confessed to Veronica that he loved her—that was something he'd never told another woman. And his confession made him vulnerable to a pain that was certain to surpass his alienation from his family and country.

Veronica opened her mouth to accept everything Kumi offered. Pleasure, pure and shocking, radiated from her mouth to every nerve in her body as she was transported to a place where she'd never been before. Her senses reeled as if short-circuited. The blood pounding in her head rushed to her heart, and then down to the lower part of her body, pooling in the sensitive area between her thighs. Her trembling knees buckled, and she slumped weakly against Kumi's solid chest. He'd aroused her to heights of desire that threatened to incinerate her with its hottest flame.

Winding her arms around his waist under his jacket, her fingertips bit into the muscles in his back through the crisp fabric of his laundered shirt. Tasting him, inhaling his distinctive male scent nearly sent her over the edge.

Kumi's ravishing mouth moved from her lips to the side of her neck, his chest rising and falling heavily. "Don't ever do that to me again," he groaned close to her ear.

Veronica went completely still, her heart pumping wildly under her breasts. "Do what?" she gasped.

Kumi's large hands slipped down her spine and cradled her hips. "Go away without telling me."

The scalding blood in her veins suddenly ran ice-cold. His words and coolly disapproving tone slapped at her while her delicate nostrils flared.

"I didn't know I was obligated to apprise you of my every move."

Easing back, he glared at her. "You're not obligated to me, but out of common courtesy you could've at least let me know you weren't going to be home." He'd made a fool of himself calling and leaving three messages on her answering machine.

The tenuous rein she had on her temper snapped and she jerked out of his embrace. "There's one thing you should know about me, Jerome Walker. I'm my own woman and I don't answer to or check in with anyone—especially *a man.*"

He winced when she called him Jerome. He'd grown up with everyone calling him Kumi—everyone except his parents. His father had attended college with a young African student who'd become his roommate and a lifelong friend. The two men had promised each other that if they ever fathered a son they would name him after the other. Years later, Lawrence kept his promise. However, it had been five-year-old Deborah Walker who had begun calling her parents' last-born Kumi, which meant *strong* in Ghana, and the name stuck.

Taking a deep breath, he forced a smile he didn't feel. "I don't want to monitor your whereabouts, Ronnie. I just want more involvement in your life."

She waved a hand. "How much more involved do you want to be? We eat together practically every day."

"I'm not talking about sharing a meal. I want to take you out. I don't like hiding out here."

"We go out," she countered hotly.

"Where, Veronica? We ride my bike," he said, answering his own question. "We've gone to one movie, then ate at a place situated so deep in the woods that even the regulars have a problem finding it in the dark."

His accusing tone stabbed her. Why was he making her the bad guy? "I didn't come to North Carolina to become involved with a man," she countered, "especially not one as young as you."

Reaching out, he caught her shoulders, pulling her to his chest. "You're back to that, aren't you? You're beginning to sound like a broken record. You're not old enough to be my mother, so I suggest you drop what has become a lame, tired-ass excuse about my being too young for you."

Rage rendered her speechless until the silence looming between them became unbearable. Veronica felt her body trembling—not from fear but a rising fury.

"Take your hands off me." Her eyes narrowed. "And I think you'd better leave before I say something I might regret later." She was surprised she sounded so calm when all she wanted to do was scream at him.

Kumi's hands fell away and he moved past her, taking long, determined strides to the door. Veronica did not turn around until she heard the soft click of the screen door closing, and then the sound of a car starting up. After he'd driven away she turned around, her golden eyes shimmering with unshed moisture.

He'd ruined it. She was ready for Kumi, ready to sleep with him, and ready for whatever they would offer each other and he'd sabotaged everything with his display of wanting to control her life. She'd believed he was mature enough to have an affair without becoming obsessive.

Turning on her heels, she headed for the staircase. Ten minutes later, dressed in jeans and a pair of running shoes, she walked out of the house and headed for the narrow path leading into a wooded area several hundred feet away. She had to think and she always thought best when she walked.

Kumi lay across his bed, in the dark, listening to the steady beats of his own heart resounding in his ears. A warning voice had whispered in his head that he was going to lose Veronica even before he claimed her—all of her. He hadn't realized what he'd said to her until after the words slipped past his lips—words he could not retract.

"I can't lose her," he whispered. Not because of a few carelessly uttered words. Sitting up, he turned on a bedside lamp, and then swung his legs over the side of the bed. He hadn't stood up to his father—to demand his respect. He'd taken the easy way out and run away, and he'd been running for fourteen years.

Pulling on a pair of jeans, a pullover cotton sweater and boots, he made his way out of the small bedroom, through the parlor and out into a lightly falling mist. Opening the door to the Camry parked under the carport, he slipped behind the wheel, turned the key in the ignition and switched on the headlights.

His expression was a mask of stone as he concentrated on navigating the dark winding road. He did not intend to give Veronica Johnson up without a fight. A muscle throbbed spasmodically in his jaw as he maneuvered up the hill to Trace Road. The half-dozen structures along the stretch of paved road were ablaze with light.

He hadn't realized how fast his heart was beating until he turned into the driveway behind Veronica's vehicle. Inhaling deeply, he cut off the engine, pushed open the door and placed a booted foot on the wet driveway. Golden light from table lamps illuminated the first floor, beckoning him closer as he made his way to the open door.

He peered through the screen at the same time he rang the bell. The melodious chiming echoed throughout the house. Waiting a full sixty seconds, he rang the bell again before trying the doorknob. It opened to his touch. She hadn't locked it.

"Veronica," he called out, stepping into the living room. He called her again as he walked through the living/dining room, into the kitchen and to the patio.

He searched the downstairs, not finding her, then headed for the staircase. "Ronnie!" His voice bounced off the walls in the hallway as he rushed in and out of bedrooms. A rising panic enveloped him; he couldn't find her. A wave of hysteria paralyzed him until he heard the familiar voice behind him.

"What are you doing here?"

Turning, he breathed out an audible sigh of relief when he saw Veronica standing less than five feet away from him; she was safe. She stood motionless, moisture dotting her velvety skin. Her silk blouse was pasted to her chest, offering him an erotic display of large dark nipples showing through a sheer bra.

Veronica stared at Kumi, light smoldering in her gold-flecked eyes as she battled the dynamic vitality he exuded. She'd fought her emotions and lost miserably. Since meeting Kumi, she had made up so many excuses, spoken and unspoken, as to why she should not permit herself to become involved with him that she was even tired of them herself.

And the reason was always the same: his age.

Why was she so fixated on his being ten years younger when she'd married a man thirty years her senior? She knew the answer as it formed in her mind. It was because she wanted to shield Kumi from what she'd experienced with Bramwell: the sly looks, whispers, alienation and the blatant references to her husband being her father. All she wanted to do was protect Kumi—she loved him that much.

A small smile of enchantment touched her lips. She loved him; that much she could admit to herself, and it was only a matter of time before she would reveal to Kumi what lay in her heart.

Kumi saw her smile, taking it as a clue that her former hostility had faded. Taking two long strides, he pulled her to his chest, burying his face in her wet hair. She smelled like a clean spring rain shower.

"Kumi?" Veronica's face was pressed against his shoulder, her arms hanging stiffly at her sides.

"Yes, sweetheart."

"Why did you come back?"

He tightened his grip on her waist. "I'm surprised you're asking that question."

The heat from Kumi's body seeped into Veronica's, warming her. She'd walked too far from the house and couldn't get back before the heavens opened, soaking her and the earth with its life-giving moisture.

"I have to ask, because I need to know."

"I came back to apologize for saying what I said." He pressed a kiss along the column of her neck. "I don't want to fight with you. Please, Ronnie, don't send me away again."

"Why shouldn't I send you away?"

"Because I love you, Veronica Johnson. I love you more than life itself."

Wrapping her arms around his slim waist, Veronica moved closer. He loved her and she loved him. Loved him despite his age and his arrogance.

Easing back, she tilted her chin, meeting his tender gaze. She could no longer deny herself his presence or his touch.

The fingers of her right hand traced the outline of his mouth. "I'm not going to send you away—at least not tonight."

Dipping his head, he brushed a kiss over her parted lips. "If that's the case, then I want to spend the night and wake up with you next to me in the morning." He wanted to tell her of the dreams that kept him from a restful night's sleep. Increasing the pressure, he deepened the kiss, his tongue parting her lips. "May I stay the night, Ronnie?"

His kiss left her weak, pulling her into a slow, drugging intimacy. Her tongue met his, testing the texture before she pulled it into her mouth, making him her willing prisoner.

Veronica kissed him back with a series of slow, shivery kisses that left his mouth burning with fire—a blaze that matched the inferno raging out of control in his groin.

Kumi groaned aloud when her fingers searched under his sweater and found his straight spine. She was touching him, but he wanted to touch her.

"Yes, Kumi," she moaned against his searching, plundering mouth. "You can stay the night."

Raising his head, he stared at her. His eyes appeared larger, near black in the diffused light in the hallway lit by wall sconces outside each bedroom. Bending slightly, he swept her up in his arms, her arms curving around his neck.

"*Merci, ma chérie.*"

Veronica rested her cheek on his shoulder, closing her eyes. There was something else she had to tell Kumi before what they shared could be taken to another level.

She opened her eyes, staring up at him. "You're right about my not being old enough to be your mother. You being ten years younger than I is really not an issue."

A slight frown furrowed his forehead as he shifted her weight. "Then what is?"

"My late husband was thirty years my senior, and there were people in Atlanta who reminded us of that in every subtle way imaginable—especially his children.

"They were vicious, Kumi, and if I hadn't been so in love with Bram I would've divorced him to spare him the insults and humiliation. I've been called everything from a hooker to high-price whore.

"I want to invite you to my family reunion in early August, but I shudder to think of the reaction from those—"

"Don't worry so much, Ronnie," he said, interrupting her. "Words are harmless."

Closing her eyes, she shook her head. "Not when you're on the receiving end," she countered. Pressing her nose to his sweater, she sneezed softly.

"We'll talk later after I get you out of these wet clothes."

She nodded. "You can put me down now."

He ignored her request, asking, "Which one is your bedroom?"

"It's the one on the left."

It took less than half a dozen steps before Kumi found himself standing in the middle of the bedroom with a four-poster mahogany bed covered with a sheer creamy drapery. His gaze swept around the space, cataloging a massive armoire carved with decorative shapes of leaves, vines and pineapples, and a matching triple dresser and rocker boasting the same design. Diaphanous sheers, flanking a double set of French doors, matched the filmy drapery falling sensuously around the bed. Soft light from a table lamp in a sitting room cast soft golden shadows throughout the large space.

He carried Veronica over to the bed, wondering if this was where she'd slept with her husband. Parting the sheer fabric, he placed her in the middle of the bed, his body following. He stared at the serene look on her face. There was no doubt she was as ready for him as he was for her.

Leaning closer, he buried his face against the side of her slender neck. "I'm not going to do anything to you you don't want me to do. If at any time you want me to stop, just say so."

Turning her head, she gave him a bold direct stare. "Will you be able to stop?"

He returned her penetrating look, nodding slowly. "With you I will."

And he could. He loved her too much not to adhere to her wishes. She'd carried pain too long for him to compound it because of his own need to pour out his passions inside her fragrant body.

Raising her arms, Veronica circled his neck, pulling his head down. Then she kissed him, offering all of herself—holding nothing back. She kissed him with a hunger that belied her outward calm. Her tongue slipped between his parted lips, tasting, testing and savoring the flavor and texture of his mouth.

Kumi kissed her, his slow, drugging kisses masking the explosive fire roaring unchecked through his body. There was something about Veronica that wanted him to forego a lingering foreplay. He hadn't known her long, but it felt as if he'd been waiting for her for years—for all of his life.

His lips continued to explore her soft, lush mouth, as his fingers were busy undoing the buttons on her blouse. The silken garment parted and he pulled back to stare at her heaving chest. A groan escaped him when he feasted on the fullness of a pair of golden breasts tipped with large nut-brown nipples clearly outlined under a sheer white bra.

The image of a child suckling from her ripe breasts—his child—flashed through his mind and he froze. Did he love Veronica enough to offer marriage? Did he love her enough to hope she would ever bear his child?

Yes, the inner voice whispered to him. He wanted Veronica as his wife and the mother of his children, but he would wait to ask her, wait until she'd come to love him as much as he loved her.

Sliding his palms under her back, he released the hook on her bra, eased the thin straps off her shoulders and then slid it off. He stared at her for a full minute before closing his eyes to conceal the lust in his gaze.

"You are perfect," he murmured in French.

Veronica lay motionless, watching the gamut of emotions cross her soon-to-be-lover's face as he continued to slowly undress her. Desire pulsed her veins like a slow-moving stream of burning lava incinerating everything in its wake.

It was her turn to close her eyes when he removed her blouse, jeans and shoes. Only her panties remained—a thin barrier concealing her femininity from his gaze and his possession. She opened her eyes and stared at him as he left the bed to undress. Watching intently, she admired the muscles in his long, ropy arms as he pulled the cotton sweater over his head.

Her mouth went suddenly dry when he bent over to remove his boots. Turning his back, he unsnapped his jeans, pushing them down over his firm hips. She breathed audibly through parted lips as he removed his briefs. He paused, retrieving the small packet of protection from a pocket of his jeans and slipping it on his redundant erection, and then turned to face her. The shadowy light from the lamp in the sitting area silhouetted his tall muscular body. Her gaze slipped down the broad expanse of chest covered with a fine layer of dark hair, flat, hard belly and then even lower to the rigid flesh jutting majestically between powerful thighs.

Eight

Veronica gasped as his blood-engorged arousal brushed her inner thigh. Instinctively, her body arched toward him, she caressing the length of his spine, and her fingernails raising goose bumps along his flesh.

Kumi's tongue explored the skin on her neck and shoulders, moving down to stake his claim on her entire body. His mouth covered the peaks of her breasts, teeth tightening on the turgid nipples. He didn't just love her—he worshiped her, ignoring her soft moans, as he tasted the taut flesh over her flat belly. Her moans escalated to gasps when he eased her panties down her hips and legs, tossing them aside.

Sitting back on his heels, Kumi surveyed the exquisite perfection of the woman with whom he'd fallen in love. He was glad he'd waited for her, because he couldn't remember the last time he'd slept with a woman.

Sinking back down to the mattress, he rested his cheek on her belly, brushing tender kisses over the velvety flesh. Moving lower, he left a trail of moisture before he buried his face between her thighs. His hot breath seared the tangled curls concealing the warm moistness of her femininity.

Veronica wasn't given the opportunity to react when she felt Kumi's tongue lathe her dormant flesh. Her body bucked as his teeth found and gently worried the swollen nodule hidden in the folds at the apex of her thighs. She writhed in exquisite ecstasy, her chest heaving from a sensual assault that made it difficult for her to draw a normal breath.

"Kumi, Kumi, Kumi..."

His voice became a litany as she felt herself drowning—drowning in a flood tide of sweetest agony that threatened to shatter her into thousands of particles of sexual bliss.

Passion pounded, whirling the blood through her heart, chest and head until she was mindless with desire for a man she hadn't planned to love.

Shock after shock slapped at her when Kumi's finger replaced his tongue once he moved up her body. His mouth swooped down over hers, permitting her to taste herself on his lips.

His hand worked its magic as he gently eased a second finger into her, moving them in and out of her tender celibate flesh in a quickening motion that matched the movement of her hips, a pulsing growing stronger with each stroke. Waves of ecstasy throbbed through Veronica and she swallowed back cries of release. She did not want it to end—not now—not when she'd waited twenty years to rediscover a passion she thought was beyond her.

Kumi felt the tight walls pulse around his fingers, and without warning he withdrew his hand and positioned his rigid flesh at the entrance to her feminine sex. Guiding his maleness with one hand, he pushed slowly, registering Veronica's gasps against his ear.

"I'll try not to hurt you," he whispered softly, gentling her, while he gritted his teeth against the passion threatening to erupt before he entered her tight body. "Relax, baby, relax," he crooned over and over as each inch of his blood-engorged flesh disappeared into the throbbing folds squeezing him like a hand in a glove a size too small.

Veronica felt Kumi's hardness fill every inch of her body, reviving her passion all over again. He pushed gently, in and out, setting a strong thrusting rhythm she followed easily. She rose to meet his thrusts, her hips moving of their own accord, their bodies in perfect harmony with one another.

Her fingernails bit into the tight flesh over his hips as she once again felt the escalating throbbing searching and seeking a means of escape. She and Kumi had become man and woman, flesh against flesh. He'd become her lover and she his, and together they found the tempo that bound their bodies together.

If possible, Kumi felt his flesh swell and become harder, as he tried to absorb Veronica into himself. Her eager response matched his, while his hunger for her intensified. He wanted to lie in her scented embrace forever; lie between her thighs for a lifetime. He wanted her more than he'd ever wanted any woman he'd ever known.

Heat rippled under his skin, settling at the base of his spine. He knew it wasn't long before it would be over. It would take less than a minute for him to spill his passions into the latex sheath protecting the woman he loved from an unplanned pregnancy.

He withdrew from her, but seconds later he anchored her legs over his shoulders. He reentered her with a strong thrust, his gaze fixed on her glistening face. The memory of her expression would be branded in his mind for an eternity as he memorized the curve of her lush parted lips, fluttering eyelids and trembling breasts, as she was aroused to a peak of desire that swept away the fear that had haunted her for two decades.

Kumi quickened his cadence and within seconds he, too, closed his eyes, lowered his head and groaned deeply in his throat as the hot tide of passion swept through him, leaving an awesome, powerful and pulsing climax that radiated from his core.

He did not know where he found the strength, but he withdrew from her body and collapsed, facedown, beside her. Draping an arm over her belly, he kissed the side of her neck.

Veronica flashed a sated smile, but didn't open her eyes. "Kumi?" He moaned softly in response. "I love you." Her voice was soft, the admission reverent.

Raising his head, he stared at her profile. In a motion too quick to follow, he pulled her over his chest, her legs resting between his. Burying his nose in her hair, he kissed her scalp.

"Thank you, my darling."

They lay together, savoring the aftermath of their lovemaking and a love that filled both with a gentle peace that promised forever.

Veronica eased out Kumi's loose grip on her body, slipping out of the bed. His soft snoring faltered, and then started up again. Grimacing, she made her way to the bathroom. She ached where she hadn't realized she had muscles.

Turning on a light in the bathroom, she closed the door softly behind her. Walking over to a black marble Jacuzzi, she pressed a dial, then brushed her teeth and rinsed her mouth before stepping into the warm swirling waters.

She lounged in the tub, the water caressing her tender flesh and unused muscles. Closing her eyes, Veronica smiled. Making love with Kumi had been an incredible experience. She thought she was going to faint when he'd put his face between her thighs.

"Would you mind if I come in and share your bath?"

Her eyes opened quickly. Kumi stood several feet away resplendently naked and magnificently male. He had the body of an ancient god sculpted by artisans in centuries past. She flashed a shy smile, sinking lower in the water to conceal her breasts.

"You're going to smell like me."

Moving closer to the oversize Jacuzzi, he stared at her, noticing the evidence of his lovemaking on her throat and along the tops of her breasts. "I already smell like you. The scent of your perfume is on my skin and the taste of you is in my mouth."

Veronica couldn't stop the wave of heat in her face as she glanced away demurely. "There're toothbrushes in the top right drawer of the dressing table."

Kumi smiled at her display of modesty. He had to remember Veronica hadn't shared her body with a man for twenty years despite the fact that she'd been married—a marriage that had been in name only.

Turning, he made his way to the dressing table and opened a drawer filled with an ample supply of toothbrushes and disposable razors. He brushed his teeth before joining Veronica in the warm water.

The black marble tub was large enough to accommodate four adults. The bathroom's ebony-and-platinum color scheme was modern and sophisticated.

Resting his arms along a ledge surrounding the Jacuzzi, he gave Veronica a penetrating stare. "Did I hurt you?"

She shook her head, limp strands of hair moving with the slight motion. "No."

The recessed ceiling lights slanted over her face, highlighting the gold in her skin and eyes. Kumi floated over to her, stood up and watched her face for a change in expression. He wanted to make love to her again; now that he'd had her he didn't think there would ever be a time when he wouldn't want to make love to her; he was certain he would want her even when he was old and gray.

Cradling her face between his palms, he eased her to her feet and pressed a kiss over each eye. "You are so incredibly beautiful, Ronnie. Beautiful and sexy."

Rising on tiptoe, she wound her smooth legs through his hair-roughened ones, making him her willing prisoner. Holding tightly to his neck, she kissed him tentatively as if sipping a cool drink.

"You make me feel sexy," she murmured, inhaling his mint-scented breath.

"No, baby, I have nothing to do with that. You *are* sexy."

His right hand moved down and cradled a breast, his head following. She gasped loudly when he took the nipple into his mouth and suckled her until she felt the pull in her womb.

She managed to free herself from his rapacious mouth, her body splayed over his. Both were breathing heavily. Waiting until her pulse slowed, she moved sinuously down his chest, her tongue sweeping over his breasts and suckling him as he had her. She moved even lower, her nose pressed against his thigh; then she registered his labored breathing as she took him into her mouth, his flaccid flesh hardening quickly.

"No, Ronnie!" His voice bounced off the walls, but it was too late. Her magical tongue caressed the length, tip and the root of him like someone savoring an exquisite dessert.

His hands curled into tight fists as he resisted the urge to explode in her mouth. The muscles bulged in his neck, shoulders and biceps. He embarrassed himself with the moans of ecstasy escaping his compressed lips. Electric shocks shook him until he convulsed uncontrollably.

His right hand moved down, his fingers entwined in her

hair, easing her head up as he spilled his seed into the swirling waters. His fingers loosened and she stood up, curled against his body, smiling.

"Now we're even," she whispered, "because the taste of you is in my mouth."

Curving a hand under her chin, he lowered his head and kissed her tenderly, his tongue meeting hers. He tasted himself on her lips, loving her even more for her selflessness.

Lifting her from the Jacuzzi, he carried her to the shower stall and together they frolicked under the flowing water like little children until it cooled and their fingers and toes wrinkled like raisins.

Half an hour later, Veronica, wrapped in a silky red robe, sat on a stool in the kitchen, watching Kumi prepare baked chicken breasts with mustard, tarragon, carrots and leeks over a serving of boiled egg noodles with an accompanying salad made with field greens.

They ate on the patio, listening to the latest Enya CD with the flowing waters of the indoor waterfall providing the perfect backdrop to the soothing selections.

Both were content to listen to the music and enjoy the comfortable solitude. What had occurred between them earlier was still too new and shockingly sensual to absorb in only a few hours.

They cleared the table, cleaned up the kitchen, then hand in hand mounted the staircase to the bedroom. Veronica straightened the twisted sheets, while Kumi stood on the veranda staring out at the night. She was in bed when he returned to the bedroom, closing the French doors behind him.

She turned in to his embrace as if she'd been doing it for years instead of a few hours. He held her protectively until she fell asleep. Sleep did not come as easily for Kumi.

Thoughts of when he would leave the States to return to Europe tortured him. For the past ten years he'd made Paris his home when he could've returned to Asheville, North Carolina. Before meeting Veronica Johnson he'd thought he would live out his life on European soil, but now he wasn't so certain.

Could he leave her? Would he return to France without her?

The questions attacked him until fatigue overtook him as he succumbed to a sleep filled with mental images of their erotic lovemaking.

Veronica came to know a different Kumi a week after they'd begun sleeping together. She'd heard the excitement in his voice when he spoke of owning and operating his own restaurant, his anxiety when he talked about returning to Paris and she also registered his pain when he revealed his strained relationship with his father.

Reaching for her hand, he threaded his fingers through hers. "How can a man reject his own flesh and blood because he refuses to follow his wishes?" he questioned.

Veronica stared up at the netting floating around the bed. Cool air filtered into the bedroom through the open French doors, and she snuggled closer to Kumi for warmth. "Because he's a control freak," she said softly, "and because he believes he knows what's best for you."

"That may have been okay when I was a child."

"Some parents never see their children as adults." Turning on her side, she smiled at him. "My mother still tries to tell me how to live my life. She doesn't like the fact that I live here alone, and she took to her bed for a month when I told her that I was marrying a man old enough to be my father."

"How do you deal with her?"

"I used to argue with her, but that got me nowhere, so now I just 'yes' her into silence. I've always been the renegade, while my younger sister has always conformed. She married a wonderful man and gave birth to two perfect children."

Releasing her hand, Kumi cradled his arm under his head. He gave Veronica a steady look. "What about you, Ronnie? Would you marry again?"

Running a finger down the middle of his furred chest, she shrugged a shoulder. "I doubt it."

His gaze widened, searching her face and reaching into her thoughts. "Would you consider marrying me?"

She wavered, trying to comprehend what she was hearing. "I don't know," she said honestly. And she didn't know. She loved Kumi, enjoyed sleeping with him, but hadn't given any thought to a permanent relationship because she knew he planned to return to France at the end of the summer.

Moving closer, he kissed her forehead. "At least you didn't say no."

"Are you proposing marriage?" she asked with a wide grin.

He hesitated, measuring her for a moment. He'd done it again—opened his mouth to say something before he'd thought it through. He did want to marry Veronica, even if she smiled at him as if he'd told her a joke.

"No," he said glibly. The tense moment passed when he reached for her and flipped her over on her back. "I want you to come with me to see my sister's place."

She lifted her eyebrows. "When?"

"Today."

Veronica shook her head. She wasn't ready to meet Kumi's family. "I don't think so."

"Please," he whispered, lowering his body over hers. "Don't make me beg, Ronnie."

She felt the crush of his muscular body bearing down on

her slender frame. Bracing her hands against the solid wall of his chest, she closed her eyes. "You're going to have to do more than beg, sweetheart."

Burying his face against the side of her neck, he nipped at a spot under her ear. "What do you want?" Curving her arms around his neck, she whispered what she wanted him to do for her. Kumi threw back his head and laughed loudly. "Of course. You're so easy to please," he crooned sensuously.

Rolling off her body, he parted the netting, scooped her off the bed and carried her into the bathroom. She'd asked that he accompany her to her family reunion in August.

He would go to Atlanta with her, while she would finally get to meet Debbie. When his sister had questioned Kumi about not being able to reach him at his cottage one night, he'd smiled at her, saying he had been occupied elsewhere.

Debbie had followed him around, taunting him until he finally blurted out that he had a friend. Flashing a smug smile, she sweetly invited him and his *friend* to come to the B and B.

Deborah had let go of some of her anxiety that Maxwell's B and B wouldn't open on its projected date, after Kumi hired the third assistant chef. Only one of the three had more than six years' experience working in a full-service kitchen. The other two were recent culinary school graduates. Kumi had offered to act as executive chef if he hadn't hired one with more than ten years' experience by opening date. He was scheduled to meet with the new hires to plan dinner menus.

Veronica waited for Kumi to come around the Lexus and open the passenger-side door for her. She hadn't realized her pulse was racing until she saw a woman standing on the wraparound porch of a magnificent Victorian house, waving at Kumi.

Veronica had given special attention to her appearance. She blew out her hair, and then pinned it up off her neck in a chic chignon. Her dress was a simple sleeveless black silk sheath that barely skimmed the curves of her body, while Kumi had elected to wear a pair of black tailored linen gabardine slacks, jacket, and a banded collar white silk shirt. He looked incredibly handsome with his freshly shaven face and neatly brushed hair.

Veronica liked Kumi's sister on sight. She was tiny— barely five-two—and very pretty. Her delicate features, large dark eyes, and quick smile made her appear almost doll-like.

Arching eyebrows lifted in a face the color of rich cinnamon, she peered closely at Veronica. "Now I see why my brother needs a pager to monitor his whereabouts. You're absolutely gorgeous."

Veronica couldn't stop the flush darkening her cheeks. Pulling her hand from Kumi's loose grip, she extended it. "Thank you, Deborah. I'm Veronica Johnson."

Deborah shook her hand, smiling up at the taller woman. "My pleasure, Veronica. Please, come in." Still holding Veronica's hand, she pulled her into the large house.

Pushing his hands into the pockets of his slacks, Kumi followed the two women, a hint of a smile playing at the corners of his mouth. Bubbly, spontaneous Debbie could get the most uptight person to relax. She would be the perfect hostess for Maxwell's. His smile was still in place as he headed for the kitchen.

Veronica was awed by the interiors of the proposed bed-and-breakfast as Deborah led her in and out of every room on the first and second levels. Highly waxed bleached oak floors gleamed under the brilliance of chandeliers, windows framed in stained glass sparkled from bright sunlight and walls were graced with patterns of wallpaper made popular at the beginning of the last century.

Veronica ran her fingers over the smooth surface of a desk in the sitting room of one of the larger bedroom suites. "This piece is exquisite." There was no doubt it was an original.

Crossing her arms under her small breasts, Deborah gave Veronica a curious look. "You have a good eye for antiques." Veronica nodded, her fingers tracing the outline of one of the five leaf- and scroll-carved cabriole legs ending in hairy paw feet.

Turning, she stared at Deborah. "And you have exquisite taste in decorating."

It was Deborah's turn to nod. "And you have wonderful taste in men."

Veronica lifted an eyebrow. "I assume you're talking about Kumi?"

"But of course."

"It doesn't bother you that I'm older than he is?"

"Does it bother my brother?"

"Not in the least."

"Then it's fine with me. I'm five years older than Kumi, and I had always assumed the responsibility of protecting him from my father. But then Kumi went away, and when he didn't come back after his tour with the Marine Corps I blamed myself.

"Dad was consumed with Kumi becoming a doctor because my two older brothers were better suited for careers in business. Larry is an actuary and Marvin is branch manager of a local bank. We all knew Kumi was gifted when he was able to read at three. Dad used to brag to his colleagues that his youngest son was able to solve mathematical and chemical equations in his head even before he entered high school.

"There's been a Dr. Walker in our family for three generations, so the responsibility fell on Kumi to continue the tradition. I'm certain he would've gone to medical school if Dad hadn't been so controlling.

"I kept saying I should've done more, said more." She shrugged a shoulder, exhaling audibly. "I beat myself up for years until Kumi made me realize that we can't change people, and if they don't change, then you accept them for who they are.

"Dad's not too old to change, it's just that he doesn't want to change." Dropping her gaze, Deborah bit down on her lower lip. "I know that I've been running off at the mouth. I said all that to say that if Kumi wants you in his life, then who am I to question his decision? He's never spoken or written to me about a woman before, therefore, you must be very special for him to introduce you to us."

Veronica flashed a warm smile. "I'm very fond of Kumi."

Deborah gave her a skeptical look. "Fond?"

"Yes, fond." She didn't know Deborah well enough to bare her soul to her. She had to know that she and Kumi were sleeping together, therefore, Veronica decided to let Deborah draw her own conclusions.

Deborah glanced at the watch on her wrist. They'd been gone for almost three quarters of an hour. She grinned mischievously. "Mom should be here now."

Veronica recoiled as if she'd been punched in the stomach. "Kumi didn't tell me he wanted me to meet his mother."

"He doesn't know I invited her. I wanted it to be a surprise."

"What about your father?"

"He went fishing with a few of his retired friends. He'll be away for at least three days."

Deborah clasped her hands together. "We'd better get back downstairs." She winked at Veronica. "Your *boyfriend* has offered to do the cooking."

She followed Deborah across a carpeted hallway and

down a staircase with a solid oak banister and massive newel posts. She was certain Kumi would be surprised to see his mother, but Veronica wondered how Mrs. Walker would react when he introduced her to his *friend*.

Nine

Veronica walked into the dining room, her footsteps muffled in a thick forest-green carpet as she met Kumi's gaze over his mother's shoulder. His near-black eyes burned her face with their intensity. She stopped less than three feet away, her arching eyebrows lifting in a questioning expression. He had changed from his jacket and shirt into the white tunic favored by chefs. All he was missing was the *toque blanche* for his head.

Smiling, Kumi placed both hands on his mother's shoulders, turning her around. "Mother, I'd like you to meet a good friend of mine, Veronica Johnson. Ronnie, this is my mother, Mrs. Jeanette Walker."

Veronica successfully bit back a knowing smile when she registered the older woman's stunned expression. Walking forward, she offered her hand. "I'm honored, Mrs. Walker."

Jeanette placed a tiny manicured hand over her throat. Recovering quickly, she shook the proffered hand. "It's nice meeting you, Veronica. How long have you known my son?"

This time she did smile. Now she knew from whom Kumi had gotten his direct in-your-face attitude. "A month."

Jeanette glanced over her shoulder at her son, who stared down at her with a pair of large dark eyes that mirrored her own. "Oh, really...that long?" Her tone was soft *and* accusatory.

Curving an arm around Jeanette's narrow waist, he kissed the top of her head. "Come along, Mother." He winked at Deborah. "We can sit down to eat now."

Kumi extended his free hand to Veronica, leading her and Jeanette to the only table covered with a snowy-white linen cloth. Place settings for four were set with fine-bone china, monogrammed silver bearing a bold M, and crystal, along with bottles of white and red wine, as well as sparkling water. He seated his mother, Veronica and finally Deborah.

"Where's Orrin?" Jeanette asked Deborah after Kumi retreated to the kitchen. Deborah's husband was missing.

"He went to Waynesville to pick up several quilts I want to use as wall hangings." She glanced at her watch. "He called me from his truck about an hour ago, saying he was going to stop and look at some vintage doorknobs at Hargan's Hardware."

Veronica studied Kumi's mother. She estimated Jeanette to be in her late sixties, but her natural beauty hadn't faded with age. And despite bearing four children, her body was still slender. Her naturally wavy stylishly coiffed short silver hair was elegant and sophisticated, her face a smooth red-brown, while her large dark eyes were bright, alert. It was only when she smiled that attractive lines were visible around those penetrating eyes.

Jeanette cocked her head and smiled at Veronica, who returned it with a warm one of her own. She was more than curious about the woman whom Jerome had invited to meet his family. It was apparent she was older than her son, but what she had to reluctantly admit to herself was that Veronica Johnson was perfectly turned out: from her sleek hairstyle, subtly applied makeup to her choice of attire. Her musings were interrupted when her son returned, balancing a large tray on his left shoulder.

"I've sampled everything Kumi's prepared thus far," Deborah announced proudly.

"What are we eating, Jerome?" Jeanette asked.

He placed several serving dishes on the table. "You have a choice between *noisettes d'Agneau, coquilles St. Jacques* or *entrecôte Bercy.* The salad is *salade frisée aux lardons.*"

"Everything looks delicious, but will you kindly translate what you just said, Jerome?"

Placing the tray on a nearby table, Kumi sat down opposite Veronica. "Ronnie, will you please translate for my mother and sister what I just said."

She smiled and said, "We have lamb cutlets sautéed in butter and served with mushrooms and an herb-and-garlic butter." She pointed to another dish. "These are sea scallops cooked in a little butter. Their orange tails, containing edible roe, are delicious. Over here is rib steak cooked in a white wine sauce. And of course the salad, which is made up of endive with diced fried bacon."

There was a stunned silence until Deborah asked, "You speak French?"

Veronica smiled across the table at her lover. "Not as well as your brother, but I manage to get by."

"Don't be so modest, sweetheart," Kumi crooned. "You speak it beautifully." The endearment had slipped out so smoothly that he hadn't realized its import until he saw Jeanette's startled look.

Picking up her napkin, Jeanette placed it on her lap, while staring at her son under her lashes. Seconds later she redirected her penetrating gaze on Veronica. She hadn't missed the sensual exchange when they shared a secret smile. It was a look she was familiar with—one she'd shared with Lawrence Walker more than forty years ago.

She didn't know who this Veronica Johnson was and where she'd come from. But it was apparent she made Jerome happy. And that's all she'd ever wanted for her brilliant son since he was a child—peace and happiness.

The soft sound of music from a mini stereo system in the sitting room and flickering votives on a table created a magical backdrop for the two lovers sharing the king-size bed.

Veronica lay in Kumi's protective embrace, her back pressed to his chest. She placed her hands over the larger pair resting over her belly.

"Your mother is very charming," she said in a quiet voice.

Kumi chuckled, the sound rumbling deep in his wide chest. "My mother is a snob."

Tilting her chin, she glanced up at him over her shoulder. "How can you say that? I thought you loved your mother."

"I do love her, but I can say that because I know Jeanette Walker née Tillman. It was you who charmed her. You said all of the right things, but more than that you exemplify what she considers a proper young woman. The way you styled your hair, your dress and jewelry were perfect in her eyes. You're educated, well traveled and speak more than one language. All that aside, you're stunningly beautiful, so what is there not to like?"

Turning over, Veronica pressed her naked breasts to his chest. She couldn't quite make out his expression in the darkened bedroom. The afternoon she'd spent with Kumi's mother and sister was perfect. They'd sampled the dishes Kumi had prepared, finding each one more delicious than the other. Orrin Maxwell arrived a quarter of an hour after they'd sat down to dine. He quickly showered, changed his clothes and joined them in the dining room.

Veronica had liked Orrin immediately. He was friendly and unpretentious. He was a tall, light-skinned slender man who was eight years older than his wife. She'd noticed he was still quite formal with his mother-in-law even though he and Deborah had recently celebrated their twelfth wedding anniversary.

"Are you saying I passed inspection?"

Kumi's fingers tightened slightly on her shoulders, pulling her up until her face was level with his. "It wouldn't have mattered what my mother thought of you, because you're the one I love. The day I left home for the Marine Corps I stopped seeking my parents' approval. All that matters is what—"

Veronica's explosive kiss stopped his words as her tongue plundered the moist recesses of his mouth. Everything that was Jerome Kumi Walker seeped into her, and she writhed against him like a cat in heat.

Her hands were as busy as her mouth, sweeping over his chest, down his arms and to his muscled thighs. Raising her hips slightly, she searched for and cradled him in her hand. He hardened quickly with the stroking motion. Flipping her quickly onto her back, he entered her without his usually prolonged session of foreplay.

The outside world ceased to exist as they used every inch of the bed, each drawing from the other what they'd never given another living, breathing person. Kumi withdrew from her moist heat long enough to kiss every inch of her velvety body from her head to her feet.

Veronica reciprocated, her rapacious tongue wringing deep moans from Kumi as she took all of him into her mouth. His head thrashed from side to side while he gripped the sheets, pulling them from their fastenings. It all ended as she slid up the length of his moist body, rubbing her distended nipples against his chest while kissing him fully on the mouth. Then she straddled him, his hands cupping the fullness of her buttocks, and established a rhythm that he matched stroke for stroke. He rose to meet her, she taking every inch of him into her body as she rode out the storm sweeping over them.

"Yes, Kumi. Oh, yes," she chanted over and over, her husky approval drowning out the soft strains of music. Their breathing quickened, and Veronica did not know where she began or where he ended. She was transported to another time and place as she surrendered to the hard pulsing flesh sliding in and out between her thighs.

Kumi was offering her what Bram had given her—love and protection. But then he'd given her something her much older husband wasn't able to elicit—sexual fulfillment.

Burying her face against the column of his strong neck, she closed her eyes and melted all over him as he climaxed, his body convulsing violently as he left his hot seed buried deep in her womb.

Kumi stroked Veronica's damp hair as he lay, eyes closed, completely awed by the display of raw, uninhibited sensuality he'd just shared with the woman in his embrace.

He loved her, more than his own life. He felt hot tears burn the backs of his eyelids. He couldn't leave her. Not now, because he knew he could not return to Paris without her.

Before meeting Veronica Johnson he knew exactly what he wanted and where he wanted to be, but all of that had changed the moment he shared her bed.

He opened his eyes, determination shining from their obsidian depths. A confident smile tilted the corners of his strong male mouth as he made a silent vow that Veronica would become a part of his life, whether in the States or in Europe.

* * *

The weeks sped by quickly with Kumi caught up in a sur-real world of complete enchantment and fulfillment. He spent every night at Veronica's house, leaving by eight the following morning, but only after they'd shared breakfast.

He had finally hired an experienced chef for Maxwell's. He conducted six-hour, four-day-a-week cooking classes for the three men and one woman, checking and rechecking their efforts when they prepared the classic French dishes he had decided to serve the inn's guests. He'd also set up ac-counts with green grocers, butchers and vendors who sold the finest wines, cordials, imported cheeses and olive oil.

Veronica had accompanied him when he drove to New Orleans to confer with a fishing establishment who had built their impeccable reputation on shipping freshly caught seafood overnight to restaurants along the East Coast.

They spent two nights in New Orleans, taking in the sights and sampling the dishes that had made the city famous for its gastronomical opulence. The sweltering heat and op-pressive humidity did not dampen Veronica's enthusiasm as they stayed up well into the night, visiting several of the pop-ular jazz clubs. They'd returned to North Carolina ex-hausted and a few pounds heavier.

Maxwell's opened for business mid-July. The event was announced in the local newspapers, and Asheville's mayor and several high-ranking members of his inner circle at-tended the celebration along with the ubiquitous reporters and photographers. Deborah had managed to get several photographs and a brief article about Maxwell's unique dec-orating style featured in the latest issue of *Country Inns*.

A restaurant critic had declared the food, service and am-bience exquisite, recommending dining at Maxwell's B and B as an experience "not to be missed during one's lifetime."

During the day Kumi smiled when he didn't want to because Veronica, pleading a headache, had stayed home. At first he believed her, but as the night wore on, a nagging voice in the back of his head whispered that she'd elected to stay away because the event had become a family affair. Lawrence and Jeanette Walker, their sons, daughters-in-law and grandchildren had all turned out to support and celebrate Orrin and Deborah Maxwell's new business venture.

Kumi was reunited with two nieces and three nephews who had been toddlers and preschoolers when he'd entered the marines. His youngest nephew, a handsome thirteen-year-old, hadn't been born at the time.

He gave them a tour of the kitchen, making certain they stayed out of the way of the chefs, who were chopping, sautéeing, stirring and expertly preparing dishes that were not only pleasing to the palate but also to the eye.

Marvin Walker's sixteen-year-old daughter, transfixed by the activity in the large kitchen, caught the sleeve of Kumi's tunic. "Uncle Kumi," she said tentatively, "can you teach me to cook like they do?"

Curving an arm around her shoulders, he smiled down at the expectant expression on her youthful face. She was a very attractive young woman who had inherited her mother's delicate beauty.

"You're going to have to ask your parents if they'll let you come visit me in Paris."

Biting down on her lower lip, she shook her head. "They won't let me drive to the mall by myself, so I know going abroad is out."

"Maybe in two years when you've graduated high school, you can come visit me for the summer before you go to college."

"Really?"

He nodded, smiling broadly. "Really."

She hugged him, surprising Kumi with her impulsiveness. Marlena hadn't celebrated her second birthday the last time he saw her, but she had always been special to him. It was with her birth that he'd become an uncle for the first time.

Turning on his heel, he made his way to a room off the kitchen the staff used as their dressing room. He changed out of the white tunic and checkered pants and into a black silk V-neck pullover and a pair of black slacks. The color emphasized the slimness of his waist and hips, but could not disguise the depth of his solid chest or broad shoulders. At thirty-two he was physically in the best shape he'd ever been in his life. He was stronger and more mentally balanced than he'd been even after he'd completed the Marine Corps' rigorous basic training at Parris Island, South Carolina.

He walked through the spacious lobby of the bed-and-breakfast, coming face-to-face with his father. When he attempted to step around the tall man with slightly stooping shoulders, he felt his egress thwarted.

"Excuse me, please." He was surprised that his voice was so calm when all he wanted to do was brush past the older man as if he were a stranger.

Lawrence Walker placed a heavily veined hand on his son's arm. "I'd like a word with you, Jerome."

Kumi froze, staring at the hand resting on his arm—a hand that had comforted sick patients for forty years until Lawrence's retirement earlier that year, a hand that had caressed his forehead whenever he was sick and a hand that had patted his head in approval whenever he brought home an exam with a perfect score.

"You want to talk *now?*" A frown creased his high, smooth forehead at the same time he shook his head. "Sorry, I'm on my way out."

Lawrence's grip tightened. "Please, Jerome, hear me out." There was a pleading in his father's voice Kumi had never heard before. Proud, arrogant Dr. Lawrence Walker asking permission to be heard was something he never thought he would witness in his lifetime.

Giving his father a long, penetrating stare, he motioned with his head. "We can sit over there."

Lawrence dropped his hand and walked slowly over to a pair of facing club chairs covered in a soft beige watered silk fabric, Kumi following. He sat down, his shoulders appearing more stooped than usual.

Kumi sat, staring intently at his father, and for the first time in fourteen years he realized that the man before him wasn't aging well. An even six feet in height, his taupe-colored skin was dotted with age spots that resembled flecks of dark brown paint. His once-coarse dark hair was now sparse, completely white, and his green-gray eyes were no longer bright and penetrating. Lawrence was only sixty-nine, the same age as his wife, but looked years older.

Crossing one leg over the other knee, Kumi folded his arms over his chest, waiting for his father to speak. Tense seconds turned into a full minute. "What do you want to talk about?" he asked through clenched teeth.

Closing his eyes, Lawrence pressed his head to the chair's back. "I want to thank you for helping Deborah."

"I don't need you to thank me. Debbie did that already."

Lawrence opened his eyes, fire gleaming from their depths. "Dammit, Jerome, don't make this harder for me than it needs to be."

Dropping his arms, Kumi splayed long fingers over the chair's armrests. "You? Why is it always about you, Dad?"

"It's not about me—not this time." Lawrence flashed a tired smile. "It's about you, son. You and me."

A muscle twitched in Kumi's jaw. "What about us?"

He wasn't going to make it easy for his father because it had never been easy for him. The alienation had nearly destroyed him—an alienation that had spread to his older brothers who had always sought their father's approval. Only his mother and sister challenged Lawrence Walker, and had successfully escaped his wrath.

"I can't turn back the clock," Lawrence began slowly, "but I'm willing to begin anew—tonight." He extended his right hand. "I'm sorry."

Kumi stared at the hand as if it were a venomous reptile. He stared at it so long, he expected the older man to withdraw his peace offer. But he didn't.

Reluctantly, Kumi placed his hand in his father's, pulling him gently to his feet. He wrapped his arms around his body, registering the frailty in the slender frame.

"It's okay, Dad," he said close to his ear. Then he kissed his cheek, unaware of the tears filling Lawrence's eyes.

Taking a deep breath, Lawrence smiled, easing out of his son's comforting embrace. He reached into a pocket of his trousers and pulled out a handkerchief, wiping away the tears before they stained his face.

"Your mother said you've met someone who's very special to you."

Kumi nodded, smiling. "Yes, I have."

Lawrence's smile matched Kumi's. "Why don't you bring her with you when you come for Sunday dinner? We're having a cookout."

"I didn't know I was invited for Sunday dinner," he countered.

"Well, you are. And so is your lady."

"Are you asking or ordering me to come?"

A sheepish expression softened the harsh lines in Lawrence's face. "I'm asking, Jerome."

Kumi inclined his head. "I'll have to ask Veronica if she's free on Sunday."

Standing up straighter, Lawrence pulled back his shoulders and stared at his youngest child. "I know you haven't heard me say this in a very long time, but I'm very proud of you, son."

The beginnings of a smile touched Kumi's mouth before becoming a wide grin. "Thank you, Dad."

Lawrence nodded. "You're welcome, Jerome."

Kumi drove up Trace Road, feeling as if he'd been reborn. The single headlight from the bike lit up the darkened countryside, matching the brilliance of the full moon overhead. Tonight there were no shadows across the clear summer nighttime sky, or in his heart.

He parked the Harley alongside the house and removed his helmet. Tucking it under his arm, he walked to the front door and rang the bell.

Veronica was slow in answering the bell, but when he saw her face he knew she hadn't lied to him. Her eyes were red and puffy as if she'd been crying.

He stepped into the entry, placed his helmet on the floor and then swept her up in his arms. Shifting her in his embrace, he closed and locked the door before heading for the staircase.

"How are you feeling?"

She moaned softly. "A little better."

He dropped a kiss on the top of her silver hair. "Your head still hurts?"

"Not anymore. It's now my back and legs."

"Do you want me to call a doctor?"

"No. It'll pass in a couple of days."

Walking into her bedroom, he stared at her as she closed her eyes. "You've gone through this before?"

"It usually hits me several times a year. It's PMS."

"What is it?"

"Premenstrual syndrome. Headache, bloating, backache, sore breasts and on occasion temporary insanity."

He placed her on the bed, sinking down to the mattress beside her. "Do you want me to fix you something to eat or drink?"

"I've been drinking mint tea."

He kissed her gently on her lips. "Have you eaten?"

She started to shake her head, but thought better of it. "I'm not hungry. How was Maxwell's grand opening?" She'd smoothly changed the subject.

"Wonderful. Everything went off without a hitch. By the way, my father invited us to Sunday dinner."

Veronica opened her eyes. "You spoke to your father?"

"He spoke to me."

"Does this mean you've declared a truce?"

He ran his finger down the length of her nose. "It only means we're talking to each other."

"That's a start."

"That it is," he confirmed, kissing her again. "Do you want me to stay with you tonight?"

"Yes."

"Do you want more tea?"

"Yes, please."

Pushing off the bed, he smiled at the dreamy expression on her face. "Don't run away. I'll bring you your tea."

Kumi didn't want her to run away, and she didn't want him to go away. But he was going to go away in another eight weeks. He was scheduled to return to Paris September 19—exactly ten days before she celebrated her forty-third birthday.

Closing her eyes, she did what she hadn't done in months—she prayed. Prayed for an answer because she loved Kumi Walker. She began and ended her day in his arms. He'd given her everything she needed as a woman and even more that she hadn't known she needed.

She was astonished at the sense of fulfillment she felt whenever they were together, and the harder she tried to ignore the truth, the more it persisted: she wanted Kumi in her life beyond the summer. She wanted him for all the summers, springs and seasons in between until she drew her last breath.

Ten

Kumi's right arm curved around Veronica's waist, leading her around to the back of the imposing Regency-style pale pink limestone structure where he'd spent the first eighteen years of his life. The fingers of his left hand tightened on the handle of a large container of chocolate cream-filled petits fours, coated with dark and light couverture and an exquisite truffle torte filled with a light chocolate cream.

All or most of the Walkers were extreme chocoholics, and he'd decided to fulfill their dessert fantasies with his contributions to what had become the traditional Sunday afternoon cookout.

His parents had been cooking outdoors on Sunday afternoons whenever the weather permitted for as long as he could remember. Unlike many Southern black families who sat down together for dinner after church services ended, Jeanette and her husband preferred the more informal approach. The only exception had been inclement weather or if his parents had invited guests to share their roof and table with their four children.

He'd gotten up an hour before sunrise, kissing a still-sleeping Veronica, and had returned to his cottage where he'd showered, changed his clothes and then had headed for Maxwell's. By the time the daytime chef had arrived to begin the task of preparing breakfast for the guests at the bed-and-breakfast, he'd finished the petits fours and had been pressing the chocolate flakes to the sides of the cream-filled torte.

Assisting the chef, Kumi had chopped the ingredients needed for omelets, and had rolled out several trays of what would become fluffy biscuits. The chef, one of two recent culinary school graduates, was talented and creative.

They'd spent more than an hour discussing cooking techniques, and before leaving to return to check on Veronica, Kumi had left a note for the pastry chef to include an assortment of chocolate candies for the dessert menu. The suggestions had included cognac balls, kirsch rolls, croquant peaks and the ever-popular chocolate truffles. Preparing the chocolate and inhaling its aroma of chocolate had triggered his craving for what had been referred to as "food of the gods."

Veronica now heard the sounds of laughter and raised voices before she saw Kumi's immediate family. The PMS had eased with the onset of her menses. She hadn't thought she would be so thrilled by the obvious sign when she'd left her bed earlier that morning; a lingering fear had gripped her after she and Kumi had made love without protection the day she'd shared lunch with Jeanette and Deborah at Maxwell's.

At forty-two I'm much too old to think about having a baby. Her declaration to her sister had haunted her once she'd realized the recklessness of her actions. She loved Kumi, but she wasn't certain she loved him enough to bear his child.

* * *

Sixteen-year-old Marlena Walker spied her uncle first. "Uncle Kumi's here," she announced in a loud voice.

A petite slender woman, an older version of the teenage girl, shifted on her webbed lounger, frowning. "Marlena Denise Walker, please. It's not becoming for a young lady to scream like that."

Marlena's smile faded quickly and she rolled her eyes upward. "Give it a rest, Mom," she said under her breath.

Bending slightly, Kumi kissed his niece's cheek. "Chill," he warned softly. Glancing at Veronica's composed expression, he silently admired her flawless skin. She had foregone makeup with the exception of lipstick. She'd brushed her hair back, securing it in a ponytail. She was appropriately dressed for the occasion: a pair of black linen slacks, matching ballet-slipper shoes and a sleeveless white cotton blouse that revealed her toned upper arms.

"Veronica, this little minx is my niece Marlena. Marlena, I'd like for you to meet Miss Veronica Johnson."

Marlena smiled. "Nice meeting you. You're very pretty. I like your hair color." The words rushed out like a run-on sentence.

Veronica returned the friendly open smile. "It's a pleasure to meet you, Marlena. And thank you for your compliment."

"Well, it's true," the teenager insisted.

Kumi handed her the large container. "Please take this into the house and refrigerate it for me, princess. Don't tilt it," he warned softly.

"I bet it's chocolate."

"And don't open it," Kumi called after her as she turned and retreated to the house.

Over the next quarter of an hour Veronica was introduced to Dr. Lawrence and Jeanette Walker's children and grandchildren. Kumi's older brothers—Lawrence, Jr., whom everyone called Larry, and Marvin, were exact physical replicas of their father. Both were tall, slender and had inherited the older man's complexion, eye coloring and slightly stooped shoulders. Their collective offspring of four boys and two girls had compromised—the boys resembling their fathers and the girls their mothers. Both of Kumi's sisters-in-law were petite women with delicate features. She found everyone friendly, but curious, judging by surreptitious glances whenever her gaze was elsewhere.

Veronica sat on a webbed lounge chair, staring at Kumi through the lenses of the dark glasses she'd placed on her nose to shield her eyes from the harmful rays of the hot summer sun, while taking furtive sips of an icy lemon-lime concoction through a straw. Kumi wore a pair of khaki walking shorts with a navy blue tank top. His youngest nephew had stopped him, pointing to the small tattoo on his left bicep. She smiled when he translated the two words that made up the Latin motto of the United States Marine Corps: *Semper Fidelis—Always Faithful.*

His eyes widened as his gaze went from the tattoo to his uncle's smiling face. "Mama," he said loudly. "I want a tattoo like Uncle Kumi."

Marvin's wife glared at her son, then turned to her husband. "I think you'd better talk to that child or he won't be around for his fourteenth birthday."

Marvin, who had assumed the responsibility for grilling meats, waved to his youngest child. "Come here, Sean. Kumi, please take over while I have a heart-to-heart with my son."

Larry patted Kumi's back. "Go to it, brother. I don't know why Marvin thinks he can cook, but every once in a while we humor him and let him think he's doing something."

"I heard that," Marvin called out.

"Good," Larry countered. "Now that Kumi's here, we really don't need your *expertise*."

The eating and drinking continued well into the afternoon and early evening. Veronica sat at a long wooden table with all the Walkers, enjoying their camaraderie. There was an underlying formality about them, as if they feared letting go of their inhibitions. It was if they had to be careful of how others viewed them. Then, she remembered Kumi telling her that his mother was a snob. Having the right family pedigree was very important to Jeanette; however, it appeared as if some of her grandchildren exhibited streaks of rebellion—a trait that was so apparent in Jerome Kumi Walker.

There was a lull in conversation as everyone concentrated on eating mounds of meats, vegetables and salads set out in serving platters. Veronica had sampled Jeanette's delicious potato salad, declaring it one of the best she'd ever eaten. Kumi, assuming the grilling duties from Marvin, grilled rock lobster tail with a red chili butter dipping sauce, swordfish, chicken, butterflied lamb and filet mignon with a brandy-peppercorn sauce.

Marlena wiped her hands and mouth, then said, "I think I want to become a chef."

Her mother's jaw dropped. "I thought you wanted to become a lawyer."

"I've changed my mind. You know I love to cook."

"We'll talk about it later," Marvin said, smiling.

"Really, Daddy?"

"Really, princess," he confirmed, ignoring his wife's scowl.

Leaning closer to Kumi, her bare shoulder touching his, Veronica whispered for his ears only, "I think you're responsible for spawning the next generation of insurgents."

Turning his head, he smiled down at her. "I believe you're right," he said softly. "Tattoos and cooking instead of medicine and law. What are the Walkers coming to?"

She smiled and wrinkled her nose. "What would you do if your son decided he wanted to become a ballet dancer?"

Lowering his head, his mouth grazed her earlobe. "Have my son and you'll find out."

Veronica stared at Kumi as if he'd touched her bare flesh with an electrified rod. He wanted her to have a baby—his child. He wanted a child, but it was he who had always assumed the responsibility of protecting her whenever they made love—all except the one time she had initiated the act. The one time she hadn't been able to hold back—the one time she'd risked becoming pregnant because it had been her most fertile time during her menstrual cycle. But her menses had come on schedule, belaying her anxiety that she might be carrying his child.

"That's not going to become a reality."

Kumi recoiled as if she'd slapped him. He stood up, stepping over the wooden bench, while at the same time anchoring a hand under Veronica's shoulder and gently pulling her up.

"Please excuse us," he said to the assembled group staring mutely at them. "I have to talk to Veronica."

If there was ever a time she wanted to scream at him, it was now. Whatever he wanted to talk to her about could have waited until they returned home.

Kumi led Veronica across the spacious backyard and into the flower garden. Sitting down on a stone bench, he eased her down beside him, his arm circling her waist.

Unconsciously, she rested her head against his shoulder. "What do you want to talk about that couldn't be discussed at another time?"

"Us."

"What about us?"

There was slight pause before Kumi spoke again. "I love

you, Ronnie, and you love me. But where are we going with this? Our feelings for each other?"

Raising her head, she stared at his composed expression. "What is it you want from me?"

"I want you to marry me, Veronica Johnson. I want you to become my wife and the mother of my children," he said smoothly, with no expression on his face.

"I'm too old to have children—"

"Then *one* child!" he snapped angrily, interrupting her.

A slight frown marred her smooth forehead. "There's no need to take that tone with me, Kumi." Her father had never raised his voice to her, and she would not tolerate the same from any man.

His shoulders slumped. "I'm sorry, Ronnie." His voice was softer, apologetic. "Wanting you in my life permanently is eating me up inside. I think I'm losing my mind."

Closing her eyes, she bit down hard on her lower lip. Kumi was offering her what every normal woman wanted— a man who loved her enough to offer marriage and children. He wanted to marry her when too many men were willing to sleep with or live with a woman without committing to a future with them.

She opened her eyes, forcing a smile she did not feel. "Will you give me time to consider your proposal?"

An irresistibly devastating grin softened his stoic expression. Shifting, he picked her up, settling her across his lap. "Of course, sweetheart." He curbed the urge to pull her down to the grass and make love to her.

When he'd returned to her house earlier that morning she'd given him the news that she wasn't pregnant, and it wasn't until after he'd recalled the time they'd made love and he hadn't protected her that he understood her revelation. He wanted Veronica to have his child, but only after she committed to sharing her life with him.

Cradling her face between his palms, his lips brushed against hers as he spoke. "Thank you for even considering me."

Veronica felt his lips touch hers like a whisper. "You honor me with your proposal."

"No," he argued softly. "I'm honored that you've permitted me to become a part of your existence." *Even if it is only temporary,* he added silently. There was still the remotest possibility that she would reject him. And what he had to do was prepare himself for that time, because it was just six weeks before he was to return to Paris either with or without Veronica Johnson.

"Make a left at the next corner."

Kumi followed Veronica's directions, after they'd left a security gatehouse in a private community, overwhelmed by the magnificence of the structures situated five miles north of downtown Atlanta, spreading outward from the nexus of Peachtree Street, Roswell and West Paces Ferry Roads. He'd visited Atlanta the year before he'd applied to Morehouse College, but he hadn't been to Georgia's capital city's wealthiest neighborhood.

He'd agreed to accompany Veronica to her family reunion, committing to spend a week with her before returning to North Carolina. He'd also agreed to drive her Lexus back to North Carolina, because she had planned to fly back a week later. He maneuvered around the corner she indicated, his gaze widening as he encountered a cul-de-sac. Four large, imposing Colonial-style structures were set on the dead-end street, each a gleaming white in the brilliant Atlanta summer sun.

"I'm the first one on the right."

Kumi stared numbly through the windshield. A sloping sculpted lawn, precisely cut hedges, a quartet of towering trees and thick flowering shrubs provided the perfect reception for the place Veronica and Bram had called home.

Veronica reached under the visor and pushed a button on an automatic garage opener. The door to a three-car garage slid open silently. Kumi drove into the garage next to a Volkswagen Passat and turned off the engine, while she removed another small device from her purse and pressed several buttons, deactivating a sophisticated alarm system.

Kumi got out of the truck, coming around to open the passenger-side door for Veronica. She smiled at him when he curved an arm around her waist and helped her down.

"It's going to take at least an hour to cool the place to where it's comfortable."

He nodded. It was as if the words were stuck in his throat. It was as if he were seeing Veronica for the first time. He hadn't even seen the interior of this house, but he knew instinctively that it would be nothing like the one on Trace Road. That one was modest while this one quietly shouted opulence. He did not have to read a real estate listing to know that the homes in the cul-de-sac were probably appraised for a million or more.

Veronica opened a side door, leading into the house, while he lingered to retrieve his luggage from the cargo area. He followed her into the house, mounting three steps and walking into a spacious kitchen. He didn't know what to expect, but he went completely still, staring at a kitchen that could've been in any French farmhouse. A massive cast-iron stove from another era took up half a wall.

He walked numbly through the kitchen and into a hallway that led in four directions. Antique tables, chairs and priceless lamps were displayed for the admiring eye. Shifting his luggage, Kumi ambled around the downstairs, peering into a living and dining room decorated in the recurring country French design. A smile crinkled his eyes. It was apparent Veronica hadn't let go her love for France as evidenced by her home's furnishings. He made his way up a flight of stairs, feeling the cool air flowing from baseboard and ceiling vents.

"I'm in here," Veronica called out from a room near the top of the carpeted staircase.

He entered a large bedroom boasting a queen-size mahogany sleigh bed. All of the furnishings in the room were white: a counterpane with feathery lace, a nest of piled high gossamer pillows, embroidered sheers at the tall windows and the cutwork cloths covering the two bedside tables.

Staring at her smiling face, Kumi felt a fist of fear knot up his chest. Veronica's home and its furnishings were priceless. And if she married him, would she be willing to leave it all behind?

Veronica smiled up a Kumi as they made their way up the path to Bette Hall's house. They had to park on a side street because of the number of cars and trucks lining the Halls' circular driveway. Veronica's and Kumi's arms were filled with desserts they'd made earlier that morning. She'd baked two sour-cream pound cakes and a sweet potato pie. Kumi had put his professional touches on a *gâteau des rois,* a marzipan-filled puff French pastry that was served on the final feast of Christmas—Twelfth Night—to mark the arrival of the Three Kings to Bethlehem, and a traditional American chocolate pecan pie.

The screen door opened with their approach and Veronica came face-to-face with her sister and brother-in-law, who had just arrived. The spacious entryway and living room were filled with people of varying ages. Infants in their parents' arms cried and squirmed; toddlers were scampering about, seeing what mischief they could get into; teenagers with earphones from disc players and portable tape players gyrated to the music blasting in their ears.

Candace's gaze lingered briefly on Kumi before she turned her attention to Veronica. Curving an arm around her neck, she kissed her cheek. "Hey, big sis. Who is *he?*" she whispered sotto voce.

A mysterious smile touched Kumi's mouth. There was no doubt Veronica would be asked the same question over and over before the day ended.

"Kumi, this is my sister, Candace, and brother-in-law Ivan Yarborough. Candace, Ivan, Kumi Walker."

Kumi flashed his hundred-watt smile, charming Candace immediately. "My pleasure."

"Oh, no," Candace crooned, "It's *my* pleasure."

Ivan and Kumi nodded to each other, exchanging polite greetings as Candace and Veronica carried the desserts into the kitchen where every inch of counter space and tables were with filled platters and pots emanating mouthwatering aromas.

Half a dozen fried turkeys, hundreds of pounds of fried chicken and countless slabs of spareribs were transported from the kitchen to the backyard by relatives Veronica hadn't seen in a year. Candace clutched her arm, pulling her out of the path of people coming and going in the large kitchen.

"He's gorgeous. Where on earth did you find him?"

Veronica stared at Candace, baffled. "What are you talking about?"

"Kumi. That is his name, isn't it?"

"Yes. Why?"

Candace shook her head. "What am I going to do with you? I can't believe you brought your man to a family re-union where every woman from eight to eighty will be drooling, analyzing and dissecting him within the first five minutes of his arrival. And you know how Aunt Bette likes young men."

"Kumi will be able to take care of himself."

"It looks as if he's been taking good care of you, Veronica."

Heat stole into her face, burning her cheeks and for once she did not have a comeback. "Let's go outside," she said instead.

Bette Hall's house was built on five acres of land, most of which had remained undeveloped. She'd had a landscaping company cut the grass, and she'd set up eight tents to accommodate the eighty-three family members who were confirmed to attend the annual gathering.

The weather had cooperated. The early afternoon temperature was in the low eighties, and a light breeze offset the intense heat from the sun in a near cloudless sky.

Veronica was handed an oversize T-shirt with Wardlaw Family Reunion inscribed on the back, along with the date. She slipped it on over her shorts and tank top, the hem coming to her knees.

Reaching for a pair of sunglasses from the small crocheted purse slung over her chest, she put them on the bridge of her nose. She waved to a cousin who'd traveled from Ohio, before moving around the grounds to find her parents. She found them in a tent with several other older couples.

She kissed her mother, then her father. "I have someone I'd like you to meet," she said mysteriously.

"Who?" Irma asked, smiling.

"Don't move."

Veronica left the tent, searching for Kumi. She spied him with Aunt Bette's teenage granddaughter. It was obvious the scantily dressed young woman was openly flirting with him, despite his impassive expression.

"Excuse me, Chantel, but I'd like to borrow Kumi for a few minutes."

Chantel Hall's jaw dropped when Veronica curved her

arm through Kumi's and led him away. She was still standing with her mouth open when an older cousin came over to her.

Chantel sucked her teeth while rolling her head on her neck. "Isn't he too young for her?"

"Don't be catty, cuz. If he can drive, vote, buy cigarettes, liquor, serve in the military and not be drinking Similac or wearing Pampers, then he's not too young."

Chantel sucked her teeth again, rolled her eyes and walked away with an exaggerated sway of her generous hips.

Veronica led Kumi into the tent where her parents sat on folding chairs, drinking iced tea. All conversations ended abruptly at the same time all gazes were trained on the tall man with Veronica Johnson-Hamlin.

"Mother, Daddy—" her voice was low and composed "—I'd like you to meet a very good friend, Kumi Walker. Kumi, my parents, Harold and Irma Johnson."

Leaning over, Kumi smiled at Irma, who stared up at him as if he had a horn growing out the center of his forehead. The spell was broken when she returned his sensual smile.

"I'm so glad you came with Veronica."

His smile widened appreciably. "So am I, Mrs. Johnson." He extended his hand to Veronica's father, who rose to his feet and grasped his fingers in a strong grip.

"Nice meeting you, Kumi."

Everyone stared at Veronica in suspended anticipation. She ended the suspense, saying, "This is Kumi Walker. Kumi, these wonderful people are my aunts and uncles."

There was a chorus of mixed greetings before several put their heads together and whispered about their niece's choice in male companionship.

It was something Veronica overhead many more times before night descended on the assembled. Most of the younger women whispered about how "hot" and "fine" he was, but the older ones shook their heads claiming Veronica had gone from one extreme to the other. First she'd taken up with an old man, and now a young boy. Poor Irma must be so embarrassed.

Dusk came, taking with it the heat, while the volume of music escalated. The hired deejay played the latest number-one hip-hop tune and couples jumped up to dance.

Veronica sat on the grass, supporting her back against a tree, watching her extended family enjoying themselves while Kumi lay on the grass beside her, eyes closed.

She stared at him. "Don't go to sleep on me, darling. I'll never be able to move you."

He smiled, not opening his eyes. "I'm just resting. I think I ate too much."

"You're not the only one."

"I like your family, Ronnie. They're a lot less uptight than mine."

"That's because we have a few scalawags and riffraff who managed to sneak in under the guise that they were respectable ladies and gentlemen. Personally, I think it's good because they add a lot of flavor to the mix."

"Who made the punch?"

Veronica laughed, the sound low and seductive in the encroaching darkness. "That had to be cousin Emerson. His grandfather used to make moonshine during *and* after Prohibition. The recipe was passed down from grandfather to son, and finally to grandson."

Kumi blew out his breath. "That stuff is potent."

"How much did you drink?"

"At least two, maybe even three glasses."

"It's no wonder you can't move. Didn't somebody warn you?"

"Nope. At least I wasn't doing shots like some of the others."

"Kumi! Were you trying to kill yourself?"

He opened his eyes, a sensuous smile curving his strong mouth. "No. I'm not ready to die—at least not for a long, long time."

Eleven

Kumi lay quietly, watching Veronica stretch like a graceful feline. She turned to her left, throwing her right leg over his and snuggled against his shoulder. A soft sigh escaped her parted lips at the same time her eyes opened.

Cradling the back of her head in one hand, he pressed his mouth to her vanilla-scented hair. "Good morning, sweetheart."

Inching closer to Kumi's hard body, Veronica smiled. "Good morning." She noticed the abundance of sunlight pouring into the bedroom through the lace sheers. It was apparent she'd overslept. "What time is it?" Her voice was heavy with sleep.

Kumi turned, peering at the clock on his side of the bed. "Eight-ten."

"It's not that late," she moaned.

"What time are you scheduled to get your hair done?"

"Eleven."

She and Kumi had been in Georgia for three days and they were invited to attend a fund-raising dinner dance to bene-

fit AIDS victims in the Atlanta area. It was one of many or-
ganizations she'd joined after she'd married Bramwell.

Kumi pulled Veronica closer and settled her over his chest.
Attending the formal affair would give him a glimpse of
what his life would be like if he married Veronica and relo-
cated to Georgia. She'd been forthcoming when she revealed
what her marriage to Dr. Bramwell Hamlin had been like.

Even though Kumi hadn't lived in the States for a decade,
he had been familiar with her late husband's name. And after
spending time with Veronica in her hometown he'd come to
understand who she was.

They'd shared dinner with her parents and with her sister's family, and the contents of their respective homes were
comparable to the furnishings in Veronica's. It didn't take
him long to conclude that the Wardlaws and Johnsons were
a product of old-black Southern aristocracy, much like his
own family lineage, concluding their backgrounds were
more similar than dissimilar.

His right hand moved up and down her spine, lingering
over her hips. A slight smile curved his mouth. She was putting on weight. He'd noticed the night before when she'd undressed in front of him that her breasts were fuller, the
nipples darker and more prominent.

The muscles in his stomach contracted when he recalled
the vision of her lush body in the warm golden glow of a
table lamp. The flesh between his thighs stirred as it hardened with his erotic musings. He wanted her, and since
they'd begun sleeping together there was never a time when
he did not want her.

Veronica felt Kumi's arousal and as his passion swelled,
so did hers.

Writhing sensuously atop him, she pressed a kiss under
his ear. "Don't start what you can't finish," she murmured.

The words had just left her lips when she found herself

on her back, staring up at Kumi. His large eyes captured her gaze, holding her prisoner. He smiled as he lowered his body and brushed a kiss over her parted lips. She closed her eyes, letting her senses take over as he kissed her chin, throat before moving slowly down her chest.

He eased down her body, leaving light whispery kisses over her belly. Her respiration quickened, fingers curling into tight fists as she struggled not to touch him. His moist breath swept over her thighs and she swallowed back a moan. This was a different kind of lovemaking—one in which the only part of his body that touched her was his mouth.

He kissed her inner thighs, she rising slightly off the mattress. This time she did moan audibly. Turning her over, he explored the backs of her knees, leaving her shaking uncontrollably. He was torturing her, and at that moment if Kumi had asked her for anything she would've given it to him.

It all ended when he moved up and staked his claim on her breasts, she keening like someone in excruciating pain. She felt the sensations in her womb.

"Kumi?"

"Yes, baby?" A turgid nipple was caught between his teeth.

"Please."

He released her breast and stared at her. "What is it?"

She opened her eyes. They were shimmering with moisture. "Don't torture me."

Holding her close, he glared at her. "Why shouldn't I? You torture me, Veronica. You've tortured me every day since I first saw you."

Closing her eyes against his intense stare, she shook her head. "What do you want?"

Burying his face between her scented neck and shoulder, he said, "You know what I want."

She knew exactly what he wanted. He wanted a wife and a child. He wanted her.

And she wanted to be his wife and the mother of his children.

"Yes, Kumi," she whispered.

"Yes, what, Ronnie?"

She took a deep breath, held it and then let it out slowly. "I will marry you."

First he kissed the tip of her nose, then her eyes and finally he kissed her soft mouth. "I love you so much," he whispered as his hands moved slowly over her body. "Thank you, thank you, thank you." His voice was thick with emotion.

Lifting his hips, he eased his thick long length into her awaiting body, both sighing as her flesh closed possessively around his. Knowing they'd committed to sharing their lives and futures made their coming together all the more sweet.

A deep feeling of peace entered Veronica. Her whole being was flooded with a desire that filled her heart with a love she'd never known. Passion radiated from the soft core of her body, igniting a fire in Kumi's loins. He moved sensuously against her, his hips keeping perfect rhythm with hers.

They were no longer man and woman, but soon-to-be husband and wife—one.

Her body vibrated liquid fire and she wanted to yield to the burning passion that seemed to incinerate her with the hottest fire. Kumi quickened his movements, taking her with him as they were swept up in the hysteria of ecstasy holding them captive.

Great gusts of desire shook her from head to toe, and her lips quivered with silent words of unspoken passion.

Tears streaked her cheeks and she moaned over and over when she surrendered to the hot tides of love carrying her out to a weightless sea where she welcomed drowning in the delight of a never-ending love.

Kumi's passions overlapped Veronica's and seconds later

he groaned out his own awesome climax. It was the second time in his life that he'd made love to a woman without using protection. Both times it had been with Veronica Johnson. But that was inconsequential because he would willingly repeat the act over and over until her belly swelled with his child.

Veronica entered the brightly lit ballroom, her hand resting lightly on the sleeve of Kumi's white dinner jacket. A brilliant diamond butterfly pin on the strap of her one-shoulder black crepe de chine dress glittered under the prisms of light from two massive chandeliers. The pin was a preengagement gift from Kumi. He sheepishly admitted he had selected the delicate piece of jewelry while waiting for the slacks to a rented tuxedo to be altered.

She'd wanted to admonish him for spending his money, but quickly changed her mind. She hadn't wanted to appear ungrateful nor bruise his pride. She'd thanked him instead, kissing him passionately. They'd stopped just in time or they never would've made it to the fund-raiser on time.

She took a surreptitious glance at his distinctive profile, her breath catching in her chest. His good looks were complemented by a self-confident presence that elicited an inquisitive glance or smile from several formally dressed women standing around in the ballroom talking quietly or sipping from champagne flutes.

While Veronica had spent four hours at a full-service salon wherein she'd had the roots of her hair touched up with a relaxer, her face hydrated by a European facial, followed by a manicure and pedicure, Kumi had visited the adjacent barbershop to have his curly hair cut and the stubble of an emerging beard removed from his face with a professional shave. He then went to select formal wear for the fund-raiser before he returned to pick her up from the salon.

When he'd walked in, all conversation had come to a

complete halt, and gazes were fixed on his smooth face and tall, muscular body. Veronica had risen from her sitting position in the reception area, curved her arm through his amid whispered choruses of "Damn!" and "Oh, no, she didn't!"

She hadn't expected the rush of pride filling her as she clung to his arm, and it was not for the first time she'd found it difficult to believe that she had fallen in love with Kumi—that she had pledged her future to his.

Kumi's right hand covered the small one resting on his sleeve, his admiring gaze lingering on Veronica's swept-up hairdo. Wearing her hair off her neck gave him an unobstructed view of her long, slender, silken neck. She hadn't worn any jewelry except for a pair of brilliant diamond studs and his gift.

Filled with masculine pride, he noticed men turning and staring at the woman on his arm. The soft fabric of her dress draped her body as if it had been made expressly for her. The garment bared a shoulder and the expanse of her back. The single strap crossed her velvety back, ending at her narrow waist; a generous display of long shapely legs were exposed by a back slit each time she took a step. Dropping her hand, he splayed the fingers of his left one across her bare back. The possessive gesture was not lost on those who were shocked to see Veronica Johnson-Hamlin in attendance with a man. Since her husband's death she had continued to attend the annual fund-raiser, but had elected to come unescorted.

Lowering his head, Kumi asked, "Would you like something to eat or drink?"

Waiters, balancing trays on their fingertips, weaved their way through the burgeoning crowd, offering a plethora of hors d'oeuvres and glasses of sparkling champagne. The annual fund-raiser was a sellout.

"I'd like a seltzer, thank you."

Leaning closer, he pressed his lips to her forehead. "Wait here for me. I don't want to lose you."

Nodding, she positioned herself with her back against a massive column, watching Kumi as he made his way toward one of the bars set up at either end of the expansive ballroom of a former antebellum plantation house.

She exchanged polite smiles and greetings with people she'd known for years and others she'd met once she married Bram. Her late husband had been medical adviser for the foundation for several years after documented cases of the disease increased with rising fears and ignorance of the epidemic affecting the African-American population.

"I'm surprised to see you here, Veronica," drawled a familiar male voice. "I was told you had gone to the mountains for the summer."

Turning to her right, Veronica looked at the man who had prompted her to leave Atlanta. Regarding her with impassive coldness was Clinton Hamlin, Bramwell Hamlin's eldest son.

Older than Veronica by only three years, she'd been initially attracted to his lean face with its perfectly balanced features. His smooth mocha-colored face was tanned from the hot summer sun, which brought out the shimmering lights in his dark gray eyes. Tall, slender and impeccably attired, Clinton was a masculine version of his once-beautiful mother before she embarked on a slow descent into a world of substance abuse.

She affected a polite smile. "You should know that this event is very important to me—to all of our people."

Vertical lines appeared between his eyes. "What I do know is that you're a *slut*." He spat out the last word. "You seduced my father, got him to marry you and now you come here and flaunt your pimp in front of everyone. Thank God my mother isn't here to witness this."

Veronica recoiled as if Clinton had slapped her. She wanted to scream at him that his mother couldn't witness anything because she probably was too drunk to even get out of bed.

Of Bram's three children, Clinton had been the only one to befriend her once his father announced his decision to marry a much-younger woman. But his conciliatory attitude changed abruptly with the disclosure of his father's last will and testament. He'd had to share three million dollars with his brother and sister—the amount a pittance compared to what Veronica had received, and he was convinced she'd talked his father into leaving half his estate to whom he referred to as "hood rats."

Only pride kept her from arguing with Clinton. "Thank you for the compliment," she drawled facetiously. She glanced over his shoulder to see Kumi coming toward them. "Now I suggest you leave before my *pimp* gets here. He has a rather nasty temper."

Clinton turned in the direction of her gaze. The man who'd come with his stepmother was formidable-looking, even in formal attire. "We'll talk again," he warned softly.

"No, Clinton, we *won't* talk again," she countered. "The last thing I'm going to say to you is get some help for your problem."

Leaning closer, he said between clenched teeth, "I don't have a problem."

"Right now the only Hamlin who doesn't have a *problem* is your sister."

Rage darkened his face under his deep tan. "You'll pay for that remark." Turning on his heels, he stalked away, his fingers curling into tight fists.

She was still staring at Clinton's stiff back when Kumi handed her a glass filled with her beverage. She missed her lover's narrowed gaze as he studied her impassive expression.

Kumi didn't know why, but he felt a sudden uneasiness that hadn't been there when he first walked into the ballroom with Veronica. There was something about her expression, the stiffness in her body that bode trouble. Had the man who'd walked away with his approach said something to upset her? Was he one of the ones whom she'd spoken about who had sought to defame her character?

Shifting his own glass of sparkling water to his left hand, he curved his right arm around her waist, pulling her closer to his side. He would not leave her alone again for the rest of the night. If anyone had anything disparaging to say to Veronica Johnson, then they would have to deal with him.

Veronica scrawled her signature across several documents that gave her lawyer power of attorney to negotiate and finalize the sale of her properties. It had taken almost a week to list her Atlanta and North Carolina holdings with a Realtor before she set up an appointment with an appraiser to catalog the contents of her Buckhead home. All that remained was the transfer of the titles of her cars to her sister and brother-in-law.

The night before Kumi left Atlanta to return to Asheville, they'd lain in bed, holding hands, planning their future. Her disclosure that she would live with him in France had rendered him mute. Once he'd recovered from her startling revelation, he told her he would make certain she would never regret her decision to leave her home and family.

Replacing the top on the pen, she dropped it into her purse, a knowing smile softening her mouth. In two days she was scheduled to return to her mountaintop retreat and the man she loved.

She and Kumi had planned to marry in North Carolina on September 18—a day before they were scheduled to leave for France, a day before she would board a flight with her husband to begin a new life in another country and eleven days before she would celebrate her forty-third birthday.

Kumi had called his sister with the news of their upcoming nuptials, and Deborah had offered Maxwell's for the reception and lodging for family members and out-of-town guests. Veronica was adamant that she wanted a small gathering, with only immediate family members in attendance.

Leaving the documents with the lawyer's administrative assistant, Veronica walked out of his office, making her way to the parking lot to pick up her car. She'd just opened the door and slipped behind the wheel when it swept over her. A wave of nausea threatened to make her lose her breakfast. A light film of perspiration covered her face as she struggled not to regurgitate. Turning the key in the ignition, Veronica switched the fan to the highest speed, and waited for the cold air to cool down her face and body. What had made her sick? Was it something she'd eaten?

She sat in the car for ten minutes before she felt herself back in control. Reaching for her cell phone, she dialed Candace's number, canceling their luncheon date. Half an hour later she lay in her own bed, swallowing back the waves of nausea that attacked when she least expected.

It was late afternoon before she finally called her doctor's office, explaining her symptoms to the nurse, who told her that the doctor had had a cancellation and could see her at five-thirty.

Veronica sat in the darkened kitchen not bothering to turn on a light, staring across the large space with unseeing eyes. A single tear rolled down a silken cheek, followed by another until they flowed unchecked.

She was pregnant!

She'd argued with the doctor that she'd had her period in July—although scant—but that she couldn't be pregnant.

The young internist reassured her that the test was ninety-five percent accurate before he cautioned her because she was high-risk, she should see her gynecologist as soon as possible if she planned to carry her baby to term.

The shock that she was going to be mother eased, replaced by a quiet, healing sense of joy. Kumi would get his wish: a wife and a child.

Kumi waited at the Asheville Airport for Veronica's flight to touch down. A bright smile lit up his face when he spied her. Waving to her, he gently pushed his way through the crowd. Curving an arm around her waist, he swept her off her feet and kissed her.

Veronica tightened her hold around his strong neck, melting into him. "Please, don't squeeze me too tight," she murmured against his searching parted lips.

Easing his hold on her body, he noted the liquid gold glints in her clear brown eyes. "Did you hurt yourself?" He knew he hadn't held her that tightly.

She shook her head, saying, "I'll tell you once we get back to the house."

He gave her a questioning look. "Are you okay?"

A smile fired her sun-lit eyes. "I'm wonderful." And she was. After she'd gotten over the initial shock that a tiny life was growing under her heart, she found it difficult to conceal her joy from her sister and parents. However, she'd decided to tell Kumi first before announcing her condition to others.

Kumi swung Veronica effortlessly up into his arms, spinning her around in the middle of her living room. He'd missed her—more than he thought he ever would.

"What is it you want to tell me?"

Holding on to his neck and resting her head against his shoulder, Veronica smiled. "We're going to have a baby."

Kumi went completely still at the same time his heart pumped painfully in his chest. He registered a roaring in his head and suddenly felt as if he was going to faint. His knees buckled slightly as he eased down to the floor holding Veronica.

He sat on the floor, her cradled on his lap and held her to his heart. "I don't believe it," he said over and over. "Thank you, darling. Thank you," he whispered hoarsely.

Her hands cupped his face as she kissed his lips. Seconds later, she began to cry as they shared a joy that neither had ever experienced in their lives.

Twelve

Veronica stared at her ripening figure in the full-length mirror, praying she would be able to fit into the dress she'd selected for her wedding. She was nine weeks into her term, and gaining weight at a rate of a pound a week. Her Atlanta gynecologist had referred her to a colleague in Asheville, who had put her through a series of tests. At eight weeks she'd undergone a transvaginal ultrasound for a better view of her baby and placenta, and the results revealed not one fetus but two. She and Kumi were expecting twins.

Her moods vacillated with the changes in her body—she'd be screaming at her fiancé, and then sobbing in his arms seconds later. The realization that she was going to permanently leave her home, her family and the country of her birth had washed over her like a cold ocean wave, adding to the stress of planning a wedding. The night before, she'd threatened to cancel the ceremony, eliciting an outburst of anger from Kumi that left her with her mouth gaping after he'd stormed out of her house, slamming the door violently behind him. Forty minutes after his departure he'd called her, apologizing. She'd accepted his apology, and then offered her own, pleading for patience. They'd ended the call declaring their undying love for each other.

All of the arrangements for the wedding were finalized: the license, rings, flowers, menu and lodging arrangements for out-of-town guests. She'd decided to exchange vows in North Carolina rather than Atlanta, because she wanted to begin her life as Mrs. Jerome Walker without whispers and innuendos. Jeanette Walker had contacted the minister at the church where the Walkers had worshiped for generations, asking him to perform the ceremony. Deborah and Orrin had offered Maxwell's for the ceremony and the reception dinner. Veronica had chosen Candace as her matron of honor and Kumi had asked his father to be his best man.

Her dress was a Victorian-inspired tunic over a full-length slip in shimmering platinum. The Chantilly lace overblouse, sprinkled with pearl and crystal embroidery, added romantic elegance to a garment reminiscent of a treasured heirloom.

Glancing at the clock on a bedside table, she noted the time. Her parents, sister, brother-in-law and nephews were expected to arrive from Atlanta within the hour. Deborah had made arrangements for them to stay over at Maxwell's instead of at a nearby hotel.

Veronica buttoned the shirt that had belonged to Kumi. She'd begun wearing his shirts because they were more comfortable than her own. After they arrived in Paris she planned to purchase enough clothes to accommodate her rapidly changing figure.

The chiming of the doorbell echoed melodiously throughout the house. Turning on her heel she headed for the staircase. Kumi had promised to pick her up and take her to his parents' house to meet several of his cousins who had come in early for the wedding. Then everyone would retreat to Maxwell's for dinner.

She opened the door, her eyes widening in surprise when she stared through the screen door at Clinton Hamlin. "What are you doing here?"

He affected a polite smile. "May I come in? I'd like to talk to you."

Her gaze shifted to a racy sports car parked alongside her SUV. "You drove all the way from Atlanta just to talk to me? You know my telephone number. Why didn't you call me?"

Clinton shrugged his shoulders and ducked his head. "What I'd like to talk to you about is better discussed in person."

She pushed it open, permitting him to come in. He took several steps, then turned and stared at her. There was something about the way he looked at her that made Veronica feel uncomfortable. It was as if he could see through her oversize shirt to see her expanding waistline and ripening breasts. But she was being ridiculous. Only her family and Kumi's knew she was pregnant.

"What do you want to talk to me about?"

He lifted an eyebrow. "Where are your manners, *Mrs. Hamlin?* Aren't you going to invite me to sit down?"

"No, I'm not, because you should know better than to come to a person's home without an invitation."

His gray eyes glittered like sparks of lightning. "Your *home?* You keep forgetting that this was my father's home. Just like the place in Buckhead. My father purchased that place before you seduced him and turned him against his own children."

Veronica pushed open the door. "You can leave now." She wasn't going to permit Clinton to insult her—not in *her* home.

Clinton shook his head. "I'm not going anywhere until you give me what's due me, my brother and my sister."

"Get out!" The two words were forced out between clenched teeth.

A rush of blood suffused his face. A feral grin distorted his handsome features as he moved closer. Without warning, his right hand came up, holding her upper arm in a savage grip. "Not until I get what I want. What you're going to do is get your checkbook and write me a check for my share of my father's estate."

Veronica struggled to control her temper. "You got your share."

"I got nothing!"

"Your father left you almost a million dollars," she argued.

"And you got almost three," he countered. "And because of you he left those worthless hood rats five million."

She tried extracting herself from his punishing grip. "This discussion is over. Now, get out before I call the police and have you arrested for trespassing."

Clinton's fingers tightened savagely. "I have nothing to lose. Either it's the police or my bookie."

Veronica went completely still, and then swung at Clinton, her fist grazing a cheekbone. Howling, he let go of her arm, but came after her as she raced to a table in the living room to pick up a cordless telephone resting on its console. The phone was ripped from her hand and flung across the room. It hit a wall and bounced to the floor.

Veronica turned to face Clinton, seeing rage and fear in the dark gray eyes. In that instant she felt a shiver of fear shake her. She feared for herself and that of her unborn children. She took a step backward as he moved toward her. Where could she run? There was no way to escape him.

"Think about what you're about to do." Her voice was low, soothing.

He shook his head. "I've thought about it, Veronica. I've thought about it a long time, and it has to end this way. If I don't come up with a hundred thousand dollars by tomorrow, then I'm not going to be around to face another sunrise."

Her heart pounded painfully in her chest. She had to reason with him—had to get him to see that hurting her would not solve anything. "I can't write you a check."

Clinton's hands curled into tight fists. "And why the hell not?" he shouted as veins bulged in his neck.

"I've invested it." And she had, along with the proceeds from the sale of her art gallery.

He stopped his stalking, glaring at her. "You don't have a checking account?"

She nodded. "Yes. But I don't have a hundred thousand in it."

"How much do you have?"

"I have about eleven thousand in one and about eight in another."

"I'll take it," he snapped.

Closing her eyes, she nodded. She would agree to anything to get him to leave. "Wait here while I get my purse."

"How stupid do you think I am, Veronica? Do you actually think I'm going to let you out of my sight?"

You are stupid, she thought. Didn't he know that she could place a stop on the checks with one telephone call? "My purse is upstairs."

He followed her as she mounted the staircase. He was close enough for her to feel his breath on her neck. She retrieved her purse, extracted a check and filled out an approximate amount for the balance. Walking over to the armoire, she withdrew another checkbook from a drawer and filled it in, making it payable to Clinton Hamlin.

Snatching the checks from her outstretched fingers, he inclined his head. "I'll be back for the rest. You'd better contact your investment banker and tell him you need to make an early withdrawal."

She forced a smile she did not feel. "Don't push your luck, Clinton."

"You're the one whose luck has just run out."

"I beg to differ with you," came a strong male voice several feet away.

"Kumi!" The relief in Veronica's voice was evident. He had arrived just in time.

"It's all right, Ronnie." He'd spoken to Veronica, but his gaze was fixed on the back of Clinton Hamlin's head.

Clinton spun around, but before he could blink he found himself sprawled on the floor with a knee pressed to his throat. It had taken less than three seconds for Kumi to toss him over his hip and pin him to the floor.

The fingers of Kumi's right hand replaced his knee as he forcibly pulled Clinton to his feet. "You better call the police, Ronnie, or I'll forget that I'm getting married in two days and snap this piece of vermin's scrawny neck."

"Don't hurt me," Clinton pleaded, gasping. "Please don't hurt me."

Kumi released his throat and slapped him savagely across the face. "Shut up before I make you sorry you ever drew breath."

Veronica walked over to a bedside table and picked up the telephone. She made the call, one hand resting over her slightly rounded belly. The call completed, she made her way over to her sitting room and sank down in the cushioned rocker. Her gaze met Kumi's before he caught the front of Clinton's shirt and led him out of the bedroom. It wasn't until the police arrived that she went downstairs and gave them a report of what had happened. Clinton was read his rights and led away in handcuffs. What she did not tell the senior officer was that she would come in and drop the charges of trespassing and extortion before she and Kumi left for Europe.

Kumi closed the door behind the departing police officers. Turning he smiled, holding out his arms and he wasn't disappointed when Veronica came into his protective embrace.

Lowering his head, he kissed the end of her nose. "Are you all right, sweetheart?"

She smiled up at him. "I don't think I'll be all right until I'm Mrs. Jerome Walker."

He lifted his eyebrows. "We only have another forty-eight hours before that will become a reality."

Resting her head over his heart, she closed her eyes. "I can't wait."

Kumi chuckled softly. "Neither can I."

"I can't wait to see who our babies are going to look like," she said in a soft voice.

"I bet they'll look like you."

She gave him a saucy grin. "How much do you want to bet?"

He ran a finger down the length of nose. "I'm not even going there," he said laughing. "We'll just have to wait and see, won't we?"

"Yes." She sighed.

Kumi released Veronica long enough to pull the checks she'd given Clinton out of a pocket of his slacks. Tearing them into minute pieces, he let them float to the floor like confetti.

"Let's go, sweetheart. Our families are waiting for us."

She followed him out of the house and into the cool night. It was only mid-September, but fall came early in the mountains. She inhaled a lungful of air, savoring it. In another two days she would marry, and the next day she would leave for her new home with her new husband.

She had come to the mountains to heal but found love instead.

Kumi was right: God does set the time for sorrow and the time for joy.

This was her time for joy.

Epilogue

A year later

Kumi cradled his son in the crook of his arm while he extended a free hand to his wife. She smiled up at him while she held an identical little boy against her breasts.

The babies had arrived early to the much-anticipated grand opening of Café Veronique. Veronica had planned to stay for an hour before she returned home to put her five-month-old sons to bed.

Her pregnancy had been difficult—she'd spent the last month in bed. The strain of carrying two babies who'd weighed six and a half pounds each at birth had taken its toll on her back and legs. The infants were delivered naturally after the doctor induced her labor, and when she saw her babies for the first time she couldn't stop crying. They looked enough like Kumi to have been his clones.

Curving an arm around Veronica's waist, Kumi pressed a kiss to her short silver hair. She'd cut her hair after the twins' birth because she claimed it was easier to maintain. The new style was very chic. She'd lost most of the weight she'd gained during her confinement, but her body had changed. It was fuller and more lush. And there was never a time when he didn't want to make love to her.

Jerome Kumi Walker still found it hard to believe his life was so perfect. He'd married a woman he loved, who'd given him two healthy sons to carry on his name, and he'd finally realized his dream to open his own restaurant.

Not bad, he mused.

No, he hadn't done too badly for a guy who'd left home because of a domineering father. He didn't ride a motorcycle anymore, because he was now a family man. He'd taken a vow before God and man to protect his loved ones. And that was one vow he intended to keep.

* * * * *

Pleae turn the page for a preview of

THE CHASE IS ON
by
Brenda Jackson

Coming to Silhouette Desire
November 2005!

Prologue

"Never trust a Graham."

Sixteen-year-old Chase Westmoreland slid onto the stool at the counter in his grandfather's restaurant when the old man turned and spoke while placing a huge glass of milk and a plate filled with cookies in front of him.

"Why? What's wrong, Gramps?" Chase asked as he immediately attacked the stack of cookies. Chocolate chip were his favorite and after a vigorous varsity basketball practice, he needed to get as much chocolate into his system as he could. He believed in the theory that chocolate gave you energy.

"What's wrong? I'll tell you what's wrong. Carlton Graham stole some of the Westmorelands' secret recipes and passed them on to Donald Schuster."

Chase stopped eating as his eyes grew large. He knew how his grandfather felt about the Westmoreland secret family recipes that had been in the family for generations. "But Mr. Graham is your friend."

Scott Westmoreland frowned at his grandson. "Not anymore he isn't. We haven't been friends since we ended our partnership two weeks ago, but I never thought I'd live to see the day he would betray me this way."

Chase downed a huge gulp of milk and then asked, "Are you sure he did it?"

Scott Westmoreland nodded, his features tired and full of hurt, pain and disappointment. "Yes, I'm sure. I'd heard that Schuster had added a couple of new dishes to his menu, and some people claimed they tasted just like mine. So I went to investigate for myself."

Chase nodded. "And?"

"They're mine, all right, and although Schuster won't say where he got the recipes, I heard from a very reliable source that Graham gave them to him."

Chase sadly shook his head. He'd always liked Mr. Graham, and his chocolate-chip cookies were the best. His grandfather's were all right, but Mr. Graham's had a special ingredient that made them mouthwateringly delicious. No one baked chocolate-chip cookies the way Carlton Graham did. "Did you ask him about it?"

"Of course I did and he denies everything, but I know he's lying, since he's the only other person who knew exactly what ingredients to use. He knows what he did, and that's probably the reason he's not wasting any time moving his family out of town."

Chase's eyes widened. "The Grahams are moving away?"

"Yes, and good riddance. It wouldn't bother me any if I never saw another Graham again. Like I said, they can't be trusted. Always remember that."

One

He needed an attitude adjustment.

That thought flashed through Chase Westmoreland's mind as he turned the corner to pull into his restaurant's parking lot. A six-month abstinence, he concluded, had to be the reason he'd been in such a bad mood lately.

He was convinced his mood had nothing to do with the fact that over a three-year period his four brothers and baby sister had gotten married. Nor did it have anything to do with the fact that of all people, his cousin Jared, the die-hard bachelor attorney, had also recently fallen to matrimony. Chase was sick and tired of various family members looking at him with a "you're next" smile on their lips. If they were waiting for that to happen, then they had a long wait.

And it didn't help matters that his brothers had the audacity to smirk and say he would change his mind when the right woman came along. His comeback to them was always quick and confident. There was no such animal that walked on two legs, no matter how great those legs might look.

"What the hell!" He brought his car to a sudden stop. The parking lot where his restaurant was located was full of activity. He had forgotten that someone had purchased the building a few doors from Chase's Place, and from the way things looked they were moving in.

He had received notice a few weeks ago that he would have a new neighbor. If he remembered correctly, someone would be opening a confectionery.

When he'd first heard about it, the news had whetted his craving for chocolate, but now, seeing the mass of confusion surrounding him, all thoughts of sweets suddenly turned sour.

Moving trucks were everywhere, taking up the parking spaces he needed for his own customers. It was barely six in the morning, so what was going on? He always had a huge breakfast crowd, and the last thing he needed was someone messing with the availability of parking. It was a good thing he had a reserved spot in front of his restaurant or he, too, would be out of a parking space.

Forcing himself to breathe calmly, he sat in his car to wait until the truck in front of him decided to move. This was Monday—not a good day for his patience to be tested. He was just about to hit his horn when his attention was drawn to a woman who walked out of the building. For a moment he forgot his anger. Hell, he even forgot to breathe. But even without breathing he was able to release a deep, appreciative sigh.

She was talking to the driver of the truck that was blocking his path, and she was a prime specimen of a woman. She was dressed in a short baker's smock, and he hoped she had on a pair of shorts, since a good gust of wind would show him and anyone else what was or was not underneath her smock. A smile drifted over his lips. Even with the smock he could tell she had one hell of a figure. And when his gaze lit on her face...

His skin suddenly felt overheated when he looked into a face too beautiful for words. She had a pair of honey-brown eyes and full, moist lips covered in what looked like juicy red strawberry.

He frowned. What woman wore lipstick this time of the morning? And as if she had committed an ungodly sin, he wanted to get out of his car, walk over to her and kiss the coloring right off her lips. Then there was her hair, a mass of dark brown curls that tumbled over her shoulders, and for the first time in quite a while he was actually physically affected by a woman.

That thought made him take a deep breath, and he forced himself to pull back. To be this attracted to someone was the last thing he needed. Like the next guy he didn't mind looking his fill, but he knew the buck stopped there. He was a thirty-four-year-old, hot-blooded male and there was nothing wrong with responding to visual stimuli. But the last thing he needed was a gorgeous face to scatter his wits. All he had to do was remember his last year at Duke University and Iris Nelson. Thinking of Iris made warning bells go off...his sound of reason.

Sighing deeply, he let his gaze drift over the woman once more before deciding to back up and move around the truck. He blew out a breath, glad he was breathing again. As soon as he got inside his restaurant he would drink a calming cup of strong black coffee.

The one thing he had noticed was the absence of a wedding ring on her finger. He smiled at the thought of that, and then just as quickly a frown crept back into his features.

* * *

Jessica Claiborne smiled as she looked around her shop. Two days after moving in she was ready for the shop's grand opening tomorrow morning. She had spent the day doing last-minute checks on inventory and confirming arrangements for deliveries. She had hired two high school students to pass out flyers about her business around the community. She had made a call to the Children's Hospital and offered to donate any treats she didn't sell tomorrow, since she intended all her products to be baked fresh daily. Also, she had contracted with a couple of the hotels around town to work on an outsource basis as their pastry chef.

She glanced out the window. It was a beautiful day in early October. The media had predicted rain, but she had wished differently and her wish had come true. It had turned out to be a beautiful day. The movers had gotten everything set up on Monday and she had hired an artist that morning to paint her shop's name on the display window. Delicious Cravings was the name she had decided on. She would be forever thankful to her grandmother for making her dream come true.

Sadness settled in her heart whenever she thought about the grandmother she'd simply adored and the inheritance she had left her when she'd died last year on Jessica's twenty-fifth birthday. The money had made it possible to walk away from her stressful job in Sacramento as a corporate attorney and to accomplish what she'd always wanted to do, which was to own a confectionery.

She sniffed the air, enjoying the smell of chocolate cooking. Already today she had made a batch of assorted pastries as well as éclairs and tarts. But what she had enjoyed more than anything was whipping up the chocolate nut clusters and an assortment of cookies for the neighbors she had inconvenienced while moving in.

Mrs. Morrison, who owned the seamstress shop next door, had accepted her apology but declined her treats, since she was allergic to chocolate. However, the older woman had promised to try her rum balls. The Wright brothers, who owned the karate school, had accepted her gift and apology graciously, welcomed her to the strip and said they looked forward to patronizing her shop. The only person left was the owner of the restaurant Chase's Place. Jessica hoped the man was just as understanding as Mrs. Morrison and the Wright brothers had been and that he had a sweet tooth.

Grabbing the box she had filled with sweet treats, she walked out the door and locked it behind her. She had hired a part-time helper, an elderly woman who would come in during the busy lunchtime hours.

It was early afternoon, but she could tell the restaurant was packed and hoped the business would eventually trickle to her when everyone realized she was open for business. Before she got within ten feet of the restaurant she could smell the mouthwatering food and realized she hadn't eaten anything since breakfast.

She walked into Chase's Place, immediately liking what she saw. It was a very upscale restaurant that somehow maintained a homey atmosphere. Lanterns adorned each table and the tablecloths matched the curtains on the window. There was a huge counter with bar stools that matched the chairs at the tables, and soft jazzy music was coming from a speaker located somewhere in the back.

"Welcome to Chase's Place, where you're guaranteed to get the finest in soul food. Are you eating in or carrying out?"

Jessica smiled at the young woman who greeted her. "I'm the owner of the shop a few doors down and wanted to bring the owner a gift for any inconvenience he might have encountered while I was moving in."

The woman nodded. "That would be Chase, and he's in his office. If you follow me I'll show you the way."

"Thanks."

Jessica followed the woman down a hall that led to the back of the restaurant. Everything looked tidy, even the storage room they passed. The woman knocked when they reached a door. "Who is it?" a deep, husky voice called out.

"It's Donna. Someone is here to see you."

"Hell, I'm surprised anyone can get through with all that chaos that's been going on in the parking lot. I have a good mind to go over there and give that inconsiderate woman who owns that confectionery a piece of my mind for all the problems she's caused me the last couple of days. I couldn't get my own deliveries through for—"

Chase stopped talking when his door swung open and the woman he had checked out Monday morning walked into his office past a speechless Donna. "I guess I saved you a trip, since here I am, the inconsiderate woman who you want to give a piece of your mind. I would think, considering the circumstances, you would have been just as understanding as my other neighbors and..."

Whatever the woman was saying was lost on Chase. He had stopped listening moments before, within mere seconds of her walking into his office. Heat flared through all parts of his body when his full concentration centered on her and the shorts and tank top she was wearing.

Up close she was even more alluring than she had seemed on Monday morning. He blinked. She had crossed the room and was now in his face. That didn't help matters any, because the closer she got the better she looked, especially those strawberry moist lips he remembered. She was angry and sexy as hell.

In addition to the honey-brown eyes and curly dark brown hair that tumbled around her nut-brown face, she possessed perfect cheekbones and a cute perky nose. He couldn't help noticing that the mouth that was moving was beautifully shaped and ready to be kissed.

"And I hope you choke on these!"

He was jolted from his lust-filled thoughts when a box was suddenly shoved against his chest, and it took only a split second for him to realize his visitor was leaving. When the door slammed he moved his attention to Donna, and although she had a silly smirk on her face, he couldn't help but ask, "What the hell did she say?"

He watched Donna's smirk increase. "I think, boss, that you've been thoroughly read. I can't believe you weren't listening."

No, he hadn't been listening. He looked down at the box.

"That was supposed to be a peace offering," Donna explained. "She figured you were inconvenienced the past couple of days and wanted to give you a gift. I think that was downright neighborly of her. I guess she expected you to be more understanding about the chaos she caused while moving in."

Chase nodded, suddenly filled with regret that he hadn't been more understanding. But he'd been in a foul mood for the past week and had wrongly directed his anger at her. After all, she was a woman, and a woman—or lately for him the lack of one—was the root of his problem.

Granted, he wasn't the ladies' man his twin brother, Storm, had been, but all he had to do was to pull out his little phone book and contact any number of women who, like him, were more interested in getting down than getting married. Unfortunately, the last woman he'd dated had read more into the relationship and he'd had one hell of a time convincing her that bedding her had not been a prerequisite to wedding her. He wasn't into serious relationships of any kind and had told her that in the beginning.

Evidently somewhere along the way she had developed amnesia.

He dragged a weary hand down his face. Some women saw him and his single Westmoreland cousins as challenges. Storm's theory—before Jayla had entered his life—had been that he enjoyed women too much to settle down with just one. Chase's take on things was that when it came to a woman you learned from your mistakes, and his mistake had been a woman by the name of Iris Nelson.

While in college at Duke he had played basketball and seemed headed for a pro basketball career when an injury ended his dreams. He found himself facing an endless future when Iris, the girl he had fallen in love with, decided that with no chance at the pros he was no longer a good prospect.

Over the years he'd come to think of women as opportunists who only entered relationships to find out what was in it for them. Mostly, when the going got tough, they got going. Making women secondary in his life was the best way and eliminated the chance of a repeat heartbreak.

"So what are you going to do?" Donna asked, interrupting his thoughts.

He didn't have a clue. One thing was for certain—he did owe his new neighbor an apology. "Tell Kirk to prepare today's special to go and be generous with the servings."

Chuckling, Donna nodded. "You think you'll find her soft spot with food?"

He looked down at the box he held in his hand and inhaled the aroma of chocolate. "Wasn't that her game plan?"

Donna gave him a long look before slowly shaking her head and closing the door behind her as she left.

Chase placed the box on his desk. The top was marked with the name Delicious Cravings. He thought about how she'd looked Monday morning when he had first seen her, as well as the sight of her standing in the middle of his office just moments ago, and thought the name was definitely appropriate.

He opened the box and immediately fell in love—not with the deliverer but with the contents of the box. Yes, he definitely owed the woman an apology, and before the evening ended he would make sure she got one.

She hadn't liked the man's attitude.

Jessica took a deep breath, refusing to get any more upset than she already was. The nerve of him saying she was inconsiderate. She was one of the most considerate people there was, which was one of the reasons she had walked away from her high-paying job as a corporate attorney.

She had gotten fed up with taking stands on things she hadn't agreed with, pushing policies that ruined people's lives and being forced in the name of earning a high income to put corporate profits before the consumers' best interests.

Also, being considerate was the only reason—once she got settled—she planned to seek out members of the Westmoreland family to right a wrong made against her family years ago. The nerve of them implying her grandfather had been a dishonest man. He had been one of the most honest men she knew and if it was left up to her, she would give the Westmorelands a good piece of her mind and tell them just what she thought of their accusations. But her grandmother had made her promise to put aside her bitterness while dealing with them. It had been her grandmother's request before taking her final breath that she come to Atlanta to clear the Graham name, and she intended to do just that.

She sighed as her thoughts drifted back to the man who had called her inconsiderate. He had reminded her of dark, rich chocolate, and she knew one of the reasons she had gone off on him as she had was that she couldn't afford to get caught up in the sheer beauty of him. Even with his horrible attitude she had to admit that he was handsome as sin. Tall and well built, he had features that took your breath away. He had reminded her that she was still a woman, something she often tried to forget.

And she didn't like being reminded of her vulnerability, especially by him.

The last thing she needed was to be attracted to a man. She refused to get so carried away that she forgot how deceitful they were. She had learned her lesson, even if her mother had not. All it took was to remember Jeff Claiborne, the man who had fathered her. He was also the man who had kept her mother dangling on a string for over fifteen years with promises of marriage. When Jessica had been born he had given her his name, but her mother's last name had remained Graham.

It had taken her grandfather's paid investigator to deliver the news that there was no way Jeff Claiborne would ever marry Janice Graham. He was already married to another woman and had a family in Philadelphia. The news had been such a blow to her mother that she had ended up taking her life.

At the age of fifteen Jessica had stood and watched as her mother's coffin was lowered into the ground and had vowed to never give her heart to someone the way her mother had; a man who could turn out to be as deceitful as her father had been; a man who had taken her mother's undying love and abused it in the worse possible way.

Her grandfather, angry and hurt over what Jeff Claiborne had done, had made sure the man didn't get away unscathed. He had paid a visit to Jeff Claiborne's wife and had presented her with documented proof of her husband's duplicity. Jennifer Claiborne, a good woman, hadn't wasted any time filing for a divorce and leaving her husband of eighteen years. And Jennifer had gone one step further by welcoming Jessica into her family, making sure she got to know her sister and brother, as well as making sure Jeff Claiborne contributed to her support. She knew Jennifer had been instrumental in helping to set up the college fund that had been there when she had graduated from high school.

Savannah and Rico were as close to her as a brother and sister could be. And Jennifer was like a second mother to her. Whenever things had gotten too rough in California, she'd known she could always go visit her extended family in Philadelphia.

She turned upon hearing the knock at the door and frowned. Dusk was settling in, but she could plainly see through her display window that her unexpected visitor was the man from the restaurant.

She had a good mind to ignore him, since he definitely put a not-so-positive spin on the term *good neighbor*. For the past couple of weeks, since her move to Atlanta, she had begun thinking she had finally found peace, but now he was convincing her otherwise.

She heard his knock again and decided that she wouldn't hide. Like everything else in life she would deal with it, and in this case, *it* was him. He had sought her out, and this building was not only the place she would work but, thanks to space above the shop, it would also be her home.

Deciding she had let him linger long enough, she made her way to the door and unlocked it. She took a deep breath before opening it. "What do you want?"

He had been standing with his back to her, looking up at the sky. The day had been beautiful, but it seemed that tonight it would rain. He turned around upon hearing her voice, and as soon as their gazes locked she felt the temperature surrounding them go up about one hundred degrees.

He still reminded her of rich, dark chocolate, but now something else had been added to the mixture, she thought as her gaze moved from the baseball cap on his head to the features of his face. A slight indention in the bridge of his nose indicated it may have been broken at one time, but she didn't even consider that a flaw. Nothing, and she meant nothing, distracted from this man's good looks.

Jeez. That wasn't a good sign.

And to make matters worse, he had the audacity to smile with a smile that was so potent she was forced to grip the doorknob to support her suddenly wobbly knees. Forcing her eyes away from that smile, she met his gaze once more and it angered her that he had this kind of effect on her. "I repeat, what do you want?" she all but snapped.

His smile widened. He was either oblivious to her less-than-friendly mood or he chose to ignore it. "I came to apologize," he said, widening that killer-watt smile while holding up a bag he held in his hand. The aroma from the bag indicated there was food in it. Delicious food, no doubt.

"I was out of line earlier," he said. "And I do understand how it is moving in, and the only excuse I can give for my behavior is the fact this has been one hell of a week, though my problems are not your fault."

His apology surprised her, but it didn't captivate her as he evidently assumed it would do. Long ago she had learned to be cautious of smooth-talking men.

"Will you accept my apology?"

She jutted her chin. "Why should I?"

"Because it will prove that you're a much nicer person than I am and someone with a forgiving spirit."

Jessica leaned against the doorjamb, thinking that she was definitely a much nicer person, but she wasn't all that sure that she had such a forgiving spirit. She inhaled deeply, deciding she didn't want to accept his apology. She didn't like the chemistry she felt flowing between them and she also decided she didn't like him. She knew it all sounded irrational, but at the moment she didn't care. "There are a lot of things I can overlook, but rudeness isn't one of them."

Chase lifted a brow and frowned. "So you aren't going to accept my apology?"

She glared at him. "At the moment, no."

His frown deepened as he peered down at her. "Why?"

"Because I don't feel like it. Now, if you'll excuse me I need to—"

He held up a hand, cutting her off. "Because you don't feel like it?"

"That's what I said."

Chase felt frustration take over his body. He had dealt with many unreasonable people, but this woman gave new meaning to the word. Okay, he'd been rude, but he had apologized, hadn't he?

"Look," he said slowly while trying to overlook the irritation plastered on her face, "I know things got off to a bad start between us, and for that I apologize. And you're right. I was rude, but now you're the one who is being unreasonable."

Jessica sighed deeply. The dark brown eyes focused on hers were intense, sharp and to-die-for, but still…

But still nothing, Jessica Lynn, she could hear her grandmother saying in the recesses of her mind. *You can't judge every man by your father. You can't continue to put up this brick wall against any man who gets close.*

Sighing again, she smoothed a hand down her face. Her grandmother had been right, but the need to protect herself had always been elemental and for some reason she had an inkling that the man standing before her was someone she should avoid at all cost.

"And in addition to accepting my apology, will you also accept my peace offering, as I did yours?" Chase asked, interrupting her thoughts. "Everything was delicious, especially the chocolate-chip cookies. They are my favorite, and I haven't tasted chocolate-chip cookies that delicious in years. They were melt-in-your-mouth good." He slanted her a smile. "And I didn't choke on any of them."

"Too bad," she said dryly. Their gazes held for a moment and she knew she was a puzzle he was trying to figure out. No doubt other women didn't cause him any trouble. He flashed his smile and got whatever he wanted. Just as her father had done so many times.

She wrapped her arms around herself, knowing he didn't intend to leave until she accepted his apology. "Okay, I accept your apology. Now goodbye."

He grabbed the door before she could slam it in his face. Holding up the bag, he smiled. "And the peace offering?"

She snorted a breath. "And the peace offering," she said, reaching for the bag.

Chase chuckled. "Now we're getting somewhere." Instead of giving her the bag, he held his hand out to her. "We haven't been properly introduced. I'm Chase Westmoreland, and you are?" he asked, taking her hand.

Jessica knew if she had a lighter skin tone he would have seen all the blood drain from her face. "Westmoreland?"

He grinned. "Yes, does the name ring a bell? There's a bunch of us living in Atlanta."

Deciding she wasn't ready to tell him just how much of a bell it rang, she shook her head. "No, it doesn't ring a bell. I recently moved here from California."

He nodded and after a few moments he said, smiling, "You never told me your name."

She blinked, recalling that she hadn't. "I'm Jessica Claiborne."

His smile widened. "Welcome to Atlanta, Jessica. Do you have family here?"

"No," she answered truthfully, "I have no family living

here." Her head was still spinning at the realization that he was a Westmoreland.

There was a bit of silence between them when Chase remembered the bag he was holding. "Oops, I almost forgot. Here you go," he said, handing the bag to Jessica. "It's today's special and I hope you enjoy it."

"Thanks."

He hesitated for a moment, then said, "I guess I'd better go back, since the dinner crowd is arriving. Will you be living up top?"

"Yes," she said, gripping the bag in both hands. She needed to get away from him to think.

"Well, every once in a while if it's a late night, I sleep up top my place, too, so if you ever need anything, just let me know."

Don't hold your breath for that to happen, she thought. "Thanks."

"See you later."

She watched as he turned to leave. According to her grandmother, the Grahams and the Westmorelands had become bitter enemies years ago.

She couldn't help but smile when she wondered how Chase Westmoreland would handle it when he discovered she was one of the "lying and deceiving Grahams."

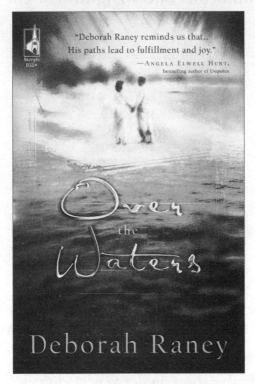

Imagine not knowing if your next meal may be your last.

This is the fate of Yelenda, the food taster for a leader who is the target of every assassin in the land. As Yelenda struggles to save her own mortality, she learns she has undiscovered powers that may hold the fate of the world.

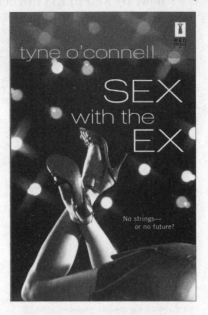

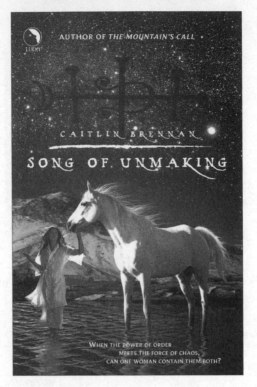